THE DEVIL HIMSELF

BB EASTON

Copyright © 2024 by BB Easton
Published by Art by Easton
All rights reserved.

ISBN: 979-8-9887494-7-9
Special Edition Paperback ISBN: 979-8-9887494-8-6
Special Edition Hardcover ISBN: 979-8-2185048-6-1
eBook ISBN: 979-8-9887494-6-2

Cover Design by Damonza
Cover Photography by Ren Saliba
Content Editing by Nicole McCurdy, Traci Finlay,
and Adele Halpin
Copyediting and Formatting by Jovana Shirley,
Unforeseen Editing, www.unforeseenediting.com

AUTHOR'S NOTE

My dear, sweet, beloved reader,

It is my absolute pleasure to welcome you back to the world of *Devil of Dublin*.

On this new adventure, you and I are going to experience the intoxicating highs and heart-wrenching lows of a star-crossed romance that would make Romeo and Juliet weep. We're going to traverse across Ireland in the midst of a Mafia war, venturing from the wildflower-capped cliffs of Howth to the mystical forest of County Kerry to the war-torn streets of Dublin. We're going to run for our lives, fight to the death, and love like there's no tomorrow. It will be the journey of a lifetime, a romance for the ages, but it will not be for everyone.

If you enjoyed *Devil of Dublin*, then rest assured that the adventure you are about to embark on was tailor-made for you. The dark themes, graphic violence, emotional intensity, explicit sexual content, mystical folklore, gorgeous Irish scenery, and ethereal romance you're about to experience were written with you in mind every step of the way. But if you're curious about specific triggers or you've had certain life events take place that have made you a more sensitive reader since the last time you were here, please consult the content warning on my website before going any further.

https://www.artbyeaston.com/devil-of-dublin-content-warning

Now that we've established that it's safe for you to proceed, there's one more thing I need you to do before you press play on chapter one. I need you to take a deep breath, leave all your expectations right here, and go in with an open mind. This story is not what you think. It's more.

It's … *everything*.

Welcome back to Glenshire.

XO,

BB

GLOSSARY

The following is a list of definitions for some of the Irish, Russian, and naval terms that appear in this book.

Aston Quay—a street in central Dublin that borders the south side of the River Liffey

bin—trash can

Bratva—the Russian Mafia

bulkhead—the wall of a ship

deck— the uppermost level of a ship, uncovered

fifth class—the equivalent of sixth grade in America

first floor—the second story of a building

gaff—house

gee—slang for a vagina

hatch—door or doorway on a ship

helm—the part of a boat that houses equipment for driving and steering

hold—the cargo storage area in the bottom of a ship

jumper—sweater or sweatshirt

kashdie—(pronounced KAHSH-dee) Russian word for "everyone"

knickers—female underwear

lift—elevator

lough—(pronounced LOCK) Irish word for "lake"

oilskins—waterproof garments, usually overalls or jackets and pants, worn by fishermen

peet—Russian word for "sing"

petrol—gasoline

primary school—elementary school

President—In Ireland, this position is more of a ceremonial role with limited powers and is expected to remain politically neutral.

prosnut'sya—(pronounced pros-NOOT-suh) Russian word for "wake up"

runners—sneakers

second floor—the third story of a building

secondary school—high school

sixth year—the equivalent of twelfth grade in America

sláinte—(pronounced SLAWN-cha) an Irish toast meaning "good health"

smer-nah—(pronounced SMEAR-nuh) Russian military command meaning "at attention"

Taoiseach—(pronounced TAY-shuh) the head of government or prime minister of Ireland

the Eye—nickname for Ireland's Eye, a small, uninhabited island off the coast of Howth

the Liffey—the River Liffey, the main river that runs through central Dublin

the Poddle—The River Poddle is a tributary of the River Liffey in Dublin that runs mostly through underground tunnels beneath the city.

torch—flashlight

trawler—a type of commercial fishing boat designed to drag a trawl net to catch fish

United Irish Brotherhood (UIB)—a fictional Irish organized crime outfit/political party, similar to the Irish Republican Army (IRA)

ura—(pronounced OOH-rah) Russian military battle cry

wellies—rubber boots

zip—zipper

In the hills at the foot of a plum mountain peak
Lies a sleepy old town where the dead never sleep.
The villagers know to stay out of the wood.
That's where the spirits are up to no good.
Especially one, they confess with a shiver.
Born with the Devil inside him, they whisper.
Eyes gray as smoke, hair like black flames.
He killed the town priest and died with him that day.
Damned for eternity, refusing to burn,
He waits in the woods for his love to return.
Out where the bluebells grow high as your knee
And the clover and moss blanket every tree
Lies a ring made of stone where no fairies dare tread.
That's where you'll find him, the ghost of the glen.

—Darby Donovan, *The Ghost of Glenshire*

CHAPTER 1

DARBY

The end.

I held my breath as I stared at those words, as if a single exhalation could blow them right off the screen. They were so small—just six little letters—but their significance was enormous. Time seemed to stand still as I admired the very shape of that sentence—tall letters on the outside, short letters on the inside, a space right in the middle. It looked like a smile that was missing a front tooth. I smiled back at it, lost in the moment, until the subtle blink of the cursor at the end of that sentence reminded me that time was most definitely *not* standing still, and based on the encroaching darkness of the woods and the pinks and corals sliding down the sky behind them, I didn't have much of it left.

Once I saved my final edits in at least fifteen different places and emailed them to my publisher, I closed my laptop and waited for my bleary, aching eyes to adjust to the soft lighting and dreamy colors of Glenshire Lough at sunset. The view was stunning on a regular day, but after staring at the harsh blue glow of a computer for hours on end, it was absolutely delicious.

Perfect really. I was in my favorite place, sitting on my favorite bench, which had been carved for me by my favorite person, doing my favorite thing—*okay, maybe my second-favorite thing*—and thanks to my agent, I was actually going to get paid for it.

I could still see the announcement in *Publishers Weekly*.

Ableman Publishing Group bought Darby Donovan's debut middle-grades series, Legend Has It, in a preemptive four-book agreement. The series is a collection of spooky fairy tales based on the folklore of Glenshire, a mysterious farming village in County Kerry, Ireland.

Kate, Kellen's mom, had been so excited that she printed it out and framed it for me … causing me to immediately burst into tears. No one had celebrated an achievement of mine since my own mother had passed away. I'd forgotten how amazing it felt.

Kellen, on the other hand, was having a much harder time accepting Kate's love. After she'd abandoned him at the age of five—leaving him in the care of the sick, sadistic priest who'd impregnated her—Kellen would never fully trust Kate again. He couldn't. It didn't matter that she had been a child herself, with no one to turn to and no idea that Father Henry would actually keep him rather than put him up for adoption. After everything he'd been through, the damage was done. But Kate kept showing up, week after week, with a smile on her face and a fresh box of pastries in her trembling hands.

I knew the hug she wanted was from him, but the one she got was always from me. She'd lost a child, and I'd lost a mother, so whenever we embraced, it felt like a fresh bandage being wrapped around an old wound.

Plus, having a bakery owner for a mother-in-law was a nice perk, especially considering the sugar cravings I'd been having recently.

I smiled, picturing the white stick with two pink lines on it that I'd hidden in my bathroom drawer that morning.

I'd wanted to tell Kellen right away, but he was out, making deliveries at the time, and I had edits to finish, so I'd decided to wait until I could tell him in person.

When I'd told him that I wanted to try for a baby once I graduated from college, I'd expected him to ask for more time. We were still young, and after everything he'd been through with both of his parents, I didn't expect him to be too eager to become a parent himself. But much to my surprise, Kellen had said yes.

Actually, he'd pulled me into his arms, kissed the top of my head, and held me like that for what felt like an eternity. So, it hadn't been a yes exactly, but it hadn't been a no either.

I knew Kellen was scared to be a father, but the past was finally behind us. We'd finished turning the barn into a workshop for him. He was making good money with his custom wood-carving business. I had my first book deal. He'd severed all ties with the United Irish Brotherhood. The Bratva kingpin who'd wanted him dead was behind bars. And Kellen's hacker friend, The Butcher, was making sure we stayed untraceable online in case any other enemies of Kellen's might come looking for us. After a lifetime of struggle, of pain and terror and powerlessness and violence, we were finally free from it all. We were safe. We were settled.

And now, before the ink was even dry on my creative writing degree, we were pregnant.

As thrilled as I was, a little part of me worried about how Kellen would react. He'd seemed paranoid lately, more so than usual, and I wondered if it was because there was a possibility that I might be pregnant or if maybe something else was going on.

My joints creaked and muscles groaned as I stood and stretched. Kellen's bench wasn't nearly as comfortable as it was beautiful, but there was no better place to go when I really needed to concentrate. The woods behind my grandfather's house had a way of transporting me into a completely different world.

Plus, I thought Saoirse might like the company.

Plucking a handful of blackberries off one of the bushes next to the bench, I popped one into my mouth and tossed the rest into the water. The thousand-year-old lake spirit was partial to much shinier gifts, but honestly, I thought she liked the attention that came with getting a present more than anything. She had a pretty lonely existence down there, and her only friend, other than me, was a creepy old forest witch that I'd only seen once.

Walking up to the edge of the lake, I clutched the laptop to my chest and smiled down at the berries floating on the surface. "I finished my final edits, Saoirse. All four books are done. Can you believe it? I'll bring you a set once they're published. They're gonna turn them into fancy hardbacks with gold foiling. You'll love them."

As excited as I was about the books, it was my next piece of news that had me grinning like an idiot. Crouching down next to the water, I dropped my voice to a whisper and added, "Also … I'm pregnant."

I knew that would get her attention. An iridescent blue sheen rippled across the darkening lake, shimmering like the northern lights in January.

I ran my fingertips over the glowing water, grinning as the light brightened beneath my touch. It reminded me of the way a cat arched its back against your hand when you petted it … when it wasn't trying to bite your fingers off. That was Saoirse.

"We're gonna have a baby."

I laughed, tears pricking my eyes as I placed my palm flat on the cool surface. Cobalt energy pulsed and bubbled beneath it, tickling my hand with the same giddy effervescence as the butterflies in my stomach.

I'd never seen her so happy.

After saying my goodbyes, I hauled ass up the hill, hoping to make it out of the woods before it got too dark to see the trail. Past the crumbling stone cottage Kellen and I had played in as kids, through the patch of bluebells I'd once thought was a field of fairy hats, and past a thousand mushrooms and moss-covered trees, I finally made it to the pasture behind our blue farmhouse, where Vlad was grazing by the gate, waiting for me to return.

I gave his black woolly head a few pats, but I was too distracted by what I saw behind him to greet him properly.

The light was on in the woodshop.

Kellen was home.

Vlad trotted behind me as I ran across the pasture to the converted barn.

When I stopped outside the door, my heart pounded as I listened to make sure Kellen wasn't using any power tools. I was always careful not to barge in on him when he was sawing or sanding. He startled easily, thanks to a lifetime spent in survival mode, and I would hate for him to lose a finger because of me.

I was partial to *all* of his appendages.

The only sounds I heard inside were some clanking and thudding, no heavy machinery, so I knocked on the door and pushed the creaky, old thing open.

I smiled as the sweet scent of sawdust filled my lungs, but the moment my eyes landed on Kellen, I released that breath, as well as my laptop, with a startled gasp.

"Darby!" he snapped, tucking the pistol he'd just pointed at me into the waistband of his jeans before rushing over to apologize. "Sorry. Shite. I didn't hear ya knock."

I bent over to pick up my computer, hoping to give myself a second to wipe the terror off my face, but Kellen's strong, scarred hands beat me to it.

Standing, he brushed the sawdust off my device before returning the laptop and his attention to me. Callous fingers reached up to trace the side of my face as glacial-gray eyes took in the rest of me. It didn't matter how many years I'd known Kellen or how much we'd been through together; his gaze never failed to send a chill up my spine. It was silent and still. Haunting and haunted.

But what truly froze me to the spot was his appearance. It was as if I'd stepped through that doorway and into a time that I never wanted to experience again.

As a child, Kellen had had the most beautiful crown of loose black curls. To me, it made him look like a handsome fairy prince. But Father Henry hated it. So much so that when Kellen came home with a French braid one day after playing hair salon with me in the woods, Father Henry had beaten him unconscious and shaved his head.

Kellen had kept his hair short after that to prove to everyone that it hadn't bothered him. That he actually liked it that way. The look became part of his persona—the tough exterior he projected to the world. But when I had returned to Glenshire as an adult, our reunion had reminded him of who he used to be, before the world had made him hard. He hadn't cut his hair since.

Until now.

I would never forget the way he'd looked the night that I came back. Bulging veins extended up his temples into his black buzz cut. Black beard stubble dusted his clenched jaw. And white skin covered his shaking knuckles as they tightened around my abusive fiancé's neck. Kellen's cold gray eyes had bored into mine while the life drained from John's.

And I was looking into the face of that killer again.

Confused and terrified, I glanced around the converted barn, half-expecting to find myself in a kitchen with John's lifeless body on the ground next to me. But it wasn't a flashback, and it wasn't a dream. Kellen—my Kellen—was gone, and in his place stood a man I hadn't seen in two and a half years.

Black buzz cut.

Black beard stubble.

Black soul swirling behind ghastly gray eyes.

The Devil of Dublin was back.

Panic exploded through my nervous system, making my hands shake and my heart race as the deadliest man in Ireland reached over my shoulder and pushed the door shut behind me.

The click of the latch made my entire body jump.

I stood, clutching my computer, as Kellen stalked back over to his workbench, where a collection of guns lay scattered on the massive table.

"Kellen, what's going on?"

"We have to leave. Now." He didn't look up as he placed the weapons into a plain black backpack. I knew he kept guns in the house. I just hadn't known it was that many. "I'm sorry, angel. I'm so fuckin' sorry."

Kellen slammed a full magazine into a machine gun, making me jump.

"Sorry for what?" I asked, taking a few shaky steps in his direction. I squeezed my laptop harder to stop my hands from trembling as I mustered the courage to ask, "What's going on?"

Picking up a shotgun, Kellen cursed and dug through the tool chest behind him until he found a box of ammunition.

"We never shoulda stayed here," he muttered to himself, pumping round after round into the chamber. "We shoulda left the country when we had the fuckin' chance. I knew you loved this place, and I couldn't make ya leave"—he snapped the barrel closed and ran a hand over his freshly buzzed head, pushing curls back that no longer existed—"but I shoulda made you fuckin' leave."

"Kellen, what are you talking about? We're happy here."

"But we're not fuckin' safe!" He slammed his hand on the table, his irate expression immediately contorting into remorse over my startled response.

I could feel my heartbeat pounding in my throat, behind my eyes, deep inside my spinning head. "I … I don't understand. I thought we were safe. I thought The Butcher was keeping us off the grid."

"The Butcher's fuckin' dead."

The ground beneath my feet began to tilt.

"Found him myself. He hadn't been answerin' my calls, so I paid him a little visit while I was in Dublin this mornin'." Kellen shoved the sawed-off shotgun into the bag and zipped it up. "The place had been ransacked. Doors blasted open. Dead guards. Missin' computers. Found him on the floor of the server room, shot in the back."

My hand flew to my mouth as the gravity of this new information set in. The Butcher had our entire lives filed away on those computers—our birth certificates, passports, marriage license, *address*. If that information got into the wrong hands …

"Who did it?" I asked, feeling the blood draining from my face. "The UIB?"

"Worse." Kellen slung the heavy backpack over one shoulder and came around the table, extending his hand toward me as he approached. "I'll tell ya 'bout it in the car. Right now, we gotta—"

A deafening blast rang out behind me, peppering my back with shards of wood as I ducked and covered my head.

When the ringing in my ears finally stopped, I opened my eyes to find my laptop on the ground again. But this time, Kellen didn't come to pick it up.

I looked up and found him standing a few feet away, gun drawn, teeth clenched, eyes wild, like a cornered animal, darting back and forth between the people I heard shuffling in behind me.

The click of a pistol being cocked next to my head explained Kellen's reluctance to shoot, and the deep, sinister chuckle that echoed through the rafters told me exactly who was holding the gun.

Alexi Abramov.

A Bratva leader who'd been so hell-bent on revenge for the murder of his uncle that he vowed war against the United Irish Brotherhood unless they handed over the hit man who'd done the job—the notorious Devil of Dublin. And the UIB, the only family Kellen had ever known, agreed. For days, Kellen and I had raced across Ireland, running from both the UIB and the Bratva, until one wrong move on my part got us both captured. But I'd learned from the best. The Devil of Dublin had taught me to fight back, to take control, to use every resource I had, so after escaping from the UIB and framing their leader, Séamus Rooney, for the death of my fiancé, I'd enlisted my detective uncle to help me rescue Kellen and take down both Alexi and Séamus at the same time.

Alexi had been given three consecutive life sentences—one for false imprisonment and attempted human trafficking, one for possession of contraband guns with the intent to distribute, and one for the murder of four police officers during the shoot-out.

Séamus had been given eighty years.

I should have known that it was just a matter of time until the Bratva found a way to get him out.

I should have listened when Kellen told me we needed to leave the country.

I should have asked him what was going on days ago instead of dismissing his behavior as paranoid.

But as I stood, staring at my husband's beautiful, hateful, fearful face, I couldn't bring myself to regret it.

There would never be any other life for me. Glenshire was my home just as much as Kellen was. As much as this little person inside of me. And all three of them were worth fighting for.

"Devil," Alexi purred with that thick Russian accent. "Ve meet again." Cold metal pressed against the back of my head as another chuckle rumbled through the air. "Be good boy. Drop zhe gun. You shoot vone of us, ve shoot zhe girl …"

Kellen's pupils were trained on Alexi's face like a pair of laser scopes as he lowered the gun to the ground.

"Nikolai, take zhat … and zhe bag."

A machine gun–carrying henchman with a shaved head and a black tracksuit darted over to Kellen and jerked the backpack off his shoulder. He cursed and said something in Russian, obviously surprised by the weight as he hoisted it onto his own shoulder.

"Two years, I sit in cell … zhinking of vays to keel you. Torture you. Make you scream. But now, I see you …" I could almost hear the smile on Alexi's ruddy, evil, pockmarked face. "I zhink of new vay."

The barrel of Alexi's gun disappeared from my head, but before I could sigh in relief, pain exploded through my right inner thigh. It was so intense that I couldn't hear, couldn't see. It was just darkness and screaming, mind-erasing agony as my senses lost all contact with the outside world. I must have been falling because the next thing I felt was Kellen's arms catching me, cradling me to his chest as he slid to his knees at Alexi's feet.

"Torture begin now."

The Russian's voice sounded distant, muffled. Even Kellen felt far away, like I was perceiving him through the glass of a fishbowl.

Forcing my eyes open, I tried to focus on staying conscious, to focus on Kellen, stay with him, keep him safe.

"Vhat is English vord?" Alexi asked one of his henchmen as the sculpted ridges and valleys of Kellen's perfect, panicked face began to blur together.

"Artillery? Artery? Artery."

Alexi walked over to the workbench, pulled a stool out from underneath, and had a seat. I watched him over Kellen's shoulder as he leaned back and rested his elbows on the wooden table. The pistol in his right hand dangled casually from his thick, pale fingers as he glanced at the watch on his opposite wrist.

"She bleed out in … mmm … five minutes." He chuckled. "Seven if pregnant. Zhey have more blood, you know."

Kellen's wide, watery eyes fell to my stomach before colliding with mine for confirmation. A fraction of a nod and a hint of a smile were all I could muster, but the way his chest rose and fell in response, the way his jaw clenched and his nostrils flared, made me wish that I hadn't.

"It's … okay," I whispered. The pain was beginning to fade, along with my vision around the edges and my sense of fear.

It would be okay. I knew it. I just needed Kellen to know it too.

Tearing his gaze away from mine, Kellen unbuckled his belt one-handed and wrapped it around my upper thigh. I could see from the tension on his face that he was pulling it tight, but I couldn't feel the pressure. I couldn't feel anything other than the agony of watching Kellen's heart break before my very eyes.

Raising my hand, I felt as though I were trying to control someone else's arm as I ran my fingers over his freshly buzzed scalp. It was soft to the touch. I could feel that, but barely.

"You cannot stop zhis, Devil. You just make more time, more pain." He laughed again. "*You* do torture now."

Kellen's rough cheek dragged across mine as he buried his face in the crook of my neck. Everything below my waist was numb, but I could feel the moisture of Kellen's tears on my skin, feel the shudder of his weeping body wrapped around mine.

There was so much I wanted to say to him. That I was going to be okay. That I believed in him. That I'd seen him take out three armed men before. That he could do it again.

But the only word I managed to rasp was, "Fight."

"I know, angel," he whispered with a nod. "I know yer fightin'."

Kellen clutched me tighter, rocking me back and forth in a way that made staying conscious almost impossible. I was trying so hard to hold on. To resist the pull of the darkness that was dragging me away from him.

"But he's right. This is torture."

I heard the clank and swish of a belt being unfastened and felt a sudden rush to the head.

"Shh … it's okay. You don't have to fight anymore, darlin'. Neither of us does." He kissed my forehead, my eyelids, my nose, my lips. " 'Cause "I'm comin' with ya, angel. Ya understand? I'm not lettin' you go. I'll never fuckin' let go."

His voice broke as he lifted my left hand to his lips and pressed a shaky kiss to the freckles on my ring finger. The ones that he bore as well.

"No." I shook my dizzy, throbbing head. It wasn't over. It couldn't be. Not when we were so close to having everything we'd ever wanted.

Kellen could save us. All three of us. I knew he could.

Bored, Alexi's men walked past us to the workbench and began speaking and laughing with their boss in Russian.

I clung to Kellen's body as if it were the only thing tethering me to my own and turned my mouth toward his ear. "Knife," I whispered, clutching his shirt in my fists.

Kellen kept a blade in his boot. Never walked out the door without it. He was still armed. We still had a chance.

Kellen nodded in understanding, and my entire body sagged in relief.

It would be okay.

It had to be.

With his hand clutching my jaw, Kellen pressed his tear-soaked lips to mine, and the world darkened around me until he was the only thing I could sense. His woodsy scent, his silent strength, his unbreakable, unwavering devotion—I sank into it like a warm bed.

But just before the darkness pulled me completely under, Kellen whispered something that I hadn't heard since the day he'd offered his life to the UIB in exchange for mine. Something that pulled me back from the brink of unconsciousness, flooding what was left of my bloodstream with panic.

"Is fíor bhur ngrá," he rasped, dropping his forehead to mine.

Saoirse's blessing.

My eyes shot open as Kellen pulled the knife out of his boot and turned to face Alexi, and with defiance in his eyes and a scream on my lips, he plunged the blade straight into his own heart.

CHAPTER 2

CLOVER

TWENTY-ONE YEARS LATER

Giving the bundle of knotted rope in my hands an exasperated shake, I let my head fall back with a groan.

I'd never be able to prove it, but I suspected that Da took great pleasure in tangling up his own fishing nets. He was probably spying on me at that very moment, laughing his arse off while I struggled to straighten them back out.

Arsehole.

I stared up at the overcast sky and prayed for an afternoon shower, one so heavy that I'd finally be allowed to come inside and take a break. But all I got was a single drop of rain—one perfectly timed *splat*, right between the eyes. It felt like the almighty himself had just spat in my face.

Which was fitting, considering that I was in my own personal hell. Actually, in my version of hell, I wouldn't be standing in front of a house that resembled a crusty white barnacle growing on top of a cliff overlooking the Irish Sea. I'd be standing in front of a mountain. One so tall that it broke through the swirling thunderclouds overhead. So wide that it wrapped around me on both sides, caging me in. But this monstrosity wouldn't be made of stone or ice or flows of lava. No, the mountain of *my* nightmares would be formed from something far more horrifying.

An endless hellscape of reeking, knotted fishing nets.

With a defeated sigh, I dropped my head, wiped my rain-splattered nose on my shoulder, and allowed my attention to drift toward the sea. I could only resist that view for so long, and the more monotonous my chores were, the more difficult it became.

The wind was relentless as I trudged over to the cliff's edge, dragging the heap of tangled rope behind me. I'd thrown on a pair of shorts that morning, thinking, surely, it would be warm enough for them in mid-June—a decision that I was now regretting. Goose bumps covered my exposed legs, and every strand of hair that hadn't made it into my messy bun lashed me in the face, but I was too distracted to notice.

Dropping the net, I pulled the hem of my jumper down with one hand and shielded my eyes with the other.

I'd lived on the Howth peninsula my entire life, but the sight of the sea and the grassy little island that sparkled just offshore never failed to take my breath away. Ireland's Eye, as the island was called, felt like an oasis that was always just beyond my reach—a tiny, tranquil, floating hill, abandoned by civilization. The only buildings on the Eye were two small stone ruins, and the only creatures that lived there were a few rats and rabbits and sea birds and a colony of plump gray seals who liked to sunbathe on the rocky beach.

As beautiful as it was, the island wasn't what drew my attention to the sea day after day. It was hope. Dumb, stupid, pointless hope.

I still remembered the exact moment when I'd learned what a selkie was. It was my first day back at school after Ma's accident, and I had no real concept of where she'd gone. I was only seven at the time, and no one had bothered to explain to me what had happened. I'd just woken up one morning to the sound of Da breaking things. He was fall-down drunk, slurring about Ma being "gone" and "not coming back."

Then, for the next few days, he just sat slumped over in his armchair, staring blankly at the TV with drool in his beard and a bottle of Jameson in his fist. He couldn't even sober up long enough to go to the funeral. My aunt and uncle took me, but they didn't want to talk about what had happened either. Everybody had just cried a lot and hugged me a lot and said that they were sorry and that I'd see her again one day.

When?

When will I see her?

Where did she go?

Can I call her?

Can I visit?

Can I go live with her instead of Da?

He was so scary now that she wasn't around. And mean. He said he couldn't stand how much I looked like her. He told me to stay in my room so that he wouldn't have to see my face.

Why did she have to leave me with him?

There were so many questions that I'd been too afraid to ask. Not only because I was terrified of upsetting my father, but because I was even more terrified that someone might tell me the truth. That she really was gone. Forever.

"A selkie," Ms. Bell announced, pointing to an illustration on the screen in the front of the classroom, *"is a mythological creature, believed to live in the waters of Scotland and Ireland. It looks like a seal, but when it removes its seal coat, it looks human."*

The class gasped.

"Legend has it that fishermen will sometimes find these creatures in their human forms, and they'll fall so in love with them that they'll hide the selkie's seal coat so that it can't shift back. Then, they'll take them home, marry them, and sometimes even start a family with them. But a selkie's place is in the sea, so they never stop searching for their missing skin. And once they find it, they'll disappear into the water and never be seen or heard from again."

My eyes watered, and my throat burned as an explanation more palatable than the truth took root in the cracks of my broken heart.

"Clover?"

I hadn't realized that I'd raised my hand until every face in the room was pointed in my direction.

I hadn't spoken to a soul since the funeral, and I wasn't sure that I was ready to start, but when I looked into Ms. Bell's concerned brown eyes, the words just tumbled out of my mouth. "Ms. Bell, I think me Ma is a selkie."

Thirteen years later, the cruel laughter of two dozen seven-year-olds still echoed in my ears as I scanned the island for seals, hoping one of them would show a glimmer of recognition. Nod in my direction. Maybe even wave.

But the seals were gone, just like I knew they would be. Because right behind the island, anchored about a hundred yards offshore, was a cruise ship the size of Mount Brandon.

Nine months out of the year, Ireland's Eye was Howth's little secret, but every summer, the tourists descended upon it in swarms. You could practically watch the island sink under the weight of all those Nike-wearing, picture-taking, flower-crushing foreigners. But the worst part was that their boats scared away the seals.

And the fish.

Which turned my da into an even bigger arsehole than he already was.

Most of the fishermen gave up on fishing during the summer months, using their boats to give tours of the island instead, but Oliver Doyle was "no fucking tour guide."

He wasn't much of a father either.

As if he were conjured by that thought alone, the sound of a van door slamming shut yanked me from the past back into the present with a violent, terrifying jerk.

Still decked out in his oilskins and wellies, my father walked to the back of the van, his boots crunching in the gravel driveway next to the house, and he pulled out a bundle of ropes as big as a washing machine.

My heart slid into my stomach, but not because of the nets. It was his posture, the scowl beneath his wiry blond beard, the stoop of his hulking shoulders.

The catch hadn't been good. It never was in the summer.

And *I* was going to pay for it.

I walked as quickly and quietly as I could from the cliff's edge back to my spot behind our house, but when my father's gaze landed on me—tiptoeing through a patch of grass with a net that was very much still knotted in my arms—I felt like a deer that had been caught in the crosshairs.

"Where the fuck have you been?"

I could feel my pulse in my throat as Oliver stomped over to me with joyous wrath in his bloodshot eyes. He was looking for someone to take his frustrations out on, and by not having my chores done, I'd just served myself up to him on a silver platter.

I looked down at the net that I was frantically trying to untangle as he approached, too terrified to hold his stare.

"Nowhere, Da." I tilted my head in the direction of the cliff without looking up. "I was just watchin' the boats while I worked. This last net's givin' me trouble."

"Watchin' the boats, were ya?" He mimicked in a high-pitched voice before snapping, "Look at me when I'm talkin', girl!" Oliver's black wellies appeared in my line of sight just before his meaty, callous hand wrapped around the nape of my neck and jerked my head back.

I gripped the rope tighter and swallowed a whimper as he forced me to make eye contact with him.

"*I* was *on* one of those fuckin' boats, workin' me arse off all day, while you were up here, doin' what? *Lookin' fer selkies and merfolk?*"

I pulled my gaze away from his blazing blue eyes and glanced over at a stack of neatly folded fishing nets piled next to the shed. It was the least confrontational way I could think of to answer his question about what I'd been doing all day, but when his head followed my line of sight, the tightening of his grip on the back of my neck told me that I'd made a terrible mistake.

Oliver didn't want to see that I'd been working too. He wanted to be angry with me, and now, thanks to that simple glance, he was.

Oliver shoved me to the ground so fast and so hard that the wind was knocked out of me before I had the chance to scream. I landed on my side in the rocks, and the bone-crunching pain in my ribs immediately brought tears to my eyes.

Don't cry. Don't cry. Don't cry. Don't cry …

Straddling my body, Oliver pushed me onto my back and clutched my face with one hard, rough hand. The gray clouds seemed to gather overhead, watching the spectacle.

"Ya think yer too good fer this now, don't cha? 'Cause yer goin' to some fancy fuckin' college. Ya think yer better 'n' me?" He released me just long enough to pull that hand back, flatten his palm, and slap me across the face.

The worst part about being hit wasn't the sting, not for me; it was the sound. That smack would ring in my ears for hours, sometimes days—long after the swelling went down—reminding me that I was weak, humiliating me over and over again, from the inside out. The sharp clap of skin hitting skin was the soundtrack of my youth. The vibration of my soul. And the source of all my shame.

I barely heard the rest of his speech over the sound of it repeating like a broken record in my head.

"Ya won't be thinkin' yer better than me when I put yer arse out on the street, now will ya? The only reason yer still here is 'cause Sheila begged me to let ya stay until you could afford a place of yer own. But yer twenty goddamn years old now, darlin'. I can kick you out whenever the fuck I want. So, maybe think about that the next time ya feel like bein' smart with me."

My cheek throbbed, my eyes burned, and panic took hold once I realized what was happening. I couldn't cry. Crying only made him angrier. I had to hold it in. I had to.

Widening my eyes to keep from accidentally blinking out a tear, I stared straight ahead at Oliver's heaving whiskey barrel of a chest. A stray beam of sunlight had broken through the clouds, making the side of his bushy blond beard glow like hay that was about to catch fire.

I wished that it would.

"Ollie?"

Da pulled me to my feet so fast that the world spun out from under me and went black. The heap of green rope tumbled out of my arms and onto the ground as I struggled to stay upright and conscious. I felt his arm wrap around my shoulders as Oliver's girlfriend, Sheila, stepped through the back door, bouncing their thrashing toddler on her hip.

I hadn't even known Oliver had been seeing anyone until Sheila showed up on our doorstep, pregnant with his baby and crying because her husband had just kicked her out. She'd been a permanent fixture at our house ever since, and honestly, she was the best thing that had ever happened to us. I tried to stay within earshot of her at all times because Da never raised a hand to me when he knew she was around.

The downside of Sheila's arrival was that she'd given Oliver a son, which only solidified his disdain for me. He had a new family now. A new child. One that could carry on the Doyle name and wasn't a walking, talking redheaded reminder of the woman who'd shattered his heart.

"Can I borrow Clo for a minute?" Sheila asked, grimacing as my half-brother whined and wriggled in her spindly arms. "Odie's fightin' his nap again, and I need her to work her magic."

Odie was short for Odin, the Norse god of war. That name was one hundred percent my father's doing. He prided himself on his Viking blood. Sometimes, when I saw him standing on the bow of his fishing boat, I could almost picture him leading the longship full of Norsemen who had raided Howth all those centuries ago.

He would have fit right in.

Da tightened his grip around me in a fake show of fatherly affection, squeezing my injured shoulder with his viselike hand. It was a warning. Oliver didn't like it when I got involved with anything related to his new family. As far as he was concerned,

Sheila belonged to him and Odie alone. She was *their* special mother figure, not mine. And the sooner I got out of his life, the sooner he could start pretending like my mother had never existed.

The feeling was mutual. After two years of working part-time at the Trinity College bookshop, had almost saved enough money to put a deposit down on an apartment and afford some basic furnishings. Honestly, I probably had enough already, but I couldn't leave Odie. Not yet. Not until he was old enough to tell me if Oliver ever tried to hurt him …

Or make him untangle those goddamn fishing nets.

"Ten minutes," Da said, giving my shoulder a shake that made my freshly bruised ribs scream in pain. "Then, this one has to go check the lobster traps."

I could almost hear his smug grin.

More chores.

Sheila gave me a sympathetic half-smile as Oliver steered me across the yard and into the house. I didn't know how much she'd seen or heard, but it didn't matter. She knew. She knew what went on, and she pitied me for it. But I pitied her even more. Because once I left, she'd most likely be taking my place as his punching bag. And unlike me, he'd never let her get away. Ma had tried to do it, and look where it had gotten her.

The back door led into the kitchen, where Oliver left his wellies on a rubber mat and hung his oilskin coveralls on a hook above them. Beside the hook was one of Sheila's coastal-chic additions to the house—a wooden anchor with the words *Life's a Beach* painted on it. Like living on a rocky cliff next to the freezing cold sea in rainy Ireland was the same as having a beach house in the Caribbean.

Sheila tried to hand me the wailing one-year-old, but Odie clung to her with a high-pitched shriek. It felt as if he were crying all the tears I was trying to hold back. My ribs and cheek throbbed, my eyes stung and my throat burned, but what hurt the most was the fact that I had to pretend as if nothing hurt at all.

"Shut him up, will ya?" Oliver grumbled as he shuffled into the sitting room, popping the tab on a can of Guinness.

"He's just overtired." Sheila winced, prying his chubby fist out of her limp brown hair. "Nothin' his big sister can't fix."

"Well, she'd better fix it fast if she's gonna check those traps before dinner," Oliver sneered, flopping into a blue recliner that was at least a decade older than me. The springs groaned and squeaked beneath him as he yanked on the lever, extending the footrest.

As soon as Sheila extracted the last of Odie's fingers from her hair, I whisked him into my arms. Turning his body sideways, I pressed his belly against mine and began twisting my torso back and forth while making a shushing sound. He went still immediately. It wasn't magic—I was simply the only one in the house who'd bothered to research how to get a baby to stop crying.

With Odie taken care of, Sheila plopped down on the couch, her small frame landing in a pile of seashell-shaped pillows—another one of her design touches.

Da turned on the TV, and while the two of them watched the glowing screen, I stood behind them, rocking and shushing and soothing *myself*. Lifting Odie's sleeping body to my chest, I clutched him like a teddy bear as one of the tears I'd been trying so hard to suppress finally slid down the swollen side of my face.

Stop it, I scolded myself, wiping my wet cheek on Odie's soft head. *If Oliver sees you crying, it's gonna be so much worse.*

"In breaking news," Mia Patel, a BBC newscaster, announced, "a report released by the Irish Directorate of Military Intelligence indicates that a Russian invasion of Ireland might be imminent."

"What?" Sheila sat up with a jolt.

"Bah." Oliver waved a dismissive hand at the TV. "Don't be an eejit. Nobody's invadin' shite."

"According to the minister of defense, Ireland's recent conflict with the United Kingdom and hostile annexation of Northern Ireland—spearheaded by Ireland's Taoiseach Séamus Rooney and members of his radical nationalist party, the United

Irish Brotherhood—has left the small island nation alienated from the rest of the world. By making an enemy of the United Kingdom and its vast network of powerful allies, the Republic of Ireland is now relatively defenseless against the iron fist of Russian President Alexi Abramov, who has declared a personal vendetta against the UIB."

"Listen to this gobshite, will ya?" Oliver gestured toward the newscast with his half-empty can. "We finally take back what's rightfully ours, and we're the fuckin' bad guys."

"Anyone living within twenty kilometers of Dublin, an international airport, or a major harbor are advised to evacuate until—"

"Da, we live near all of those—"

"Clo!" Oliver's sudden shout brought a fresh wave of startled tears to my eyes. Turning around in his chair, he glared at me as I widened my eyes to hold in the moisture. "For Christ's sake, go check the fuckin' traps already. Didn't ya hear?" He grinned like a madman through his wild blond beard as he thrust a hand in the direction of the TV. "The Russians are comin' for dinner!"

CHAPTER 3

DAMIEN

"Smer-nah!"

The deafening rabble of Russian voices, screaming drills, and clanging socket wrenches fell silent as a hundred crewmen darted out from behind the tanks they had been servicing and stood at perfect attention.

Facing me.

It was a show of respect that I hadn't earned and damn sure didn't deserve. And they all knew it.

"Topside. Now," I barked in Russian, reigniting the noise and activity in the belly of Russia's most prized warship.

The sound of tools crashing into bins and boots marching across the floor echoed off the metal bulkheads until the last man disappeared into the stairwell and the hatch slammed shut behind him.

And then the hold was silent again.

I was supposed to be in that stairwell with them, but I couldn't make myself move. There were no windows in the hold. No sights or sounds that might remind me of where I was. Down there, I could pretend like we were anchored somewhere else.

Literally anywhere else.

It had been five years since I'd stepped foot on Irish soil, but it felt like five lifetimes. Every day that I'd spent sparring with Bratva soldiers in the Siberian snow instead of playing football in Phoenix Park, every day that I heard the guttural grunts of Russian instead of the songlike cadence of Irish, every day that I ate shchi and kasha instead of soda bread and shepherd's pie, I felt another piece of the boy that I'd once been burn away. Now, all that remained was a single charred cinder—a brittle, unwanted reminder of who I used to be.

Of who I would never be again.

Remembering that they had cameras on every inch of that ship, I clasped my hands behind my back and began walking between the rows of tanks. My eyes swept over the machines as if I were inspecting them for fuck knew what, but all I could really see was a merciless onslaught of memories from my childhood in Dublin.

For five years, coming home to Ireland had been my only goal—my singular obsession, my sole reason for living—but now that I was finally back, I couldn't even bring myself to look at it.

"Lieutenant," a man shouted in Russian over the intercom, causing me to stand at attention and face the security camera on the bulkhead beside me.

"This is Senior Lieutenant Petrov."

Petrov. My superior. I pictured the brass buttons on his overly decorated jacket straining to contain his swollen beer gut.

"What the *fuck* are you doing down there? The captain wants you topside for his speech. *Now*."

I answered with nothing more than a salute. I knew he would see it—he was obviously watching me—but I also tried to limit all conversation as much as possible. I'd been taught to speak Russian without a detectable accent as part of my father's rigorous training, but I didn't want to press my luck. I'd been warned that no Russian—Bratva or military—would ever trust me if they found out where I was from.

And honestly, they probably shouldn't.

I wasn't one of them, and I never would be. I'd been taken against my will at the age of fifteen—the second my father found out he had a bastard son in Dublin—and thrown into an underground Bratva development program called the Kletka. It meant *cage*, and that was exactly what the fuck it was. A prison-like boot camp in the frozen tundra of Siberia, where the organization trained their potential new soldiers to fight, kill, and most importantly, obey. I was fed a steady diet of steroids and beatings until I was big enough to fight back. And then … the real training began.

Because my father had no other sons, he saw me as his only chance at immortality—an angry, hateful lump of clay that he could mold into his own disgusting image. Initially, he'd been training me to take over the Bratva and carry on the family's gun running, drug muling, and human trafficking businesses, but when Russia began planning to invade Ireland, he enlisted me in the Navy and pulled enough strings to have me start as a lieutenant. He didn't want me engaged in actual combat—I was far too valuable for that. He'd just wanted to solidify my identity as a Russian by making me participate in the destruction of my own homeland.

It was a ten-story climb from the hold of the ship to the deck, but I wished that it were ten thousand. I stared down at my boots as I ascended the stairs, focused on their rhythmic stomping, but all too soon, the dull black leather began to glow gray. The moment I lifted my head and saw that overcast Irish sky through the porthole, my heart began to pound against my ribs like a prisoner thrashing against the bars of its cell. The final glowing cinder of my boyhood longed to see home, but the betrayed, burned-out husk of a man that I'd become knew better.

Seeing it would only make what I'd been sent there to do that much harder.

With a deep breath and an even deeper sense of dread, I opened the topside hatch and stepped out onto the deck. I knew I wouldn't be able to see that green coastline without wanting to scream, so I shut everything out, except for what was directly in front of me. I didn't feel the summer breeze on my skin, I didn't taste the salt of the Irish Sea in the air, and I refused to hear the cries of the gulls I'd once fed as a boy. Instead, I did what I'd been doing at the Kletka since the day I'd realized that there was no escape.

I accepted my situation, and I armored the fuck up.

By the time I reached the stage, my longing, my rage, my powerlessness and despair were all safely locked away behind the numb, bulletproof facade of a Bratva-trained killer.

Captain Orlov watched me take my place in line next to the other officers with an impatient scowl on his vodka-flushed face, but he didn't reprimand me. Either my mask was terrifying enough to make him think twice or he was too excited about starting a war to waste his time on me.

Senior Lieutenant Petrov, who'd barked at me over the intercom, stood to my left, back stiff and belly out, leaving nothing to my right but the one fucking place I couldn't afford to acknowledge.

So, I stared straight ahead at the two thousand troops gathered shoulder to shoulder on the deck. This was what they'd been waiting for, what they'd been promised when they were drafted. The pay was shite. The conditions were worse. But on that shore, they'd be given complete immunity to rape, steal, maim, or kill anything and everything that crossed their path. And judging by the gritted teeth and wild eyes of the men staring back at me, their patience was wearing thin.

"Comrades," Captain Orlov's voice boomed through the loudspeakers, and two thousand hands immediately shot up in salute.

Including mine.

Like a fucking puppet.

I could almost feel my father tugging on the invisible marionette strings above me, lifting my chin, squaring my shoulders.

"Today, we fight not for Russia, but for the honor of President Abramov himself!"

Every saluting hand sliced forward with a guttural, "Ura!"

I felt nothing.

"Over twenty years ago, the United Irish Brotherhood ordered the murder of President Abramov's uncle, Dmitry. But when Alexi came here to avenge his uncle's death, like a man of courage, of honor, the UIB behaved like cowards. They had him arrested—*framed*—for unspeakable, heinous crimes."

The troops booed and spat on the ground, as if their precious president hadn't done *exactly* what the fuck he was accused of. Human trafficking, murder, arms dealing—that was probably the least of it. Everyone knew that Alexi Abramov was a Bratva kingpin who'd hijacked last year's election and taken the Kremlin by force. We just weren't supposed to say it out loud.

"President Abramov spent two years locked in a prison cell because of these deceitful, lying bastards." Captain Orlov thrust a hand in the direction of the shore, and without thinking, my gaze followed.

The sight of the Irish coast hit me like a sucker punch, forcing the air from my lungs in a sudden, nauseating rush. Gray stone cliffs sloped down to the sea, blanketed with green grass and dripping with wildflowers. Waves crashed against the rocks hypnotically, like the rhythmic curl of a beckoning finger, calling me home. And behind them, gray clouds gathered where the cliffs met the sky. It looked like smoke.

Like the cliffs were on fire.

An onslaught of childhood memories played over a soundtrack of my own silent, self-hating screams, and for one torturous second, I felt everything. Every useless, agonizing emotion I'd refused to feel for the last five years flooded my body like boiling toxic waste, scalding my skin from the inside out before I finally pulled my mental armor back on and clung to the numbness.

That's exactly what he wants, I reminded myself. *To hurt me. To break me. To control me once and for all.*

"Since then, the UIB has branded itself a *political party*, and like a virus, it has infiltrated every level of the Irish government. They promised to reclaim Northern Ireland from the UK, but in delivering on that promise, they have made themselves weaker than ever. Their military is depleted. Their allies have vanished. They are isolated, defenseless, and ours for the taking!" Orlov roared as the troops shouted and thrust their fists in the air.

I hoped that if anyone noticed my distraction, they'd assume that I was scanning the coastline for threats because I was incapable of tearing my eyes away from that sight. I followed the cliffs as they sloped down to sea level, the rocky beach giving way to a pier that stretched out into the water, dotted with barnacle-crusted fishing boats and a lighthouse that hadn't functioned in years.

Howth Harbour. I'd been there as a lad. We took a school trip to Ireland's Eye to see the ruins of a monastery that the Vikings had raided. I'd never been on a boat before that day.

Now, I was back, on a very different boat, and this time, I was the one doing the raiding.

Bile seared the back of my throat, but I forced that down too.

"Like a Trojan horse, this converted cruise ship has already allowed us to breach their defenses. She is too big to take into Dublin Bay without drawing suspicion, so from here, we'll take Howth peninsula and push through to Dublin by land."

I scanned the boats, the docks, the paths, the beaches—searching for signs of life and praying that I wouldn't find any.

The boats were all docked. The pavements were empty. The windows of every house, shop, and restaurant were dark. And a seed of desperate, masochistic hope took root in my chest.

Howth was a ghost town. We weren't sneak-attacking them—the residents had already left.

"Crewmen, deploy the tanks and head straight to the harbor. Infantry and intelligence, follow in the rafts. Once the bombing has stopped, set up an encampment, establish roadblocks, and deploy the drones to look for survivors. Artillery troops, remain on deck and report to your assigned officer.

"Tonight, we show the UIB that a crime against President Abramov is a crime against Russia, and Russia … never … forgets!"

The cheering was deafening, but I didn't feel a fucking thing.

"Lieutenant," Petrov bellowed, clapping me on the shoulder as he steered me off the stage. "You are a lucky man. Your platoon has been assigned to short-range shelling." He swept his sausage-like fingers over the Howth coastline. "It is much more fun when you can see the shit that you are blowing up, no?" He laughed, giving my shoulder a series of shakes. "My men on the rocket launchers will be jealous."

I wanted to rip his hand off and stab him in the throat with the severed bone.

Instead, those marionette strings forced my own hand to lift in a salute and my legs to march over to the artillery guns, where my platoon was awaiting my instruction.

I couldn't change what was about to happen. Despite the authority implied by my officer's uniform and the patches on my chest, I had no power here. I was just as much a prisoner on this ship as I had been in the Kletka. The only thing I had control over was whether or not they broke me. And at that, I would never fail. I would bury my humanity so deep that even I couldn't find it. I would carve out my heart, snuff out my soul, if that was what it took to deny them the satisfaction of my pain.

And that was exactly what I did. I took solace in the fact that the town had been evacuated, I accepted the situation, and I armored the fuck up.

CHAPTER 4

CLOVER

I tried to avoid looking at the decor in Odie's nursery as I placed him in his crib. In fact, I tried to avoid going into that room as much as possible. It wasn't that I disliked Sheila's coastal-chic theme—although the vintage fishing nets hanging from the ceiling did make my skin crawl, for personal reasons; it was what those decorations signified that was so hard to stomach. Every starfish and seashell reminded me that Odie had a mother who loved him very much.

And I didn't.

As soon as he was settled, I practically sprinted back down the hall, thankful that my bedroom door was shut so that I wouldn't have to see the faded field of green and purple lining the room. My ma had painted a garden of clover and bluebells along the bottom of my walls before I was born, knowing that she was going to name me after a quote from her favorite poem, but now, the sight of them made my chest ache. Those chipped, cracked leaves and flowers were the only things left in the house that still looked like *her*.

Other than me. A fact that had made me the target of my father's rage since the day she'd died.

In the sitting room, Sheila clutched a crab-shaped pillow to her chest and stared at the news in horror while Oliver continued his diatribe about how this new Russian threat was "just made up by the BBC to scare all of us because they're still fucked off about us taking Northern Ireland back." Neither of them gave me so much as a glance as I bolted through the room and out the back door, which was a relief because my tears had already begun to fall.

By the time I pulled the door closed behind me, I could feel the sob climbing its way out of my throat. I ran to the shed and barely made it inside before I sank to my knees and let it all out. I hated that he made me feel that way. I hated that I was too weak to stand up to him. But mostly, I hated how much I wanted him to love me. It only made it hurt that much more when he reminded me that he didn't.

With a deep, shaky sigh, I wiped my eyes on my sleeve, pulled myself off the ground, grabbed a net big enough to hold a few lobsters—God willing—and tucked a handful of rubber bands into my pocket.

Then, I shoved my feet into my ma's old yellow wellies and headed off toward the cliff trail.

Scanning the sea, the sky, and Ireland's Eye, I was surprised to find that the cruise ship was the only vessel in the water. After that news report, I'd expected to see Russian warships closing in from all sides and fighter jets zooming overhead—we were that close to Dublin. Our house was on the northern side of Howth Head peninsula, the sea side, but the southern side bordered Dublin Bay, which funneled right into the heart of the city.

Maybe Da was right, I thought, feeling the tiniest bit of relief. *Maybe the news really is full of shite.*

The cliff path meandered around the edge of the peninsula, flanked on both sides by wispy purple heather and waist-high yellow gorse bushes. I usually had to duck and weave through the photo-taking tourists this time of year, but the trail was eerily empty. Just as I began to appreciate having it all to myself again, a swell of familiar voices came rolling over the next hill.

Unfortunately, those voices were followed by the arseholes they belonged to—Liv, Sophie, Caiden, and Cash. They lived near the golf course and didn't have chores or jobs … or a single redeeming quality among the four of them. As soon as they saw me, their voices dropped to a whisper, but I could hear everything they said, thanks to the sea winds barreling up the path.

"Ah, look. It's Crazy Clover."

"Where the hell do ya s'pose she's goin'?"

"We're under evacuation orders, and she's out here, takin' her imaginary friend for a walk."

They all burst out laughing.

Crazy Clover. I'd had that nickname since second class. And they were right; I did have an imaginary friend. At least, I had back then. He was the main character from one of the books Ma used to read to me at night—a handsome young fairy prince who could be found in the forest of Glenshire, a small farming village where the author lived. The author's descriptions had been so vivid that I could practically feel the velvety fuzz of the moss covering every tree trunk, the tickle of the bluebells against my bare legs. I could taste the sour burst of blackberries on my tongue. And I could definitely picture the boy.

He didn't have wings or pointy ears, but he looked special nonetheless, both because of his beauty and because he was completely colorless—wild black hair; pale, porcelain skin; and eyes the color of smoke, if you were lucky enough to see them. He never spoke, but he liked to play. The author said she often found him playing in the ruins of an old stone cottage out in the woods, and although it was a very serious offense for a fairy to allow themselves to be seen by a human, for a few vanilla custard creams, he could be persuaded to let her play with him.

After Ma died, I'd needed a friend so badly that I began imagining that the fairy boy was with *me*, in my world, all the time. I told myself that he had to stay hidden so that he wouldn't get in trouble, but I knew he was there. I could feel him.

But between my unpredictable crying fits, my insistence that my mother was actually a selkie, and my imaginary fairy friend, it wasn't long before the whole town began calling me Crazy Clover. Including my da.

The teasing got so bad that I stopped talking to everyone, including the boy. I had nightmares about car crashes and freshly dug graves, walls closing in and waves pulling me under, cruel children and crueler adults. I picked at my lips and cuticles until they bled. I pulled out my eyebrows and eyelashes completely. I withdrew into my fairy-tale books, and whenever I did emerge, I wished that I hadn't. Life was just easier once everyone forgot that I existed.

But by secondary school, everything had changed. My eyelashes and eyebrows had grown back in. My auburn hair was nearly down to my waist, thanks to Oliver never bothering to get it cut. And my scrawny body had filled out in new places. Suddenly, I wasn't invisible anymore.

Quite the opposite.

Boys who'd once tripped me in the hallway began cornering me at my locker. They'd ask me out on dates, take me places alone. They'd kiss me and touch me and tell me nice things when no one was around, but in front of other people, they pretended like they didn't know me. It hurt, so much, but it felt better than being invisible *all the time*, so I let them do it.

I'd let them do anything they wanted.

A fact that Cash McNalley had taken full advantage of the summer before sixth year. When he'd driven me to the Baily lighthouse after dark, I assumed that he had romantic intentions. Maybe we'd look at the stars, I thought, tell each other our deepest, darkest secrets. Instead, he invited me to sit in the backseat with him, where he took my virginity in seven minutes or less. As soon as it was over, he tossed the condom out the window and drove me home. I cried myself to sleep that night. *Quietly.* Oliver hated crying.

And because I was no longer invisible to the boys, I was no longer invisible to the girls either. They'd glare at me and chat shite about me and laugh whenever I walked by. I'd thought it would end when I finished secondary school, but ... no such luck.

Sophie held up a rose-gold phone, which glimmered almost as brightly as her cruel eyes and icy-blonde hair. "Forty-seven notifications to evacuate, and Clover here decides to"—her gaze flicked down to the lobster net in my hand—"go fishin' with her invisible boyfriend."

"Very *on brand*," Liv added with a smirk while the two boys looked around uncomfortably.

I stepped off the trail to give them enough room to pass, careful not to trample the heather, and stood facing the water so that my red, swollen cheek would be out of view.

The cruise ship was still there, and that gave me hope. They probably had all kinds of technology that would tell them about other ships nearby. If they weren't worried about the Russians, then I decided I wouldn't be either.

"Seriously? Yer just gonna stand there, staring at the water, and not say anything?" Sophie rolled her eyes as they approached, but Cash's gaze locked on to mine and held it.

There was an apology in his stare, but he'd never say it out loud. Not in front of them.

"She's so weird," Liv whispered, loud enough for me to hear.

"And she smells like fish." Sophie giggled, causing both girls to erupt into a fit of laughter.

"Maybe that's just her gee. Cash would know, wouldn't ya?" Caiden gave his brother a playful shove.

Cash immediately shoved him back much harder. "Fuck off, arsehole."

For one brief moment, I thought he might be defending me, but I knew better. Cash was defending *himself*. God forbid anyone find out that he'd stooped so low as to sleep with Crazy Clover Doyle.

The second they passed, I turned and walked in the opposite direction, the aching knot in my stomach throbbing in time with my bruised cheek and battered ego.

A few more meters down the trail, hidden between two yellow gorse bushes, was where *my* trail began. I had to be careful not to let anyone see me take it. If the tourists discovered a path leading from the cliff to the sea with a charming little cave at the bottom, it would be all over the travel sites in a heartbeat. And then we'd be done for. That cave and the lobster I caught inside were the only things that kept us afloat in the summer.

The cliff was steep, but there were enough jutting rocks and grassy patches to form a skinny trail down. Climbing back up with a few kilos of wet lobster thrown over your shoulder … now, that was trickier.

In fact, Oliver couldn't take my trail at all—he was far too big. He could only access the cave by anchoring his boat outside the entrance and either swimming in or taking a small, inflatable raft. It was a pain in the arse, which was why he insisted on making me do it.

I'd never admit it to him, but I actually loved checking the traps. That cave was my favorite place in the entire world.

As a kid, I'd read that in ancient Ireland, caves were thought to be portals to the otherworld—the magical realm where fairies and other mythical creatures lived. So, when Oliver began making me check the lobster traps on my own, I was elated. I'd scour every inch of that cave, looking for a secret passage, a hidden door, a symbol, a code, anything that might take me away from there and deliver me to the world of my silver-eyed friend. I never found it, of course, but I never gave up. Every time I went down there, I did a lap around the cave, exploring the farthest, darkest corners, pressing on stones and feeling for cracks. I'd kept searching long after I stopped believing in fairies.

Because hope was the only drug I could afford.

I descended the cliff with sure-footed steps, grasping at stones and bushes on the trickier parts. The trail ended on a flat patch of rock, maybe two meters above sea level, which, to most people, would seem like the final destination. But I knew there was more under that stone. So much more.

Scaling the slope on the far side of the landing, I ducked under the capstone and made my way in. The left side of the cave entrance had a narrow ledge I could walk on, just a few centimeters below sea level, but the ceiling was so low that I had to crouch to keep from bumping my head. The right side of the cave entrance was a narrow channel of deep seawater—the perfect little hiding place for lobsters trying to avoid predators.

With every wave that crashed against the rocks outside, a burst of salty mist peppered my back, and a swell of cold seawater swirled around my ankles, chilling my feet, even through my rubber boots.

Soon, the entryway opened up, and I was finally able to stand upright again. The light coming in through the cave entrance bounced off the water, casting glittery sparkles and shimmering shadows on every stone surface inside. The narrow ledge I'd been walking on expanded into a pebbled beach that curled around the left side of the cavern, stretched across the back, and ended in a dramatic spray of jagged boulders on the right. And behind those rocks was where I stored my most precious belongings in the whole entire world.

As I worked my way around the edge of the cave, sliding my hand along the stone wall out of habit, I made sure to watch my step. Radiating out from the edge of the water was a web of red ropes, each anchored to a heavy rock. There were twelve in total, and I hoped that on the other end of at least half of them, I'd find an unsuspecting lobster trapped in a cage.

But first, I had to check on my babies.

Once I made it to the farthest, darkest corner of the cave, I squatted next to a boulder and reached around behind it. Groping the cool stone wall until I found a crevice, I shoved my hand in and pulled out a simple black backpack.

In fifth class, I was mortified by my own backpack—a pink and purple nightmare that I'd been carrying since I was a little kid. Oliver refused to buy me a new one, no matter how much I begged, so after seeing that jet black backpack on the lost-and-found table at school every day for a month, my desire got the better of me, and I stole it. I realized on the way home that Oliver would beat me black and blue if he caught me with something that didn't belong to me, so I hid it in the cave.

And eventually, I'd filled it with other things that I wanted to hide from Oliver—things I loved, things I'd stolen, things I would need if I ever found a portal to the otherworld and decided to run away.

Sitting on my favorite boulder—the one with a chunk broken off, forming a seat—I placed the canvas bag on the ground and unzipped it with a flutter in my chest that made me forget all about arseholes like Cash and his friends and my da and the Russians. None of them could hurt me in the cave. In here, it was just me, the sound of the waves, the shimmer on the water, and all my favorite things—stored in clear plastic resealable bags to keep them dry and mildew-free.

The first bag I pulled out of the backpack contained a pack of matches from The Bloody Stream pub and four of Oliver's cheap cigars. I'd taken them one at a time so that he wouldn't notice.

After making a hole in the end of one cigar with my thumbnail, I toasted the other end with a match and placed it between my lips. I'd learned how to light them from watching Oliver. Puff, rotate, puff, rotate. The smoke tasted gross and made my head spin, but the smell? The smell was intoxicating. Powerful men smoked cigars, and there, in my secret hideaway, I could pretend like I was powerful too.

Balancing the lit cigar on the edge of the boulder, I dug through the rest of my belongings—a framed picture of Ma, extra clothes, a few bottles of water, and some long-expired snacks—until I finally reached the heart of my trove. There, at the bottom of the bag, was the entirety of my book collection— the Legend Has It series by Darby Donovan.

My mother had been gone thirteen years, but I still got misty-eyed every time I saw those books. I pulled them out one by one, running my fingers over the gilded titles through the plastic bags I kept them in. They had dark green linen hardcovers, like vintage books, with gold foiled titles and haunting hand-drawn illustrations inside. They were my most prized possessions, and between those pages, in the forest of Glenshire, I felt more at home than I did in my own house.

I wished I could stay out there all night, reading and smoking and avoiding my father, but it was getting late, and those traps weren't going to empty themselves.

After placing everything back in its designated spot, I gave the backpack a firm hug and returned it to its secret hidey-hole.

Then, with Oliver's cigar between my teeth and one eye squeezed shut to keep out the smoke, I knelt down at the water's edge and used both hands to reel in the first of the traps. It felt heavy, which gave me hope, but when I peered into the water to see what was inside, it was the reflection of the sky on the surface that caught my attention.

Or rather the streaks of fire shooting across it.

CHAPTER 5

CLOVER

Even thirty meters below ground, the explosions were deafening. Oliver's cigar tumbled from my gasping mouth and hit the water with a hiss as the cave began to shake. It floated there in front of me, unlike the loose rocks that fell from the cavern ceiling. Those pummeled the surface like a hailstorm, dousing me with frigid seawater and crashing on the pebbled beach all around me. Covering my head with both hands, I darted over to the cave entrance and ducked inside the narrow tunnel that would lead me out.

The bombing was relentless. With every concussion, my heartbeat stuttered, my eyes squeezed shut, my body jerked, and my lips mumbled a prayer that the cave wouldn't collapse before I made it out. But as I approached the mouth of the tunnel and that first whiff of smoke filled my lungs, I realized that the cave might be the safest place on the entire peninsula.

It couldn't have been later than seven, but it looked like midnight outside. Plumes of gray smoke and ash billowed in the sky, torn and punctured by the endless barrage of missiles that came screaming off the deck of the cruise ship. Smoke swirled on the surface of the water as well, but not where a fleet of boat-like tanks sliced through it on their way from the belly of the ship to the harbor. Every panicked breath I took was answered with a violent cough as the thick, sulfuric air suffocated me. I had to get to higher ground. I had to get to Odie. But when I turned and stared up at the cliff behind me, I realized that my mental image of hell from earlier had been wrong.

Hell wasn't a mountain of fishing nets. It was a burning cliff separating you from the people you loved.

Blast after blast rattled my chest as I climbed up the trail, constantly scanning the ground for my next step or handhold. Fire licked at the edges of the path and reached for me with crackling fingers, but I refused to look anywhere but straight ahead.

How many minutes had it been since the bombing had started? Three? Five? Maybe they were okay. Maybe they'd gotten out. I didn't hear any screaming.

My stomach dropped.

I don't hear any screaming.

I had just begun to panic when my body came to a sudden halt. The bush that hid the entrance of my secret trail was completely engulfed in flames. In fact, *everything* on top of the cliff was engulfed in flames. My mouth fell open as I tried to make sense of what I was seeing. What had been an idyllic sea of purple and yellow wildflowers swaying in the breeze just half an hour before was now a fiery, blazing wasteland. I couldn't see a single house—they had either been demolished or were shrouded in smoke so thick that I couldn't tell if they were still standing. And off in the distance, the rolling hills of Howth appeared to be boiling—everywhere a shell landed, an orange fireball swelled and popped, spewing a cloud of sparks and black smoke.

Pulling the neck of my shirt up over my mouth and nose, I leaped over a shorter bush and sprinted down the path. I could hardly see anything up ahead, but the fire closing in on the trail illuminated my steps as I ran. It was so hot; I expected to find my wellies melted onto my feet by the time I got home.

If I still had a home.

Pushing that thought away, I glanced over my shoulder in the direction of the cruise ship. I could only tell it was still there because its generic white paint color glowed through the haze and ash like the blurry essence of a ghost ship. Flashes of orange burst from the cannons on its deck, and after each one, a nearby explosion seized my heart and made me flinch. They never landed in the same spot twice, which was why it shouldn't have surprised me when one screaming missile careened directly into the cliff in front of me.

Rocks and earth exploded in all directions as a blinding heat seared my face and sent me flying backward. I landed in the unforgiving arms of a burning gorse bush. Its sharp, flaming branches punctured my skin and singed my clothes before I rolled onto the ground, gasping for air. Clumps of dirt and grass rained down on me from the blast as I struggled to suck in a breath. I couldn't hear anything, but everything was loud. I couldn't feel anything, but everything hurt. I couldn't see anything …

Until my unfocused eyes landed on a heap of green fishing nets.

Dragging myself toward it, I blinked and coughed and squinted into the smoke, desperately searching for something familiar within all that fire and debris. The nets were strewn about on a pile of rubble, which I crawled over, ignoring the shards of wood biting into my knees and palms.

"Odie …" I called, my voice barely above a whisper.

I didn't know why I was being so quiet, but I suspected it was because I wanted to hold on to that last shred of hope a little longer. If I whispered his name and he didn't cry out, I could tell myself that he just hadn't heard me. But if I shouted at the top of my lungs and he didn't answer …

A sob swelled in the back of my throat as the ropes and wood beneath my palms transitioned to chunks of stucco and shards of roofing tiles. I could feel the heat from a nearby fire, but the smoke was so thick that it didn't provide much light.

"Odie …" I coughed. "It's me, Clo." My voice was louder that time. More frantic.

When no one responded, I began to dig and claw and tear at the pile of rubble that now spread out around me in all directions.

"Odie!" I coughed harder. "Da! Sheila!"

Wooden beams as long as my arm went sailing across the yard as I attacked the pile, choking on smoke and ash and my own unspoken fears.

"Da, answer me! I know you're in there!"

Lifting half of our once-yellow door with both hands, I hurled it to the side and found my answer lying just beneath it.

A woman's arm, severed at the elbow.

With my da's key ring dangling from its finger.

Time stopped.

The explosions stopped.

The only sounds I could hear were the crackling of a thousand fires and the rumbling of a dozen tanks.

And my own mind, as it shattered into a million jagged pieces that would never fit together again.

It was a nightmare that I couldn't wake up from. It didn't feel real. How could it be? Less than an hour earlier, I'd been standing in that exact same spot, holding my baby brother. We'd all been together, watching TV. And now, I was crawling through a smoky wasteland, staring at …

I squeezed my eyes shut and willed myself to wake up.

This is real, a sinister voice whispered from somewhere deep inside my own skull. *This is real, and it's all your fault.*

Wake up, Clover.

You knew you should have evacuated when you heard the news, but you were too scared to argue with Oliver.

Wake up!

You didn't even try. Odie was right there in your arms. You could have just grabbed Oliver's keys, and—

I grasped both sides of my head and opened my mouth to scream when a blinding white light flooded my vision. Squeezing my eyes shut, I tilted my face toward the source with a shuddering sob of relief. I didn't know if I had died and was traveling into the light or if the morning sun had come to wake me from my nightmare. And I didn't care. All that mattered was that it was about to be over.

Or so I thought.

"This is a message from President Abramov."

Blinking in confusion, I shielded my eyes and squinted into the light. It wasn't coming from the sun or a tunnel welcoming me into heaven. The beam was coming from a single spot, hovering a few meters above me. A drone.

And it was talking.

"Your city has been captured by the Armed Forces of the Russian Federation," the robotic voice continued. "This is your only chance to surrender. You have ten seconds to raise your hands above your head and follow this device to the nearest encampment. Refusal to do so will be considered an act of war and will result in your termination."

My mind reeled as I struggled to process the words that had just been spoken to me.

Captured.

Surrender.

Encampment.

War.

Termination.

I was dreaming. I had to be. That was the only rational explanation.

"Ten."

But I wasn't waking up.

"Nine."

Why wasn't I waking up?

"Eight."

My eyes darted all over the wreckage, now illuminated by the spotlight, and the nightmare morphed into a horror film. In the light, I could see that the rubble I'd been digging through was splattered with blood. Everywhere I looked, I saw pulpy chunks of flesh, clumps of hair, severed fingers, splintered bone.

And I was kneeling in it.

My gaze landed on Sheila's hand again—my father's key ring still looped over her knuckle—and a voice inside of me screamed, *Take it!*

Shoving my hand into the pile of plaster and wood in front of me, I held my breath as my fingers brushed Sheila's. A wave of nausea swelled in my throat at how real it felt. How cold and rubbery and limp.

"Seven."

I slid the key ring off her finger and scrambled over the debris toward the area where I thought Oliver's van was parked. It was hard to tell where I was with all the smoke and rubble. Nothing looked familiar. Nothing but the keys in my hand. The drone and its spotlight followed me effortlessly, lighting my way.

"Six."

Butterflies of elation took flight in my belly as soon as the van came into view, but they quickly died, along with any hope I had of escape, when I realized that the driver's side of the vehicle had been completely crushed under our chimney.

"Five."

I stopped and stared at that wreckage as if I were staring into my own freshly dug grave. That van had been my only chance. I couldn't outrun a drone, not for long. But I couldn't force myself to lift my hands and surrender either. I watched the news. I knew what happened to female prisoners of war.

"Four."

That was it then. I'd made my choice. Maybe there would be an afterlife and I'd get to see my family again, or maybe there'd be nothing but an endless black abyss. Either way, my suffering would be over in …

"Three."

I held my breath and closed my eyelids, waiting to see my short, miserable life flash behind them. But it wasn't my life I saw at all. It was *him*.

Steely-gray eyes shone up at me as I sat, perched on the branch of an oak tree. The fairy prince was shirtless and shoulder deep in the lake where we used to play—the one deep in the forest that was surrounded by blackberry bushes. The sky above him churned like a witch's cauldron. The mist on the water rose toward it in curling tendrils. But there, in the center, was the eye of the storm. Calm. Powerful. Focused solely on me. The boy had become a man, and the sight of him twisted a knife of longing in my belly. The pain was sharp and deep as I gazed upon his hardened features. His cut hair. His square jaw, held high. A face that had once blushed bashfully under soft curls now gazed upon me with cold, masculine confidence.

"Jump," he commanded, extending his sculpted, muscular arms toward me.

I'd never heard his voice before. The sound of it was so velvety and hypnotic that it took me an extra second to register what he'd said.

An extra second that I didn't have.

"One."

Throwing the keys on the ground, I turned and ran. The smoke and rubble in my path seemed to part for me, clearing the way so that every step landed sure and true. I heard the drone open fire behind me, felt the whoosh of bullets zipping past, but I wasn't afraid. I saw the bushes engulfed in flames up ahead, but I knew they wouldn't burn me. A sense of peace, of *rightness*, that I'd never felt before pulled me toward the cliff like a siren song. And every cell in my body listened, pushing me to get there faster. I never doubted, never wavered, and when I reached the cliff's edge, I pictured my prince waiting to catch me below, arms outstretched, an impish smirk softening the hard angles of his face. I didn't care if I lived or died beyond that leap.

And evidently, I wasn't the only one.

As soon as I pushed off from the rocks—suspended and weightless in a spray of bullets—my gaze locked on to a moving shadow directly across the water. With my heart in my throat, I watched the figure jump off the top deck of the warship at the exact same time as me. Their body was just a black silhouette against the ghastly white of that death machine, but I could tell that we were facing one another as we fell.

And for one brief moment, I didn't feel so alone.

CHAPTER 6

DAMIEN

THIRTY MINUTES EARLIER

I was on autopilot. No thoughts. No feelings. Just action, authority, and indifference. That was how I'd survived in the Kletka, and that was how I would survive this.

They couldn't break something that didn't exist.

I focused on the task at hand, spoke as little as possible, and instructed my men to load and prepare the artillery. When we got the signal, it was my platoon that fired first.

Striking the Howth Harbour lighthouse dead fucking center.

The relic exploded like a firework, spewing fire and shooting three-hundred-year-old granite in all directions.

It was the first strike against Ireland, a declaration of war, and I might as well have pulled the trigger myself.

But I felt nothing.

As the crew cheered, I watched my childhood crumble and fall into the sea through a cold, impenetrable shield. Detached. Devoid. And completely fucking alone.

That lighthouse broke the seal. Within seconds, every gun on the deck was pumping out missiles, rockets, or shells as fast as their crews could get them loaded and aimed. The deck of the ship filled with smoke and shuddered with every deafening blast, along with my heart, which felt like it might seize at any moment from the brutal concussions pounding through my chest.

And for possibly the first time in my life, I wished that it would. My obsession with finding my way back home had kept me alive, kept me going all those years in the Kletka. But now that Ireland was disappearing before my eyes, being consumed, bite by bite, by the same machine that had consumed me, what was left to live for?

These were the morbid thoughts going through my head as my gunners worked their way from the harbor to the cliffs. Building by building, house by house, it was like shooting cans off a fence post. But at least they were empty cans.

Or so I'd thought.

The smoke and flames climbing up the cliffs from the harbor had become so thick that I needed binoculars to make sure my gunners were hitting their targets. I swept over the coastline, confirming each hit, but when I looked farther ahead at what hadn't been struck yet, what I saw broke through my mask of indifference like a hammer through a sheet of ice.

The next house in the line of fire was a tiny white thing—as old as the cliffs themselves—with a bright yellow door. The color was what stopped me. It seemed so familiar, just like the woman who stepped out of it, dripping with luggage and holding a baby boy.

I couldn't make out her features, but she was thin with dark hair and fair skin.

Just like my ma.

My reaction was immediate and involuntary. With both hands, I shoved the crew member to my right away from the artillery, but I was too late. He'd already pulled the lanyard, and the blast felt like a sledgehammer against my skull. Fire tore through the smoke-filled sky. And all I could do was watch in horror as the white house with the yellow door—and the mother and child in front of it—were consumed by a billowing fireball of death.

"What are you doing?" I screamed, thrashing against the meaty hands holding me in place as a second Bratva soldier entered through the front door of our apartment.

He stomped toward my mother, who was standing on the other side of our tiny sitting room.

"Let him go!" she shouted, holding her ground as the goon approached. She was off work that day, so her long, dark hair was pulled back in a ponytail and the purple bags under her eyes weren't hidden beneath a centimeter of makeup. Neither was her terror. I could feel it in the air. "We had a deal," she said, glancing from them to me.

The soldier made no attempt to argue with her. He simply placed his hands on either side of her face and jerked her head to the side so hard that her neck snapped. I'd never forget the sound. That sudden, unexpected crunch.

"Deal's off." He chuckled, tossing her lifeless body onto the couch.

She landed on her side, and the last thing I remembered before they hauled me away was the haunting emptiness in her pale blue eyes as they stared straight through me.

"What are you doing?" Five years later, I was screaming those words again, this time at the sailor whose shirt was in my fist. "There was a woman up there! With a fucking baby!"

Half of my platoon went still, and they stared at me, too, but their stares weren't vacant—they were shocked and suspicious and ready to attack. They stared at me like I'd spoken to them in a foreign language.

Because I had.

Shite.

Releasing the sailor, I took a step back.

"What the fuck was that?" he shouted, allowing his comrades to help him stand. The rest of my platoon kept firing, too absorbed in their tasks and obscured by smoke to notice our standoff.

"He sounded like one of *them*."

"Maybe he's working for them."

"That's impossible. His father is—"

"I know what I heard."

"I'm your fucking lieutenant," I shouted—in Russian this time—"and you'll address me as such."

"You just attacked Antonov and screamed at him in English, *sir*," one of the men who'd helped the gunner stand up said, still clutching his arm.

"Spy!" Antonov shouted, shoving a finger in my direction. "He's a fucking Irish spy!"

I didn't know who drew first, but in the blink of an eye, my pistol was pressed against the gunner's temple, and five more were aimed directly at me.

"Stand down!" I yelled, realizing a moment later that the words had come out in English again.

Whatever the fuck I'd been pretending to be had turned to water in my fists. I couldn't hold on to it much longer, and honestly, I didn't want to.

"Stand down!" I repeated in Russian. "That's a direct order!"

The crewmen looked at one another, confused and conflicted.

"Any sailor who does not holster his weapon immediately will be charged with insubordination. This is your final warning."

As the men hesitantly lowered their weapons, I glanced back up at the smoldering remains of the white house with the yellow door. No one could have survived that blast, so I wasn't expecting to find any signs of life. But that was exactly what I saw. A silhouetted speck of a person, possibly a woman or a child, was running along the top of the cliff.

And directly into our line of fire.

Charging toward the other artillery gun under my command, I dived for that gunner just as he yanked on the lanyard, sending a shell screaming into the side of the cliff. As we crashed into the plexiglass deck railing, I kept my eyes on the silhouette, up until the moment it disappeared behind a geyser of rocks and earth.

The toxic rage that had been festering inside of me for five fucking years ignited and boiled over, flooding my veins with a hatred so thick and so hot that it burned away the last tattered remains of the lie I'd been living.

Pinning the gunner on the ground, I unleashed my fury, my agony, and my guilt through my fists, relishing the pain in my knuckles as they collided with bone and split open on teeth. All that time, I'd been putting on armor to protect myself—to keep me numb, to hide my humanity—but now that it was gone, I realized that it had also been protecting them.

From *me*.

Countless hands seized my arms, wrenching them behind my back as they hauled me away from the bloody pulp of a man on the deck. My chest heaved, and my body shook as they shoved me against the wall of a storage room and pummeled me with their fists, their knees, the soles of their boots, but I barely registered the blows. Because at that very moment, a spotlight beamed down on the ruins of the house with the yellow door.

Someone had survived.

Relief washed over me as I squinted into the darkness, moving my head to get a better view around the helmets of the men who were restraining me. I was desperate for proof that I'd finally done something right, that my actions had saved at least one innocent life, but as soon as I remembered what that spotlight meant, what it was attached to, that fleeting joy was replaced with a frantic, nauseating sense of dread.

The drones were programmed to *find* survivors, not rescue them. Whoever was still alive up there wouldn't be for long. They'd either die in ten seconds by gunfire or in two weeks after being raped and tortured to death. But either way, that beam of light was a death sentence.

And I'd just blown my cover for nothing.

"What is the meaning of this?" Captain Orlov boomed.

A silence more deafening than artillery fire fell over the ship as every crew member turned toward the stage and saluted their leader.

I couldn't see him through the crush of sailors surrounding me, but I knew that at any moment, Orlov would descend from his pedestal and push through the crowd, haul me off to a cell, let all the officers on the ship take turns beating and torturing me, and then send whatever was left of me back to my father, whose punishment would make the Kletka look like summer camp.

I should have been terrified, but I was too busy counting the seconds in my head to care.

Seven.

A black silhouette, small and quick, darted away from the pile of rubble, and I knew that it had to be the runner. They were still alive.

"He's an Irish spy, Captain."

"It's true, sir."

Six.

The beam of light followed the survivor effortlessly as they approached a vehicle parked next to the rubble.

Don't do it. You'll never get away in that. You'll just become a bigger target.

"He assaulted two artillery gunners, sir."

"He put a gun to my head, Captain."

Five.

The survivor stopped running and stood perfectly still, staring at the van.

No. No, no, no. Don't surrender. It'll be so much worse. Fuck.

"He screamed at us in English, sir."

"He sounded just like one of *them*."

Four.

Run! Hide somewhere that'll mask your body heat. Go!

My heart slammed against the bars of its permanent prison as I scanned the coastline in vain. There was nowhere to hide from a heatseeking drone. Nowhere except …

My gaze dropped to the moonlit waves crashing against the rocks below.

Three.

My entire awareness shrank to the size of that spotlight on top of the cliff. The ship, the sea, the smoke-filled sky—it all faded away, darkening and flickering until I felt as though I were looking up at that light from the bottom of a deep, murky lake. I swam toward it in my mind—watched it expand as I grew closer—and when I finally broke through the surface, I was no longer in Howth.

I was standing in a lake, in a forest, staring up at an oak tree …
And into the eyes of a girl perched on its lowest branch.
The sight of her took my breath away. She was clutching a rope swing and wearing nothing but her bra and knickers. Soft copper waves cascaded around her body like a veil, and when her big, terrified eyes landed on me, something inside of me cracked open, allowing a need that I had long ago buried to claw its way out of my rotten, putrid soul.
I didn't just need her. I needed to protect her. I needed to get her down from there. I needed her in the water, in my arms, immediately and forever.
Standing to my full height, I lifted my hands, but a tightness in my throat prevented me from speaking. I couldn't force more than a single word through the blockage. A single word to convey my inexplicable longing, my fear, my desperation … my love.
"Jump!"

But another word slipped through the crack in my consciousness right after it. A word that reeled me back into my body like the snap of a rubber band.

Two.

The light was once again just a slash of white on the other side of the sea, but standing in it was my salvation. If this stranger lived, then it would've all been worth it. If I could trade my hopeless, miserable life for theirs, then my treason wouldn't have been in vain.

"Jump," I whispered.

Please.

"Show me this traitor," Captain Orlov demanded. "Move. Now!"

As the crowd of sailors parted before me, making a path for their leader to come administer his wrath, I felt a frantic, overwhelming need to go back into the light. To find the girl who'd been waiting for me on the other side of it and never let her go. I'd thought that the home I was longing for was Ireland, but I'd been wrong. It was a girl with copper hair, whom I'd never met.

But she was so close that I could taste the blackberries bursting on my tongue.

One.

Streaks of orange fired from the drone as the figure turned and sprinted toward the cliff. And without thinking, without a plan, without hope of survival or fear of death, I did the same.

"Seize him!" Orlov shouted.

A sick, electrifying thrill coursed through my veins like the end of a lit fuse, burning away those marionette strings and setting that last forgotten, charred ember of life inside of me ablaze.

The path in front of me opened wider as men got out of the way to allow those behind me to open fire. I hardly noticed the bullets whizzing past my head—my entire focus was on the runner on the cliff.

Make it. Please. You have to make it.

A bolt of pain tore through my side as I leaped over the railing, but when I saw that the runner had made the leap too—as we plummeted, together, into uncertain waters—all I could feel was the exhilaration of freedom and the weightlessness of relief.

I didn't know if I would survive the jump, and honestly, I didn't care.

Dead or alive, I was finally coming home.

CHAPTER 7

CLOVER

The waves pummeled me as I swam along the edge of the cliff over to the cave, spilling over my head in merciless torrents and shoving my body into the rocks. The sea was always freezing, even in June, and the shock of being repeatedly doused by that frigid water made it nearly impossible to think about anything other than getting the fuck out of it.

By the time I found the entrance and hauled my soaking wet, half-drowned arse onto the narrow ledge outside of it, all I could do was lie there and gasp and stare up at the sky. For a few moments, it was just me, my burning lungs, and my shivering body. Nothing else. No thoughts. No feelings. Just the sound of the sea, the smell of my burning town, and the hollow echo of my soul. I was simply too depleted to think or feel.

I hoped it would last forever.

But soon, another sound joined the rhythmic lapping of the waves, one that was alarming enough to break through my exhausted, traumatized fog—the deep roar of rapidly approaching jets.

Finally, I thought. The Air Corps were coming.

I continued to stare at the sky above me as three smoke-spewing missiles sliced across the starless night, followed by the planes that had fired them. I rolled my foggy head toward the cruise ship just in time to see it return fire. The Russian missiles crossed paths with ours in the air, their contrails nearly kissing, and then … night turned into day.

I threw my arm over my face as an inferno of heat and light enveloped me. The explosions were so loud that they rattled the bones in my chest, the sounds more terrifying than anything I could have ever imagined. Grinding metal and groaning steel. Squealing engines and screaming men. A plane plunged into the water a hundred meters in front of me, and I had to scramble up on top of the cave entrance to avoid being washed out to sea by the massive wave it'd created.

From there, I could see that the entire deck of the ship was on fire, and there was a gaping hole right in the center. But even as the ship burned and slowly split in half, even as its engulfed crew threw their flaming bodies into the sea, it somehow kept pumping missiles into the air.

Another jet went down out past the Eye, but I couldn't see where it landed through the black smoke billowing out of the belly of the ship. I turned my gaze skyward, looking for the third plane, when the right side of the ship suddenly erupted in an explosion so powerful that it knocked me on my arse. The fire must have reached the ship's cache of ammunition because the detonations kept happening, one after the other in that exact same spot, producing a fireball the size of a hot-air balloon that kept being refilled. It was so bright that it illuminated everything from the island to the cliff.

Including the lifeless body of a man drifting toward the rocks.

The pilot.

Nothing about him suggested that he might be alive. He was floating face up, arms motionless, legs submerged, and I'd seen that crash. No one could have survived that. But the second I saw him, my exhaustion, my emptiness, my complete and utter depletion were forgotten, replenished with fresh energy and pulsing with purpose.

I felt that same pull—that urgent, desperate, unexplainable need—that I'd felt on the cliff.

Jump, it commanded again.

And just like before, my body responded without question.

Compared to the thirty-meter plunge I'd just made, the leap off the cave's entrance felt like nothing. I was already freezing, so my muscles and lungs didn't even seize from the cold. And I wasn't running for my life this time.

I was swimming toward his.

The waves were relentless, but so was I, diving under the surface between breaths where the water was easier to cut through. Even though it felt like I was swimming in place, for every meter of progress I fought to make, the current carried him three meters closer to me.

The need to wrap my arms around him propelled me. I pictured myself embracing him as I hauled him to safety. Anticipated the moment when my chest would be pressed against his, when his body would be draped over mine. I couldn't explain it. I didn't know this person. I didn't even know if he was still alive.

In fact, I was so focused on reaching him that when I came up for my next breath, I didn't notice the massive swell of water surging toward me until it was almost too late. Diving beneath the surface just before it crashed over my head, I felt the weight of the churning water shove me violently into the deep. It tossed my body like a rag doll, rolling and spinning me toward the rocky sea floor, but when it finally passed, I somehow found my way back to the surface.

The pilot did not. I knew it before my head even breached the water.

The ship was now completely engulfed in flames, illuminating the choppy black sea and airplane wreckage floating around me, so it only took a split second for my eyes to verify what my gut already knew. Then, with a deep breath and a renewed sense of determination, I dived back under.

He was down there somewhere, and I was going to find him. His presence was a warm breeze on my skin—I could tell which direction it was coming from even though I couldn't see it. Chasing that sensation, I drove myself deeper, muscles pumping, lungs burning. And with every passing second, I felt less and less in control of my actions.

After everything I'd survived that day, everything I'd already lost, I was going to drown in the sea, trying to rescue a stranger who was probably already dead. And there was nothing I could do to stop myself.

I'd barely had a single conscious thought since I'd jumped off that cliff. My heart and mind were a pair of traumatized voids, vacant hostages inside a body that was propelling them straight toward the ocean floor.

My lungs begged for air, and my nerves twitched with frantic commands that my muscles ignored, but a spark of blue light behind my closed eyelids distracted me from the fear. Again and again, it flashed, like lightning during a storm, and in those split-second illuminations, it was as if it was showing me a parallel universe.

Flash.

Blue light spilled over the sea floor, revealing a treasure trove of trinkets and jewelry rather than seashells and starfish.

Flash.

I was standing on the bottom instead of swimming toward it, weighed down by some invisible force.

Flash.

The blue glow surrounded me in this alternate reality, pulsing and surging, taunting and teasing. It was the force holding me captive, and it was enjoying itself immensely.

Flash.

I was going to inhale. I could feel it. At any second, I was going to lose the battle between my need to breathe and my will to live.

Flash.

With my jaw clenched shut, my muscles jerking violently from the cold, and every cell in my body screaming in panic, I pulled a ring off my finger and held it out to the greedy blue glow. An offering, a plea, in exchange for my life.

Flash.

With a swirl of bubbles, the ring disappeared. The light disappeared. The invisible weights around my feet disappeared. And when I reached into the void it'd left behind …

He was there.

Even with my eyes closed and the sea blacker than midnight, my arms slipped around his waist as if I could see him in the dark. The size and shape of his body felt perfect and familiar against mine, and I pushed off the sea floor without realizing that I was even close to it. The pilot and I shot up effortlessly, as if propelled by another invisible force, but the moment our heads broke through the surface, only one of us gasped in relief.

Panic raced through my veins, pushing me to swim harder as I struggled to keep both of our heads above water. The current did most of the work, guiding us into the mouth of the cave as the nightmarish sounds of the ship breaking in half ricocheted off the stone walls.

Finding a foothold in the side of the inlet, I pushed our upper bodies out of the water and dropped the man onto his back on the pebbled beach. I didn't know what I'd expected to find, but when I finally gazed down at the stranger's face, mine contorted into a silent wail.

He was dead.

And he was the most beautiful corpse I'd ever seen.

Even with nothing more than the ambient firelight reflecting off the water, I could tell that the smooth skin covering his high cheekbones and square jaw was drained of all color.

That his full, unbreathing lips were as purple as a deep bruise.

That his closed eyelids, rimmed in thick black lashes, didn't so much as flutter.

And that the water streaming down the side of his face was red instead of clear.

"No!" I shouted, giving his shoulder a shove. "No! Wake up!"

I slammed my fists down on his unbreathing chest. "Wake up! *Please!*"

Again and again, I pounded on the hard muscle above his cold, dead heart. A strike for every person I'd lost. For every person I'd been too late or too weak or too afraid to save.

Ma.

Odin.

Sheila.

Da.

Him.

"Why?" I screamed, my voice cracking along with my mind as I grabbed his jacket with both hands. "Why are you doing this to me?"

I didn't know who I was yelling at, and I didn't know what else to do, but I knew that accepting another loss simply wasn't an option. So, in a sudden act of desperation, I threw myself forward, slammed my mouth over his, and blew.

The moment our lips touched, a warm, giddy golden glow seeped into the marrow of my bones. It spread through my body, lighting everything in its path. It turned me on, made me hum. I felt like a neon sign that had been plugged in for the very first time. My fragile, forgotten, hollow soul now sang with life, radiating heat and vibrant color.

I exhaled every bit of my wonder and confusion and pain and need through our sealed lips, and as soon as the pilot's lungs expanded under my fisted hands, he jerked away from me, rolling onto his side and heaving a bellyful of seawater onto the pebbled ground.

I laughed in relief as he coughed and gasped, a tingly rush of joy dancing over my damp skin. His life felt like a gift from God, just for me—a consolation after so much death.

Until I noticed that the jacket of his uniform was hanging halfway off, and underneath, staining the crisp blue-and-white striped shirt below, was a massive puddle of blood.

Dread slithered up my spine and coiled around my heart.

Not because of the blood.

But because of the stripes.

I'd been watching the Irish military on the news for the last year while they battled England for control of Northern Ireland, and *none* of their uniforms had ever looked like that. Especially not their fighter pilots. They wore dark green jumpsuits. Always.

This man wasn't my salvation. My glimmer of sunshine in the midst of a storm.

He was the goddamn lightning.

I recoiled from him so fast that I lost my foothold and slipped back into the inlet. Swimming backward to get away from him, I didn't stop until my shoulder hit the opposite wall.

What had I done?

What the hell had I done?

That cave was the only reason I was still alive, the only hope I had of staying that way, and I'd just welcomed a potential killer inside with open arms.

Clinging to the rocks, I stared at the back of his foreign uniform, rising and falling with every raspy, ragged breath, as tears of hatred blurred my vision.

I pictured Odie's sweet, round cheeks. Da's big, blond beard. Sheila's severed arm, lying in the smoldering, blood-smeared wreckage of my home. A drone telling me to surrender or die.

In my mind, this stranger morphed into the singular embodiment of the entire Russian military. *He* was the reason my family was dead. *He* was the man behind the machine. *He* was the missiles and the ship and the tanks and the drones.

And *he* deserved to die. Not them.

Shoving off from the wall, I crossed the inlet in two strokes and hauled myself out of the water. Squatting down in front of the sailor—or officer, based on the fanciness of his uniform—who was still lying unconscious on his side, I gave his shoulder a hard shove. He rolled onto his back without a fight, eyelids closed and lips parted.

I tore my gaze away from his hauntingly handsome face and focused instead on the patches and medallions decorating his chest—the ones that told me who he really was.

The ones that reminded me what he'd taken from me.

I knew I was freezing by the way my fingers shook as I wrapped them around his left bicep, but all I could feel was a blinding-hot lava flow of rage as I yanked on his arm, desperate to roll him into the inlet.

"Get … out!" I grunted, pulling and shoving, but he was too heavy, and I was too exhausted. I'd lost my wellies in the sea after my cliff jump, so every push and shove caused my knees and bare feet to grind harder against the pebbles on the beach until they eventually slid out from under me completely.

I landed with a shriek on the Russian's chest, and when he didn't move, I lay there, draped over his unconscious, bleeding body, and wept.

CHAPTER 8

DAMIEN

I knew I was dreaming the moment I saw her again, but everything felt different. Wrong.

We weren't in the forest anymore—we were in a house. A house that made my skin crawl and my heart race. A house that felt alive and evil. Something bad had happened there. A man ...

My head throbbed, and my ribs ached, and a few of my knuckles felt broken. The intensity of the pain confused me. I normally couldn't feel pain in my dreams.

Even the girl seemed different. She was younger now, but every bit as beautiful. She stood in the middle of a tobacco-stained kitchen, staring at me with big, worried eyes—eyes that I could now tell were as green as the forest where I'd first met her—before she glanced down at a lock of black hair in her tiny, trembling fist.

Reaching up, I touched the side of my head and immediately hissed in pain. Not only was my hair completely gone, but the wound I found there was laid open and oozing blood.

Taking a slow step toward me, the girl's eyes glistened with unshed tears, and her full lips quivered as they pulled into a frown. I wanted to kiss them, to make them curve the other way ... until she reached up to touch my butchered head.

I jerked away immediately. Embarrassed. Ashamed. I didn't want her to pity me. I didn't want her to know what had happened. I couldn't exactly remember myself, but I knew it was shameful. I knew it would make her look at me differently. So, I glared at her and watched as her sad, stunning face crumpled in response. Throwing the lock of hair on the floor, the girl turned and sprinted toward the front door.

She yelled something at me, a few things, but all I could process was that final look on her face and the hurt in her voice just before she slammed the door shut behind her.

I couldn't let her leave like that. I'd just gotten her back. If I didn't catch her, didn't make things right, I might never see her again.

Bolting out the door, I found myself free from the grimy grayscale of the evil house and plunged into a Technicolor dream world. The girl's hair glimmered in the sun like spun cooper as she sprinted across a green cemetery under a cloudless blue sky. Birds sang, and church bells rang, and my blood thrummed in my veins as I pushed myself to run faster. The closer I got to her, the more my pain faded until we were just a tangle of arms and legs rolling in the soft grass.

Turning onto my back, I pulled her against my chest and—after a few seconds of struggle—felt her tense body surrender and melt into mine. It was unlike anything I'd ever experienced. Like warm water being poured over a block of ice. I would have held her like that forever if I could have, but the edges of my awareness were already starting to blur.

There was so much I wanted to say before I woke up. So many questions I wanted to ask. Who was she? When would I see her again? How did I know her? Why did she make me feel this way? But just like the last time I'd seen her, the words seemed to slam against a steel door in my throat. So, I fought harder to push them out. When the colors began to fade, I held her tighter, refusing to let go. When I could no longer feel the weight of her on my chest, I coiled her hair around my fist and pressed my lips to the top of her head.

And when the girl in my arms finally vanished, along with the bolts and locks around my throat, I whispered into the darkness between our two worlds, "Remember me. Please … please come back."

Everything hurt. Inside. Outside. My lungs, my throat. My head, my side. My injuries were the same as the ones from my dream, only amplified. Excruciating. And instead of warm summer grass, it felt as though I were lying in a bed of cold broken glass.

I didn't know where I was, but I knew that I would die there. Soon. My brain was too foggy to think, my body too broken to move. I tried to remember what had happened, but nothing surfaced. My mind was a void. A vast black tunnel with no light at the end, only the wide-open gates of hell, ready and waiting.

Just then, a small sound and a slight twitch caused my labored breathing to stop altogether. Something was on me. Something heavy and alive.

Lifting my head slowly, I gritted my teeth as a sharp pain tore through my temple and lifted one eyelid just enough to see the creature sleeping on my chest.

I didn't understand what I was looking at. I blinked down at the angel sprawled across my body, waiting for a thought to form, for some logical explanation to surface, but my brain was an oxygen-deprived wasteland. It wasn't capable of anything more than basic observation, but my heart didn't care. It had *her*. It didn't need an explanation.

Lifting my hand to her head, I ran my scabbed knuckles over the long, soft waves cascading down her back. Her hair was damp and cold. Her eyelids fluttered at my touch. And the early morning sun bouncing off the water next to us illuminated every freckle on her beautiful face. This was no dream. She was really here, in the flesh, and for a moment, I thought I'd died and gone to heaven.

But I was in too much pain to be in heaven. Perhaps I'd pulled her out of the dream world after all, and now, we were stuck in some kind of purgatory, some in-between place. I didn't know, but the more I tried to process it, the more my skull throbbed and my vision blurred.

Dropping my head back onto the rocky ground, I stared up at the stone ceiling overhead and marveled at the rise and fall of her back under my splayed hand. I had no memories of the past and no capacity to think about the future. All I could do was try to stay conscious long enough to appreciate the sensation of her warm body draped over mine.

As I stroked her hair, she shifted sleepily, nuzzling my chest with a soft moan as her hand slid across my stomach. My abs flexed violently beneath her featherlight touch, causing pain to shoot out in all directions from my side, but it was a dull roar compared to the sensation of her lazy fingertips drifting over to my hip. My heart stopped, and my cock swelled as she unfastened something on my belt—the anticipation of her next move almost more excruciating than my injuries. But then, with a quiet *snap* and a flick of her wrist, she was gone.

The sound of crunching pebbles echoed off the stone walls as I winced and lifted my head again. The girl ran to the farthest corner of the cave and plastered her back against it. Then, she lifted a gun—*my* gun—and aimed it directly at my face. I couldn't remember what I'd done to upset her. I didn't even know where I was. But when I opened my mouth to apologize, to reassure her, the words wouldn't come out. I cleared my throat and coughed and groaned, but all that accomplished was making my injuries hurt infinitely worse. Glancing down at my side, which felt like it had been run through with a rusty bayonet, I saw that half of my uniform was soaked with blood.

Glancing back at the girl, I reached for her in desperation, tried again to speak, to call to her, but the words were just beyond my grasp, lingering at the edges of my consciousness where the darkness was closing in.

The last thing I saw before I surrendered to the void was her perfect face contorting into a silent sob as her knees buckled and her back slid down the wall.

I was wrong, I thought as the nothingness cracked open and swallowed me whole.

I'm not on my way to hell.

I'm already there.

CHAPTER 9

CLOVER

I sat and stared at the body lying in front of me for what felt like hours, trying to process what had just happened.

I'd thought that waking up on the blood-soaked chest of a Russian officer was terrifying, but it was nothing compared to the moment when I finally saw his eyes. Because in that moment, I feared my own mind even more than I feared him.

Only one person had eyes like that—gray as the cave walls on a cloudy day—and he was a figment of my imagination. So, if I was seeing him in the flesh, that could only mean one thing.

It was happening again.

"Ah, look. Here comes Crazy Clover. She talks to an invisible fairy, that one."

"Aye, and she claims her ma's a selkie."

"Poor lass. Cute as a button, but mad as a box of frogs."

"Hey, Clo, where's yer imaginary friend? I'm not steppin' on him, am I?"

I'd been delusional after my ma died. I understood that now, but when I looked back, it was scary how real it had all seemed. How my mind had the power to trick me into believing whatever might make me feel better, no matter how fantastical. I'd been convinced that a real-life fairy was with me at all times, hidden just out of sight, offering his silent sympathy and companionship. I'd been absolutely sure of it.

So, it made sense that, now that I'd lost the rest of my family, I was hallucinating him again.

But the realization was terrifying.

If my brain was capable of projecting the face of my childhood imaginary friend onto a stranger who wanted to kill me and destroy my entire country, then I had to get as far away from him—and anyone else who might want to hurt me—as possible before it happened again.

Standing up, I tucked the gun I'd taken from him into the back of my shorts and tiptoed across the cave floor. The man was unconscious, but I still moved as quietly as possible, hoping the distant explosions and clanking of plane wreckage washing up against the cliff outside would mask what little noise I did make.

Once I reached the cluster of boulders in the back corner of the cave, I reached into my hiding spot with trembling fingers. The contents inside of my secret backpack had always been precious to me, but now …

Now, they were all I had left.

The straps were too tight when I slid the bag onto my shoulders, still adjusted to fit my eleven-year-old body, but I kept them that way. It felt more secure.

As I walked back along the wall toward the cave entrance, the heavy bag rubbed against the gun tucked into my shorts, reminding me with every step just how much danger I was in. Not that I needed the reminder—one of the men responsible for killing my entire family was lying between me and the exit.

I didn't look at him as I passed. I knew that if I did, I might see something that wasn't there. Something that would lure me right back into his clutches. So, instead, I kept my eyes fixed on the waves crashing against the rocks outside. A storm was coming.

Grand.

As soon as I emerged from the tunnel, I was greeted by a splash of cold seawater and a clap of thunder so loud that it made me gasp and cover my head. I was immediately taken back to the night before, when bombs had rattled the cave walls and sent rocks plummeting into the inlet. It felt like my heart was trying to escape through my throat as I scrambled up on top of the capstone to avoid being splashed again. My eyes darted in all directions.

The first thing I noticed was that both planes that had been shot down and most of the ship was completely submerged now. All that was left was the bow of the ship, which pointed straight up at the churning gray sky like the tip of an iceberg. I pictured the bodies of the men who'd been on board scattered across the bottom of the sea. They were probably washing up on the beach by the dozen. Luckily, my cave was on the cliff side of the peninsula. The water was deep there, so the only debris I could see was what floated on the surface—plastic containers and hoses, hollow metal airplane parts, foam seats, a pack of Russian cigarettes. The waves smashed the rubbish against the cliffs over and over as a gust of wind threatened to do the same to me.

I began my climb, but between the ten kilos of books and bottled water and miscellaneous stolen items strapped to my back and the fact that every clap of thunder caused me to freeze and cover my head before I could keep going, it took far longer than I'd expected to reach the top. I was so grateful I'd made it without falling that for one second, one blissful moment of relief, I forgot what I'd made it to.

The wall of charred bushes at the top of the trail was my first reminder.

My hands began to shake, and a river of acid filled my empty stomach as I stepped between the two skeletal shrubs that had once hidden my trail and walked out onto the well-worn cliff path. Where green grass and swaying wildflowers had been the day before now lay a scorched wasteland, punctuated by a few crackling fires and dusted with a steady snowfall of ash.

I could hear bombs exploding over in Dublin. A formation of planes flew overhead, probably on their way to drop more. So, I knew I wasn't the last person on earth, but from where I stood, it sure felt like it.

Maybe I was just the last person in Howth. The Russians were probably all fighting in Dublin by now. There was no reason for them to occupy such a small town when the capital was right next door.

A glimmer of hope took root.

If they were gone, then I was safe. If they were gone, then I could find shelter—some place with running water and all its walls intact. Maybe I'd go back home, see if the shed was still standing. I could live in there until …

A sudden flashbulb image of Sheila's severed arm caused me to slam my eyes closed and drop to my knees. Bile rose in my throat, along with a scream that clawed its way out of my body like a demon being exorcised. The sound was inhuman—a guttural, broken wail that would be heard by no one but the dead.

Or so I'd thought.

The wind was so strong and the rumbling of thunder so constant that I didn't notice the soft whir of propeller blades until the drone was almost on top of me. By the time I registered the high-pitched hum of the motor and lifted my head, it was too late.

I'd been spotted.

The black device descended upon me like a bird of prey, swooping out of the gray sky with its spotlight aimed and its belly full of bullets. That beam had barely grazed my elbow before I dived through the bushes and back onto the cliff trail, but I leaped with too much force.

"This is a message from President Abramov."

Propelled by the weight of my backpack, I slid right off the side of the trail, headfirst. Barreling through charred bushes, over rocks and off steep drop-offs, I tumbled down the nearly vertical cliff face with the grace of a rag doll.

"Your city has been captured by the Armed Forces of the Russian Federation."

Branches tore at my jumper and sliced into my bare legs. Rocks and sticks punctured my palms and bare feet as I grasped at anything that might slow my fall. The Russian's gun slipped out of my shorts and clattered onto the rocks below—a preview of what would happen to me if I didn't find a way to stop my fall. After the next sudden drop-off, my backpack surged forward and slammed into the base of my skull. White light blinded me, and I didn't know if it was from the blow I'd just taken to the head or Satan's spotlight shining in my face.

"This is your only chance to surrender. You have ten seconds to raise your hands above your head and follow this device to the nearest encampment."

Finally, I careened into a patch of bushes that hadn't been burned. Gripping them with both hands, I held fast as the momentum carried my body right over them. I thought my shoulders were going to rip out of their sockets as I flipped over the shrubs, slamming backpack-first into the stone cliff with my arms twisted above me in the air.

"Refusal to do so will be considered an act of war and will result in your termination."

My heart raced, and my feet groped at the mossy stone cliff as I dangled ten meters above a pile of rocks and airplane wreckage.

The light in my face became even more intense as the drone settled directly in front of me, mocking my struggle to live. My pathetic human adherence to gravity.

"Ten."

"Ugh!" Thrashing with both legs, I finally found a foothold and felt my heart leap in my chest.

"Nine."

Twisting my body so that I was now facing the cliff, I began to climb sideways, using rocks and roots for footholds and shrub branches for handholds. I did not look down. I did not breathe.

And by the time the drone said, "Six," I was placing my bloody, bare feet back on my well-worn cliff trail.

"Five."

I ran down the path so quickly that I slipped and fell on my arse, sliding the last few meters down to the capstone.

"Three."

I didn't know what to do. I'd been so focused on getting back to the cave that I hadn't thought about the fact that the drone could simply follow me in.

Then, I glanced out at the open sea and heard a familiar voice whisper the same word that had saved me the night before.

"Jump."

Clinging to the straps cinched tightly over my shoulders, I took a deep breath and a running leap as the drone robotically announced my last second on earth.

I dived in headfirst, blowing all the air out of my lungs as the weight from the pack propelled me toward the bottom. The *thwip-thwip-thwip* of bullets piercing the surface pushed me to kick faster, swim harder. Once my ears began to ache from the depth, I turned and swam back toward the hidden inlet that cut into the side of the cliff. It was infinitely harder to do with a sack full of dead weight on my back, and between the extreme cold of the water and the sting of the salt in my abrasions, I felt as though I'd been beaten with a hammer and skinned alive. Pain consumed me as I forced my bruised, contracted muscles to keep moving, as I struggled to hold my breath long enough to make it to the end of the narrow channel. But I did. And when I finally broke the surface and sucked in a lungful of damp cave air, the sound of machine-gun fire had stopped.

I should have been relieved—proud even—but as I pulled myself out of the freezing cold sea for the third time in less than twenty-four hours, all I felt was the absolute mortification of failure and a seeping, oozing, smothering sense of dread. I'd accomplished nothing by leaving the cave, other than almost getting myself killed—*again*; letting the Russians know that there was a survivor on the peninsula; scraping, cutting, and/or bruising most of my body; losing my only means of self-defense; and soaking the last of my earthly possessions in seawater.

Actually, I *had* accomplished one thing: I'd learned that escape was not an option. I was stuck in that cave, with that monster, indefinitely.

And the sooner he died, the better.

CHAPTER 10

CLOVER

I didn't look at my new roommate when I got out of the water. I didn't trust myself to. Instead, I stayed on my side of the inlet, hidden behind the family of boulders, as I removed the contents of my bag and laid them out to dry.

I must have assumed the otherworld would have plenty to eat and drink when I was a kid because the supplies I'd squirreled away in the event that I ever escaped from this reality were embarrassingly inadequate.

Three bottles of water.

One bottle of whiskey that I'd stolen from my da.

An out-of-date pack of vanilla custard creams.

A handful of smooshed granola bars, also out of date.

Some sopping wet child-sized clothes that I'd taken from the lost and found in primary school.

A previously framed picture of my mother that Da had broken and thrown in the bin after she died.

Three cigars and a pack of matches.

And four books, all sealed in plastic zip-top bags.

I couldn't survive on books and stale biscuits for long.

My heavy heart plummeted deeper into the black hole of failure that was now eating me from the inside out.

But then I pictured the little girl who'd packed that bag, and I felt even worse. She wasn't a failure. She was resourceful. She was hopeful. And because of her, I still had a chance. What would that girl have done in this situation?

Besides hallucinate an imaginary friend? Already did that.

A clap of thunder rattled the cave walls, just before the sky went dark and the sound of raindrops drumming against the metal wreckage outside drowned out my negative thoughts.

My prayer for rain had finally been answered. A day late, but right on time.

After pulling the plastic bags off everything I owned, I held them up over my head as I quietly slipped into the inlet and swam down to the cave entrance. I could have walked out and avoided the pain of the cold and the salt in my wounds, but I would have had to go past the Russian to do that, and my new rule was that I did *not* look at the Russian.

Hiding just inside the mouth of the tunnel, I held a shiny piece of airplane wreckage as far out as my arm would reach so that I could scan the cliff for signs of danger. It was hard to see anything through the pouring rain, but when my hand wasn't instantly blown off by a drone, I decided that the coast was clear. But I couldn't move. What I needed to do would only take a few seconds—a minute at most—but I was paralyzed with fear. The last two times I'd left that cave, I'd been chased off a cliff and nearly shot. But I had to risk it. If I didn't, I would die of thirst in a few days, and honestly, a machine-gun execution would be a much better way to go.

Motivated by that morbid thought, I pulled myself up onto the ledge, gasping as the rain and waves pummeled me from all sides. I hobbled over to the sloped side of the tunnel—my body so battered from my fall that I couldn't tell where one bruise ended and the next began—but I managed to climb to the top of the capstone and get to work.

Thunder rumbled, and lightning flashed, causing my heart to stop and my body to involuntarily duck and cover every few seconds, but I pushed through the panic. I had to. After dropping a few rocks into the bottom of each plastic bag to keep them from blowing away, I set them out on the flat capstone and rolled their tops down to keep them open. By the time I was done, I had a dozen little containers set up to collect drinking water, and they were filling up fast.

It was a tiny victory in a sea of grief, but I clung to it like a life preserver.

I'm going to be okay, I thought, wringing out my hair as I crept along the ledge of the tunnel.

I could drink rainwater. I could catch lobster. I had shelter. No warm clothes, but …

Stepping out of the tunnel and onto dry stone, I was so distracted by my own thoughts that I completely forgot about my new rule.

I glanced over at the man.

And nearly screamed.

I'd never seen so much blood in my entire life. It soaked his shirt and jacket, ran down the side of his face, pooled on the rocks beneath his writhing body. He was propped up on one elbow, trying to sit, trying to stand, but his every move, even breathing, seemed to cause him excruciating pain. His teeth were gritted; dry, cracked lips pulled back in a snarl; his dark brows were knitted together; and when he met my gaze, the eyes that stared back didn't belong to him. They belonged to *me*. To *my* imagination. To my very soul. I stared into those molten steel pools as if I'd been forged from them. As if you could cut me and I'd bleed gray.

I knew I was hallucinating. I knew the man writhing in front of me wasn't really him, but that didn't make it any easier to stand there and watch my friend die. The one who'd been there for me when everyone else cast me out. The one who comforted me when no one else cared. The one who'd given me the courage to jump. He was a part of me, and his suffering was mine too.

Rushing over, I knelt by his side and brushed the pebbles out from behind him. "Shh. Lie back down. Please."

He continued to struggle, jaw clenched in pain as those eyes stayed fixed on mine. Begging. Pleading. The intensity of his stare, of those silver irises fixed on mine, was almost hypnotizing. It took everything I had to tear my gaze away and assess the damage.

"I'm going to lift your shirt, okay?"

He nodded, and for a moment, I let myself believe that he spoke English instead of Russian. That he really was who I wanted him to be. Always listening. Never speaking.

Lifting his woolen jacket out of the way, I untucked and unbuttoned his shirt as quickly as my shaking fingers would allow. Then, I pulled the sides open and gasped as a beam of light shone through a shredded hole in the blue-and-white striped fabric. It was the same size and shape as the wound underneath—a mangled, jagged starburst, like something had exploded out of him.

Oh my God.

Reaching around his side, I felt the corresponding spot on his back and immediately found what I was looking for. A few centimeters below his rib cage, on his left side, was a small, mushy hole the size of my fingertip.

My stomach lurched the moment I touched it, and the man sucked in a sharp breath through his teeth.

"Sorry. I'm so sorry," I muttered, wiping my bloody finger on his navy-blue jacket.

I glanced back up at him, but the words of encouragement on my tongue simply vanished as I found myself face-to-face with the proof of my own insanity. The illusion didn't falter that close up. In fact, it only became more convincing. More familiar. I knew how soft his hair would feel without ever having touched it. How scratchy his day's growth of beard was. I knew the exact angle of his eyebrows and soft fullness of his lips before I'd even studied them, but then again, I would, wouldn't I? I'd put all of those things there in my own mind.

His pupils swelled, and his dry, cracked lips curled at the corners as he drank me in, but the moment he lifted his hand to touch me, his face contorted into a grimace of agony.

"Don't move," I begged, tearing myself away from him to go grab my supplies.

I returned in seconds, tossing everything on the ground and trying not to blush from the relief I saw on his face when I came back. The sound of a cap being unscrewed was the only warning I gave him before I tipped Da's bottle of Jameson over and poured straight whiskey directly into his wound.

The man gasped and grunted and breathed hard through his nose as I pressed a white long-sleeved shirt against his wound and tied the sleeves around his waist to keep it in place. Then, I glanced at the wound on the side of his head.

With his teeth gritted and his eyes screwed shut in anticipation, he nodded his consent.

And I poured the amber liquid over his gash without hesitation. He breathed like a dragon through flared nostrils, squeezing a handful of pebbles in his fist, but I don't think I was breathing at all. Because the moment he reopened his eyes, they rolled skyward, and his body began to fall. Darting behind him, I caught his shoulders before he hit the ground and guided his head onto my lap with my heart in my throat.

"Stay with me," I begged, patting his cheek as panic shot through my veins. "Please. *Please.*"

Grabbing a bottle of water, I twisted the cap off with my teeth and spat it to the side.

Saliva pooled in my mouth instantly. I realized I hadn't had anything to drink either, not since … *before.*

"I'm gonna sit you up, okay? You need water." As I rose up onto my knees, the man's upper body lifted along with me, his head rolling to one side.

"Hey." I reached down and wrapped my left hand under his chin to turn his head, and the scrape of his stubble against my palm brought tears to my eyes. It felt exactly the way I'd imagined.

I pushed my classmates' jeers of, "Crazy Clover," to the back of my mind as I brought the bottle to his parted lips. I didn't know what to expect as I began to pour. I was afraid I might drown him, but the moment that cool water hit his tongue, the man began to swallow, and he didn't stop. I sighed as his throat bobbed against my splayed fingers, and when he lifted his hand to the bottle and wrapped it around mine, a bolt of tingles shot up my arm, leaving a trail of goose bumps in its wake.

I watched him drink through a wall of grateful tears. His black eyelashes, his bloody knuckles—every detail became blurry and distorted. Every detail except for the red, blue, and white flag emblazoned across the swell of his bicep. That I could see clear as day. It was like a tear in the fabric of my fever dream. A slash of reality reminding me that this man was not who I so desperately wanted him to be. Not even close.

He was the enemy.

He'd destroyed my town.

He'd killed my family.

And I was officially out of my goddamn mind.

Shoving away from him, I grabbed my things and ran back to my side of the inlet, yelping in pain as I stepped down on a particularly sharp pebble before careening into the cave wall behind the boulders. Curling into a ball where he couldn't see me, I pulled my knees up to my chest like a shield.

"Stay away!" I screamed over the deafening roar of the storm outside. "Don't come any closer! I have yer gun!" My voice broke on that lie as I realized how vulnerable I truly was. How deluded. How weak. "I'll kill you," I tried to yell, but the words came out no louder than a strained whisper, hoarse and heard by no one but me. I repeated them over and over again as I rocked in my corner, tears streaming down my already-wet face.

I didn't know what I was more upset about losing. My mind ...

Or *him*.

CHAPTER 11

CLOVER

That night felt like it would never end.

I'd been in survival mode ever since the moment the first bomb had dropped, but with a granola bar in my belly, a collection of rainwater on the roof, shelter over my head, and an enemy who was too injured and unconscious to hurt me, the only basic needs I had left to focus on were the ones I couldn't meet.

Warmth.

And love.

I was used to living without the latter. I'd learned that I didn't actually need love to survive. But what I did need, what I'd really lost in the explosion, was the *hope* of love. That was what had kept me going day after day. The hope that if I was good enough, quiet enough, hardworking enough, forgiving enough, Da would stop hating me. The hope that Odie would grow up to become my best friend—my only friend. The hope that, if I did what I was told and smiled through my tears and inconvenienced no one, I could convince my family to love me. Eventually. I just had to do better. Be better.

Now, that possibility was gone.

I tucked my knees inside my jumper in an attempt to stay warm, but the knitted material was so burned and torn that it did little to stop my shivering.

But honestly, I didn't want it to stop.

The discomfort of being cold, the aches and pains of lying curled up on a rock, the gnawing in my nearly empty belly—those were the only distractions I had from the absolute agony of realizing that the family I'd lost … wouldn't have cared if they'd lost me.

And the worst part was that there was nothing I could do to let that feeling out.

I wanted to scream. I wanted to wail. I wanted to hit and kick and break things until I expelled the poison boiling over inside of me. But making that kind of noise in this new world was a death sentence, so I had to just lie there and let the pain consume me, fill me up until it leaked out through my tear ducts and between my gritted teeth like the high-pitched whistle of a teakettle.

It was excruciating, and the longer I lay there, the louder and more uncontrollable my crying and shivering became. I covered my mouth with my hands to try to muffle it, clenched my jaw shut, curled in on myself tighter, but fighting it was exhausting, and I was already so, so tired.

Fear gripped the back of my neck, turning my shivers into full-body tremors when I realized that I couldn't stop my sobbing. It felt like vomiting. My body was expelling the pain whether I liked it or not, and it was not a quiet process. Burying my face in my elbow, I rolled onto my knees to muffle the sound, but it wasn't enough.

I began shushing myself between every desperate, wailing gasp of air, but my attempt to self-soothe only made me cry harder.

Because it made me realize how completely and utterly alone I was.

Turning my head, I bit my bicep as hard as I could, and my howls of grief finally quieted to whimpers of pain. But what made me go completely silent was what I heard in that stillness. Something was moving in the cave.

At first, I feared that it was the hum of drone blades, but when it stopped and started again, I realized that it was something even more terrifying. The slow, gravely scrape of a body dragging itself across stone.

I glanced up from the arm my face was buried in, but the cave was pitch-black. I couldn't see the man approaching, but I could hear him getting closer with every push and pull of his massive body.

My heart beat so hard I could feel it behind my straining eyes, which darted in all directions, desperate to catch a flash of a brass button or gleaming white teeth. Anything that would help me prepare for what was about to happen.

I can outrun him, I told myself. If he touched me, I would jab at his injuries, grab my bag, and follow the cave wall to the entrance as fast as I fucking could.

But the truth was that I couldn't have moved if my life depended on it. The terror had sent my body into a freeze mode so intense that it bordered on paralysis. I could hardly breathe. Hardly blink. Running was an impossibility.

With blood thumping in my ears and a whimper of fear lodged in my throat, I stared helplessly into the darkness as the scraping sound got closer. Then, once it was practically on top of me, it stopped. I widened my eyes and held my breath as I waited for something to happen. And with a grunt and a groan and a sharp hiss of pain, it did. The form of a man began to take shape in front of me, so close I could feel the warmth of his torso on my face. The brass buttons on his blazer seemed to glow in the dark as he reached up with thick fingers and unbuttoned each one.

Stomach acid seared the back of my throat as I watched those fingers do the same thing to the buttons on his white striped shirt.

I begged my body to move, to run, to kick and shove, but it simply curled in on itself even tighter as a tiny, panicked yelp slipped past my defenses.

The man then removed his shirt and jacket in one motion, and I couldn't take it anymore. Slamming my eyes shut, I sucked in a lungful of air and debated letting it out with a scream. I had the power to stop this. To make it all just go away. The fear, the pain, the grief, the hopelessness. One scream, and it would all be over.

But I hesitated.

Because the next move the man made wasn't to unbuckle his belt or unzip his trousers.

It was to drape his bloodstained shirt and jacket over my trembling ball of a body.

His clothes landed on me like a wool blanket on a raging fire, extinguishing my fear, my despair, and my shivering on contact. And it had nothing to do with the warmth of his body. It was the warmth of his gesture that had made all the difference.

Because for the second time in two days, I didn't feel completely alone.

CHAPTER 12

DAMIEN

I hardly noticed the rain as I marched through a blackened forest, dodging every branch and boulder on instinct rather than sight. I didn't know where I was going, but my body did. It navigated those woods as if it were being steered by someone else.

Someone who obviously knew where to find my girl.

I could feel the pull of her. The urgency to move faster, the almost-panicked need to see her again.

When I finally crested a hill and emerged from the woods, I was standing at the edge of a pasture, staring at a house that I knew I had never been welcome in. But she was in there—I could feel it—and welcome or not, I was going in.

As I trudged through the gate and across the pasture, I knew in my gut that something bad was about to happen. Everything felt wrong. The storm. The golf ball–sized hail scattered across the ground. The unfamiliar car parked in the driveway. Even my jacket. I went to zip it up and realized that I wasn't wearing it. I always wore it.

The wind howled, and the rain roared, but that all faded away the moment I heard her scream.

Breaking into a sprint, I charged around the side of the house and burst through the door, hoping that I was overreacting. Hoping I'd find her standing on a chair, pointing at a spider. But what I saw was worse than anything I could have imagined. On the far side of the kitchen, with her face pressed against the floor and her bare arse up in the air, my girl was being restrained and forcibly fucked by a man who was about to die.

Something happened to me as I crossed that kitchen. A relaxing. A letting go. It was as if there was so much darkness inside of me that freeing it was easier than keeping it at bay. A sense of calm washed over me as I wrapped that piece of shite's silk tie around his fragile neck and pulled it taut. As I glanced down at my girl's perfect face, now badly bruised and staring up at me in shock. As her swollen lips parted and whispered my name.

Those two syllables felt like petrol in my veins, fueling my rage, igniting my wrath. Standing up to my full height, I lifted that rapist pig off his knees, napalm pumping through my muscles as I tightened the noose. And as the life drained out of his worthless body, the girl never once took her eyes off of mine. She had a front-row seat to the freak show—the monster that I'd been molded into was unleashed and on full display—and she accepted it. She looked at me like a savior instead of a psycho, and it felt fucking amazing.

But not nearly as amazing as the way I felt when I realized she was wearing my jacket.

Pain, sharp and swift, ripped through my side, and I sat up with a jolt.

"Sorry," a feminine voice said. "You were bleedin' through your bandage."

With my heart still pounding, I glanced down and found the redhead kneeling beside me. Her hair was different—darker, more bronze than copper—but the way it spilled down the back of my uniform made me feel the exact same surge of pride that I'd felt in my dream seconds before.

She was wearing my jacket.

Until that moment, I'd honestly thought I was in hell—the thirst, the hunger, the incessant pain, and the hours I'd spent lying awake in the dark, listening to this girl's muffled sobs and chattering teeth. I hadn't been able to see her, or speak to her, or get up and walk to her, but I could hear her.

The Devil had made sure of that.

When I couldn't fucking take it anymore, I'd rolled onto my good side and used my forearm and legs to drag and push myself, meter by meter, toward the source of the sound. The pain was so intense that I would have vomited if there'd been anything in my stomach, but the agony didn't stop me. It only fueled me more.

Pain had been a way of life in the Kletka. They inflicted it to remind me of their power, and I fought through it to remind them of mine. For five years, pain had been my constant companion, but those five years had been nothing compared to the few hours I spent listening to that redhead suffer.

When I'd finally dragged myself over to the boulders where her tiny body was huddled in a ball, I'd collapsed at her feet, unable to see through the blinding agony I'd just inflicted upon myself. I sensed her body stiffen next to me, heard her yelp in fear, and hoped for a moment that she would shoot me like she'd promised—put me out of my misery—but I knew I wouldn't get that lucky.

I was in hell after all.

The world threatened to spin out from under me as I pulled off my jacket and shirt and draped them over her trembling body. They were stiff with dried blood and smelled like death, but I knew they were warm. I was on fucking fire.

Once her shivering stopped, I pushed and dragged my worthless body back over to my side of the cave, bile searing the back of my throat from the pain. Panting and sweating and shaking from exertion, I crumbled against the stone wall and waited for the relief to follow. The triumph. I'd thought my act of defiance would feel like a *fuck you* to Satan himself, but instead, I could practically hear him laughing at me from his throne of lies.

Because silence, it turned out, was the worst torture of all.

"Ya scared the shite outta me last night," the girl said, her head still bowed as she untied the shirt wrapped around my waist. "I thought you were gonna …" Her shoulders shuddered as her voice trailed off, and after the nightmare I'd just had, I knew exactly what she'd been afraid of.

The fact that she thought I might be capable of something like that hurt worse than being shot. It was like she didn't know me at all, but I knew her. At least, I felt like I did. I knew her smile, even though I hadn't seen it in this place. I knew the exact color of her eyes—even though she wouldn't look at me—and I knew that she pursed her lips when she was thinking or trying not to laugh.

"You shouldn't have done that, ya know." She kept her eyes down, speaking to herself as she doused what looked like a pair of pink cotton shorts with Jameson. "Draggin' yourself across the cave like that. You were finally startin' to heal, and now, look at ya."

Something wasn't right. The longer I watched her work, the more differences I began to notice between this girl and the one in my dreams. Her hair color was wrong, her attitude, even the way she smelled—salty instead of sweet, like seawater. Maybe she wasn't the same girl after all. Maybe she was an imposter, created by the Devil himself just to torture me.

I didn't know where I was, who I was, or if I was alive or dead, but I knew better than to trust a fucking soul, human or demon, who wasn't *her*.

And this girl was not her.

I hissed through my teeth as she pressed the whiskey-soaked fabric against the gaping hole in my side.

"But thanks anyway," she muttered. "Ya probably have no idea what I'm sayin', but … what ya did last night was … really nice."

Then, she glanced back and forth between the shirt that had been wrapped around my waist and the fabric she was holding against my wound. "Em … shite. How do I … I need a third hand."

I placed my hand on top of hers, wincing from that simple movement, and the girl gasped in surprise.

"You understand English?"

I nodded, gazing at her downcast face, the thick lashes fanned out over her freckled cheekbones, the way my sleeves swallowed her hands as she worked. She wasn't my girl, but she was just as beautiful.

It felt like a trick.

Sliding her fingers out from under mine, she set to work, tying the bloodstained shirt from the day before around my waist to hold the new bandage in place.

"What's your name?"

I opened my mouth to tell her, but nothing came out. It was as if my lips and tongue had forgotten how to form words. I could at least hear them in my head again. That was an improvement. My confusion was beginning to lift, but …

I groaned in frustration and scrubbed a hand over my broken fucking skull. I couldn't remember what had happened. My entire life was just … gone.

"It's okay," she said, placing a hand on my bare shoulder before turning her attention to the wound on the side of my head.

Her touch was so gentle. No one had touched me like that since … well, I couldn't fucking remember when. But it made something in my chest throb worse than the head wound she was dabbing with alcohol.

"There was a woman in our town," she said, still avoiding my gaze, "the wife of a fisherman. She slipped at the harbor and hit her head so hard she couldn't remember a thing for days. Not even how to talk, other than curse words, which was pretty funny 'cause she was such a God-fearin' woman. They thought she might have brain damage, but come next Sunday, she was back at church, singin' in the choir like nothin' had happened."

The pain subsided as I closed my eyes and tried to process what she was saying.

Her fingertips caressed my jaw, turning my head to the side with the lightest of touches. "You could use a few stitches—can't help ya there—but once the swellin' goes down, ya might be okay."

A head injury. Memory loss. Was I alive then? Was this place real? Was she?

"Do ya know how ya got here?" Her voice turned icy as she pulled away from me. Sitting back on her heels, she picked at the label of the whiskey bottle in her hands, avoiding my stare.

Dread seeped into my veins as I shook my head slowly.

"You're in the Russian Navy," she replied, her voice hard and accusing. "Ya showed up here in a warship disguised as a cruise ship. Then, ya bombed my entire town, my house, my …" Her voice trailed off as she swiped a tear away from her scowling face. "It doesn't matter. It's not like you care. I just need ya to hurry up and get better so you can get the hell out of my cave."

Fuck.

The Navy.

The ship.

The shelling.

Fuck. Fuck. Fuck.

Images from that night assaulted me rapid-fire, but the only thing I could focus on was a pink welt on the girl's cheekbone. It was just like the one I'd seen in my dream. Someone had hurt her. Someone was going to die.

Or maybe they already had.

Fuck!

As she turned away and walked back to her side, I wanted to tell her she was wrong. That I did care. That I'd tried to stop it. That I was sorry. That I'd do anything to go back and make it right. But all that came out were grunts and coughs and the word *fuck*, clear as a bell, just like she'd said it would be.

If she was an imposter created by the Devil to torture me, it was fucking working. I was losing her again, and there was nothing I could do about it. I didn't want to drag myself back over there when she'd just finished patching me up from my last dumb attempt to move. I couldn't speak to her. Could I write?

I looked around and found a full bottle of water and a granola bar that she must have brought over when she'd come to dress my wounds. The sound of quiet crying pierced my soul as I tore the label off the bottle and stared at the blank underside, waiting for letters and words to form in my mind.

"Fuck," I muttered again, picturing her face buried in her hands on the other side of that boulder while I sat there and did nothing.

Her face. That was it. I could see it in my mind like a photograph. Every line, every freckle. I just needed …

Looking around, I noticed a smear of blood on the shirt she had tied around my waist. Gritting my teeth, I dipped my finger beneath the bandage and exhaled in relief when it came out red.

I didn't have to speak. I didn't have to spell. All I had to do was close my eyes, and there she was. My finger swooped across the label with no conscious thought from me. Two closed eyes, brow furrowed in pain. Two full lips, turned down at the corners. Two freckled cheeks—one tearstained and one bruised. A heart-shaped face. A wavy mane of hair, bronze instead of copper.

Wrapping the portrait around a small rock, I said a silent prayer and tossed it across the inlet and into the cluster of boulders she was hiding behind. My injuries screamed in protest over that single motion. When I saw that my gift had landed where I wanted, I dropped my head back against the wall and waited.

I heard the sounds of pebbles rustling, a plastic label being unwrapped, and then nothing.

The girl stopped crying.

And I was back in the silence. Again.

CHAPTER 13

CLOVER

I never thought the chemical stench of burning plastic would make me so happy.

I'd pulled two lobsters out of the inlet that morning as well as a floating piece of metal sharp enough to butterfly them, but with everything outside being soaked from the rain, I had to find something inside the cave to burn. Which was a problem because the only dry, flammable things in the cave were my books and my clothes, and I was going to have to be a lot closer to death before I lit either of those on fire.

Luckily, a plastic ammunition box had floated in during the night. It took four matches before it finally lit, which was concerning because I'd only had ten to start with, but once it caught, I knew it would burn for hours. Maybe even days. I'd once read an article about a plastic factory that caught fire and burned for almost a week.

A week. I couldn't even wrap my mind around that amount of time now. I was the type of person who always had a long-term plan, a backup plan, and a fantasy just-in-case-I-find-a-portal-to-the-otherworld plan, but now, all I had was the present moment.

And a mute, murderous roommate who hadn't looked at me all day.

I watched him out of the corner of my eye while I cooked the shellfish over the open flame—inhaling enough plastic fumes to shave years off whatever life I had left. When I'd woken up that morning, I'd found him sitting over by the tunnel, slumped against the wall and staring out at the sea. I was happy to see him upright and moving around a bit, but he'd had his back to me all day, and I hated how much that bothered me.

I'd managed to follow my rule about not looking him in the eye for four days now, and it had definitely helped me feel less crazy. Only allowing myself to look at his legs, his wounds, his bare and bloodstained torso … his abs. God. I knew fellas in the military were fit, but he looked like he'd been chiseled straight from the cave wall. It shouldn't have affected me as much as it did, but with his shirt off, it was easier to forget who I was talking to. Who I was touching. Who was drawing portraits of me in his own blood to comfort me. With no gray eyes to remind me of my insanity and no Russian patches to remind me of his reality, we were just two lonely, broken people in a desperate situation, and honestly, that was the most dangerous illusion of all.

An illusion that was getting harder and harder to recognize with him staring out at the island like that. How many hours had I spent doing the exact same thing after Ma died? It had been thirteen years, and I still found myself searching the sea for something I'd never get back.

We aren't that different, my mind whispered.

He was hurting too. Maybe he wasn't so bad after all. Maybe …

I tore my eyes away and stared down at the stiff woolen jacket I was using to hold the piping hot lobster tails. I was hoping a patch might be visible, maybe a medal—some Russian insignia that would snap me out of my commiseration. But all I found was a bullet hole.

Which had quite the opposite effect.

Carrying our lunch over to the tunnel, I walked past the collection of water bottles and bars I'd brought him over the past few days. All sat untouched, where I'd left them.

That wasn't good.

My hands were full of shellfish, so I bent over and picked up a water bottle with my forearms along the way.

"Hey," I said, squatting down next to him.

I didn't want to sit because sitting felt like we were having lunch together, and that was something friends did, not mortal enemies. I faced the water, like him, and from there, I could see that he was really staring at the ship—or what was left of it.

I hadn't even thought about all the people he must have lost on that boat. I'd lost three people I cared about the night of the attack—he might have lost hundreds.

I held one of the lobsters out to him while keeping my gaze safely on the horizon. I expected it to vanish from my hand, but instead, I found my arm being gently pushed back toward my body.

Glancing down at the bloodstained fingers wrapped around my forearm, I felt my cheeks flush. I wasn't sure if it was in response to his touch or in anger over him rejecting my offer. Maybe both.

"Eat," I snapped, extending the lobster toward him again. "Ya haven't had a bite of food since ya got here, and the only water you've had is what I poured down your throat."

His breathing became heavier. Then, he swallowed audibly and cleared his throat. He was trying to speak again and still struggling. I immediately regretted my tone.

With a frustrated sigh, he pushed my arm away from him again, this time guiding my hand up until the lobster grazed my parted lips.

"Ya want *me* to eat it?"

He released my arm with a single nod before leaning his head against the cave wall again.

For a moment, I assumed he must be too proud to take charity or too hateful to accept help from the Irish, but that couldn't be it. The man had given me the shirt and jacket off his back. And he'd let me bandage him. He'd accepted my help in other ways. This was specifically about the food and water.

Then, it occurred to me.

"You don't think I have enough."

He shook his head, and I sat down immediately, practically collapsing under the weight of what he'd just communicated.

He was *choosing* not to eat or drink, willfully risking his own life, so that I would have more.

"There's plenty," I assured him, my voice rough with emotion. "See those ropes lyin' on the cave floor? Each one is attached to a lobster trap. This inlet's full of 'em, so we're not gonna starve. And I've been collecting rainwater outside, so there's plenty to drink."

Cracking one of the butterflied lobster tails open even wider, I pulled out a tender piece of meat and quickly glanced at the side of his face. His eyes were closed, so I relaxed and held the morsel up to his dry, parted lips.

"Eat," I whispered. "Please. If ya don't, you're gonna die, and then I'll be stuck in here with your smelly corpse because you're too heavy for me to push into the inlet. I already tried."

A glimmer of a smile illuminated his face, a sliver of white teeth, and before I knew it, I was hypnotized, watching two curtains of black lashes lift in slow motion.

At the first flash of gray, I slammed my eyes shut, breathing heavily from that close call. Then, I felt his warm lips close around my fingertips, and I stopped breathing altogether.

But soon they were gone, along with my offering, and the sound that rumbled in the back of his throat made my empty stomach flutter.

"Good?" I smiled, dropping my gaze to the shellfish in my hands. Then, I pulled off another piece and popped it into my own mouth just to give myself something to do other than watch his square, stubble-covered jaw flex as he chewed.

"Mmhmm." Those two syllables hung in the air like sunshine, warming me from the inside out.

"That was almost a word." I smiled as I offered him another piece, keeping my gaze fixed solely on the shellfish in my lap. I could feel his eyes on me, and my cheeks flushed under this stare.

His teeth grazed the soft pad of my finger.

I could tell from his energy that one almost word would not be enough to ease his pain. I only wished I knew which kind of pain he was in. Physical or emotional.

"Are you sad about the people you lost … on the boat?" I lifted my chin toward the bow of his warship, protruding from the sea like a giant steel shark fin.

He shook his head.

"No?" I asked in surprise.

No.

I held another morsel out for him and felt the warmth of his gaze as it roamed over my body. First my face, then my lap where his jacket had fallen, then my bare legs. I held my breath as he reached toward my thigh but released it a moment later when nothing happened. Looking down, I saw that he was pointing at a particularly deep gash in a sea of cuts and bruises and puncture wounds.

"Oh, that? I, em, took a tumble down the cliff a few days ago."

His lips closed around a bite of food that I'd forgotten I was holding out, and my breath hitched in my throat.

"I went out to look for better shelter, or supplies, whatever I could find, but … a drone found me first."

His whole body stiffened. He knew about the drones too.

Because he was one of the arseholes who'd brought them here.

My stomach soured.

Glancing down at the hand that had just been dangerously close to touching me, I placed what was left of his lobster in it and drew my knees up to my chest.

He hadn't been staring out at that water, thinking about the people he'd lost—he'd said so himself. He'd probably been thinking about the people he'd left behind. Back in *Russia.*

This man is not your friend, I reminded myself.

He is not like you.

His family's still alive.
And yours isn't because of him.

Setting my untouched lobster aside, I shook out his jacket and folded the torn, bloodstained material into a square, making sure to drape the sleeve with the Russian flag patch over the top.

"You miss home, don't ya?" I asked, my voice cold and sharp.

After a moment's hesitation, he nodded slowly.

"Yeah." I stood up. "Me too."

Then, I dropped his jacket on the ground next to him and turned to walk away.

I hadn't taken a single step before a hand shot out and wrapped around mine.

"S-s," he stuttered, squeezing my hand harder as he struggled to find the words.

I closed my eyes and waited, trying to block out the sympathy pain I felt every time he tried to speak.

"Sorry."

That single word, deep and raspy and laced with regret, landed on my soul like that woolen jacket, snuffing out my anger, soothing my grief.

I stood with my back to him, paralyzed by indecision as a battle broke out between my heart and my pride. My pride demanded that I storm off, that I continue to hate him and punish him for what he'd done. But my heart … my heart was fixated on the slow, rough drag of his thumb over my knuckles. The warmth of his skin on mine. The sincerity of his apology and the way it felt to be seen as a human being for once, rather than a sex object or a servant girl or the silly little laughingstock of Howth Head peninsula. My heart needed what he was offering far more than my pride needed to deny me of it.

So, without another word, I sat back down, my shoulder grazing his, and together, we finished our lunch.

CHAPTER 14

DAMIEN

I dreaded nightfall. It was torture—the way she'd hide from me, the crying, or worse, the silence—but something had changed between us.

Everything had changed.

Instead of cowering behind a boulder as far away from me as she could get, the girl was out where I could see her, reclined against the wall and reading by the light of a burning ammo box.

And the silence wasn't agonizing anymore. It was almost … content. The crackle of the fire and hiss of melting plastic. The turning of her pages and scratching of my rock against the sheet of metal I'd pulled out of the inlet. The sun had already set, but there was enough twilight left for me to finish my etching. Once it was done, I planned on giving it to her. Not that it was enough.

The girl had saved my life, dressed my wounds, given me shelter, water, food, and all I had to offer in return was the bloodstained shirt off my back and a few primitive drawings. I felt like a fucking animal. But there were words forming on the tip of my tongue—I was thinking clearly again and was pretty sure I'd be able to speak if I tried. With food in my belly and water in my veins, I'd managed to stay conscious the entire day, and the pain was now more of a dull throb than a stabbing agony.

Setting the sketch down next to me, I watched the sky darken over the sea. Now that I remembered where I was and how I'd gotten there, I couldn't stop staring at the aftermath. I was home, but I was homeless. I was alive, but I had nothing to live for. I was healing, but I was so fucking broken.

"Done with your drawing?"

I glanced over at the girl and watched the firelight dance across her innocent features, her eyes never lifting from the book on her lap. I stared at those nearly closed lids so hard I could almost see the emerald-green irises hidden underneath. I remembered their exact size and shape, and if I let my vision blur and my imagination take over, it felt like she was looking at me again.

The way she did every night in my dreams.

"I could read to ya, if you're bored," she said without looking up.

Yet another kindness that I didn't deserve, but was too fucking selfish to refuse.

Leaning back against the wall, I stretched my legs out in front of me, wincing slightly from the pain.

"This story's called *The Ghost of Glenshire*." She closed the book and gazed at the cover with a wistful smile. "My ma used to read it to me. It's from a series of fairy tales about this little village in County Kerry called Glenshire. The author's note says that all of her books are based on folklore from the area, and the way she describes it …" She shook her head. "I want to go there so bad."

Her smile faded. "It's sad though. The author died before the series was published. She and her husband were murdered, right there in Glenshire, and they never found out who did it. Can you believe that? She was only twenty-two."

Jesus Christ.

"Darby Donovan," she said, gently touching the letters on the cover.

"Darby." I spoke the word not from my mind or my mouth, but from the depths of my fucking soul. It tasted familiar, like dark berries and sweet vanilla.

The girl's eyes shot up in surprise but didn't make it any higher than my chest before she jerked her head away, like a hand that had almost touched a hot stove. "You spoke again." She smiled weakly, her voice still laced with sadness. "See? You're gonna be singin' in the choir by Sunday."

"Darby?" I tasted the sounds again, clung to them, but they floated away from me like ripples on the surface of a lake, the accent changing from Irish to American as they faded into the darkness.

"Me? No, I'm Clover. Clover Doyle." Her face fell as she glanced down at the book in her lap. "I wish I were Darby Donovan—I would love to write like her one day—but … she died before I was born."

I slumped back against the wall, my head suddenly pounding.

The girl, Clover, began to read, and with every passing page, the coals of rage that had been smoldering inside of me since I was fifteen years old burned hotter and brighter until they eventually caught flame. By the last few pages, it became brutally clear that this was, in fact, my own personal hell, and Satan was using this girl to mock me.

Her sweet voice and slender fingers read directly from the story of my dreams—a gray-eyed boy and a green-eyed girl, the woods, the farm, the lake, the cemetery, the evil house, and the man who lived there. The visions I'd been having since returning to Ireland came pouring out of her pink lips, only in her version, everything was wrong. It was despondent and demonizing. Tragic and hopeless. The boy didn't get the girl in this version— she abandoned him. Then, after years of abuse and solitude, he finally became the monster everyone in the village believed him to be. He killed his own father and burned his house to the ground. The villagers suspected the boy had died in that fire as well, and now, his ghost haunted the forest of Glenshire, still waiting for his one true love to return.

I didn't have many good memories, and the ones I did have never really happened. They were fading glimmers of dreams that I clung to because without them, my life would be just as tragic as that story. Which was the whole fucking point. The Devil had found the one remaining source of pure happiness in my life—my dreams—and he'd corrupted that too. I could hear his laughter in my head as I pushed myself to stand.

"Fuck," I sneered, bracing my forearm against the wall as the earth tilted beneath me.

"What are you doing?" Clover asked as my vision went black around the edges.

Pressing my forehead to the cool stone, I took a deep breath, waiting for the dizziness to pass. I didn't know what was beyond that cave, but it had to be better than the psychological torture of being hated, feared, cared for, and mocked by a demon who was impersonating an angel.

My angel.

"Christ, you're gonna fall."

Keeping one shoulder pressed against the stone, I took a single step and exhaled in relief when it was easier than I'd expected. Less painful. Once the dizziness subsided, I would leave. I needed to fucking leave.

The sound of crunching gravel filled the cave as the imposter leaped up and sprinted over to me. "At least let me help ya."

I wanted to scream at her. I wanted to rip her face off and expose the lying monster underneath. I wanted to burn every shred of this illusion to the ground and show the Devil that I knew exactly what the fuck he was doing.

But mostly, I wanted to go to sleep and never wake up again so that I could find the redhead—the real one—and stay in her world forever.

The girl appeared on my right, slipping between me and the stone. Wrapping her arm around my back, she fit against my side as if she'd been carved from it, and some angry, empty space inside of me felt the same way. My rage evaporated. My wrath simmered. And when I pushed away from the wall and draped my arm over her shoulders, allowing her to help me stand, a new pain demanded my attention—a searing burn behind my eyes.

I could feel her heart pounding against my ribs, feel the rise and fall of her lungs, just as hard and fast as mine. And I could sense her hesitation before her cheek pressed against my chest and her chin began to quiver.

This was no fucking demon. This was a human being who was in even more pain than me.

I held my breath and lifted my arms as she wrapped herself around my torso, my muscles tensing violently as they prepared to fight back. The only times I'd been grabbed round the middle were during sparring matches in the Kletka, after which the fucker would find himself on his back with my knee inside his rib cage. My heart rate skyrocketed as I closed my eyes and forced myself to breathe through it, to focus on her scent, her size, her soft hands, and her shuddering breaths.

Even as a kid, no one had touched me like that. My ma had worked nights as a dancer, and when she was home, the last thing she'd wanted was another arsehole grabbing at her. I thought that had helped me survive in the Kletka. I'd learned to live without human touch long before I got there.

But this girl hadn't. She was so desperate for comfort that she was seeking it from the same man who'd destroyed her life. I'd *never* been in that much pain. I would let my father torture me before I ever let him touch me.

My father.

Jesus Christ, I had done to this girl exactly what my father had done to me. Killed her family. Ripped her away from her home. Put her in a cage where survival was a daily challenge.

I felt fucking sick.

I'd thought I'd won. By forsaking my own humanity, by suppressing my basic instincts, my moral compass, I thought I'd been denying him the satisfaction of breaking me. But really, I'd done exactly what he wanted all along.

I'd become just like him.

Lowering my arms, I wrapped them around Clover's shoulders stiffly, mechanically. My muscles throbbed with unspent adrenaline. My hands balled into fists. My rapid, heavy breathing ruffled her hair as I fought an all-out war against my urge to defend myself. But Clover didn't seem to notice.

She was busy fighting her own battle. I could feel the weight of it, of everything I'd taken from her, pulling her toward the ground. Her fingertips dug into my upper back as a silent sob racked her body. A few moments before, I'd hardly been able to stand, but if Clover needed me to, I would help her carry that burden forever.

It was the least I could fucking do.

I held her like that until the grief finally retreated. Once her shoulders stopped shaking and her legs could bear weight again, Clover released me and wiped her eyes with the sleeves of her jumper. A cooling wave of relief washed over me as soon as she let go—my body still interpreted human contact as threat—but I found myself leaning toward her rather than pulling away.

Touching her might have felt like a war, but some wars were worth fighting.

"Sorry." She sniffled, keeping her gaze cast down. "I came over here to help you, and instead, I ..."

"Don't."

Grasping her chin, I tilted her face up until I could see the shame all over her sweet, tormented face. She avoided looking at me at first, but when I made no move to release her, those dark brown lashes eventually lifted, revealing two endless emerald pools.

A riot of images exploded in the space between us. Blackberry bushes next to a lake, water in a teapot, biscuits in a sugar bowl. Trees and mushrooms and crumbling stone cottages. Missing teeth and freckled cheeks. Big green eyes ...

Like the ones that were looking at me now.

I knew in that moment that I'd been right—this *was* an illusion. And the illusion was that we were strangers. I knew those eyes. They might have been set in a different face, surrounded by a mane of different hair, but every fleck of gold and facet of green was exactly the way I remembered—like the sun shining through a canopy of trees.

But I remembered them smiling. These eyes weren't smiling. They were glistening with tears that spilled over the moment she tore them away.

"Sorry," she apologized again, ducking her face and shielding it from me with her hand. "I can't look at you. You remind me of someone, but he doesn't exist, so—"

"I feel the same way," I interrupted. The words came so easily that it was as if I had channeled them from somewhere else.

Clover froze at the sound of my voice, pursing her lips and tilting her head. "Can you say that again?"

I hesitated, unsure if I could speak while I was consciously thinking about it.

"It's fine if ya can't. It's just … the way you said that sounded … Irish."

One hopeful green eye peeked through two splayed fingers, and when I answered her unspoken question with a nod, the grin that followed enslaved me on sight.

"No. You're Irish?" Clover's squeal echoed through the cave as her eyes darted from my face to my wounds to my empty gun holster to my heart, which was beating its way out of my goddamn chest.

"Oh my God!" She beamed. "This makes perfect sense. When I found you, the Russians hadn't made landfall yet, so I didn't understand why you'd already been beaten and shot, but it's because *the Russians* did that to you … on the ship!"

I could see the gears spinning in her head as she fabricated a story almost as far from the truth as the one she'd just read to me.

"Maybe you were wearing their uniform to sneak on board, or maybe you were deep undercover, like a spy—I don't know, but they must have found out who you were and attacked. Maybe they even threw you overboard or—"

Her mouth fell open as her wide, round eyes shot back up to mine.

"It was you … that night, during the bombing. I was on the cliff"—her gaze fell away as the joy drained from her face—"and a drone found me."

It *was* her. The girl I'd seen on the cliff. The one I'd risked everything to save. My injuries were for *her*, not some heroic spy mission. And they'd been fucking worth it.

"I was gonna let it kill me." She swallowed. "Everything was destroyed—my home, my … family." Her voice broke. "I just wanted to die along with them."

Her eyes stared a hole through my chest as the memory hijacked her vision, but it felt as if she were staring directly at my heart, watching it splinter with every word she spoke.

"But then I saw you. In my mind. You were standing in a lake, and you looked so handsome." Color rushed to her cheeks as she smiled. "You held up your arms, and you told me to—"

"Jump." The word spilled from my lips as I pictured her the way I had that night. Lighter hair, perched in a tree, too far for me to hold … or save. That single word encompassed everything I was feeling—the hope and the hopelessness, the regret and need for redemption, the desire and the fear.

And when she lifted her eyes, smiling through the tears, she echoed my plea with a whispered, "Jump."

Past and present, life and death, heaven and hell—it all blurred into meaningless nothingness as I stood, suspended in her grateful, awestruck gaze.

I used to want to come back to Ireland. Now, all I wanted was to make *that* girl look at me *that* way as often as possible for the rest of my life. Or eternity, if I was, in fact, already dead.

The world around us burned away as I dived headfirst into the flames.

Clover and I collided in a space that felt untouched by the past. When she wrapped her arms around the back of my neck, I didn't want to push her away; I wanted to pull her closer. When she pressed her lips to mine, I didn't taste the salt of her tears; I tasted the sweetness of who she had been before all that pain. But when she parted those lips and slid a shy tongue along the seam of my mouth, something inside of me cracked open, allowing the past to come rushing back in.

Gripping her hair in my fist, I kissed her back with an urgency that bordered on panic. I knew at any moment, the Devil was going to snap his fingers and send her running back behind the boulders. Remind her of what I was, what I'd done. I knew I'd spend another night listening to her cry as she cowered from the monster who'd ruined her life. And she should.

I wasn't some heroic Irish spy, like she was telling herself. I was the sole heir of the Russian Bratva. I was a lieutenant on the ship that had bombed her town. I'd given the order. I'd led the charge. I was a fucking monster, and by allowing her to think otherwise, I was proving it.

But I was powerless to stop myself. Clover was my first taste of heaven after five long years of hell, and no amount of guilt could have pulled me away.

She might have been desperate, but I was fucking starving.

Tilting her head back, I devoured her trust, feasted on the version of me that she saw in her mind. I wanted to digest him, embody him, so that one day, I might become worthy of the admiration and gratitude I tasted on her lips.

"Tell me you're real," she whispered against my mouth, clutching the sides of my neck as if I might disappear. As if she was just as afraid of losing this as I was. "Tell me I'm not crazy."

Twisting my hands in her hair, I dropped my forehead to hers and willed myself to say the words she longed to hear. But I couldn't. Not because they wouldn't come, but because they would be a lie. Nothing about me was real, not the version she saw anyway. So, instead, I pressed her back against the cave wall and poured every word I couldn't say directly down her fucking throat.

I'm sorry.

I need you.

Don't hate me.

Clover's tears of joy seeped into my tongue as she smiled against my mouth. They tasted like a drug I'd never had, but had been born addicted to, and any hope I had of behaving like a better man disappeared the moment she gripped my shoulder blades and arched her body against mine.

We became a desperate riot of pleasure and pain, soothing tongues and ravenous teeth, clawing hands and tender lips. Bracing myself on the wall with my forearm, I sucked a trail of starving kisses along her jaw as Clover draped her battered thigh over my hip and pulled my body flush against hers. She was still seeking comfort, seeking an escape from her pain, and I was too far gone to deny her.

A sharp pain throbbed in my side as I ground against her, but it was nothing compared to the invisible blade that pierced my heart a moment later when the Devil finally came to collect, ripping Clover out of my arms with a single flash of lightning.

The earthshaking clap of thunder that followed was drowned out by Clover's terrified scream as she dropped to the ground and covered her head with both hands.

The next boom made her jump and curl in on herself even more.

I stared at her in absolute horror as the realization of what was happening slowly took hold.

I had done this to her.

And she didn't even know it.

Sitting against the wall next to her, I debated what to do before I finally pulled the cowering girl into my lap, gritting my teeth as pain shot through my side.

"They're back," Clover cried, burying her face in my neck.

They.

As if I wasn't one of them. As if I hadn't led the fucking charge.

Guilt twisted in my guts as I lifted a finger and pointed at the entrance of the cave and the darkness beyond.

"Look," I managed to say through the vise closing around my throat. "It's just thunder. See?"

Clover lifted her head just in time to see the next flash of lightning, and after tensing in fear, she suddenly relaxed. Slumping against my chest, exhausted and embarrassed from her panic attack, Clover hid her face against my neck and apologized.

I'd broken her, and she was apologizing for it.

Cradling her tear-streaked cheek, I rested my chin on the top of her head and stroked her arm with my free hand. I comforted her like I should have before, and with every stroke, I silently begged for her forgiveness.

Clover clung to my body and drank in my remorse, not realizing what it was. I wasn't the enemy to her anymore—I was a hero, a good guy—and suddenly, I understood why the Devil had let me kiss her.

At first, my punishment had been her suffering.

Then, it had been her silence.

Now, it was my guilt, which ate away at me like a thousand maggots as the victim of my crimes lay shattered in my arms.

CHAPTER 15

CLOVER

I still wasn't convinced that he was real, and honestly, I didn't even care anymore. Because when I woke up, cradled in his arms, our bodies painted pink by the sunrise over the sea, it was the first time I'd felt safe since I had been seven years old.

I lay with him for as long as I could, listening to him breathe, feeling the reassuring warmth of his skin and thump of his heart under my cheek, memorizing every line and swoop of the intricate Celtic knot he'd etched into a sheet of metal the night before, but when my bladder refused to be ignored any longer, I quietly slipped out of his embrace.

As I stood and stretched, I glanced at the man over my shoulder—both to make sure I hadn't woken him up and simply because I could. I was no longer afraid of what I might find staring back. But perhaps I should have been. Because the moment I took in his handsome face, my hopeful heart plummeted into my empty stomach. His skin was ashen, lips dry and cracked, and the shorts tied around his waist were dotted with fresh blood.

Shite.

I flashed back to the night before—him trying to walk, him holding me up while I fell apart, him pulling my body onto his lap—and shame flooded my cheeks. He'd needed my help, but I was so fucking broken that I ended up using him to meet my own emotional needs instead. I'd managed to hurt him worse than he would have hurt himself if I'd just left him alone.

I had to make it right.

Hunger and guilt gnawed at the lining of my stomach as I tried to figure out what to do. I had no more clean clothes to dress his wounds. I was almost out of whiskey. And despite what I'd told him the day before, there weren't enough lobsters in that inlet to feed us both for very long. The bombings and plane crashes and shipwreck must have scared them away.

It was settled then. I would go look for food and medical supplies and, God willing, a house to squat in, and once he was better …

I smiled to myself before quickly shutting down that line of thought.

One thing at a time.

I'd found him.

Now, I had to keep him alive.

I hardly felt the chill of the water or the sting of the salt as it lapped at my battered feet in the tunnel. The sun was warm on my legs. The gulls squawked as they fought over shiny objects in the water. And the ship was a meter or two away from becoming just another bad memory.

I gazed at the Eye as I relieved myself outside the cave entrance, and in another remarkable first, I realized that I hadn't been scanning the beaches for seals.

I'd simply been taking in the view.

But as soon as I climbed on top of the tunnel, my early morning reverie was punched in the gut by the harsh truth of my new reality.

Every bag of water had been completely pummeled by the storm. The rocks inside kept them from blowing away, but the sides had collapsed, and the contents had almost completely spilled out. All that was left were a few sips caught in the corners.

As I glanced up at the sky, my mood only soured. It was blue as far as the eye could see. Buckets of water had fallen over the past three days, and all I had to show for it was a dozen wet plastic bags.

Any second thoughts I'd had about risking another trip up the cliff suddenly became irrelevant. My life expectancy in the cave—our life expectancies—had just dropped from a few weeks to a few bleeding days. Drones or no drones, I was going up.

I didn't have a choice.

Pouring what little water remained into one bag, I took a careful sip before sealing it to carry with me. Then, I pocketed the empties and set off up the trail.

I climbed slowly, careful not to make any loud noises. Both times that I'd encountered a drone, it was after I'd screamed or cried out. I wouldn't make that mistake again.

Most of the trail was untouched by the fire. Every rock and root and wisp of heather looked exactly the way I remembered. It felt as if I'd gone back in time—back to when I was carrying a wet net full of lobster rather than a plastic bag full of rainwater. It was comforting—the familiarity—but frightening too. That climb had always been an anxious one. I'd never known what kind of fresh hell would be waiting for me when I got home.

I still didn't.

When the bushes turned to charred black stumps, I knew I was close to the top. I slowed down and listened this time before I crept onto the main path. I stayed low. Scanned the skies. When the coast was clear, I took a deep breath, preparing myself for what I would see when I stood up.

I was ready for it this time. The scorched earth. The green and yellow and purple hills, now drained of all life and color.

I didn't dwell on it, and I didn't turn right. Home was to the right, so I forged straight ahead, across the main path and up the steep rise to Howth Head Peak, the barren pinnacle of rock that overlooked the rest of the peninsula. Not even the tourists climbed to the top very often, so the path was narrow and overgrown with gorse bushes and thorny vines. They tore at my bare, already-battered legs, which shook from exertion by the time I got to the top. There was nothing in my stomach to fuel a climb from sea level to Howth Head Peak in one go, but when I finally dragged myself onto the bald stone crest, all of my physical pain disappeared, severed from my awareness by the swift stab of shock.

I stared through the numbness at a place I didn't recognize. The valley below used to be filled with life—lush green meadows covered in cows and sheep, clusters of trees filled with birds, tightly packed houses and townhouses beyond the farmland, carved into the steep hills at odd angles, all vying for a glimpse of the sea. Now, my entire town, my entire *life*, lay smoking before me like a bed of hot ashes that had been left out in the rain.

I wondered how many of those piles of rubble were splattered with blood and hair and teeth, like the one I used to call home.

No. I shook my head, blinking away the images from that night. *Everyone else evacuated. It's fine. There's nothing to be afraid of. It's fine.*

I continued this internal pep talk as I walked down the hill into the valley, scanning the sea of devastation for any homes that might be inhabitable as I tried to ignore the way the brittle, burned grass turned to dust beneath my feet. Other than the distant rumble of explosions, the town was as still and silent as a cemetery.

See? There's nobody here. Not even the Russians. They've pushed through to Dublin. You're totally safe.

As I got closer to the valley floor, I noticed a few sheep grazing in Mr. Kearney's field. My heart leaped at the sight of something so normal, so ... alive. Until I realized that they weren't. Their lifeless bodies were scattered across the muddy field like soggy cotton balls, blasted as far and wide as the debris from their barn.

Jesus Christ.

Tears begin to well in my eyes, but I forced them back down and kept walking. I had the rest of my life to cry about this nightmare, but if I didn't find food and water soon, that life was going to be very, very short.

Once I made it to the bottom of the hill, I decided to cut across the farmland as quickly as possible and head for the townhouses on the other side. Or what was left of them. Not only did I want to spend as little time as possible out in the open, but at the townhouses, I could search more homes at once and hopefully find more supplies in the process.

I kept my eyes on the ground as I squished through the grass, careful not to step on a nail or a sheep or shard of barnwood. I made it about halfway across Mr. Kearney's field when I first heard the voices.

My heart stopped as I froze and listened. The voices were muffled and distant, but after my last two trips outside of the cave, I wasn't going to take any chances.

There was a small patch of trees on the edge of Mr. Kearney's farm, next to the low stone wall separating his land from Mr. McCormick's, so I sprinted over to it and crouched down beside the wall, hidden behind the cluster of trunks.

I scarcely breathed as I listened for the sound again. I didn't hear footsteps approaching or drone blades whirring overhead, so that calmed my nerves a bit, and when I finally heard the voices again, they weren't shouting like angry foreign soldiers. They were laughing.

Lifting my head, I peered over the wall and found that most of Mr. McCormick's house was still intact. The right side of it was blown off, but the rest remained standing, and there were lights on inside.

Laughter rang out from the direction of the house, and I smiled as if I were in on the joke. I'd always liked the McCormicks. Mr. McCormick was the nicest, funniest man in the town, and his wife had been my music teacher in primary school. They'd never had any children of their own, and I'd often fantasized about running away and living with them whenever things got especially bad with Da.

A figure passed by the kitchen window, and I pictured Mr. McCormick shuffling into the sitting room with a cup of tea, cheerfully defying evacuation orders, as his wife followed on his heels, nagging him about fixing all the broken windows.

Climbing over the wall, I practically sprinted across the mushy meadow, and my heart skipped right along with me. The McCormicks would help us. I knew it. I could hardly wait to get back to the cave and tell … I paused mid-step, realizing that I didn't even know the man's name. I put that on my mental to-do list for the day.

Find food, water, shelter, and medical supplies.

Bathe. With soap.

Don't get killed by a drone.

Find out beautiful Irishman's name.

Maybe kiss him again without *crying or having a panic attack.*

My lips tingled as I remembered the way he'd thrown me against the cave wall the night before. I could still feel the scrape of his stubble along my jaw, his teeth on my throat.

The echo of his voice vibrated through me, dampening my knickers as I relived the feeling of him grinding against that very spot. The intensity. The connection. I'd never felt that way in my entire life. My cheeks heated as I imagined what would have come next, but then they flushed even harder, with mortification, when I remembered how it had actually ended.

And how fucked up I actually was.

Straightening my filthy jumper and tossing my matted hair over my shoulders, I lifted my chin, took a deep breath, and knocked. But when the door swung open, it wasn't a friendly smile or a warm hug that greeted me. It was a nameless, faceless man in a camouflage shirt, his hairy knuckles shooting out and grabbing me before I had the chance to scream.

I reacted immediately, slamming one hand against the doorframe to keep from being pulled inside the house and swinging the only weapon I had—a bag of water—with the other. The flimsy bag connected with the side of the man's wiry black beard and exploded on contact, surprising him just enough to loosen his grip. And when he did, I was gone.

I'd never run so fast in my life. A pair of deep Russian voices and their heavy, wet footfalls crashed through the silence behind me as my eyes darted left and right, desperately searching for a place to hide. But there was nothing. Other than that single clump of trees, the valley was a flat, grassy quilt, crudely divided into rectangular patches by low, crumbling stone walls. One of which I was rapidly approaching.

I'd gotten a head start, but if I tried to scale the wall, I'd have to slow down, and they'd catch me. If I tried to jump it like a hurdle, I'd fall, and they'd catch me. The only option that left me with was diving over it headfirst. Whether I would tuck and roll when I landed on the other side or slide on my belly, I wasn't sure, and I never got the chance to find out. Because as soon as I pushed off the ground and sailed halfway over the wall, two rough hands clamped around my ankle, halting my jump in midair. My body slammed down onto the stones like an egg being cracked in half, forcing the air from my lungs as a sharp, crunching pain exploded through my rib cage. Then, I was yanked backward.

I scrambled to grab hold of the wall as it slid out from under me, but the man was too strong. Too fast. Within a second, my body was falling again, this time face-first onto the wet earth.

And then they were on me.

The one who'd caught me by the ankle tried to pin my legs to the ground as I rolled onto my back and kicked at his sneering, bearded face. His friend grasped my thrashing arms, bloodshot blue eyes flaring with excitement just before he flipped me back onto my stomach and pressed his shin across my shoulder blades.

I continued to thrash, but when the other man wrenched my legs apart and knelt between them to keep them open, a bolt of panic sliced through my mind. It threatened to sever me from my thoughts, reduce me to an animal caught in a trap, but I fought against that too. I'd been living in a state of fear my entire life. I knew how to push it down, how to keep my wits about me in the presence of a violent man.

But not two.

Turning my face to the side, I scanned the field for anything I could use as a weapon. I scanned the hills for any sign of *him.*

But I knew he wasn't coming. Even if he had the strength to climb the cliff, he'd never find me in time. I was on my own.

As usual.

The bearded bastard knelt on the backs of my legs, holding them open, as he unfastened his belt and trousers. A wave of nausea purged my stomach of the only thing I'd put in it that day—a single sip of water—mixed with stomach acid. It burned my throat like liquid fire, reminding me that it was still raw from the guttural scream I'd let out that night after finding Sheila.

That scream.

My eyes widened.

I knew how to get a gun.

Thick fingers, cruel and rough, fisted the material between my legs, pulling the crotch of my shorts and knickers to one side, and I let out a scream so loud and so long that it echoed off the hills and shredded what was left of my vocal chords.

I screamed until the man holding my wrists eventually released one of them, but only so that he could punch me in the back of the head to make it stop.

And it did.

For one serene moment, the world was quiet again. Blissfully dark. Mercifully still. There were no hands on my body. No weight shackling me to the earth. Just a murky, watery oblivion. I didn't know how long I stayed suspended in that nothingness, but I knew if I could just find my way to the surface, I would see him there, arms outstretched, gray eyes glinting like moonlit steel as he commanded me to jump.

But there was no surface, and the next voice I heard wasn't his.

It wasn't even human.

"This is a message from President Abramov."

Scrambling sounds brought me back into my body. A hasty zip, a jingling buckle.

I then heard the voices of my attackers, barking angry orders at each other or possibly at the drone, but it wasn't listening to them. It was there for *me*. And if they didn't get off me in the next ten seconds, I was going to let it pump all three of us full of bullets.

The pig who'd just refastened his trousers pulled a gun identical to the one I'd stolen out of his own holster and pointed it over his shoulder at the drone.

"*Nyet! Nyet! Nyet!*" His comrade released my wrists, allowing me to turn just enough to see him holding his hands up in a panic as the drone's machine-gun barrel swiveled from the back of my head to the bearded face of the man holding the gun.

"Nine," the robotic recording continued.

The gunman lowered his pistol, but continued to yell at the drone, as if he were talking to a real person on the other side of that camera lens.

The drone ignored him, retraining its aim on me, and I sucked in a relieved breath as both men begrudgingly removed their knees from my thighs and shoulder blades.

"Seven."

Then, I coughed it back out as a boot careened into my side.

Gasping for air, I pushed up onto my hands and knees and felt another kick, this time to my stomach. My body collapsed and curled into the fetal position, my arms flying up to cover my head as more kicks landed, maybe three, maybe ten, before the bang of a gun brought everything to a standstill.

"Five."

Cracking one eyelid open, I peeked through the crook of my elbow and saw that both men were now facing the drone with their hands up. It must have fired a warning shot to get them to stop attacking me.

"Four."

But my relief immediately morphed into dread when the machine's attention fell on me again, blinding my open eye with its all-seeing spotlight. My heart seized, my body aching in a dozen different places, as I squeezed my eyes closed again, desperately searching for that blissful nothingness. But the beam penetrated through my closed lids, plunging me into an endless expanse of white. It was so tempting, that tunnel of light, the promise of a swift end to all this pain. All I had to do was stay still for three more seconds, and it would be over. I could see my family again, escape this nightmare once and for all, but I couldn't do it. Because deep down, I didn't want to go to heaven. I wanted to stay there, in hell, with *him*.

Delusion or not, I'd found something worth living for, and when I pulled myself into a sitting position and raised my shaky hands above my head, I prayed that he really *was* just a delusion.

If he was a figment of my imagination, then I could take him with me.

If he wasn't …

"You have surrendered to the Armed Forces of the Russian Federation. Follow this drone to the nearest encampment, where you will be detained as a prisoner of war. Failure to cooperate will result in your immediate termination."

If he wasn't, then we were both fucked.

CHAPTER 16

CLOVER

As I followed the drone through the ashes of Howth, down shattered streets half-buried under rubble, the two men followed *me*. I hadn't saved myself from them at all; I'd only delayed the inevitable and pissed them off in the process. They shoved me, spat on me, squeezed my arse, and grabbed at my breasts. With every bloody step, my legs shook harder, both from fear and from hunger, but somehow, they kept pulling me forward, delivering me to my doom. I ignored the taunts from the men behind me, ignored the leveled homes on either side of me, and stared straight ahead at Ireland's Eye.

Searching for a selkie that didn't exist.

Once we reached the harbor, I was shocked to find that most of the boats and several of the buildings there were still intact. The pier, the restaurants lining it, and the warehouse-like fish market where Da had sold his daily catch were all still standing. Probably because the Russians were using those buildings as some kind of headquarters. Tanks that looked like armored boats lined the main street. Tents crushed every blade of grass in the park next to the pier. But everything else had been destroyed.

Except for the boats in the harbor.

I stared at the faded red trawler at the end of the pier, and for the first time that I could remember, I wanted my da.

The drone led us past the loading dock behind the fish market and around to the main entrance facing the harbor. Men in camouflage watched me pass, their eyes lingering on my bare legs before flicking to the faces of the arseholes behind me with an appreciative sneer. My feet began to drag, my body recoiling from the hell that awaited me inside that building, but two viselike hands around my upper arms propelled me forward.

Just before we reached the door, it slammed open and stayed that way as a sailor or soldier struggled to pull something heavy out from inside. Releasing me to hold the door, the blue-eyed man with the buzz cut exchanged words with the stranger as the object he was dragging came into view.

First a foot, then the leg it was attached to, and then the rest of the naked young woman came sliding out the door, as unwieldy and unwanted as a bag of garbage. And almost as badly soiled. Multiple streams of blood ran down the length of her inner thigh, some dried and smeared, some shimmering red. Her torso and bare breasts were covered in burns, lashes, bites, and bruises. And when her pale gray face finally came into view, it was beaten beyond recognition and half-covered with a bloodstained matting of icy-blonde hair.

Sophie.

My empty stomach lurched violently as I turned away, dry-heaving on a startled sob. It was the single most horrifying thing I'd ever seen, and it had happened to someone I knew. A regular girl, like me.

And I was going to be next.

The drone began beeping in what I assumed was a warning that we needed to keep moving, so with a huff of impatience, the bearded man released my other arm and helped his comrade fling my classmate's lifeless body into the harbor.

I'd made a mistake.

I'd made a horrible fucking mistake.

I should have let that drone kill me the very first night. Now, I was going to be tortured and raped to death, and for what? So that the man I'd saved could die of thirst or infection or starvation while he waited for me to return?

The speed of the beeping increased, like a bomb that was about to explode, and for the first time in a week, that didn't scare me.

But what was waiting for me inside that building did.

I was frozen to the spot. I couldn't run, even though I was temporarily unrestrained, and when the bearded man's fist closed around my bicep again, I couldn't make myself walk either. Jerking on my arm, the arsehole shouted at me in Russian before he finally leaned over, planted his shoulder in my stomach, and lifted me off the ground.

"No!" I screamed, kicking and thrashing as the other two men joined him in wrestling me into the building, but my efforts were in vain.

The men were simply too strong. And as soon as the door closed behind us, I knew that I would never be coming back out.

Alive.

Between my flailing limbs and the bodies of the three men carrying me, I couldn't see much, but I could tell that the warehouse was dimly lit and smelled like a combination of fish, cigarettes, and every imaginable body fluid. Setting me down on an old wooden stool, one of the men held me still while the other two lashed my ankles to the legs with cable ties.

They shoved my torso forward so that my wrists would reach the front legs, which meant that I couldn't sit all the way up, but also that if I got tired and leaned too far forward, I'd fall face-first onto the concrete floor. In fact, if I thrashed at all, I'd fall face-first onto the concrete floor. My only option was to try to maintain a semi-upright position, which wasn't easy with my bruised thighs, abs, back, and ribs all screaming in pain.

When I finally lifted my head, I saw that we were gathered next to the long counter where Da used to sell his fish, which was now covered with laptops instead of mackerel and lined with Russian militants instead of fishmongers. Some of the screens had maps, or spreadsheets, or pages full of Russian text on them, but most were broadcasting arial footage of various places in Howth and Dublin. The screen in front of me, however, whose operator was shouting back and forth with the men who'd carried me in, had a very different image on it—the back of a hunched-over girl in a mud-soaked jumper, lashed to a stool.

Looking over my shoulder, I watched as the drone that had led me there slowly glided past us and landed on a charging dock next to the laptop. My bewildered face, framed by two curtains of unwashed hair, stared back at me just before the screen went black.

Someone had been manning that drone after all.

My gaze shifted to the balding, middle-aged man who was stationed at that laptop. Spittle flew from his mouth as he shouted at my captors, and it became apparent that he carried some kind of seniority over them. He thrust a hand in my direction several times during his rant, but it wasn't until his eyes followed that gesture that I understood why he'd shot at his own men for beating me. Heat flared behind his crazed stare as he salivated over my filthy, battered body. His tongue slid along his slimy teeth, and I could almost see the gears in his head turning as he contemplated what to do with me.

He hadn't given a shite about them hurting me. He'd just wanted to make sure that they delivered me to him in one piece.

With the flick of his chin toward the door behind the counter, he barked at them in Russian, and my captors nodded with something that sounded a lot like, "Yes, sir."

Picking up my stool by the seat, they carried me past the rows of laptops and into the bowels of the fish market. There must have been a kitchen back there because the hallways were filled with the scent of fresh-cooked seafood. They were probably burning through Howth's entire weekly catch, trying to feed everyone stationed out in the tents. Saliva pooled in my mouth, and acid gnawed at my empty stomach as I wondered if they'd feed me too. Give me water. Put any effort into keeping me alive whatsoever.

The water question was answered a moment later when they carried me into a bright white room lined with sinks the size of small bathtubs. I imagined they had once been used to clean fish or maybe store it on ice, but now, they served as toilets and sinks for the trembling, naked prisoners handcuffed to them. The stench of vomit, piss, sweat, and shite burned my eyes as I searched their faces. Four women, hiding behind what was left of their hacked-off hair, and one old man.

"Mr. McCormick?"

The white-haired fella didn't respond—he just stared at the ground, his shriveled body curled against the wall, like a dead leaf that hadn't yet let go of its vine—but the younger woman to my right did.

"Clo?"

A familiar pair of eyes looked up from the bruised knees they'd been hidden behind, but I barely recognized them without the brutal, bullyish smirk that usually accompanied them.

"Liv?"

Her long, expensive highlights had been chopped off in random chunks, her lip was split, her arms were bruised and burned, and I knew from the emptiness in her deep brown stare that I'd probably find a smear of blood between her legs, too, if I dared to look.

Suddenly, a hand sliced across her cheek, and the sailor with the buzz cut shouted, "*Peet*!"

Sitting up, Liv stared straight ahead and, like a robot, began singing something in Russian.

"*Kashdie! Kashdie!*" he demanded, gesturing wildly for everyone else to join in.

The naked women joined in, mumbling a song in a language they didn't know as they watched the sailor circle the room with wide, terrified eyes. He sang at full volume, waving his arms like a possessed orchestra conductor and pausing only to kick the prisoners who had made mistakes—which was all of them—until he came to Mr. McCormick.

"*Peet!*" he shouted, kicking Mr. McCormick as hard as he could in the hip.

When the ol' fella didn't comply, he shoved something small and black against his ribs, causing his entire body to convulse violently. I watched in horror as the man who'd once told the best jokes in town, the one who'd always greeted me with a smile, and who'd once given Da a ride home from the pub when he was too smashed to drive slumped to the floor, unconscious.

"No!" I managed to shout just before pain shot through the side of my head and the ground rose up to meet me.

I landed sideways on the tiled floor, still attached to the stool, with my forearm crushed between the wooden seat and the ground. Panic gripped me, chasing away the pain and the sounds of the men's raucous laughter, as I prayed that the bone wasn't broken.

Grabbing my other arm, the bearded man—the one who'd just hit me—jerked me back up and righted the stool, still laughing as he brandished a knife and lunged for my chest. I squeezed my eyes shut with a whimper, but felt only a few scratches as he hacked through the wool of my jumper. In less than a minute, I was as naked as the rest of the prisoners, but unlike them, I still had my hair to hide behind. My matted, tangled, mud-caked hair.

The man with the buzz cut crouched down so that we were on eye level, but I refused to look at him. My heart thundered in my chest as he grabbed my face, jerking it from side to side as he appraised my appearance. Turning my head all the way to the right so that his comrade could look at me, too, they joked in Russian, their sexual tone punctuated by nauseating chuckles.

Buzz Cut released me and turned around, running the water in the sink behind him. With his friend preoccupied, the bearded man took his place, stepping in front of me. I held my breath as he tipped my head as far back as it could go. Then, he leaned forward and smashed his mouth against mine.

Coarse, cigarette-scented facial hair grated my skin as he probed my tightly closed lips with his tongue. When I refused to open up for him, he grabbed my face like his friend had but squeezed harder, forcing my lips to pucker just enough for his tongue to penetrate. Bile hit the back of my throat as he licked my clenched teeth, clamping his free hand around my breast in anger. My pained whimper was quickly silenced by a hand around my windpipe as an unintelligible barrage of shouts peppered my face with spit.

I couldn't breathe, and for one brief moment, I hoped that I never would again. I hoped that he'd lose control and end me right there and then, but all too soon, Buzz Cut intervened, barking something at him that made him back away. I sucked in two lungfuls of air, but before I had a chance to exhale, I sucked in even more as a bucketful of cold water cascaded over my head. Then another. And another.

From my crouched position, all I could do was stare at the drain in the floor as the men scrubbed me with dish towels, touching me everywhere, pinching and squeezing and fondling whatever they pleased. Shutting out the feeling of their hands on my flesh, their cruel laughter in my ears, I focused only on the water pouring off of me. I watched as it changed from brown to clear. I sucked in every muddy drop that streamed past my lips, but it wasn't enough to quench my thirst. If anything, it only made it worse.

Beyond the drain in the floor, I also noticed that the sink in front of me had an empty pair of handcuffs hanging from the drain pipe and a pile of white-blonde hair scattered underneath. A fresh wave of dread wash over me.

This had been Sophie's sink.

And now, it was mine.

I pictured the way her body had looked, being dragged out, limbs twisted, face smashed in. I was so distracted by it that I hardly noticed that the men had finished scrubbing me—that was, until the glint of a serrated blade caught my attention.

My eyes squeezed shut as the bearded one grasped a chunk of my hair and began sawing away at it. It felt as though he had ripped every strand out by the root before he finally released me, tossing a wet lock of auburn hair the size of a snake on the floor.

I stared at it as the metal door slammed shut behind me, and for several seconds, the room was eerily silent.

Deathly silent.

"Mr. McCormick?" I finally asked, turning my head to the left, but my heavy, wet hair blocked my view.

"It's for the best," Liv snapped.

The other prisoners that I could see nodded their heads in agreement before hugging their knees and burying their faces again.

"What do you mean? Is he ..." I turned to face Liv.

She nodded, hugging her own knees as she watched me with sunken eyes. "If he's lucky."

I thought about what she'd said and couldn't disagree. It didn't make his death any less tragic, but I was sure anyone in that room would have traded places with him if they could have.

"What happened?" I asked, scanning the downturned faces and naked bodies in the room. "I thought everyone was evacuating."

"We were," Liv answered bluntly, "but traffic got backed up with everyone trying to get off the peninsula at once, and then ... they put up roadblocks." Her deep brown eyes clouded over, as if she were seeing something I couldn't.

"They went from car to car, takin' the women ... shootin' the men."

Her face was expressionless, but I knew. Her da, her brothers ... her ma.

Oh God.

She kept talking, trying to get past that part as quickly as possible. "But some men, probably the weaker ones, got brought back here, too. They forced them to watch."

Her eyes refocused and landed on Mr. McCormick's naked husk.

"They're gonna come for you soon." Her attention shifted back to me with a sense of urgency. "When you first get here, they all take a turn. If you want my advice, fight back. Bite, scratch, kick, spit ... be such a fuckin' problem that they decide to go ahead and kill ya. Trust me. The longer you stay alive"—

her gaze drifted over to the empty handcuffs in front of me—"the worse it gets."

"Is that what Sophie did?" I asked gently. As cruel as she'd been to me all those years, I couldn't help but feel sorry for her. For all of us.

What little color was left in her face drained completely at the mention of her best friend's name. "Why do ya say that?"

I recoiled from the venom in her tone.

Liv sat straight up, pinning me with a murderous glare. "Why do ya say that, Clo? Did you see her?"

"I … I …" I shook my head slowly, hoping that she would get the message without me having to say it out loud. "I'm so sorry."

Liv slumped back against the wall, her face falling and eyes glazing over, just like Mr. McCormick's had when I got there.

And like Mr. McCormick, she didn't so much as flinch when the door shot open behind me a moment later.

CHAPTER 17

CLOVER

As they carried me through the hallways, back out the way we'd come, I tried to tell myself that it was just like the long walk home after checking the traps. I knew I was going to be punished for something, but I never knew why or how badly until I got there. It didn't matter how many lobsters I'd caught. If I came home with an empty sack, Oliver would lay into me for being a lazy failure. If I came home with a full one, I'd get it for being late or tracking dirt in the house or some other thinly veiled excuse for his anger over my success. Walking straight into certain doom was something I should have been used to. I'd done it more times than I could count. I could do it again.

At least these men were strangers.

At least when they hurt me, it wouldn't break my fucking heart.

But all my logic and bravery disappeared the moment they set my stool down in the center of the fish market and a rumble of jeers and whistles echoed through the warehouse-sized room. This wasn't one man or two. This was an entire lion's den.

And I was a wet, naked lamb on a plate.

I was suddenly grateful for the dripping ropes of hair that stuck to my face and blanketed my hunched shoulders. It prevented me from seeing their predatory stares. But I could still hear them, circling, laughing. I could still feel my captors' hands groping and kneading my body as they presented me like prize livestock. But it was one particular set of footsteps, approaching at a slow, deliberate pace, that really caused my adrenaline to spike.

These steps didn't have the same shuffling, aimless quality as the others. These were steady and heavy, and the louder they got, the quieter everyone else became until the only thing I could hear between the footfalls was my own thrashing heart, pointlessly pumping blood through my veins, screaming at my muscles to fight or flee when all they could do was tremble in their bindings.

A pair of black combat boots stopped directly in front of me, and I shrank away from them instinctively, curling in on myself as another sound replaced the footsteps—the sound of my wobbly wooden stool shaking against the concrete floor, broadcasting my fear for all to hear.

The man turned to face the crowd. Through my downturned gaze, I saw him pull a piece of paper out of his back pocket, and when he held it up, they all cheered.

Then, he turned back around and jerked my head up by my hair.

My eyes flew open in shock, landing squarely on the face of the man who'd been flying the drone—the balding one, who I assumed was my captors' superior. He sneered at me with a mouth full of tobacco-brown teeth before pursing his lips and making a kissing sound. Everyone laughed as he held up the paper again, this time showing it to me. It was a photo of Alexi Abramov, Russia's president, and no sooner had I recognized who it was than it was being smashed against my mouth. The men erupted with cheers and more kissing sounds as their boss dragged the photo over my breasts and shoved it between my legs. The edges of the paper sliced my inner thighs as he rubbed it up and down, grinning as he watched himself touching me.

I slammed my eyes shut and strained every muscle in my body as I tried to squeeze my legs closed, curl into a ball, elbow him away, but I was completely immobilized.

A scream built in the center of my chest, but I didn't dare let it out. Every time I screamed, things only got worse. But also, what would be the point?

There was no one left to save me.

My eyes, blurry with fresh tears, flew open again when I felt the stool lift off the ground. The two men who'd brought me in carried me over to the long counter. The laptops had been pushed off to the sides, and in their place lay an assortment of what I assumed were torture devices—an electric rod, a stun gun, a knife, a pair of pliers. There were more tools, some I didn't recognize, but I couldn't take them all in. The moment they set me down, the two men held my arms still as their boss used the knife to cut through my wrist restraints. Two more men stepped up to secure my lower legs, and my ankles were freed as well.

Liv's words from earlier echoed in my mind.

"Fight back."

"The longer you stay alive, the worse it gets."

I considered her advice. My muscles ached with unspent adrenaline. My helpless, violated body shook with rage, begging for an outlet, dying to explode. The urge to thrash and bite and kick and scream possessed me like a virus, clouding my thoughts and seizing my muscles. But when I closed my eyes and prepared to let it take over, I found myself right back in that cave, paralyzed at the sight of him—clutching his side, covered in blood, holding me hostage with those pleading platinum eyes.

These men weren't my only captors. They might have been in possession of my body, but my life was tethered to a man whose name I didn't even know. If I died, he died, too, only much more slowly and painfully. Thirst. Hunger. Infection. He would be in agony for days before his heart finally gave out.

So, when the men placed my feet on the ground and held them there, I didn't kick.

When they shoved my chest down on the stainless steel counter and bound my wrists to a metal shelf below it, I didn't thrash or claw or hit.

And when the first two fingers shoved inside of me—rough and hateful, a gleeful public stabbing—I damn sure didn't scream. I swallowed all the rage, all the pain, all the humiliation, just like I'd been doing since I had been seven years old.

People hurt me. That was what they did.

The only power I had was denying them the satisfaction of knowing they'd done it.

I closed my eyes and let my head hang off the end of the counter, going to that forest in my mind where the moss grew like carpet and the sun-speckled bluebells swayed in the breeze. The edges of a misty lake had just started to take shape when my head was jerked up by my hair.

This time, when my eyes flew open, the boss was in front of me again, only instead of holding a picture of his president, he was holding his own hard cock, pumping it in his fist as he tightened his grip on my hair and steered my head toward the leaking tip.

No.

I could take them violating me from behind, where I couldn't see, where I didn't have to participate. But this?

I couldn't do it. I couldn't make myself fucking do it.

Acid erupted from my empty stomach, coating the inside of my mouth with my own searing bile as my body recoiled against my will. I couldn't fight the fear any longer. I'd tried rationalizing it away, compartmentalizing it away, dissociating it away, but they'd stripped me of my final coping mechanism—my happy place—and reduced me to a panicked, caged beast.

My wet feet slid across the floor, and my delicate wrists sliced open from the cable ties as I thrashed and bucked and yanked at my bindings. Angry Russian shouts filled the room as men struggled to hold my kicking legs. Others reached for the weapons on the counter to my left and right. The clicking of a stun gun being turned on—the same sound I'd heard before Mr.

McCormick was shocked—buzzed in my ear as something cold and hard prodded against my exposed arse.

Gripping my hair even harder, the man in front of me pulled a gun out of his holster and pressed it to the side of my head. He barked a command, his fully erect cock pressing against my tightly sealed lips as a chunk of my hair tore out at the root. Everything was happening all at once, and I couldn't escape any of it. I needed to scream, to release some of the terror boiling over inside of me. So, with my jaw clamped shut and tears streaming down my face, I gave them the one thing I'd sworn I wouldn't. Without opening my mouth, I sucked in a deep breath and released a high-pitched squeal so loud and so raw that everything around me just *stopped*.

It sounded like the bats of hell were pouring out of me—a furious, inhuman, deafening shrieking—and when it was over, I realized that, aside from the hand gripping my hair, no one was touching me anymore.

Hesitantly, I glanced up at the man standing in front of me, but instead of finding his hateful, soulless blue eyes staring back, I discovered that he wasn't looking at me at all. His narrowed gaze was fixed solely on something across the room.

My head fell suddenly as he released my hair and lifted his hand in a salute. The rustling sound that spread throughout the room suggested that everyone else was doing the same. Holstering his weapon, the boss greeted their visitor with surprise in his voice and, if I wasn't mistaken, a tinge of fear.

Turning my head as slowly as possible, I glanced over my shoulder and felt my heart plummet into the acidic wasteland of my stomach.

No. No, no, no, no, no.

It was *him*. He was standing in the open doorway, a silhouette backlit by the summer sun, but I would know the shape of him anywhere. The width of his shoulders, the hard line of his jaw, the soft flips of his hair—a little too long to be a military cut—the slight stoop of his posture. To anyone else, his stance might look casual, relaxed even, but I knew that he was favoring his left side.

Because beneath that shirt and jacket, there was a gaping bullet wound.

And as soon as these people discovered that he spoke English instead of Russian, they were going to put a few more in him.

As relieved as I was to see him, as devastating grateful as I was to him for coming to find me, all I wanted to do was scream at him to run. He was outnumbered twelve to one, injured, hungry, and impersonating a Naval officer. There was no sense in both of us dying. But all I could do was watch in absolute horror as the door closed behind him, caging him in.

As he stalked into the room, the fluorescent lights sharpened his cheekbones, hollowed out his eyes, and accentuated the wrath beneath their smoky surface. That gray gaze connected with mine for no more than a heartbeat before darting to the face of the man standing with his cock out before me.

Then, he opened his mouth, and my heart stopped beating completely.

Perfect Russian poured from his sculpted lips, as brash and eloquent as that of a seasoned leader. He spoke with his chin high, eyes narrowed, hands gesturing in slices and thrusts— violent motions that punctuated the simmering anger in his velvety voice. And with every step he took forward, I felt the men in the room shrink back.

The day before, when he'd spoken to me in English, each word and sentence had seemed so effortful, but here he was, commanding a room full of Russian militants like it was second nature.

Because it is, I realized.

His gaze met mine again, but this time, it felt as if I were looking into the eyes of a stranger. An imposter. A heartless, murderous liar who would do or say anything to save his own neck.

He'd earned my trust. He let me believe that he was Irish. He held me while I cried about the family *he'd* killed. And the second he felt strong enough, the second I left him unattended, what did he do? He'd abandoned me and marched straight back to *them*.

My instincts had been right all along. He *was* just a figment of my imagination. A hologram of comfort projected onto the source of all my pain. And from the way he was looking at me, I knew he was about to prove just how delusional I'd been.

Those silvery eyes slid down the length of my naked body as he unfastened his leather belt in the span of one smooth, confident stride. I held his cold stare as he unzipped his trousers, wanting him to see the betrayal on my face. The hatred in my eyes and the hardening of my soul. But my body betrayed me, too, spilling a single tear down my freshly bruised cheek before I jerked my head away in shame.

I'd been wrong about these men.

They *could* break my heart.

A hush fell over the room as his warmth drew closer. I remembered the way it had felt just that morning, the heat of his body lulling me into a sleepy stupor of imaginary safety. But now that heat felt more like the roar of an approaching wildfire.

And I was tied to a tree.

Shoving my heel out backward with a grunt, I managed to kick his shin, but he easily sidestepped my next attempt and stood with his feet spread, bracketing my tightly closed legs. The most I could have done from that position was try to step on his boot-covered feet.

He'd won. He'd taken advantage of me in every way a man could. The actual act was just a formality.

I could feel my heartbeat in my face as I stared down at the blood dripping from my bound wrists onto the floor.

"I should have let you die," I sneered, pushing the words out through clenched teeth as I pictured his blood, pooling on the cave floor just a few days ago.

Tears blurred my vision as I realized how true that statement was. How pathetic. He'd been wearing a Russian officer's uniform, for Christ's sake. How could I have been so blind?

But deeper than my shame, than my anger and self-blame, was a place that whispered what hurt the most. What I'd always known but had been too afraid to admit.

That I was completely and utterly unlovable.

If saving a person's life wasn't enough to make them care about me or at least see me as a human being, then maybe this was all that I was.

A sex object. A servant girl. A dog to kick at the end of a hard day.

Lacing my fingers together, I closed my eyes and whispered, "I hate you."

But I didn't know if I was saying it to him or myself.

The man standing in front of me, who'd backed up one or two steps, asked something in Russian as the liar behind me gripped my hips with large, commanding hands. He answered with a short quip, and as the entire room burst into laughter, he pulled my head back by my hair and thrust himself between my legs.

My eyes shot open, but not in pain. In shock. He hadn't entered me. In fact, he wasn't even fully hard.

Leaning forward until his lips grazed the shell of my ear, he whispered, just loud enough for me to hear, "Scream."

Then, he thrust his hips against me again. My pelvis slammed against the counter, and I did as he'd said. I funneled all my rage, terror, and grief into a single bloodcurdling wail.

It felt good, that release. That unapologetic explosion of emotion. How many times had I wanted to cry out at home but had been too afraid? Or in the cave, where a drone might hear me? I didn't have to stay quiet anymore. I could let them know exactly how I felt.

I could let *him* know too.

"I hate you," I snarled again, this time at full volume as I stared at the place where the wall met the ceiling—the only thing I could see with my head pulled back. "I hate you!"

He said something in Russian that made the crowd chuckle—mocking my pain, no doubt—but if I wasn't mistaken, he was also stroking the back of my head with a single finger, covertly, beneath the mass of wet hair he was gripping. It felt like an apology, a tiny token of comfort, but I knew that was just my desperate, pathetic mind grasping for something that wasn't there.

He wasn't offering me solace; he was patronizing me. Praising me like a good little girl for putting on a good little show. By saving me from being gang-raped, he could absolve himself of any guilt he felt over using and betraying me. He could walk away, feeling like we were even when, really, he'd hurt me more than the rest of them combined.

"Get off of me!" I shouted, suddenly wanting to get as far away from him as possible. I would have rather been touched by strangers than feel his body on mine for another second, knowing that it was all for show. That he was using me again, this time to make himself feel better about everything he'd done before that. "Get off!"

I thrashed and jerked as if I could free myself from my own skin if I just fought hard enough. "I hate you!" I screamed, lifting both feet off the ground as I tried to kick him again.

Releasing my hair, he gripped my hips with both hands, holding me still as he trapped my lower legs between his knees.

Excited shouts burst from the crewmen as he fucked my thighs faster, never pulling out far enough for them to see that he wasn't inside of me.

But he was. As soon as I dropped my head, letting it hang off the end of the counter, it became flooded with images of him. His perfect body, shivering shirtless against the cave wall after he'd given me the clothes off his back. The lines of my crying face, drawn in his own blood as a token of his sympathy. The despondent shake of his head when I'd offered him food, indicating that he was willing to starve to make sure I didn't go hungry. The taste of my tears on his lips as he'd shoved me against the wall and chased away my pain.

I was doing it again. I was slipping back into the illusion— my need for love and comfort always stronger than my ability to handle the truth. I knew what was happening, but I was powerless to stop it.

I was too busy picturing the curl of his dark eyelashes against his cheekbones that morning and the way his muscular, corded arms had looked wrapped around my body. I imagined that, instead of letting me go when I'd wriggled out of his embrace, he'd pulled me closer. Touched me. Made love to me.

Promised to stay with me forever.

No longer fighting, I tilted my arse up, allowing his cock to slide across the most sensitive parts of me. He felt thick and powerful between my thighs, fully hard now, and slick with the proof of my delusion. His swollen crown grazed my entrance with every thrust, and I found myself wishing he would breach that final boundary. It was desperate and depraved, but for just a few seconds, I wanted to experience pleasure instead of pain. I wanted to disappear into my fantasy.

But mostly, I wanted to believe that he wanted me too.

His pace quickened, and his viselike hands kneaded my arse as the wet slap of our bodies announced to the room that not only was it almost their turn, but that I was a ready and willing participant. The shuffling of their impatient feet, the shoving, the shouting—it all brought the world crashing back into focus.

He hadn't saved me from them.

He'd only delayed the inevitable.

Fear rushed down my spine like poison, tensing my muscles and locking my knees as he said something in Russian to the man in front of me.

I stared at the floor as his boots stepped toward me, landing mere centimeters from the blood that had dripped from my wrists.

Again, the balding man jerked my head up, forcing me to look at him, and the grin on his pasty face was only slightly less nauseating than the noisy wad of spit he hocked into his hand before fisting his cock with it.

Wait. What?

The world tilted on its axis as I realized that the man whose warm body was now draped over mine as he rutted against me had just invited his sadistic friend to join in.

I recoiled from his cold blue gaze as he pulled his gun back out and pressed the barrel against my temple.

I couldn't breathe. I couldn't think. I couldn't believe this was happening. All I could do was blink through my tears as he jerked my head and pressed his cock against my seething, bared teeth.

Then, with a flash of movement and a blast so loud that it sounded as if it had come from inside my own head, one of the blue eyes I'd been glaring up at exploded.

CHAPTER 18

DAMIEN

I was no stranger to rage.

Some days, it was so consuming that it felt as if it had its own heartbeat, like a parasite living inside of me, eating away at my soul.

That rage had been craving an outlet since the moment I'd watched the life drain out of my mother's eyes, but there was only ever one man deserving of my wrath, and laying a finger on him was an immediate death sentence.

Even for his own son.

My father had taken everything from me—my mother, my home, my freedom, my identity—not the Bratva goons he'd sent to kidnap me, not the trainers in the Kletka or the sailors I'd enlisted with. They were all just following orders, a fact that I'd fought hard to remember every time I found my fist buried in one of their faces on the sparring mat.

These men weren't my enemies.

Not until that morning, when I'd followed Clover's muddy footprints up the cliff.

I could still see the impression of her body in the field—deep, as if there'd been a massive weight on top of her. The V of her spread legs, the profile of her face, the signs of her struggle were embedded in my mind just as deeply as they had been gouged into the wet earth.

And so were the boot prints that had led her away.

I'd been in agony when I left the cave to search for her— empty stomach, dehydration headache, stabbing pain with every step—but the moment I realized what had happened, where they were taking her …

My pain didn't just disappear; I disappeared, completely. Consumed by a blackout rage so intense that I didn't remember following their footprints back to base camp. I didn't remember feeling another second of pain from my injuries. I didn't remember buttoning my jacket and throwing open the door. But I would never forget the seething, writhing need to kill that exploded through my veins when a dozen men turned to salute me with their cocks in their hands. Because behind them, lashed to a metal counter and covered in bruises, was a naked, squealing redhead with a cock in her mouth and a gun pressed against her temple.

I'd known rage.

This was wrath.

It filled the room, swallowing every shadow as it sharpened my vision. It sucked the air from their lungs and pumped it into mine. It identified the exact location of every weapon and exit in the room within seconds, all while fluent Russian poured from my lips. And it deduced immediately that these men didn't know that I'd defected. They wore camouflage instead of sailor stripes, meaning that they were part of the Naval Infantry battalion that had come to shore in the amphibious tanks. They had no idea that I'd jumped overboard *before* the ship exploded. To them, I looked like a battle survivor. But more importantly, I looked like their superior.

And superiors got first dibs on the spoils of war.

A plan formed instantly—one that would keep the entire room distracted while I got close enough to the fucker with the gun pressed to Clover's head to take his weapon—but the reality of what I'd have to do was almost worse than the carnage that would follow. But my wrath didn't give a fuck. It wouldn't be satisfied until *my* boot prints were the ones leading Clover away—through a river of rapist blood.

As I stalked across the room, I poured all my concentration into keeping my movements fluid and my eyes focused. Every motion and sound made me want to attack. Adrenaline flooded my muscles, soaked my brain, and honed my reflexes to the point that I became a walking, talking hair trigger. But on the outside, I was exactly who my father had trained me to be.

Bratva royalty.

Power personified.

Death incarnate.

I refused to look at Clover as I unbuckled my belt, but I could feel her eyes on me. Her pain, terror, and betrayal threatened to penetrate the numbness of my wrath, but those emotions quickly vanished when my gaze landed on an electric cattle prod the size of a billy club in the hand of a man standing directly behind her.

He hadn't used it on her yet—she wouldn't have been conscious if he had—but my seething gaze still darted to her body, taking inventory of every single injury marring her freckled skin.

The ground was smeared with blood where her feet had slid across the floor, lacerated from days of walking barefoot over rocks.

Guilt gnawed at my stomach.

I should have given her my boots.

Her long, toned legs were still slashed and bruised from her fall down the cliff, but now, her arse was stained pink from their handprints as well.

My hands vibrated with self-hatred as I unzipped my trousers, preparing to touch her just like they had.

Heat radiated off my body as I followed the curve of her arse up to the valley of her back, where bruises as black as the cancer in my soul bloomed from her ribs to her spine. They were the same size and shape as a fist or the toe of a boot, and judging by the smoothness of the edges and the depth of the bruising, I assumed that it was the latter.

Water had pooled in the small of her back, fed by delicate streams running from her sopping wet hair, and I had to resist the urge to bend over, press my lips to her skin, and drink. I didn't know what I was craving more—water or the opportunity to kiss and lick and suck every injury on Clover's body until she was better. Until she no longer saw me as one of them.

When I lifted my gaze to hers, that thought, along with any hope that she could ever forgive me for what I was about to do, burst into flames of blinding murderous fury.

As Clover glared at me over her shoulder, the narrowed, hardened slant of her eyes did little to mask the single tear clinging to her bottom lashes or the swelling purple cheekbone that it finally cascaded over.

Tearing my gaze away before I did something stupid, like react, I pinned it directly on the dead man who'd been trying to fuck her face when I walked in.

He stumbled backward in response, which was the opposite of what I needed him to do. I was going to have to calm down before I could lure him back over. Be more convincing.

Clover's arms hung down the other side of the counter, tied to something I couldn't see below, and at the sound of my zip being lowered, she hung her head below the counter as well.

"I should have let you die."

Her words caused the first slice of pain I'd felt since standing in that field, but the sensation was quickly consumed by the raging inferno burning inside of me.

"What did she say?" the balding bastard asked, spitting in his hand before smearing the filth all over his already-shriveled cock.

My presence must have intimidated him more than I'd realized.

Good.

Grabbing her hips with both hands, I replied in Russian, "She said she hopes my dick is bigger than yours."

I wasn't trying to taunt him; I just needed the distraction. As soon as the room burst into laughter, I yanked her head back by her thick, wet hair and thrust myself into the seam between her tightly closed thighs.

I hated myself for being even semi-hard. She was beaten and trembling and had possibly been tortured, but she was still the most beautiful woman I'd ever seen.

And the first naked girl I'd ever touched.

They'd brought prostitutes into the Kletka every month or so to keep the men from killing each other, but every time I looked at them, all I could see was my mother. She'd been a stripper, but she also sold her body on the side. It was no secret—that's how I was conceived. She would come home early in the morning—a split lip here, a black eye there—but she never wanted my sympathy. She never wanted me to touch her at all. And one glance at the hateful eyes and defensive postures of the women in the Kletka had told me that they felt the same way.

Just like Clover must have felt when her trembling body stiffened beneath me.

But my wrath quickly shut down that line of thought and refocused.

Leaning forward—my bullet wound now a distant ache, thanks to the adrenaline pumping through my veins—I pressed my lips to the curve of her ear and whispered, "Scream."

Then, I thrust against her again. I felt the sound vibrate through her back and into my chest as it clawed its way out of her body. Every cell it passed through vibrated with the animalistic fury I heard in that scream. It was the frequency of my own soul.

I felt truly connected to her in that moment, understood in a way I hadn't thought was possible. But then she opened her mouth again and remined me *who* had made her feel that way. *Who* had taken everything from her. *Who* had reduced her to this shivering, snarling beast.

"I hate you!"

I hate you.

I hate you.

More words came pouring out of her as she thrashed, but the rest of them fell on deaf ears as my wrath turned inward.

I glanced down at the place where our bodies were joined and felt as if I were seeing myself with someone else's eyes. We weren't sharing some fucking connection—my officer's uniform was decorated with the patches of her enemy. My scabbed knuckles—sunk deep in the soft flesh of her hips—turned white as I struggled to restrain her bucking, terrified body. And my cock was now fully fucking hard, as if I got off on causing her this much pain.

I hate you.
I hate you.
I hate you.

The words echoed through the vast emptiness inside of me, only this time they were spoken in my own voice.

First a whisper, then a scream as Clover's body went limp. It was as if she'd passed out, her head dangling over the counter again. My pulse skyrocketed with concern, but while I debated what to do, what I *could* do with all these people watching, the gradual arch of her back let me know that she was still lucid. Then the tilt of her hips. Then the lift of her feet up onto her toes.

Once again, our bodies vibrated on the same frequency, this time humming in unison as something shifted between us. With a few subtle movements, Clover had positioned herself so that the head of my cock was now sliding along the seam of her, stroking her clit with every thrust. Silky and wet, she began to rock against me when I grazed her entrance, and like her fury, I understood this repressed need as well. She was seeking something to fill the chasm of emptiness inside of her.

A chasm that I'd helped create.

I wanted nothing more than to give her what she craved. After five years of only being touched in violence, of refusing the advances of desperate, hollow-eyed women, I couldn't deny that the thought of losing myself inside Clover's perfect body had become an obsession. That need whispered to me. It undermined my wrath. It told me to close my eyes. To focus on the slick, warm oblivion she was offering. A bead of cum seeped from my cock in anticipation as I kneaded her arse and drove myself along her slit faster and faster.

Do it, the need whispered. *She's beggin' for it. Feel how wet she is? She wants you to fuck her. Make her feel good. Make her come until she cries.*

Clover's hips met mine, thrust for thrust, and the sound of our bodies colliding—desperately asking for something the other wasn't willing to give—echoed off the rafters until more sounds joined them. The sounds of pushing. And shoving. And shouting. And *stroking*.

I'd let it go too far. The men had gone from being passively distracted to aggressively impatient, and their eagerness to hurt my girl reignited my wrath like a match to a fuse. I'd had a plan when I crossed that room, but now that I knew what it felt like to hold Clover down while she thrashed and screamed and begged me to stop—now that I'd felt her tremors of terror with my own hands, heard her cries of desperation with my own ears—there was no going back.

I was going to kill every motherfucker in that room or die trying.

And I was going to start with *him*.

Lifting my head, I took in his salivating, glassy-eyed gaze, his quickly jerking fist tugging on a cock he deserved to be choking on, and tried to keep my facial expression neutral. But inside, I couldn't even feel my face anymore. The wrath was taking over. It seeped from my pores like a poisonous gas. I could see it in the air, darkening the edges of my vision, blanketing Clover's naked body like a shield. It slithered out of me in smoky tentacles, wrapping itself around the necks of every man in that room. Marking them. Tethering them to me so that they couldn't get away.

"Join us," I commanded in Russian, gesturing for that limp-dick piece of shit to come closer with a flick of my chin. "Got her purring like a kitten for ya."

By the time he stepped forward and pressed the barrel of his gun to Clover's head again, I had become a spectator in my own body. Time shifted into slow motion as I watched myself reach out and snatch the pistol from his hand. His eyes went so wide they looked like blue targets with black bull's-eyes. I aimed at the one on the left and pulled the trigger. I didn't hear the blast or feel the spray of blood misting my face; I was already sliding across the counter with my arm around Clover's waist.

I dropped into a crouch behind the counter and set her down on her knees beside me. Her wrists were twisted in front of her, bound to the metal shelf post below the counter with a cable tie, but I would deal with that later. I had about ten seconds to kill eleven more sailors before the lads outside heard the gunfire and burst through that door.

Make that nine.

Clearing the shelf, I ducked under the counter and blew a hole through the stainless steel back, opening fire on a room full of men who were still trying to zip their trousers. I couldn't see my targets, but I didn't need to. It was as if my awareness had extended beyond my physical body. I knew where every man in the room was, living and dead.

Which was how I knew that one of them was coming over the counter, even before I heard Clover's scream.

Jerking back, I turned and fired at the space over her head as a sneering man with a bushy black beard launched himself at me from above. The bullet tore through his throat, causing his charging body to go limp and plummet toward mine. Covering my head, I caught the brunt of his dead weight on my forearms and tossed it aside. He landed next to the first cunt I'd killed, and their bodies immediately began to jump and twitch as a hail of bullets rained down from above, tearing through the plaster wall behind me and the men slumped against it.

Evidently, the remaining men had finally put their cocks away and found their guns.

Three of the original twelve were still out there, firing at us. I could sense their locations, just like I could sense that my gun was out of ammo without needing to check.

There was no time to unholster the bearded sailor's gun, so I grabbed the knife out of his boot—same as the one I'd had before I lost it in the sea—and turned to face all three men as they rushed the counter at the same time.

And the wrath smiled.

I'd never killed anyone before that day, but every slash, every duck, every punch and stab felt rehearsed, like a dance I could have done in my sleep. It wasn't just my training kicking in or the adrenaline sharpening my skills; it was as if I had developed muscle memory for something I'd never done. It wasn't a possession exactly. More like … an awakening.

My hands instinctively knew that a quick stab to the jugular was quicker than slitting a throat. They knew to aim for the kidney beneath the rib cage rather than go through the rib cage, looking for the heart. And when my knife was kicked out of my hand by the last man standing—that scrawny fucker with the blond buzz cut and the cattle prod—a distantly familiar surge of bloodlust shot through my veins as my hands snatched the weapon out of his grasp and jammed it deep into his belly.

He convulsed and jerked as the current tore through him, foaming at the mouth, but my wrath only grew. It wouldn't be satisfied with the simple pull of a trigger or the slash of a blade. My muscles screamed for a release that only my bare hands could deliver.

Throwing the cattle prod to the ground, I caught his falling body by the neck and felt that muscle memory take over again. I squeezed until his windpipe collapsed, knowing exactly what that crush would feel like before it happened. Just like I knew that my arms would shake from exertion and I'd need to widen my stance to support the weight of a thrashing man. I also knew what I would find shining out of Clover's glistening green eyes before I looked over at her. I'd seen it in my dream in the cave. Acceptance. Gratitude. Overwhelming relief.

But that was where my knowing ended. Once again, I was reminded that Clover was not the girl from my dreams, She wasn't staring at me like I was her hero. In fact, she wasn't looking at me at all. She was too busy using the knife I'd dropped to saw through her restraints.

If time had been moving in slow motion before, the sight of her kneeling and naked, hands bound as if in prayer, made it stop altogether. I felt as though I were gazing upon a religious painting, a masterpiece in a museum somewhere that commanded my full attention. Dark auburn hair cascaded over the curves of her body as bright red streams flowed from her pale wrists. She didn't look human. She looked … heavenly. A crimson angel of pain.

But when her eyes finally lifted to mine, the only thing I saw shining out of them was terror.

My arms went slack. The final body fell to my feet. And when the door burst open and the first of the troops filed in, guns and voices raised, I didn't even move.

I'd already been slain with a single look.

"Shit!"

"What the fuck happened?"

"Sir! Sir, are you okay?"

"Who the fuck did this?"

"Lieutenant, you've been shot."

Glancing down, I noticed that my jacket had fallen open, and my shirt was stained with fresh blood. Only this time it wasn't my own.

Clearing my throat, I lifted one trembling arm and pointed toward the back hallway. "A prisoner got her hands on a gun …" I'd planned on saying more, but I shut up the moment I realized how hard it was to form a simple fucking sentence in Russian, how quickly the pain and hunger and weakness were returning, clouding my mind, blurring my vision.

Noting my unfastened trousers, the men nodded in solemn understanding. The prisoner had obviously caught us off guard with our dicks in our hands instead of our guns. There was no judgment in their eyes, only horror.

As if it could have happened to any one of them.

"Go!" the man in front shouted, jerking his gun in the direction of the back hallway. "Find the bitch! Now!"

The second they cleared the room, Clover bolted.

I lunged for her, pulling her to the ground just before a second wave of men burst through the door. I clamped my hand over her mouth as they filed in—gasping and cursing at the massacre before them—and felt my guts twist as Clover squeezed her eyes shut and stifled a whimper.

It was the way someone would react if they'd just been pinned to the ground by a fucking bear. That was what I was to her now—a mindless, murderous animal.

Clover managed to stay silent, but she was breathing faster than a rabbit, causing her perfect tits to heave against my chest. Having her naked body beneath me was a torture I hadn't thought I'd have to endure again so soon. It was also making it hard for me to formulate a plan other than removing my hand from her mouth and kissing the shite out of her.

But that was a privilege I'd never have again.

We were right back where we'd started. I was the enemy, and she couldn't bear to look at me. Only this time it wasn't because I reminded her of someone. This time, it was because I'd just killed twelve fucking men in front of her and their blood was still splattered all over my face.

"I'm not going to hurt you," I whispered, my lips grazing the soft skin of her ear.

She flinched on contact.

Our hearts were both racing—pounding against one another through the layers of bone and flesh separating them— when the commander emerged from the hallway and instructed the new crew to fan out and search for the escaped prisoner. From that angle, he would have been able to see us if he'd looked behind the counter, but my body was so much bigger than Clover's that she was mostly hidden from view. I held perfectly still, my lips poised at her ear, and felt her body begin to tremble beneath mine.

"Shh," I whispered, my own arms beginning to shake as they held hers against her sides.

I might have been trained to kill, to engage in every form of hand-to-hand combat on earth, but nothing in my training had prepared me for the violent adrenaline crash, suffocating dread, or nauseating sense of disgust that would come after slaughtering a room full of men and then lying among their oozing bodies.

"I'll get you out of here," I promised, "as soon as they leave."

Clover's cheek brushed against mine as she shook her head, so subtly no one but me would have noticed.

As the men passed through the room, I felt their eyes peer behind the counter. I squeezed Clover's body so tight that her tremors finally stopped and held my breath until I heard the hallway door slam shut for the final time.

"Come on," I whispered, pushing up onto my elbows so that I could look into her eyes. Not that they were looking at me. Clover kept them screwed shut as she turned her head as far to the side as it would go, facing the counter.

"I have a plan."

I did. It wasn't much, but it was better than lying there, waiting for someone to discover us.

As soon as I loosened my grip on her, Clover's tremors returned. But despite her fear, she still managed to stun me with her bravery when she replied, "I can't leave without them."

Who? I didn't even ask the question out loud. I just stared at her with my eyebrows pulled together and a ticking clock in the back of my mind.

When I didn't respond, Clover's eyes finally opened. She turned her head and gazed up at me as if she were staring into the sun. As if looking at me caused her physical pain.

"There are four women back there," she whispered, eyes pleading, voice raw. "I can't just—"

The rest of that sentence went unspoken, cut off by four gunshots that sounded as if they'd been fired inside the building. Clover's face contorted from pleading concern to utter devastation in the span of a single breath. Tears filled her eyes as they widened in horror, and I felt her pain as if it were my own.

Because a week ago, it had been.

I knew what it was like to try to save someone a moment too late. I still saw the white house with the yellow door every time I closed my eyes. Which was exactly why I didn't have time to comfort her. I would not make the same mistake twice.

"Come on," I whispered, sitting back on my heels and zipping up my trousers. "Time to go."

CHAPTER 19

DAMIEN

I pushed open the front door with Clover's limp body draped over my shoulder and winced into the sunlight. Men in camo marched up and down the pier, entering and exiting every vacant shop and restaurant with their guards up and guns drawn. As soon as they saw me, they stopped and raised their hands in salute.

I opened my mouth to announce that I'd found the prisoner, but didn't get more than the first syllable out before I realized that I was about to say it in English.

Fuck.

Clearing my throat, which made the hole in my side throb worse than the lifeless body I was carrying, I started over, stating the obvious in Russian. "Got her."

Then, I walked straight to the edge of the harbor before anyone could get too close. I gave Clover's thigh one reassuring squeeze before tossing her in like a sack of flour. She did as I'd said, staying limp the entire way down, and after the splash receded, she was gone.

I should have been relieved that the water was dark, shadowed by the harbor wall and the row of boats docked next to it, but panic tugged at the edges of my awareness the second she disappeared. It whispered that she was gone forever. That she'd be floating face down in a few minutes, just like the blonde a few meters away.

"That her?" a Russian voice asked to my right, out of breath from jogging over.

I turned and glared at the commander, trying my best to remember how to look intimidating. Technically, he was my superior, but I was Bratva royalty. I had to behave like I was untouchable, not some traitorous murderer who would be dragged back to Siberia and tortured to death if anyone found out what I'd done.

I nodded once.

He lowered his hand and straightened his back. "How did you find her? We looked everywhere."

"Everywhere?" I snapped, simply repeating the last word he'd said to make sure my Russian didn't fail me again.

A crowd was beginning to form behind him. At least two dozen men approached and stood at attention, waiting for me to give them orders.

Fuck.

"Sir, what do we do now? With the bodies? What do we tell their families?"

I stared them all down as I rehearsed what I was about to say in my head. I didn't trust my Russian anymore, especially not while my mind was preoccupied with Clover's safety and my body was preoccupied with the agony of thirst, hunger, adrenaline withdrawal, a head injury, and a fucking gunshot wound.

"You tell them what happened. One of Russia's finest was tending to an injured prisoner when she took advantage of his kindness and stole his weapon. Our men hesitated to return fire because they didn't want to harm a woman, and they paid for it with their lives."

I must have spoken fluently enough because the men were nodding in agreement instead of giving each other questioning looks.

"Call the admiral's office in Saint Petersburg and arrange transport for the bodies. The rest of you …"

I was about to tell them to move the bodies into the walk-in refrigerator, if there was one, but while I tried to remember the Russian word for *refrigerator*, the front door of the fish market began to open behind them. Something about the way it moved—in slow, jerky increments—made my heart race. The crowd noticed my distraction and followed my gaze to the cracked entrance, where a man in a camouflage shirt was dragging himself out. Blood poured down his face from what I knew was a bullet wound at the top of his forehead, but the round must have clipped his skull instead of going straight through.

Fuck.

Maybe he won't remember what happened.

I couldn't remember shite for days after my head injury, which I still wasn't sure how I'd gotten. Probably hit a rock underwater after my jump.

"Where are the medics? Get this man some help," I ordered, hoping to slip away during the commotion.

Every second that Clover was out of my sight, the odds of her running away went up tenfold. She'd already tried to run from me once. I needed time to explain myself before she did it again.

But slipping away wasn't in the fucking cards.

At the sound of my voice, the man who'd dragged himself out of the fish market lifted his head and trained his one clear eye on me. "You." His voice was a guttural growl, punctuated by a bloodstained finger, pointing in my direction. "It was you!"

Ice flooded my veins, chasing away the dread as I glared at the confused faces of the men before me.

My only response was to thrust my hand in his direction and raise my eyebrows, as if to say, *What are you waiting for? Fucking help him.*

The less I spoke, the better.

A few crewmen rushed over to help him up, but he swatted them away and continued to thrust his finger in my direction.

"It was him! He fucked the redhead and went fucking crazy when Borkov wanted a turn. He killed them all to keep from … from …" He collapsed on the ground. "… sharing her."

"Redhead?" the commander asked, glancing from me to the blonde corpse in the water.

"Redhead," I repeated with an eye roll. "Poor bastard's been shot in the head. He doesn't know what the fuck he's saying."

"I saw them bring in a redhead a few hours ago," one of the crewmen announced. He was speaking to the commander, not me. That wasn't fucking good.

"I saw her too," another said. "She was so fucking hot. I was hoping to get a taste later."

My jaw clenched.

"Sailor"—the commander's eyes were on me as he prepared to ask the crewman his next question—"was this redhead chained up with the others when you searched the building?"

I felt the blood drain out of my face and surge into my extremities. My right hand vibrated with the urge to unholster a weapon. I'd grabbed a knife and a pistol from one of the bodies behind the counter before we left, but there was no way I could take on this many men on my own. Especially not when they were all armed and on high alert.

"No, sir," the crewman answered.

"Shit! Get him!"

A commotion broke out as I turned and sprinted down the pier. Every step was excruciating. Every bullet that whizzed past me, a miracle. And as I scanned the boats bobbing along the wall for the one Clover had described, every second felt like a lifetime.

Wexford Whaler.

Irish Hospitality.

Galway Girl.

Fuck, fuck, fuck!

Up ahead, all the way at the end of the pier, I finally spotted it—Clover's father's boat. The *Pride of Howth* was a rust-colored nightmare that looked like it had been raised from the bottom of the sea or possibly from the bowels of hell. Ropes and nets and fenders dripped from its hull like bandages from a mummy that had been brutally stabbed to death with a half-dozen poles and antennas.

My heart rate skyrocketed as I scanned the deck and the helm for any sign of her, but I knew she wouldn't be there. I'd known the moment she disappeared beneath the surface of the water that I would never see her again. Now that she was free, she could go wherever she wanted, which, based on her reaction in the fish market, was as far away from me as fucking possible.

Pain sliced through my chest at the thought of losing her, almost as sharp and searing as the bullet that grazed my right arm seconds later.

As the shouting and gunshots grew louder, I quickly realized that stopping to use the ladder was out of the fucking question. So, with a running jump, I plummeted three meters down onto the deck of the boat. Pain exploded in my side, but I gritted my teeth and pushed through it. Pulling the knife out of my boot, I slashed through the ropes tethering the *Pride of Howth* to the pier, and then I dived into the helm as a window shattered overhead. Glancing up at the wires beneath the wheel, I cursed and punched the bulkhead.

A metal plate covered the control panel, held on with four simple screws.

"Fuck!"

"There's a spare key under the seat cushion."

Rolling onto my good side, I glanced up and found an auburn apparition leaning over me. A wall of shimmering wet hair separated me from the madness outside, and for a moment, for a fleeting fraction of a second, I felt like a kid in a blanket fort again.

Then, another window shattered, and she was gone, crouching behind the seat with her hands over her head.

"Drive!" I shouted, pulling the pistol from my holster and launching to my feet. I stood in the hatch, shielding her with my body as the first head came into view over the harbor wall.

"I don't know how!"

"Turn the key!" I aimed and pulled the trigger as the engine roared to life.

That head and the body attached to it dropped to the ground, but was quickly replaced with another. And another.

"Do you see a lever?" I shouted between blasts.

"Em … yes! Over here!"

I fired three more rounds into the squad barreling toward the edge of the pier above us. It was enough to keep them back, but not enough to keep them from returning fire.

"Hold down the button on the handle and slide it forward."

I widened my stance to keep my balance as the boat lurched forward. It might not have looked like much, but the *Pride of Howth* had a beast of an engine. Thank fuck.

Clover screamed as a bullet flew through one of the already-broken side windows and shattered the windscreen.

"They're shooting from both piers!" she shouted.

"Stay low and steer!"

I swiveled and took out two lone infantrymen on the opposite pier before returning my attention to the squad to my left. With the choppiness of the water and the sudden acceleration, it was getting harder and harder to hit my marks, but it made us a harder target to hit as well. More bullets ripped through the helm, piercing the bulkheads and showering Clover with sparks from the radio.

By the time my clip was nearly empty, the men I hadn't hit were lowering their guns and screaming obscenities as Howth Harbor disappeared behind us. None of the amphibious tanks were fast enough to catch up, and by the time they figured out how to hot-wire another fishing boat, we'd be long gone.

I turned to face Clover with a sigh of relief, but she wasn't looking at me. She wasn't looking forward either. Her entire body was sideways in the captain's chair, and her gaze was locked on the rolling green hills of Ireland's Eye as we sped past. Saltwater misted her face through the broken windows, but Clover didn't so much as blink. Her eyes narrowed to slits as she scanned the empty island, almost as if she was searching for something.

But that small patch of land disappeared just as quickly as the harbor, and when it did, Clover turned away with a deep sigh. The afternoon sun cast her silhouette in a halo of golden light as she wrapped her arms around her naked body and shivered.

"Here." I took off my blazer—wincing as the fabric dragged across my latest injury—and draped it over her shoulders. Then, I sat on the floor and pulled off my boots and socks, slipping them onto her tiny, ice-cold feet. I would have given her my shirt as well, but it was covered in fresh blood, most of which wasn't mine.

Clover slipped her hands into the oversize sleeves of my jacket and buttoned it closed while I cinched the laces on my boots as tight as they would go. By the time I was done, her shivering had stopped.

Satisfied, I leaned back against the hatch and closed my eyes. I could feel the darkness creeping back in—the fog of unconsciousness that I'd been trying to fight off ever since my head injury. I knew Clover was watching me, but I didn't have the strength to lift my eyelids and find out why.

"They shot you again," she finally stated, her tone factual and cold.

I nodded slowly.

Silence stretched on between us as I struggled to stay awake. I knew there was more that she wanted to say, and when I finally forced my eyes open to let her know that I was still listening, she said it.

"You're one of them."

Clover was furious with me—I could see it in her stiff back and clenched jaw—but her tone gave nothing away. She was either too polite or too afraid to let it show.

I hoped it was the former, but I knew better. I'd seen the way she reacted to me back there. I was a monster to her now.

I was a monster, period. The things I'd just done, the ease with which I'd done them … I'd enjoyed killing those men. I'd *needed* it. And Clover had been a captive audience for all of it.

I'd become a lot of things that I wasn't proud of over the last five years—a liar, a puppet, a deserter, now a killer—but there was one thing that I couldn't be accused of, not anymore.

"I *was* one of them," I corrected, holding her gaze even though my eyelids felt like anchors.

"And what are you now?" She was still using that neutral tone, but she clung to the back of the captain's chair as if it were a shield.

Clover was definitely afraid of me, and that hurt worse than any of the festering injuries screaming for my attention.

Clover was the only person I'd met in five years who treated me like a human being. Who touched me out of kindness rather than violence. I would never hurt her. I was in awe of her. That night on the ship, when I'd watched her face off with a fucking drone all by herself, her defiance had awakened something in me. She'd reminded me of who I used to be, who I wanted to be again. It might have been wrong to let her believe that I was an Irish hero rather than a Russian invader, but it hadn't felt wrong. In fact, nothing had ever felt more *right*.

My purpose, my identity, my reason for living—it was all wrapped up inside my boots, socks, and blazer.

She'd asked what I was now, and the answer was simple. *Hers.*

But I'd scared her enough for one day. So, instead, I told her the only other thing I knew for sure.

"I'm just Damien," I said, my eyelids drifting closed on the weight of that statement. "Damien Hughes, at your service."

Then, I gave her a two-fingered salute and let the darkness pull me under.

CHAPTER 20

CLOVER

*D*amien Hughes.

The deep purr of his Irish accent was still vibrating through my chest when his body slumped over sideways onto the floor.

Shite.

I released the wheel, making sure it was tracking straight before I turned to assess the massive body lying unconscious behind me.

At least, I hoped he was just unconscious.

I hated him for what he and his men had done to Howth, what they'd done to my family, to me. I hated him for letting me believe a lie. He'd taken full advantage of my desperation and stupidity the night before, knowing damn well that I never would have touched him if I'd known the truth. I hated that he'd seen me naked and touched me without my permission at the fish market. Just like the rest of them. I hated the way he'd scared me back there, like my father, with his explosive rage and lack of remorse. But mostly, I hated how hard it was to hold on to that hate.

When I looked at him, I saw a friend.

When I heard his voice, I heard the green hills and rocky cliffs of home.

When I felt his touch, I knew I was safer behind enemy lines than I had been under my own roof.

And when I saw him unconscious and bleeding on the floor, all the hurt I'd been trying to hold on to dispersed into the air like a fine mist of seawater, exposing the tender, terrifying truth underneath.

"Damien." I dropped to my knees, patting his scruffy cheek as I searched his body for new injuries.

I unbuttoned his shirt and pulled it off his shoulder far enough to expose his new bullet wound. It had only grazed his arm, but the gash was deep, and he'd lost more blood. Blood that he probably couldn't replace with his current level of dehydration.

I knew from experience that his dead weight was too much for me to move, so I slipped the knife out of his boot pocket—which was now lashed to *my* ankle—and cut as much of his shirt off as I could. Visions of a white room full of naked bodies chained to sinks immediately hijacked my mind. I could suddenly smell human waste, feel the scratch of a blade down my chest, and hear the tearing of fabric as my clothes tumbled to the ground. My heart began to pound as I sliced through the blue-and-white material, tearing it into bandage-sized strips, but I pushed the images away almost as quickly as they'd appeared.

I'm the one with the knife this time, I told myself. *And I'm using it to cut up something of theirs.*

I needed whiskey and water, so I stayed the course, traveling south at full speed along Ireland's coast as I scoured every inch of my father's filthy boat. It was agony, going through his things. I hadn't been on his boat in years, but I'd spent so much time on it as a child that I still remembered every nook and cranny.

He couldn't afford childcare after Ma died, so I'd spent every summer and school holiday out on the boat with him. I wished I could say that it had given us time to bond, but instead, it just gave him more time to yell at me. I was always getting in the way or touching something I shouldn't, so by the time I turned nine, he'd decided that I was old enough to stay home alone—with a list of chores, of course—but for a year and a half, the *Pride of Howth* had been my sad, salty home away from home.

I saw my father's face in every wet, reflective surface, saw his callous knuckles in every knot. As I tore through his belongings, I braced myself for his wrath, knowing that at any moment, he was going to come barreling out of the cabin, cursing and snatching things out of my hands and shoving me to the ground—or worse—but he didn't. My heart raced, and my fingers shook as I rummaged through his storage bins, but no one came to hurt me, and the relief I felt made me sick to my stomach.

I found at least five nearly empty bottles of Jameson, dozens of crushed cans of stout, food wrappers with no food, and exactly zero bottles of water, but when I dropped to my knees in the middle of the deck—exhausted and defeated and dying of thirst—I stared at the buckets on the bow and realized that it wasn't seawater sloshing around inside of them, like it would have been after a catch. Those buckets were full of *rainwater*. In fact, they were brimming with it.

Rushing to Damien's side with my arms full of bottles, I soaked the fabric strips in what little whiskey was left and tied one around his heavy arm. The muscle immediately tensed in my hands as Damien's face contorted in pain.

"Damien … Damien, wake up."

A whisper of a smile tugged at the corner of his mouth before I tightened the knot, causing those lips to part with a baring of teeth.

"Havin' a good dream, were ya?" I asked, placing another whiskey-soaked strip of fabric, this one folded into a square, against the exit wound on his side.

A hiss followed.

"Ya said my name." That small smirk returned, melting some of the ice that had formed around my heart before Damien's features went slack and his face rolled to the side.

"Oh no. Stay with me. Come on." I slid my hands between his head and the ground—careful to avoid the scabbed-over gash on one side—and lifted. "Ya need to sit up. I found water."

Without opening his eyes, Damien pushed himself to a sitting position, and I guided him back to his original spot against the opening of the hatch. The buckets were too heavy to carry, so I'd filled two empty whiskey bottles with water.

Holding one dripping wet bottle to his lips, I held my breath as Damien took it from me and tipped it back. A stray drop of water slid from the corner of his mouth, down over his chiseled jaw, along the straining tendons in his neck, and through the planes and valleys of his chest and abs before disappearing into the waistband of his trousers.

The sight caused my mouth to water violently. Lifting my own bottle to my lips, I glanced back up at his face, where two haunting gray eyes took my breath away. Damien's throat bobbed as he drank. His stare traveled to my mouth, where twin streams cascaded down my own neck and into the woolen fabric of his jacket. My nipples hardened as those streams converged between my breasts and slid down the length of my nearly naked body. After what had just happened to me at the fish market, I didn't think anything could make me want to be touched again, but something about the way Damien was looking at me, the way my body tingled and hummed as I fed it something it desperately needed, made me realize that Damien's touch had made me feel the exact same way.

It was a need—but I could live without things that I needed. I'd been doing it since I had been seven years old.

Setting his bottle down, Damien licked his lips and tipped his head back against the hatch, watching me with hooded eyes.

A prickly heat crept up the column of my neck as I set my own bottle down and wiped my mouth with the back of his sleeve.

"Feelin' better?" I asked, keeping my eyes cast down as I pulled the deep V of his jacket closed with both hands.

I heard him lean forward, felt the swipe of his thumb, featherlight, as it collected a drop of water from the side of my lip, and my body froze on contact. My lungs were still as rocks in my chest, but my heart pounded wildly next to them as Damien's knuckle lingered under my chin. Then, in a gesture so gentle that it brought tears to my eyes, he lifted my face, encouraging me to look at him. I blinked and widened my eyes out of habit, letting the sea breeze dry my tears before the first one could fall, but when I glanced up and found soothing silver staring back at me rather than bloodshot blue, I realized that I didn't have to do that anymore. Damien might have been every bit as terrifying as Oliver and far more violent, but he'd never once lashed out at me for crying. He'd taken care of me instead. Given me the clothes off his back, drawn me pictures ... held me.

The memory of waking up that morning, safe and warm in his arms, only made me want to cry more.

"Thank you," he said, his hushed voice as sincere as his beautiful face.

"Why did you do it?" I asked, pulling away and wiping my eyes before he saw more than I was willing to show. "You're obviously Irish—your accent, your name. How could you ..." My words fell away as the sound of distant bombs rumbled over the roar of the engine.

Glancing to the right, I notice that the cliffs were gone, replaced with the wide expanse of Dublin Bay. Heavy smoke hung over the city, blocking out the summer sun as unseen fires burned and unseen missiles exploded. My eyes went wide, and my mouth fell open as I scrambled to my feet and stared out the shattered cabin window. The city was too far away to tell how much damage had been done, but the flashes and bangs were unmistakable, even from several kilometers away.

Ireland was under siege, and Damien had helped lead the charge.

I bristled as he pulled himself up and stood at my side, but the sadness radiating off of him kept me rooted to the spot. He stared at the destruction the same way I did, like someone had just reached inside of him and crushed his heart.

His gray eyes darkened. His jaw flexed beneath his stubbled skin. Then, the side of his fist shot forward, smashing out what was left of the broken window. I turned with a shriek, covering my face as he punched the glass again and again, until the entire pane was empty and our view of the nightmare happening in Dublin was unobstructed.

"Damien, what happened?" I shouted over the wind that was now whipping through the cabin, my hands shaking from his sudden outburst. "Why were you with the Russians? Talk to me, goddamn it!"

Barreling out of the cabin, like my father would have done if he were upset, Damien began to pace back and forth across the deck. I stood in the hatch and watched as he shoved a hand in the direction of our burning capital.

"I grew up there," he growled, pointing at some indistinguishable place on the horizon. "He knew that. He knew I wanted to come home, so he sent me here to watch it burn."

"Who did?" I kept most of my body inside the hatch, using it as a shield, but the precaution was unnecessary.

Damien's face paled, and he began to sway on his bare feet.

Darting across the deck, I wrapped my arm around his back and guided him to sit on the wooden storage bench in the center of the boat. His body was on fire. Leaning forward, he braced his elbows on his knees and stared across the bay, his mouth set in a hard line. It was as if he could see through the crumbling buildings, all the way into his own childhood home.

"I never knew who my father was," he said, his voice as distant as his mind appeared to be. "My ma raised me alone, did the best she could. But the older she got, the harder it was to make a living"—he hesitated—"in her line of work."

I placed a hand on his upper back in understanding.

"When she couldn't make enough to pay the rent and support her own various addictions anymore, she finally got desperate enough to contact my father. It turned out that he's an extremely powerful member of the Bratva—the Russian Mafia. My ma never wanted to see him again after … what he'd done to her, but she was willing to risk it to get him to pay her child support. To keep us from being out on the street."

I could feel the broken heart pounding beneath his fiery, hot flesh and realized that mine was keeping time with his. "What happened?"

"He sent his men to kill her and kidnap me. He has no other sons, so molding me into his successor became his number one priority. I spent the next five years in a Bratva training camp in Siberia before being shipped off to the Navy a few months ago."

My hand flew to my gasping mouth, but Damien's steely gaze stayed focused on the smoking city in the distance.

"How old were you?"

His hard gaze cut to me over his shoulder. "Fifteen."

He might have looked cold on the outside—a chiseled killing machine, honed by hate and numbed by the ice in his veins—but on the inside, he was burning alive.

Damien tore his eyes away as another series of booms echoed through the bay. I sat next to him and gripped the bench with both hands as my pulse began to climb, but there were no missiles in the sky. No screaming projectiles arching toward us. I was safe … with him. Only with him.

"Why the Navy?" I asked, my voice trembling with the fear I was trying so hard to rationalize away.

Damien's hands formed two fists where they rested between his knees. "My father hates nothing more than the fact that his only son was raised Irish, so when Russia decided to invade Ireland, he pulled some strings and got me assigned to *that* particular ship as a *fuck you*. Even made me a lieutenant so I'd have to lead the attack against my own country."

His gaze turned to me again, and I could almost see the iciness of his exterior cracking from the simmering rage within.

I couldn't imagine what it must have been like for him on that ship—surrounded by enemies who'd come to destroy his homeland, forced to keep his mouth shut and kill his own people. Kill his own dream.

"Damien, I … God, I'm so sorry." I shook my head, at a loss for words.

Sorry wasn't enough for everything this man had been through. He'd bared his soul to me, shown me his pain. The least I could do was reciprocate.

"My ma died too." Between the wind and the waves, I could barely hear my own voice, but Damien's crestfallen face told me he'd heard me loud and clear. "She got in a car accident when I was young, after a … *really* bad fight with my da. He didn't kill her, but … he did. Ya know?" My gaze drifted over to a green fishing net, hanging out of a partially closed storage bin. "I hated him so much, and I loved him so much, and now … now, he's gone too. They all are."

Despite his anger, his tensed muscles and clenched jaw, Damien stood and pulled me against his hard, heaving chest. The action wasn't gentle, and the landing wasn't soft, but his arms encircling my body felt like two bandages closing a wound I hadn't realized was bleeding. I melted into his rigid embrace, accepted what little comfort he had to give, but as the two of us stood in silence, watching our childhood homes crumble into the past, I couldn't help but widen my eyes so that the breeze would dry my tears.

CHAPTER 21

CLOVER

I'd once read that there were only two real emotions—love and fear. In my years of research, trying to understand my father's behavior, the consensus was that anger was a manifestation of fear, and that when a parent lashed out at their child, it was because they were *afraid* that someone they *loved* was going to get hurt.

Well, I didn't give a shite what those articles had said. I knew that the only two emotions Oliver Doyle had ever felt were love and *hate*. He'd lashed out at me because he hated himself for what he'd done to my ma, and he'd hated *me* for reminding him of her. And I could tell that the same two emotions were what fueled Damien Hughes. He loved Ireland. He loved his ma. And he hated his father and the Bratva and the Russian government so much for destroying them that it literally burned inside of him, making his skin hot to the touch.

Damien had said very little after that crushing embrace. Once Dublin was out of view, he'd simply taken to the helm and driven in silence, scanning the cliffs and sea for any sign of danger.

Unfortunately, I wasn't fueled by hate. I was fueled by hope and food—two things that were in short supply on the *Pride of Howth*.

Honestly, my growling stomach was but a tickle compared to the stabbing pain in my ribs and throbbing bruises that ached every time I moved, but sitting still hurt more. I thought too much when I sat still, so I busied myself trying to figure out how to trawl for fish. There was an entire system of pulleys and ropes and hooks dangling from the tall poles on either side of my father's boat, but he'd never explained to me how they worked, and none of the switches or nets were labeled.

After countless failed attempts, my energy, my pain tolerance, and the daylight all ran out at the same time. Using the last rays of light to tie the largest net I could find to the back of the boat, I watched it drag behind us—immediately becoming a tangled, twisted mess in our wake—as I drowned my sorrows in another bottle of rainwater.

When the boat suddenly slowed and the engine began to sputter and lurch, I turned to see what was going on. The cliffs of Howth were hours behind us, replaced by flat, sandy beaches that gave way to a large harbor full of boats and glowing streetlamps up ahead.

"We're running out of petrol," Damien announced, turning the wheel and easing the lever back like a seasoned seaman. The visual reminder of who he'd been was unwelcome, as was the sight of a massive gray battleship docked in the center of the harbor.

As soon as he saw it, Damien switched off the lights and killed the engine.

Causing my breathing to stop as well.

We'd just escaped from a harbor full of Russian sailors by the skin of our teeth. Damien was wanted for murdering more of them than I could count. And now, we were headed right back into the same situation?

"Damien?" I whispered, hoping for some kind of reassurance, but he had none to give.

He simply ignored me as we drifted closer to the ship in slow, agonizing silence. He was a silhouette in the glow of the harbor, but I could tell from his rigid posture and swiveling head that he was on high alert. He steered toward a row of fishing boats that were docked along the left seawall. Then, he glanced at me over his shoulder, his face obscured in the dark of the cabin, and extended a hand in my direction.

"Rope."

Tugging the closest one I could reach out of its pulley, I handed the end to Damien and watched as he quickly tied it to a hook on the side of Da's boat. We were drifting straight toward the last trawler in the row, but Damien made no attempt to straighten the wheel. Instead, he grabbed the other end of the rope, climbed onto the bow, and leaped onto the boat we were a meter away from hitting. In the span of one held breath, he dashed across the deck, scaled the ladder attached to the seawall, dug his bare feet into the ledge at the top, and pulled until the *Pride of Howth* stopped and reversed course.

Shadows settled into the valleys between his bulging muscles as he guided her backward and sideways into the empty spot behind the other trawler. Moonlight clung to his chiseled features and furrowed brow as he tied us off. And once he was satisfied—hands on his hips and head thrown back in relief—I gazed up at him in absolute awe. I felt as though I were seeing him for the first time—the real him. Damien wasn't my burden or my enemy or my grief-induced delusion anymore. He had a name. He had a story. And he had my undying gratitude.

I'd been too confused and upset to understand the magnitude of what he'd done for me at the fish market, but it was clear to me now how much he'd risked to save me. How terrifying it must have been to walk into that place, injured, unarmed, outnumbered, and how far he'd had to push himself, mentally and physically, to get us both out alive.

What wasn't clear to me was his motivation. Had it been love … or hate?

My heart sank as I weighed those options. There was no way he cared about me enough to do what he'd just done. He barely knew me, and even if he did, I wasn't the type of girl men risked their lives for. I wasn't even the type they risked being seen with in public.

Which meant that it was option number two—hate. Just like Oliver. That killing spree had probably been fueled by a personal vendetta against his father and the Bratva, and I was just along for the ride.

He probably felt obligated to save me because I'd kept him alive in the cave, and that's fine, I told myself as I clomped up the ladder to the top of the seawall in Damien's oversize boots.

It was more than anyone else would have done, I rationalized, accepting his warm, outstretched hand.

Just be grateful, make yourself useful, and don't piss him off, I thought, unable to look him in the eye as he helped me up.

I opened my mouth to say *thank you*, but before I could, Damien whisked me across the street and into the shadows of the last building in the row of shops facing the water.

We stood face-to-face, each with a shoulder against the brick, and when he released my hand, I wished that he hadn't.

"Where are we?" I whispered, trying to ignore the ache in my heart as I looked around at the empty roads and dark windows. "And why hasn't this place been destroyed? The Russians are here."

"Wexford," Damien replied, his voice as soft and gentle as a feather against my cheek. "Howth was the only coastal town the Navy had orders to destroy—they wanted to clear a path from the sea to Dublin. The rest of the ports and harbors they want to keep intact. Russia's cut off from most first-world countries, so Ireland's going to be its primary trading hub once it falls."

Once *it falls. Not if.*

"Is everyone gone?" I whispered.

"I fuckin' hope so."

I glanced up, and Damien's guarded eyes were the same color as the fog in the harbor.

"The crew will sleep on the ship—encampments are only for prisoners of war and surveillance teams—but until lights out, they'll be raiding the shelves of every pub in town."

Surveillance.

My hands began to shake.

I couldn't face another drone. I couldn't.

Just then, a crash shattered the stillness, followed by raucous laughter and booming Russian voices.

I jumped, but Damien clamped a hand over my mouth to stifle my shriek as his head twisted to the side, listening.

Without looking at me, his other hand wrapped around the back of my neck, guiding my ear toward his mouth.

"Shh … it's okay," he whispered, only loud enough for me to hear. "Some arsehole just lost a poker game … threw a chair out a pub window." He paused to listen to the men shouting, their argument spilling into the night through the broken glass. "He's accusin' somebody of cheatin'. They're not too happy about that."

Wrapping my fingers around the hand covering my mouth, I gently pulled it away, and Damien let me, turning to face me in the dark.

"They sound so close." My words were barely audible over the panicked pounding of blood in my ears.

With one hand on the back of my neck and the other being gripped by both of mine, Damien pulled me even closer and whispered, "You're okay. Just keep listenin'."

Then, he led me by my clutching hands around to the back of the building.

It was nearly pitch-black in the alley behind the shops and restaurants. Damien ran his free hand along the brick until he came to the first door in the row. He felt the surface, possibly looking for a window, and tried the handle before continuing down the alley.

"Damien, we're just getting closer to them."

"Shh. Keep listenin'," he whispered, trying the next door.

I listened, but all I heard was a horde of drunk sailors, my own heart pounding in my ears, and the sound of me failing to walk quietly in Damien's massive boots.

By the third shop, it took all the courage I had to keep going. My throat had gone dry, my legs trembled, and despite the evening chill, a trickle of nervous sweat rolled down the length of my bruised ribs. Every step we took closer to the hell we'd just escaped from made me want to scream and run in the opposite direction, but I trusted Damien's instincts more than I trusted my own. He was the only reason I was still alive—a fact I had to repeat over and over in my head to keep from bursting into frightened tears.

The muffled rumblings of male voices grew louder as Damien approached the fourth door, and I knew we had to be close to the pub that they were drinking in. Panic gripped me, and I dug my feet—still warmed by Damien's socks and boots— into the pavement, pulling him back before his fingers could graze the handle. Damien turned to face me, and as he did, the ground shook with the sudden blast of a bugle being played at full volume over a loudspeaker. A series of long, proud notes punched through my chest, filling me with even more dread. I didn't know what the song meant, but it felt like a victory cry. It was proof that no matter where I hid, they could find me, and they could terrorize me, and I was helpless to stop it.

The voices inside the building grew louder and were accompanied by the sound of glasses breaking and heavy wooden chairs being shoved across a floor. I clung to Damien's arm with both hands, listening as their shouts and grumbles spilled out into the street. But soon, their voices faded away, and on the last bugle blast, long and loud, Damien pulled out the gun he'd taken from the encampment and shattered a small window on the back door as quietly as possible.

By the time the last shard hit the ground, the trumpeting stopped, and all was quiet in Wexford again.

"They play that before lights out," Damien whispered, reaching into the black hole and unlocking the dead bolt inside. "A few patrolmen will have the night shift, but the rest will be tucked away inside the ship until sunup." He tried the handle, and the door cracked open. "As long as we're quiet and don't turn on any lights, we should be safe until then."

Safe until sunup. It wasn't much, but eight straight hours without fearing for my life sounded pretty damn good after the week I'd had.

Tucking me behind his back, Damien stood to one side of the door and opened it slowly in case a hail of gunfire was about to come pouring out. When the coast was clear, he entered before me, broken glass crunching quietly under his extremely graceful bare feet. It sounded like firecrackers under mine.

After closing the door behind us, Damien raised his gun and whispered for me to stay put. So, I stood in the dark as he disappeared down the hallway, realizing once he was out of sight that the pistol he was carrying might have been unloaded. He'd shot so many bullets during our escape from Howth.

Shite.

Pulling the sleeves of Damien's jacket over my hands and crossing my arms over my chest, I tiptoed down the hallway behind him. Up ahead, I could see that it opened into a large room with a wall of windows that let in enough light from the streetlamps to actually see what you were doing.

I wished Damien had let me keep that knife. Anyone could be in—

A hulking silhouette appeared before me, so suddenly that I ran straight into its hard, bare torso. He smelled like the sea and my father's favorite whiskey.

"Damien!" I whisper-shouted, slapping him on the chest. "Ya scared the shite outta me!"

His answering chuckle rumbled through my bones. Deep and velvety, it was the most comforting sound I'd ever heard.

"You're never gonna believe where we are, angel."

Angel.

I smiled.

Damien took my hand, and the sensation of his warm, rough fingers sliding between mine sent a flush up my neck and into my face. Tiptoeing behind him into the open room, I realized that we were in some sort of restaurant, but it wasn't a pub. Where the bar would have been, there was a counter instead. A glass counter, the kind you would see in a—

"A bakery?" I squealed as quietly as possible.

Glancing over his shoulder at me, Damien beamed, and for the first time since we'd met, it was more than just his eyes that reminded me of the fairy boy from Darby Donovan's books. A lock of disheveled black hair grazed his eyebrow, a spark of mischief ignited his smoky stare, and beneath all that dark stubble, a hint of a dimple gave me the overwhelming urge to find a mossy wood to run through just so that he would chase me.

I was so happy, so … *overwhelmed* with relief that I returned Damien's grin before breaking into a sprint. I darted across the seating area, weaving my way between the tables as I headed for the counter. My ribs and back ached with every step, but Damien's bare feet on the tiles and his soft laughter behind me were a balm that could heal any wound.

I couldn't remember the last time someone had played with me.

"It's all mine!" I whisper-giggled, stopping in the small pass-through on the side of the counter and turning to block his path.

But Damien didn't stop. He stalked toward me with hungry eyes and a sinister smirk that made my knees go weak. I suddenly felt very naked, standing there in nothing but his blazer. Needing to defend myself, I grabbed a handful of forks off the counter, but before I could throw them, Damien charged. He grabbed the backs of my thighs and lifted me off the ground, plastic cutlery flying in all directions as I threw my arms around his neck to stabilize myself. His gun dug into my hip. His breath warmed my exposed throat. His hair found its way between my fingers. And when he set me down on the counter, his body settled between my parted legs.

Still clutching my thighs, Damien held my stare as our chests rose and fell in rapid unison. I wanted to kiss him again, but it didn't feel right, not now that I knew I was only a charity case to him. My chest ached as my vision grew dark around the edges and the room began to tilt.

"Clover?" Damien's voice sounded echoey and distant.

"Hmm?" My eyes fluttered closed as his hand slid into my hair, cradling my suddenly heavy head.

"Stay with me, love. Ya need to eat."

I nodded and felt something rough slide along the length of my bottom lip.

"Open up, angel."

I did as he'd said and immediately felt a flaky pastry come to rest on the tip of my tongue. Closing my mouth around Damien's fingertips, I tasted the salt of his skin, mixed with the sweet, buttery richness of a chocolate croissant. I hummed appreciatively as I chewed—eyes closed, arms slack—feeling an immediate rush as the sugar hit my bloodstream. Cracking one eye open, I reached up and plucked the rest of the croissant out of Damien's grasp before he could react.

With another soft chuckle—my new favorite sound—he leaned forward, still cradling my head, and placed his lips next to my ear. "You're lucky they have more of those."

Taking a huge bite from the end of the pastry, I turned my head so that our cheeks nearly touched and whispered back, my mouth full of heaven, "Why? Would you fight me for it?"

I was only teasing, but the question sent an icy shiver down my spine, as did Damien's sudden seriousness as he slid his hand out of my hair and leveled me with that cold gray stare.

"No. I would do this."

That was the only warning I got before he reached for my side in a flash of movement. My hands shot out to protect my tender ribs as I doubled over with a squeal.

"Don't!" I cackled, the mere threat of being tickled sending me into hysterics, which only made my bruises hurt worse. "You can have it! I surrender!"

"I accept." Damien smirked as he plucked the croissant out of my hand and took a bite.

Then, he closed his eyes and moaned quietly, causing me to change my mind. *That* was my new favorite sound.

CHAPTER 22

DAMIEN

As I stood between Clover's spread legs—clutching her smooth thigh in one hand and a stale pastry in the other—two very different hungers were tearing me apart. I needed food, as much as I could get. My stomach twisted in pain as I swallowed the bite I'd just taken, demanding more, filling me with a sense of urgency. But seeing Clover relaxed and happy, feeling her long auburn hair brush across my bare chest as she leaned forward in laughter, watching my blazer slide off her freckled shoulder as she sat back up, staring at my chewing mouth with hooded eyes—*that* filled me with a need that was far more ravenous.

Holding the last bite of croissant to her smiling mouth, I held my breath as Clover's lips parted and wrapped around my fingertips. Her eyes closed as she pulled away, taking the bread with her, which caused both my stomach and my fully hard cock to ache at the loss.

I wanted nothing more than to shove my hand back into her hair, taste the chocolate on her tongue, and slide her hips to the edge of the display case so that we could pick up where we'd left off in Howth … *without* an audience. I could still feel her, on a very different counter, dripping wet and bucking against me. My cock was still coated with the proof of her arousal. But what had happened before and after that moment ... I had no idea how she was even functioning. I'd seen the impression her body had left in the field, legs spread, just like this.

Fuck.

I stepped away from her and wiped my suddenly sweaty palms on my trousers, pretending to peruse the baked goods in the case as I took a few much-needed breaths.

"Ya know what?" I mused, keeping my gaze locked on the assorted sweets between her dangling feet. "I think ya are gonna have to fight me for the rest of these croissants."

Clo giggled and pretended to kick me before hopping down off the display case, and I politely stumbled backward, as if I'd been struck.

But really, I just needed the space.

Sitting on the floor—her on her knees, digging things out of the display case, and me a safe distance away with my back against a cabinet—we ate for what felt like hours.

"Oh my God, these banana nut muffins ..."

"Cheesecake?! When was the last time you had cheesecake?"

"This blueberry scone might be the best thing I've ever tasted."

"I was wrong. This apple tart ..." She moaned deep in her throat. "God, what is that? Cinnamon? Cardamom?"

I had no idea if the food was good or not. I ate everything she handed me, but all of my awareness was focused on watching Clover enjoy herself. Hearing her soft moans of pleasure. Memorizing the way she wiggled and danced when she found something she liked. It was a torture far more delicious than anything in that case. But even in the presence of pure joy, the darkness caught up with me.

It always did.

It listed my crimes, over and over in my head.

Traitor. Defector. Murderer, it whispered.

They're going to find you.

You can't escape from this.

They're going to find you and turn you over to your father, and he's going to break you once and for all.

And if she's with you when you're discovered—after what you did to save her ...

I shook my head as I stared at the side of her perfect face in the moonlight. I pictured the parts of her they would present to me first. Her slender fingers, her ears, her nose. They'd make me watch, make it last for days.

"Damien?"

"Hmm?" I glanced up to find Clover frowning at me.

"What's wrong?"

I forced a smirk before glancing from her worried face to the glass case. "Just poutin' 'cause ya haven't given me one of those biscuits yet."

Clover followed my gaze and grinned.

The bleakness of my thoughts had destroyed my appetite, but I'd eat my fucking boot if I thought it would keep that smile on her face.

Grabbing two small biscuits out of the case—little beige ovals with a layer of cream filling in the middle—Clo handed one to me and crashed hers into the side of it as if they were pints of stout.

"*Sláinte!*" she cheered, taking a bite.

And with my stomach in knots, I did the same.

The moment that vanilla custard hit my tongue, the noxious cloud of dread that had been slowly suffocating me vanished, replaced by the warmth of the fucking sun on my skin. The flavor was so familiar, so ... *important*, but I couldn't place it. My mind tore through every memory I had, looking for the source, while my body hummed and buzzed with some unknown pleasure. It felt like laughter, like sex, like drugs—it was the high most people spent their entire lives chasing, and I'd found it with her, on the floor of a bakery in Wexford.

When the world finally came back into focus, Clover was kneeling in front of me with a half-eaten biscuit in her hand. I wanted to ask if she'd felt it, too, but I didn't have to. The stunned gasp on her panting lips and hopeful glimmer in her wide green eyes said it all.

My heart pumped hard and steady, like the beat of a marching drum I couldn't ignore. I knew I should leave her alone—take her upstairs and put her to bed—but my body wasn't taking orders from me anymore.

Dropping my gaze to Clover's mouth, I ran my thumb along her sugar-dusted bottom lip as I licked my own.

"Feelin' better?" I asked, already knowing the answer.

Clover nodded, leaning into my touch. Those big, round eyes were locked on mine, and the need I saw in them mirrored my own.

"You want me to kiss you, angel?"

Clo dropped her gaze as a shy smile bloomed across her face. I cupped her jaw as I waited for the nod, and the moment I felt her chin dip, I leaned forward and pressed a simple, closed-mouth kiss to the center of her fat bottom lip.

Which only made her smile wider.

Leaning back, I smirked as Clover tried and failed to regain control of her face. As badly as I needed to fuck her—and it was a *need*, had been since the moment I'd woken up with her sprawled across my chest—I couldn't imagine anything better than the swell of pride I felt over her reaction to a single fucking kiss.

"Shut up," Clo said, swatting playfully at my face before covering hers with both hands.

Reaching up, I wrapped my hands around her forearms and lowered them gently, causing her to blush even harder.

She dropped her head, trying to hide behind her wavy mane of hair as that smile turned into a laugh.

"You're so mean!"

"I just wanna see you."

"See me make an arse outta myself."

"Look at me."

"No."

"Clo ..."

"Mm-mm."

Lifting her chin, I waited for her to make eye contact with me. And she did, but only after pressing her lips between her teeth to squash her smile.

I shook my head with a chuckle as I pulled her bottom lip free with my thumb. "Don't."

"Don't what?" she asked innocently, dropping her eyes again as that smile returned.

"Don't hide. Not from me. This smile … this face …" I leaned forward and pressed my lips to hers again, reveling in the sharp gasp that passed through them the moment I was done. "You are the most beautiful thing I've ever fuckin' seen."

I kissed her again, lingering this time, and in that space, I felt the entire fucking universe hold its breath. Time seemed fluid when I was with Clover. Like a dark sea where the current moved more slowly the farther out you drifted. I hadn't sorted out how to stop it completely, but as soon as I did, I would. I'd stay like this, with her, until the last star in the sky imploded, and then I'd float with her in the stagnant abyss.

Pressing her forehead to mine, Clover's smile disappeared as she placed her hands on the sides of my face.

Then, she tilted her head and kissed me back.

CHAPTER 23

CLOVER

Stunned tears stung my eyes as I tried to absorb Damien's words. Tried to make sense of the way he was touching me, looking at me. I didn't want to believe him. Boys had told me things like that before, when no one was around, but their rough lips and punishing, impatient hands had always revealed the truth.

But not Damien's. His kisses were sweet and slow and saturated with emotion. They made me feel cherished, seen. They gave instead of took. And they turned my blood into tingly, silvery moonlight—the same color as his eyes.

Pressing my forehead to his, I tried to process what was happening between us, tried to slow my racing heart and savor the connection I felt, pulsing just beneath my skin. I didn't trust his words—I didn't trust *anyone*, not entirely—but I trusted that feeling. And I wanted more.

So, I did what I should have done the second his lips first met mine—I tilted my head, and I kissed him back.

Damien held perfectly still as I sealed my mouth over his, but the moment my tongue slid along the parted seam of his lips, he thrust his hand into my hair and devoured me with a hunger that made it clear that food had not been the sustenance he was craving.

Lightning arced across my skin as his commanding tongue swirled and sucked, licked and teased. He tasted like vanilla and chocolate and cinnamon-dusted apple tarts, but the rest of him was anything but sweet. His body felt like hot stone—chiseled and solid. I wanted to wrap myself around it, cling to it until the storm of emotion and desire I was feeling passed.

Pushing up onto my knees, I straddled Damien's outstretched legs, but he grabbed my hips before I could sit. I froze mid-kiss, the heat of rejection slithering up my neck as he held me still. Then, releasing me with one hand, Damien unbuckled his belt and slid the leather strap and holstered gun out of his belt loops in one fluid motion. He set the deadly accessory on the floor beside us. Then, he guided me to sit.

With the contraption gone, my thighs slid into place around his hips, and I gasped into his mouth as his erection pressed against my exposed clit. A rush of fizzy tingles cascaded over my body, and it reminded me of our first night in the cave, when I'd given him mouth-to-mouth. There was something about this man's touch that affected me like no one else's. Some magical spark that chased away the darkness. And I wanted to feel it *everywhere*.

Reaching up with trembling fingers, I unbuttoned Damien's blazer and let it slide off my shoulders and pool on the floor. I expected to feel the vulnerable caress of cool air on my skin, but instead, all I felt was the welcoming heat of Damien's body, beckoning me closer, like a crackling fire. Pressing his forehead against mine, Damien gazed down the length of my naked body and swallowed hard.

"Touch me," I whispered.

"Thank God," he replied.

Sealing his mouth over mine in another dizzying kiss, Damien let his hands roam up my tender ribs to cup the swell of my breasts. The warmth and weight of his palms sliding over my skin soothed everything in their path, including my heart. I felt grounded. I felt safe. And when his thumbs rolled over the tight, sensitive peaks of my nipples, I felt an incredible, insatiable need begin to build.

Tearing his mouth away from mine, Damien kissed his way down my neck and along my collarbone as I dropped my head and peered into the shadow between our rolling bodies.

"Am I hurting you?" I rasped, realizing that his bullet wound was probably only a few centimeters above my thigh.

Ignoring my question, Damien pulled one straining nipple into his mouth, and I threw my head back on a silent gasp. Hands kneading, tongue swirling, teeth grazing, Damien reduced me to a mindless, writhing, ravenous thing. I wanted to lose myself in that connection, sink to the bottom of it and never come up for air. As I reached for the button of Damien's trousers, I let my fingers slide along the length of him, just below the fabric. And Damien followed my lead. Dragging a massive hand down my back, over my arse, and between my legs, he traced the tender seam of me with two thick fingers, and suddenly, I wasn't in the bakery anymore.

Flashes of feelings, sights, and smells tore through my bliss like bullets.

The scent of fish.

The sting of plastic cable ties cutting into my wrists.

A gun digging into my temple.

A cock burrowing into my mouth.

And two thick, rough fingers, belonging to unseen hands, shoving into me from behind.

My stomach lurched, and I pushed away from him, afraid I was going to be sick. I scurried backward across the cold tiled floor until my back hit the cabinets behind the display case. Then, I pulled my knees to my chest and stared at Damien's horrified face, which I was sure mirrored my own.

"Clo?"

My breaths were coming loud and fast. I could hear them, but the air wasn't getting in. It wasn't getting in!

"Fuck, Clo. I'm sorry. I'm so fucking sorry. I shouldn't have … "

Tightening my arms around my knees, I cried out in pain when my hands closed around my wrists. Shaking, I lifted one arm and saw a deep red slice encircling it and stripes of dried blood trailing from my wrist to my knuckles.

A scream lodged in my throat.

Damien said something else, but I couldn't hear him. I couldn't hear anything but a chorus of men shouting at me in Russian.

Lifting my other hand, I found a bloody gash matching the first. It throbbed under my sudden attention, alerting me to the fact that this was no nightmare. This was real.

It had all been real. The attack in the field. The helplessness. The terror. Liv and Sophie. Mr. McCormick. The dehumanization. The violation. Damien speaking Russian. Damien killing.

And killing.

And killing.

"I was too late."

His voice pulled me back to the present, but my heart was still pounding, my throat still suffocatingly tight. I tried to focus on his face. I watched it harden in the shadows just before the side of his fist shot out and slammed into a cabinet door.

I jumped, squeezing my eyes shut and hugging my knees as I willed myself to breathe normally.

"I was too fucking late!"

I shook my head. It was the only reassurance I could give him. I wanted to smile, to put on a brave face, but I couldn't move. And when I finally opened my eyes, all I could see were my bruised legs disappearing into a pair of boots that looked just like *theirs*.

Damien was one of them.

And not just because his father had made him join. There was a dark, violent need in him that I'd seen in those men, and I was seeing it all over again as he stalked toward me on all fours. His wrathful gaze roamed over my injured body as his lip curled into a sneer and his muscles rippled with every stride.

"You weren't too late," I sputtered, scooting away from him in vain. "I'm fine. I just—"

Grabbing one of my forearms, Damien lifted it into the air as his glowing gray eyes bored into mine. "Fine?" He shook my arm in anger. "Does this look *fine?*" Then, he lifted it even higher and pointed at my blackened ribs underneath. "What about this?"

"Damien, stop it."

"Tell me what happened."

"You saved me before anything happened."

"They beat the shite outta you, Clo!"

"I know!" I snapped, snatching my hand away from him. "I was there!"

"And I fucking wasn't!"

I flinched at Damien's sudden outburst, my heart galloping in my chest as I slammed my eyes shut and braced myself for the smack—the crack of skin on skin that would ring in my ears, taunting me, laughing at me long after the blow.

But there was only silence.

Lifting one eyelid, I found Damien sitting back on his heels—lips parted and eyes wide, as if my reaction had physically punched him.

I couldn't reconcile the wounded man I saw kneeling before me—shoulders hunched in shame, brow furrowed in remorse—with the salivating beast who'd murdered a room full of men, some with his bare hands, just hours earlier. It was as if there were two men sharing the same skin—Damien Hughes, the sweet, selfless Irish boy with a hidden dimple and a talent for drawing; and the lieutenant, a commanding, merciless killing machine, forged by the Russian Mafia and destined to rule over it one day.

Damien would never hurt me. I knew that. I did.

But the lieutenant?

He hurt everything he touched.

Damien finally opened his mouth to say something, but the sound I heard next wasn't human. It was the groaning of weight on an old wooden floorboard, and it came from the stairwell in the corner of the bakery behind me.

Damien's eyes darted over my shoulder to the pitch-black doorway, and when they returned to mine, they were harder than gunmetal and twice as deadly.

The lieutenant was back.

And I hated how relieved I was to see him.

CHAPTER 24

DAMIEN

It was demented, but I was actually relieved that someone was approaching. I needed an outlet for all this rage, some Russian face that I could smash with my bare hands before I fucking exploded.

This whole time, I'd assumed that I'd gotten to her before the worst of it. That they hadn't … violated her yet. She'd seemed okay, happy even, once she felt safe and full, but … *fuck*. When I'd touched her, she'd looked at me like I was one of *them*. Cowered from me like *I* was her captor. Flinched at my raised voice like I'd beaten her myself. I was furious over what they'd done to her. I was furious over what they'd taken from *me*. But I was fucking livid with myself for letting it happen.

If I'd gone with her that morning when I heard her leave, none of this would have happened. I should have looked for her sooner. Should have asked where she was going. I'd thought she just needed some air, but now—

The wooden floors creaked again.

Now, I was going to kill whoever the fuck was coming down those stairs.

Sliding my gun out of the holster as silently as possible, I stuck it in the back of my waistband. Not that I wanted to use it. What I wanted to do was beat this fucker to death. Kick him in the ribs, like they'd done to Clo. Feel his skull collapse around my fist and hear his screams of agony as I severed each and every appendage that might have been used to hurt my girl.

Another wooden groan echoed through the stairwell. I glanced over at Clover. She watched me with wide eyes, white knuckles clasped around her naked legs. A subtle shiver ran through her, so I picked up my blazer and took a step toward her.

This time, she didn't flinch. She held my gaze as I draped the disgusting fabric over her body. It was covered in even more blood and bullet holes than before, but she smiled weakly at the gesture, which cooled my wrath. Slightly.

This fucker was still going to die.

Standing against the wall between Clo and the stairwell, I took an offensive stance, lifting my hands and waiting for the shadow to appear.

And when it did, I attacked.

A thrill shot through me as I grabbed the bastard and slammed him against the wall on the other side of the doorway. He let out a grunt, but it was hardly audible over the sound of a woman's shrieking cry, coming from the top of the stairs.

"Jacqueline!"

Jacqueline?

"Let … me … go!"

The voice of the arsehole wriggling in my grasp was definitely feminine, so I released her immediately and took several steps backward until Clover's body was safely behind my legs.

The stairs creaked and groaned rapidly now as the second woman flew down them. Barreling straight into the one she'd called Jacqueline, she wrapped her in an embrace without once stopping to assess the danger.

It was a miracle they hadn't been captured yet.

"Is there anyone else here?" I asked, listening closely for the sound of movement upstairs.

"Just you arseholes," Jacqueline said, straightening her back as she assumed a similar stance to mine, stepping in front of her woman.

They were facing the widows of the bakery, so there was enough light to see their basic features. The one standing in front had dark skin and short gray hair, faded on the sides, while the one behind her, who'd come charging down the stairs like an eejit, had fair skin and white hair, cut to her shoulders.

"Apologies," I grumbled, sounding more annoyed than remorseful. "We thought everyone was gone."

"So sorry," Clover echoed, standing behind me.

"We've been *tryin'* to lie low, but that's kinda hard to do with the two a yous here, bickerin' loud enough to wake the dead."

"Jack, be nice," the white-haired woman snapped. "Ya heard what they were sayin'. The girl's obviously been hurt or …" Her concerned eyes drifted to mine, looking for confirmation, but her words trailed off on a sudden gasp.

The woman stared at me for a second, mouth agape. Then, she swallowed and shook her head.

"Sorry." She laughed, rubbing her palms on her tightly cinched white bathrobe. "I'm Kate." Stepping out from around her partner's stiff back, Kate extended her hand. "Don't mind Jack. She's retired military. All bark and no bite."

"I'll give *you* a bite."

"Damien," I announced, giving her frail hand a single shake.

"Clover," Clo said, leaning out from behind me. She clutched the backward blazer to her chest as she reached a hand around it to shake Kate's.

"Oh, darlin'," Kate gasped, her gaze dropping to Clover's bloody wrist before traveling to her bare hip and battered legs. "What happened?"

I glared at her over my shoulder, silently asking the same thing.

Clo dropped her eyes.

"No matter. We'll get ya cleaned up." Kate took Clo's hand and tugged her gently away from me, but Clo dug in her heels, afraid to leave my side.

A tiny ember of hope flickered in the wasteland of my heart.

"It's okay," I said, turning toward her.

Then, I grasped the jacket by both shoulders, holding it open so that she could turn around and slip into it properly. Once it was on and buttoned, Clo turned back around and gave me a grateful smile.

"You have clothes she can wear?" I asked Kate, guiding Clo toward her with my hand on the small of her back.

"Clothes, toothbrushes, a hot shower … we'll get her fixed right up." Kate glanced at me quickly before ducking her chin and looking away. "Both of ya."

"Thank you," I muttered, holding Clover's worried stare as Kate led her up the stairs.

"Shouldn't you be fightin' up in Dublin right now?" Jack asked, folding a pair of thick arms across her broad chest.

"Sorry?"

"The boots on that girl's feet, your holster over there … you're in the military. Or ya *were*." Her black eyes narrowed to slits as she sized me up. "Boy, if I find out you defected, I'll drag your arse back to Dublin myself."

I turned so that my left side was visible in the light and lifted the edge of the bandage Clover had made for me on the boat. "Got shot during the attack. Full discharge."

Jack hissed at the sight of my bullet wound and wrinkled her nose. "Fuck. You're lucky to be alive."

"Am I?"

I thought about the way Clover had recoiled from my touch, flinched at my voice. How I had doomed her to a fate far worse than the one she'd faced in Howth simply by being near her. But mostly, I thought about how, once again, I'd failed to save a woman I cared about. They'd hurt her, and as soon as they found us, they were going to do it again just to torture me.

"Listen." Jack stepped forward, placing a hand on my shoulder as she steered me toward the darkness of the stairwell.

"I know how ya feel. When I retired, I felt like my whole life was over. I didn't know who I was without the Rangers. I had no family, no purpose, no fuckin' reason to live."

If my bullet wound had been able to make a sound, it would have groaned just as loud as the planks beneath my bare feet as I gritted my teeth and began to climb.

"I was so depressed that my neighbor signed me up for a baking class just to get me outta the house and encourage me to consume somethin' other than whiskey. And that's where I met my girl." Jack sucked her teeth. "I dunno why she puts up with me, but thanks to that woman, I have a reason to get outta bed now. Or not, if ya know what I mean."

Jack chuckled and elbowed me in the side as we reached the top of the stairs, eliciting a grunt of pain.

"Oh, shite. Sorry, lad."

I looked up and found one large space, about the size of the bakery downstairs, that had been sectioned into a sitting room, kitchen, and dining area. The lights were off, but the curtains were open, allowing just enough ambient light in to illuminate the edges of the furniture and cabinets.

More creaking and groaning echoed through the stairwell, and Jack and I turned to find Kate coming down from the second floor.

"Got her in the shower and put a first aid kit and some toothbrushes and spare clothes on the bed for ya. Had a few things from my son that should fit." She smiled, but the expression faded as soon as she met my gaze.

Kate looked away immediately, like she'd done downstairs, and Jack pulled her in for a hug.

"You look just like her boy," Jack explained. "Never had the pleasure of meetin' the fella, but … he was Kate's pride and joy."

Was.

Fuck.

I didn't know what to say.

"G'wan now." Jack waved me off. "Ya kept us up past our bedtime. Just keep the lights off, and for fuck's sake, try to be quiet."

"Thank you," I rasped, placing a hand on both of their shoulders.

Jack gave me a small salute before leading Kate toward their bedroom.

As I watched them go, that ember in my chest flickered.

CHAPTER 25

DAMIEN

My injuries were fucking throbbing by the time I made it to the top of the stairs, but the pain was nowhere near as bad as it had been those first few days. If I could avoid infection a little longer, I might actually be okay.

Until they find you. Then, you'll wish *you'd died of infection.*

Blowing out a breath, I dragged a hand over a week's worth of beard and glanced around the room, hoping for a distraction from the terrifying future that was breathing down my neck.

The ceiling had a steep pitch—like an attic—so the only useable space was directly in the center, where an old brass bed sat, facing the stairs. The surface was lumpy and sagged in the middle, and it probably groaned even louder than the floorboards when you sat on it, but to a lad who hadn't slept in a bed on dry land in over a week, it looked like fucking heaven.

The shorter walls, where the roof sloped down, were lined with boxes and other assorted bullshit, but on the far wall, across from me, there was nothing but a single door. Golden light and the sound of running water streamed out through the cracks.

Clover.

I wondered how she was doing. If she was still upset with me. Still stuck inside that nightmare.

Walking over to the bed, I pulled the gun out of my waistband and set it on the quilt next to the clothes and supplies Kate had laid out for us. As I stared down at them, I wanted to feel grateful, or happy, or relieved, but the sight did nothing more than stir that deep, dark, swirling void inside of me. I didn't know why Kate's act of kindness made me feel so angry, so hopeless. Maybe it was because she was trying to mother me, and it reminded me that I didn't fucking have one. Or maybe it was because those clothes had belonged to a dead man, and soon, they were going to belong to another one.

No. I wasn't that lucky. My father would rather torture me beyond the brink of insanity than kill the only heir to his Bratva reign. He wouldn't relent until he broke me. Until he shattered me completely and glued the pieces back together in his likeness.

Either way, it was over.

By sunup, every Russian soldier and sailor on the island would be on the lookout for the *Pride of Howth* and me.

And her.

Steam was beginning to filter through the cracks of the bathroom door now, illuminated by the streaks of light that escaped along with them. I noticed how the golden light forged straight ahead, never wavering, never looking back, while the silvery vapor simply … disappeared into the darkness.

That was us. Clo and me.

We'd escaped together, but now …

Now, she had to keep going, and I had to disappear.

It was me they wanted, not her. They didn't even know her name. Kate and Jack would take care of her—I knew they would—and they'd do a better fucking job than her arsehole drunk of a father ever had. This was what was best for her. If I wanted to protect her, to do what I hadn't been able to with my ma, this was the only way.

"Fuck!"

My skin felt tight as the rage swelled beneath it, pushing against the surface, looking for an outlet. I wanted to scream. I wanted to kill. But only because what I really wanted wasn't a fucking option.

It never was.

My chest ached, and my eyes burned as I tore through the room, looking for my boots. I had to get out of there before Clo finished her shower. If I saw her, I didn't know what I would do. I didn't know if I'd have the strength to leave.

After I looked under the bed and in every corner of the room, my eyes landed on the glowing bathroom door again, and I shook my head with a bitter, humorless laugh.

Of fucking course.

Turning the knob as quietly as possible, I opened the door and squinted into the light and steam. The sink was directly across from the door, and next to it, on the closed lid of the toilet, sat my neatly folded, blood-soaked blazer.

And my boots were on the floor beside it.

My throat swelled as I pictured Clo on the boat—the way my sleeves covered her fingers and my socks swallowed her feet. The way the light clung to her hair and the sea made her eyes sparkle. I'd never seen her outside in the sun before.

And you never will again, arsehole. Accept the situation and armor the fuck up. Now.

My jaw clenched, and my nostrils flared as I fought back the emotion strangling me from the inside out.

My boots were right there. All I had to do was grab them and go. But as I reached in, my heart slamming itself against my ribs in protest, I heard something beyond the white noise of the shower and the blood thundering in my ears. It was a sound I'd heard every night in the cave—the soft, shuddering gasps of Clover crying.

I stared at my boots as her jagged breaths sliced through my resolve like the teeth of a saw. There was no conscious thought, no more rationalizing or weighing my options. There was the sound of Clover crying, and then there was Clover, looking over her shoulder at me as I opened the shower door.

"Damien? What are you—"

I stepped inside and wrapped my arms around her and felt her stunned body go tense, only for a second, before she completely fell apart in my embrace. Clover clung to me like she had the night before, like even gravity was trying to tear her away from me. But this time, I didn't fight back. I didn't try to hold her up. I sank to the floor with her and held her close while she buried her face in my neck and wept.

It was the same position we'd been in downstairs—Clo naked, straddling my lap—but this time, it was *real.* There was no more pretending to be okay, no more denial or survival mode. We were both terrified of the future and terrorized by the past, but when we were together, when we stayed present, not even time itself could touch us.

Sweeping a heavy curtain of wet hair over her shoulder, I dipped my head and kissed Clover's bruised, tearstained cheek.

And her entire body went rigid with fear.

No. No, no, no.

"Shh … look at me," I instructed, gathering her hair in my hand and pulling her head back gently until we were face-to-face.

My cock throbbed between her legs with every beat of my heart, which probably only fueled her panic, but Clover did as I'd asked. She gazed up at me with wide, worried eyes—wanting to trust me, wanting to please me, but mostly, I think she wanted the same thing that I did. She wanted to believe that this time could be different. There was a glimmer of hope in those emerald depths, a silent plea that I vowed to fulfill if it was the last fucking thing I ever did.

"I'm not gonna touch you," I promised. "Not like that."

Clover nodded and glanced at my mouth. It was just a second, but I could see the conflict on her face. I felt it too. We'd only kissed twice, and both times had ended with her in the fetal position. So, this time, I wasn't going to kiss her at all.

At least not on the mouth.

"I want to start over," I said, brushing a few wet strands of hair away from her face. "When I found you at the encampment, when I saw you splayed out on that counter, ya know what I wanted to do to you?"

Clover lowered her gaze as shame stained her cheeks pink.

Dropping my forehead to hers, I had to concentrate on keeping my hands from balling into fists as I smoothed them down the length of her arms. "I wanted to kiss every bruise, every scratch and cut on your beautiful body"—I pressed my lips to her cheekbone again—"while you told me how you got each and every one." I kissed her nose as clean, warm water cascaded down my face. After being covered in dried blood, salt water, and whiskey for a week, the sensation of having it all washed away felt amazing. It felt like a fresh start, which was exactly what I wanted with Clover.

"And *then* I wanted to kill every man in that room with my bare fucking hands."

Clover glanced back up at me, full lips parting in surprise.

Taking her hand in mine, I brought it to my mouth and kissed the thin red line encircling her wrist. There were finger-shaped bruises just below it that I hadn't noticed before. My blood fucking boiled, but I forced myself to breathe through it until I was able to speak again.

"Angel, I need you to tell me what happened. *Please*. Let me make it better."

And she did.

Clover started at the beginning as I helped her to her feet, trying to ignore both my painfully hard cock and her achingly perfect tits as I kissed every bruise and cut on both arms before moving down the center of her chest. I felt her heart pound beneath my lips as she told me what had happened in the field. Felt her shudder as my hands traced the curves of her battered ribs, followed by my mouth as I kissed every black-and-blue reminder of what they'd done.

I wanted to heal everything that hurt. Worship every place they'd wounded. It wasn't sexual. It was … sacrificial—my heart in exchange for her happiness.

I worked my way down her stomach to her pelvis as she described what those men had done to her at the encampment. How they'd stripped her, restrained her, humiliated and violated her.

It took all the willpower I had not to grip her hips in anger, not to bury my face in her pussy and make her forget every motherfucker who'd dared to touch her before me. But I was trying to prove that I was different from them, both to her *and* to myself. So, I clenched my jaw until my teeth nearly cracked, and I kept fucking going.

Her long, toned legs—strong from years spent scaling the cliffs of Howth—trembled under my fingertips as I showered every scrape and gash on them with attention. I knew that she'd fallen off the path, running from a drone, and I knew her feet were fucked from going a week without shoes—a fact that I felt personally responsible for—so I turned her around to face the wall and carefully lifted each foot. I kissed the raw red pads of all ten toes, her punctured heels, her scabbed ankles. But when I dragged my tongue along the curve of her arch, her moan of pleasure was so fucking sexy that I had to unbutton the top of my trousers to make room for my swollen cock.

I couldn't even call it torture. It was a privilege to be allowed to touch her again. I'd thought I needed to fuck her, but I didn't. I'd needed to *feel* her. To hold her. To give her pleasure instead of pain.

As I worked my way up the backs of her thighs, I remembered exactly what it had felt like to be buried between them—like coming home, like a warm, soft, welcoming heaven after a lifetime spent burning in hell. I remembered what Clover's firm, round arse had felt like in my hands as she pushed back against me, begging me to make her feel good, to save her from a hell of her own.

My mouth watered as I scented her need, as I imagined dragging my tongue along the seam of her pussy, tasting what I'd felt earlier. My palms slid over the handprint-shaped bruises on her arse, followed by my lips as I lavished her with open-mouthed kisses that were meant for somewhere else.

Fuck.

Making my way up her back, I gathered her hair in one hand and slid it over her shoulder, exposing the last of the places I needed to touch. By the time I was standing again, my lips were on the top of her head, my hands had just finished working the knots out of her neck, and my hips were far enough away to avoid accidentally grazing her with my cock.

"*That's* what I wanted to do," I finally said, running my palms down her arms and pressing a kiss to her freckled shoulder.

"Thank you," Clover whispered, turning her face toward mine.

I nodded, my lips still on her shoulder and a lump in my fucking throat.

"Damien …" Clo's voice dripped with remorse as she tried to turn around, but I gripped her arms and steered her toward the shower door instead.

"Go on now. Off to bed."

Clover stood at the door, but didn't open it. She tried to turn around again, but I held her in place.

"Clo, please. Go."

"I don't want to," she huffed, lifting her arms in an attempt to shrug me off.

And I let her do it. I couldn't bear to restrain her after everything she'd just told me, but my heart sank the moment I let go. I knew the instant she turned around and saw another hard cock pointed in her direction, that would be it. She'd be triggered, and we'd be right back where we'd started.

Clover spun around before I had a chance to warn her, and the sight of her, dripping wet and flushed with need, stole the breath from my lungs. Fuck, she was perfect.

"Angel," I said, cupping her jaw in an attempt to keep her eyes on my face, "I'm trying really hard to prove to you that I'm not like them, which is why I need you to—"

Clover's gaze dropped to my waist, and her body froze as she took in what had to be the last thing she needed to see. I didn't look down, but I could feel the spray of the shower on the entire exposed head of my cock, where it rose above the top of my unbuttoned trousers.

I held my breath and waited for the flashback, the tears, the terror, but instead, Clover simply swallowed, took a deliberate breath, and tore her gaze away from my massive erection, glancing at my soaked bandage wrapped around my waist instead. Gentle fingers untied the knot, using the strip of fabric to wash the dried blood away from my bullet wound. I stared at her lowered eyelids as she worked, trying to read her mind. Then, she leaned forward, slowly, and pressed her lips to a spot just above the scab.

Her touch was featherlight, but it felt like a branding iron—excruciating, scarring, burning itself through the deepest layers of me. I would never forget that feeling. Never escape it. It would haunt me for the rest of my life. When the Bratva finally got me back, I prayed that they'd torture me enough to give me even a momentary reprieve from the agony of knowing that this feeling existed, that this *woman* existed, and I couldn't have her.

I gritted my teeth and breathed through the pain as Clover's gaze traveled up to my opposite arm. Delicately, she untied the bloody strip of blue-and-white fabric and winced at the gash underneath. The water cascading over the wound should have hurt like a bitch, but I couldn't feel a thing other than her lips on my bicep and her name being seared into my heart.

When her fingertips moved up to my jaw, turning my face so that she could lift up onto her toes and check the gash on my head, I was thankful to have an excuse to look away. Because the moment I felt her hands in my hair, the grief became unbearable. Tears burned behind my tightly closed lids as Clover washed the blood out of my hair. My chest throbbed. My throat closed, and when she sank back down onto her flat feet and pressed her tits to my chest and her lips to the side of my neck, I grabbed her biceps and jerked her away with far more force than I'd intended.

Clover's startled eyes flew to mine as I struggled to control my emotions. I couldn't speak through the lump in my throat, so I gritted my teeth and shook my head, begging her with my eyes not to push me any further. It was gut-wrenching enough that I had to leave her. I couldn't fuck her *and* leave her. I wouldn't.

Reaching past her, I opened the shower door and waited for her to go. I watched Clo's eyebrows pull together in confusion as she searched my face for an explanation, but I didn't have one to give. The truth was too painful. And if I told her, she'd try to make me stay.

Or maybe she wouldn't.

And maybe that would be worse.

Pushing past her, I stormed out of the shower and into the bedroom, dripping all over the wooden floor as I tore off my soaking wet trousers.

"Damien!"

Tossing them through the open door and into the sink, I dug through the clothes Kate had left out, looking for a pair of boxers.

"Damien, wait!"

The water shut off.

No underwear. Just black trousers and a white shirt.

"I'm sorry! I'm so sorry! Just tell me what I did, and I won't do it again. Please!"

The moment I heard that word, the invisible thread of control I'd been hanging on to snapped like a fucking trip wire.

Clover's face paled as I stalked toward her and grabbed her jaw, walking her back into the bathroom until her arse hit the sink behind her.

"Don't ever say that to me again. You have nothin' to be sorry for, Clo. Nothin'!"

Her eyes instantly widened and filled with tears.

"Fuck!" I shoved away from her and thrust my hands into my hair.

Clo reached for me, but I took another step back.

"Damien, talk to me." Her voice broke, along with my heart, as I turned and grabbed the shirt off the bed.

"Where are you going?"

I started unbuttoning it.

"You can't leave."

My hands were shaking.

"Damien, you're scaring me. Just tell me what's happening. Please!"

I had only gotten three buttons unfastened before I threw the shirt back on the bed and turned toward her with a fury she didn't deserve.

"I'm trying to save your fucking life! Every second that I stay here, that your da's boat sits in that harbor, is another second closer to them capturing you again! I can't let that happen, Clo. I can't—"

Strangled with emotion, I turned away from her and grabbed the shirt off the bed again. I couldn't look at her. Not that it mattered. I didn't need to see her face to know how devastated she looked. I didn't need to hold her to feel the panicked pounding of her heart. Clover had become a part of me, and the act of leaving her behind was about as horrifying and excruciating as severing one of my own limbs.

"You're leaving me here?"

Fuck. I was wrong. Cutting off an arm would hurt a hell of a lot less than hearing the sadness in Clover's sweet voice.

"It's the only way to keep you safe," I choked out.

"No," she said, walking toward me. "No, I'm coming with you."

"Clo!" I huffed, tossing the shirt down and grabbing her by the shoulders. I held her at arm's length even though it killed me, even though all I wanted to do was pull her close and never let go.

"Don't you get it?" I said. "They won't stop until they find me. And if you're with me when they do"—I closed my eyes and tried to block out the images of what had happened the last time my father sent for me—"they'll kill you to hurt me." My voice broke. "That's what they do. They kill everything I love and make me watch."

Two small, damp hands clasped the sides of my face, instantly cooling the inferno of rage and grief that had been burning me alive.

"You … love me?" Clover whispered, the hope in her voice extinguishing the flames completely.

I leaned into her touch, but couldn't bear to open my eyes. "Let me go, Clo," I whispered back. "Please. Let me save you."

"You already did."

Tilting my face down, Clover lifted up onto her toes and pressed her lips to mine. I held my breath, hoping that this time, I could do it. That this time, I could stop the clock forever.

But all too soon, her lips were gone, and the pain flickered back to life—like the strike of a match, ready to ignite my petrol-soaked heart the moment I walked out that door.

"This is different." I opened my eyes, hoping she would see the gravity of the situation on my face. "This is the Bratva."

"Every day, it's something different," she said, running her thumbs lightly over my scruffy cheeks. "Today, you rescued me from the encampment. Last week, I saved you from drowning and infection and dehydration. Don't you see, Damien? The only reason either of us is still alive … is because we have each other."

Hope swelled, filling the cracks of my shattered heart, as I realized that I couldn't argue with her. And I didn't want to. I felt like I was back on the ship, watching her run toward the edge of a cliff rather than accept her fate. Her bravery, her refusal to surrender, had inspired me to take the leap as well. I hadn't known whether or not we'd survive the jump, but I'd been willing to find out if it meant that I could experience two seconds of freedom with her on the way down.

Dropping my forehead to hers, I released her shoulders and slowly slid my hands down the sides of her back. "You jump, I jump?"

Clo nodded, clutching my face tighter as my palms came to rest under the swell of her arse.

"Then, jump."

Lifting her off the floor, I swallowed Clover's startled gasp as her thighs clamped around my hips and her arms wrapped around my neck.

"Your wound!" she mumbled against my lips as I carried her across the room, but the moment I pressed her back against the wall, the moment our bodies collided, Clover's concern dissolved into something carnal and craving.

A moan rumbled in her throat as she clutched my head with both hands and kissed me with a hungry, breathy need, and I realized that I hadn't just stopped time; I'd fucking reversed it. It felt like we were back in the cave, back before everything had turned to shite. It was just Clo and me and the indescribable relief of knowing that she wanted me too.

But when her hips tilted up and my cock slid along her slick, warm center, the cave disappeared, and I found myself back at the encampment, thrusting between her thighs while a platoon of eager rapists watched with their dicks in their hands.

Was she there, too, reliving that moment? Was she bent over a counter in her mind?

Squeezing my eyes shut, I broke our kiss and pressed my forehead to hers. "Stay with me," I begged, clutching her tighter. "Please, angel. Talk to me."

"What do you want me to say?" she asked, and the soft amusement in her tone, the way her lips curved as she kissed me, put me at ease.

Slowly, the dimensions of the room returned to normal, the fluorescent lights of the fish market dimmed, and the shouting, grunting crowd of men that I was about to kill faded away until it was only us.

Us and something more. Something fucking indescribable.

"Anything," I answered, my chest heaving in sync with hers. "Everything."

"How about … I love you too?"

My eyes flew open and landed on Clo's sweet, freckled face, her head tilted to one side as a reassuring smile tugged on the corners of her full lips.

Emotion coiled around my throat tighter than her thighs around my hips as she began to move against me, holding my stare with hooded eyes she slid up and down my aching shaft.

"I do. When I was captured, the only thing I could think of that was worth living for … was you. I don't want to be here without you. I *wouldn't* be here without you."

I dropped my head to her shoulder and clutched her body to mine, overwhelmed by the sincerity I saw in her deep green gaze.

She was so wet, so ready to accept me, all of me—even after seeing the rage I lived with, the murderous tendencies I fought to suppress—but I didn't know if I was ready to let her.

"They'll kill you if you stay with me," I murmured against her throat.

Lifting herself up until she was looking down at me, until her hair fell around me like a blanket and my swollen crown was pressed against her warm, welcoming slit, Clover whispered, "Damien, jump."

And I did. With a single thrust of my hips, I was falling all over again, plunging headfirst into uncharted waters.

A blinding, all-consuming bliss washed over me as Clover sank the rest of the way down, biting her bottom lip as she adjusted to my size, taking all of me until we were fully joined. And when we were, when I was as deep inside of her as I could get, fucking drowning in the sea of pleasure and emotion I found there, Clover went still, as if she was just as desperate to hold on to that moment as I was.

"Fuck, Clo," I rasped, dropping my forehead to hers.

"I know." She sucked in a shaky breath, like the shuddering sobs I'd heard every night since we'd met, and my head snapped up. Giving me an embarrassed smile, Clo wiped her tear-streaked cheek on her shoulder.

"Sorry." She laughed, and as much as I hated that word on her lips, I loved the way she looked, saying it. She looked the way I felt.

Happy.

"Good tears?" I asked, forcing the words past the lump in my throat.

Clo nodded with another self-conscious laugh, dropping her eyes as a blush so bright I could see it in the dark bloomed across her face.

Releasing her with one hand, I lifted her chin with a gentle knuckle, forcing her to look at me. "No hiding, remember?"

She nodded again, holding my gaze as another tear slid down her smiling face.

"I love you," I said, feeling as though my heart might explode. It was pounding so hard I could feel it in my jugular, vibrating through in my chest, and throbbing inside my beautiful girl.

My hips pressed against her harder, then withdrew and surged forward again.

"Mmm, God. Damien," Clo moaned, digging her nails into my shoulder blades as I filled her again. "I … mmm, fuck … I love you too."

My parted lips pulled into a smirk. I'd never heard her curse before.

"Say that again," I growled, capturing her earlobe between my teeth.

"I love you. I love you. I love you."

Clo's words were a breathy, begging prayer for more that made me absolutely fucking feral. Squeezing her arse with both hands, I claimed her mouth and devoured her whimpering cries as I thrust into her harder, faster. I wanted to give her everything I had—my body, my life, my freedom, my future. It all belonged to her, and it had since the moment I had seen her on that cliff.

And she accepted it, hungrily. There was no more pushing me away. No more fear or mistrust. Clo wanted this just as badly as I did. With every thrust, she took me deeper, and with every withdrawal, she clung on to my cock as if she didn't want to let me go. I'd never felt anything so powerful. So instantly addictive. I would be a slave to this feeling, to this woman, for the rest of my life.

"Damien," Clo panted against my lips, breathing in time with the sound of our bodies colliding. "I'm … I'm on birth control—the shot."

Her voice was a whimper, a desperate, needy plea for something only I could give her. The sound made my cock swell.

"You want my cum, angel?"

She nodded, pulling her bottom lip between her teeth as she moaned.

Fuck, that sound.

Pulling her away from the wall, I carried her over to the bed, where I sat on the edge and leaned back on my elbows. Somehow, I filled her even deeper that way, and her swollen clit throbbed where it pressed against the base of my cock.

"It's yours," I rasped, staring at the sexiest fucking thing I'd ever seen. "No one else's."

"Never?" Clover asked, holding my stare as she rocked against me.

I shook my head, transfixed by the look on her face. "Never. Take it, angel. Take what's yours."

With hooded eyes and hardened nipples, Clover held my stare as she leaned forward, sliding her hand around the back of my neck and sealing her fat pink lips over mine. Her hair surrounded me like a fortress, blocking everything out, except for the only thing that mattered—her. Us. This.

Shifting my weight to my good arm, I used my right to hold her neck and jaw, squeezing slightly as she sucked my tongue. She kept me deep inside of her as she ground against me, rolling her hips and whispering my name, and as much as I wanted to stay that way forever, I wanted to give her what she wanted more.

Lifting my hips, I let go of her jaw and grabbed her arse, pressing her into me as I fucked her back.

"Oh God. Damien. Mmm. Please."

It was the *please* that killed me. Laid me to waste as I sat up, wrapped her soft, warm body in my arms, and let it all go. A flood of indescribable pleasure and a lifetime of pain tore through me, and Clo drank it down hungrily, letting me fill her until she overflowed. Tears ran down her face as she whimpered through her release, but this time, she didn't try to hide them. This time, she laughed as I dipped my head and caught one on my tongue.

"I love you, angel."

"I love you more."

Now, it was my turn to laugh.

Clo sniffled adorably as I ran my hands over her tits and kissed the throbbing pulse point just below her jaw.

"That was …" Another sweet laugh vibrated in her throat beneath my lips. "What *was* that?"

"Magic," I hummed against her collarbone as I kissed my way over to her shoulder.

"Magic," she repeated, and the wonder in her voice had my cock swelling inside of her all over again.

"You okay?" she asked, taking my left hand in both of hers and kissing my nearly healed knuckles. "I hope that didn't hurt too bad."

"Grand," I said, grazing her shoulder with my teeth. And it was true. I'd never felt fucking better.

"Good," Clo muttered, rubbing the knuckle of my ring finger with her thumb. Then, she licked her thumb and rubbed it harder. "Damien, are these … freckles?"

Lifting my head, I glanced at the three dots slashed across the base of my finger and shrugged.

"Guess so. Why?"

Clo's face lit up in what had to be the most breathtaking smile I'd ever seen as she slapped her left hand on top of mine. There, on her ring finger, darker than all the other freckles on her hand, were three dots, just like mine.

"I read about this in one of Darby Donovan's books." She beamed. "It means we're soulmates, bonded for eternity."

She laughed, but I'd heard the sincerity in her voice. Clover believed it, and as I rolled her onto her back and clutched her body to mine and thrust into her again, I wanted to believe it too.

More than anything.

Because with the Bratva coming after us, *this* lifetime was going to be very, very short.

CHAPTER 26

CLOVER

When I woke up, I felt like I'd been hit by a bus—in the best possible way.

Everything was sore—*everything*—but all those aches and pains were just reminders of all the places Damien had kissed.

Or touched.

Or …

I smiled and burrowed deeper into the sheets, reliving my favorite moments from the night before.

Then, I added my heart to the list of body parts that were sore. It felt as if it might burst.

A ray of sunshine broke through the clouds, warming my face through one of the small attic windows. Rolling over, I reached for Damien, craving the solid grounding of his body, the intoxicating safety of his arms.

But all I found was a lumpy mattress, covered with a perfectly smooth patchwork quilt.

Sitting up, I squinted into the late morning light and found that Damien's side of the bed looked untouched. The clothes Kate had laid out for him were gone, along with his gun, his scent, his warmth. It was as if it had all been a dream, and I was suddenly thrust back into the nightmare of my reality.

Running over to the window facing the harbor, I glanced at the water below and had to clutch the windowsill to stay upright.

They were gone.

Damien and the *Pride of Howth* were both gone.

Our fight from the night before rang in my ears as I slid to the floor and stared at the bed.

"Every second that I stay here, that your da's boat sits in that harbor, is another second closer to them capturing you again! I can't let that happen, Clo. I can't—"

"You're leaving me here?"

"It's the only way to keep you safe."

I wanted to feel shocked, to feel hurt and betrayed, but the only one who'd betrayed me was me. I knew that boys left as soon as they got what they wanted. I knew that having feelings for someone only meant they could hurt me more.

I knew that I wasn't really lovable.

I'd done this to myself.

Damien had told me exactly what his plan was, and I'd ignored it.

With my elbows on my knees, I dropped my head into my hands and stared at the wooden floor between my scratched, bruised legs as a black hole of numbness chewed its way through my body like a cancer.

I had nothing.

I had no one.

I was nothing.

I was no one.

I didn't feel the boards beneath my feet as I walked back over to the bed. Didn't feel my bruises ache as I put on the yellow sundress Kate had left out for me. And I didn't feel the scrapes and puncture wounds on my feet as I shoved them into a pair of dirty white runners.

I went through my morning routine mechanically, as if I were driving someone else's body. Brushing someone else's teeth. Washing someone else's face. I straightened up the bathroom and shoved Damien's wet trousers into the bin, but I couldn't bear to leave his blazer. I might not have been able to feel the satin lining slide over my bare arms, but I could smell it—a heartbreaking mixture of sea and blood and *him*. A sharp pang of loss stabbed me in the heart, but the black hole swallowed that too.

Looking around, I realized that there was nothing left to do. No more distractions, no more tasks to be done. The urge to leave was overwhelming. To lock my feelings in that attic and run as far away from them as I could get.

I was so focused on getting out of there that I didn't process the smells and sounds coming from the floor below until I was already halfway down the first flight of stairs.

The scent of blueberry muffins.

The unintelligible murmuring of a television newscaster.

Jack's blunt but cautiously quiet voice, asking a question.

And a deep, masculine response that made my throat tighten and my eyes burn.

I couldn't hear what they were saying, but the cadence of Damien's speech, his relaxed tone and timbre, indicated that he wasn't going anywhere anytime soon.

He'd stayed.

He'd actually stayed.

All the emotions I'd been running away from slammed into me as I stood there on the stairs—the worthlessness, the grief, the self-hatred, the shame. I was so embarrassed by my overreaction. So embarrassed that they were going to see how absolutely broken I was. But I needed to see Damien more than I wanted to hide from him, so with a shaky breath, I let my feet carry me the rest of the way down.

Sun filled the cozy sitting room, illuminating a treasure trove of photos and books and art and old furniture. And over in the open kitchen, huddled around the glowing screen of a tablet and a basket full of muffins, Kate, Jack, and Damien turned their heads and smiled at me.

And I immediately burst into tears.

"Oh, honey."

"I told ya that bed was uncomfortable."

"Angel …"

Before I could wipe my eyes, Damien had crossed the room, pulled me into his arms, and pressed his lips to the top of my head. He smelled like soap and felt like home.

"Shh …" he hushed, smoothing a hand over my hair.

"I …" I shook my head, burying my face in the white shirt he was wearing. "I thought you'd left."

Holding me at arm's length, Damien glared at me, but his gray eyes were softer than usual.

"After last night?" He smirked. "Impossible."

That dimple was on full display now, making me realize that he'd shaved while I was asleep. I pictured him using one of Kate's pink razors and laughed, wiping a mortified tear from the corner of my eye.

"I'm sor—"

"Don't," he warned. "Don't even think it. Come on. Kate made breakfast."

Kate gave me a sympathetic smile as Damien sat me in the empty chair next to his. "That dress looks nice on ya."

Jack simply cleared her throat as she slid a mug of hot tea over to me.

"Thank you," I said to both of them with a sniffle, feeling my cheeks flush as I lifted the mug.

"Damien told us … about your family." Kate's smile faded as her own eyes began to glisten. "You're welcome to stay with us as long as ya like."

"Are ya fuckin' serious?" Jack mused. "As loud as these arseholes are? Kept us up half the night with their fuckin' and fightin'."

Now, Kate was blushing too.

"We'll head out today." Damien squeezed my leg. "You've been more than generous. Thank you."

I stared at the side of his face in trepidation.

"Where are we gonna go?" I asked, trying to keep the panic out of my voice. "Where's the boat?"

Jack snorted knowingly as she plucked a muffin from the basket.

"At the bottom of the harbor," Damien stated, glancing at me out of the corner of his eye.

I nearly spat out my tea.

"I sank it … early this mornin'."

I blinked at him as I struggled to process what he was saying.

"Took longer than I'd expected, but she was all the way under by sunup."

Reaching across the table, Kate clasped my hand. "He had to, love. It woulda led 'em right to ya."

"To *us*," Jack added with her mouth full.

To us.

As much as it hurt to lose another part of myself, of my family, I looked around the table and realized that what I had gained was worth so much more than some rusty, old boat.

Squeezing Kate's and Damien's hands at the same time, I responded to his worried gaze with one of overwhelming gratitude.

"Thank you," I whispered, feeling like an eejit. "I should have thought of that. Leaving that boat out there put everybody at risk. I'm so—"

"Breaking news in the war with Russia." The British newscaster staring at us from the tablet on the table interrupted my apology even faster than Damien. "Officials report that the Irish death toll has just surpassed one thousand. Most of these casualties have been military personnel, which is a devastating blow to the already-depleted Irish Defence Forces. During last year's conflict in Northern Ireland, it is estimated that the country's total military strength was reduced to fewer than eight thousand active personnel."

"Fuck!" Jack shoved her chair away from the table, causing the glowing tablet to fall forward on its face.

Kate gently propped it back up.

"The Irish Defence Forces have chosen to concentrate their efforts on maintaining control of Dublin, leaving all other major ports and cities undefended. Most residents in these areas have fled to rural villages that have yet to be invaded, but several of those who did not get out in time have been captured and taken to makeshift prison camps. According to our war correspondents, Irish detainees are being subjected to daily beatings and ill treatment."

"Ill treatment," Jack scoffed, pacing across the kitchen.

Damien slid my chair next to his and wrapped his arm around me.

"Because of Ireland's unprovoked attack on UK soil last year," the newscaster continued as scenes from the now-infamous Battle of Belfast played on a green screen behind him, "it has alienated itself from all of England's allies. Thus, the majority of European and North American countries have closed their borders to Irish refugees."

"What did I tell ya? What the fuck did I tell ya when the UIB took office?" Jack spat. "I said those gangsters were gonna run this place into the ground."

"Shh!" Kate hushed, turning up the volume.

"However, in a bold act of defiance against the Crown, the mayor of Boston, Dr. Kendall Fitzpatrick, held a press conference yesterday to announce that she is opening her city to Irish refugees."

The screen changed to a woman standing at a podium, wearing a helmet of strawberry-blonde hair and a red pantsuit that was just as stiff. A river, bridge, and cityscape glittered behind her.

Dr. Fitzpatrick smiled into the camera and spread her arms as wide as her suit would allow. "Ireland, look behind me. Everything you see here—every bridge, building, and byway—was built with the blood, sweat, and tears of Irish immigrants. Your ancestors came here by the thousands during the Great Famine, bravely forging a new life for themselves and their families. To this day, twenty percent of our citizens claim to be of Irish decent. One hundred percent on St. Patrick's Day," she added with a smirk. "So, your history is our history. Your blood runs in our veins. *You* are family, and you will *always* be welcome here in Boston."

Tears welled in my eyes as they lifted and locked on to Damien's.

Boston.

The idea was exhilarating and terrifying. I'd never even left the island before. I had no money. No friends in America. But we would be safe there, and there was nothing I wanted more than to curl up in Damien's arms without the fear of being bombed or captured or killed.

"When asked to comment, American President Samuel Torres announced that he will not only allow Boston to accept Irish refugees, but he will facilitate the evacuation effort by sending his largest ships and military aircraft to transport those who wish to leave. In a statement directly following Mayor Fitzpatrick's, President Torres said, quote, 'What's happening in Ireland is a humanitarian disaster that defies politics. We do not support the United Irish Brotherhood, nor do we recognize them as a legitimate political party. The UIB is an organized crime syndicate that has hijacked a country, akin to the Bratva in Russia. The conflict between these two countries is a glorified gang war, plain and simple, and our support lies solely with the innocent Irish people whose lives and livelihoods are at risk because of it.' "

Jack scoffed.

"And in what is only his second-recorded appearance since the invasion began, Taoiseach Séamus Rooney has also issued a statement."

The screen cut to an image of Rooney, red-faced and sweatier than ever, sitting in some kind of windowless bunker. He was wearing a camouflage army uniform—as if he'd ever seen a second of any of the battles he had caused—and was lit as if he were under interrogation.

"People of Ireland," Rooney sneered, "I speak on behalf of the United Irish Brotherhood, the brave men and women fightin' on the front lines, and the generations of Irish rebels who came before ya when I say that we are *disgusted* by the way yous all have been actin' since this little skirmish began."

"Disgusted?" Jack snapped.

"Little skirmish," I whispered, picturing scorched hills covered in dead sheep and leveled houses.

"Fleein' yer cities. Runnin' off to the country—or worse, *America*. After everything we just went through to unite our island again, yer just gonna roll over and let another colonizer take it from ya without a feckin' fight?"

Jack laughed maniacally and pinched the bridge of her nose.

Rooney continued, "Yeah, sure, Abramov likes to brag that he's got a two-million-man army. Ours might not be that big—"

"Not that big?! We're down to eight thousand, ya fuckin' muppet!"

"But we've got *five million* men, women, and children on this island who can all join the fight."

"Children?" Kate echoed, shaking her head as she stared at the screen with sad, unfocused eyes.

"So, get yer arses to Dublin and bring all the weapons ya got. Yer country needs ya, ya <bleep> cowards!"

Pausing the broadcast, Kate looked at Jack. "What do we do?"

"You should get off the island," Damien responded, his voice deep and commanding. "Right now, Abramov is focused on the capital, but as soon as there's a Russian flag flyin' over Dublin Castle, he'll take the rest of the country."

"How do ya know that?" Jack asked, coming to stand behind Kate.

Damien shrugged. "We have our sources."

He was letting them believe he was in the Irish military, just like he'd done with me. I'd felt so betrayed by that omission, but now, I understood why'd he done it. Damien was one of us, no matter what the patches on his jacket said.

Shite.

I glanced down at the Russian flag on my arm and turned that side of my body farther away from our hosts.

"We're not leavin'," Jack stated bluntly, gripping the back of Kate's chair. "This is my home, and I'm gonna defend it."

"What are you gonna do?" Kate asked quietly.

She didn't look at either of us, but I could tell that her question was directed at Damien. She behaved the same way around him that I had in the cave. Like it hurt her to look at him. Like it hurt her not to.

He opened his mouth to answer, but the next voice we heard wasn't his.

And it wasn't speaking English.

Damien and Jack locked eyes as the sound of two men laughing and speaking Russian echoed up the stairs from the bakery.

"Hide," Damien whispered.

"No!" Jack hissed. "Nobody move. These floors squeak like rusty gates. They'll hear ya."

Kate's eyes went wide with terror as they darted from Jack to Damien.

"Ya have a gun?" Damien asked.

"In the bedroom. Too far."

Something shattered downstairs, like a plate or a pane of glass. The men laughed and broke something else.

"Motherfuckers," Jack spat.

Kate's hand began to shake in mine, but Damien was as calm and quiet as the harbor fog. Standing up in his chair, he pulled the gun from his waistband and stepped onto the table. It creaked a bit under his weight, but not enough to hear all the way downstairs. Crouching to keep from hitting his head on the ceiling, Damien stepped from the table to the counter, then over to the kitchen island. There, he dropped to his knees and silently lifted a barstool, placing it back down as far out as he could reach. With it, he bridged the gap between the kitchen and the sitting room, ending up on a blue velvet couch that sat across from the stairwell. Kneeling on the seat, Damien leaned over the back, staring down the barrel of his gun into the shadowy void below.

No, not Damien.

The lieutenant.

Someone was about to die.

The sound of things breaking downstairs stopped, and the laughter grew louder. *Closer.*

"Get down." Jack motioned at Kate and me.

Kate complied immediately, her white hair disappearing below the table, but I couldn't take my eyes off the man with the gun.

I'd only ever seen him bleeding, starving, disheveled, and exhausted, and even then I'd thought he was the most captivating creature on earth. But I'd had no idea. Seeing him cleaned up—a crisp white shirt stretched over hard muscle, his clean-shaven jaw clenched in concentration—made me realize what a force of nature he really was. Damien exuded power and confidence, filled the room with his perfectly composed potential to strike. It was like being in the presence of a king cobra—hypnotizingly beautiful and every bit as deadly.

So, when the voices grew louder and the stairs began to creak, I wasn't afraid.

But I should have been.

Because after Damien fired his first shot and I heard a body tumble down the stairs, his gun only clicked.

Plaster exploded above his head as the second sailor returned fire. Damien ducked in front of the sofa as bullets spewed from the stairwell, disappearing around the far side of it as the Russian charged into the sitting room. The moment his boots hit the landing, Damien tackled him from the side.

My heart leaped into my throat as I watched him pound the man's face with the butt of his pistol. The sound was unlike anything I'd ever heard before. A sick, dull crunching. I thought the man was already dead. I thought Damien was unleashing all of his training and torment on a corpse. But when I noticed the Russian's arm move, my entire world narrowed to the size of the object in his hand.

"Damien!" I screamed. "Gun!"

The moment I said his name, Damien's gaze cut over to mine, and like water on a blacksmith's blade, every glowing ember of warmth I'd felt from him moments earlier was extinguished, blackened, honed into a weapon of solid steel. The

Russian lifted his hand and shoved the barrel of his pistol under Damien's chin, and in that split second, I thought the bullet was going to pierce my own heart. A scream lodged in my throat as Damien jerked the sailor's hand away, his cold, calculating stare darting to something over my shoulder in the process.

A rush of air ruffled my hair as a butcher knife sailed past me, spinning end over end before sinking into the side of the sailor's skull, causing his entire body to jerk and his gun to go off.

Plaster dust rained down on them as Damien stared at his attacker, chest heaving, fist squeezing the man's wrist so hard that his knuckles turned white.

"Couldn't let ya have all the fun now, could I?" Jack teased, walking over to him.

But Damien wasn't looking at her. His gaze slid from the dead body beneath him over to me, and I knew that no matter how relieved and awestruck and grateful I felt, the only reaction he would see on my face was pure horror. I was sick to my stomach over almost losing him, over the focused, unflinching way he'd bashed that man's skull in. I could still hear the crunching, Damien's soft grunts of force, the sudden, wet chop of metal through bone.

But mostly, I was horrified because I knew we'd summoned another threat, one that filled me with more dread than our two unexpected visitors combined.

"Shh!" I called out as the hair on the back of my arms stood up. I *felt* the hum rather than heard it. Felt it in every bruise. Every knife scratch and nearly broken rib vibrated at the same frequency as the death machine coming to investigate. "Hide in the stairs! Now!"

Damien didn't hesitate. As I grabbed Kate and ran to the stairwell, he and Jack dragged the body in behind us. I had to clamp my hand over my mouth to keep from shrieking as his cleaved head bumped down the stairs next to me, butcher knife still lodged in place.

No sooner had his last boot disappeared into the shadows than a beam of light illuminated the spot where it had just been.

The curtains were closed, but they were sheer enough that the drone hovering outside could no doubt see in. And so could the Russian surveillance team operating it.

I didn't realize I was hyperventilating until Kate squeezed my shaking hands.

"Breathe," she whispered. "It's gone, love. It's gone."

I couldn't speak. All I could do was shake my head and pray for someone to read my thoughts. My heart was racing, my breaths were ragged, and I was suddenly freezing. My whole body shivered as Damien appeared at my side.

Gasping for air, I reached for him, pushing two words out between my insufficient, panicked breaths. "Not … gone."

Nodding, Damien pulled me into his lap and pressed his lips to my forehead. "She's right," he announced to the women. "If the drone's here, that means they heard the shots. They'll keep searchin' till they find the source … and the bodies when they realize they're missing."

"I hate these fuckers." Jack gave the body sprawled out on the stairs a kick.

Kate pressed her fingertips to her lips, a vacant look in her unfocused eyes. "What do we do?"

"We give 'em what they're lookin' for." The steady tone of Damien's voice had already begun to calm my terror. He would fix this.

He has to.

"Jack, find a mirror and a window where you can keep an eye on the drone without being seen. Give me a signal if it comes back."

Jack answered with a salute.

"Kate, I need ya to clean up the blood and find a damn good hiding spot in case any more troops come through here."

Kate nodded as she stared at the unmoving chest of the man sprawled out between us.

"Clo …" Damien stood and helped me to my feet as well, keeping a steady hand on my body the entire time. "Pack us a bag and get ready to run."

"With a fuckin' drone on the loose?" Jack whispered.

"Yes," Damien stated. "I'm gonna move the bodies to the pub through the back door. The front window's already broken, so once they start lookin' for the missing sailors, the drone will be able to fly right in and find them. If their surveillance catches us fleein' the city, they'll assume we killed the bastards, and you two will stay off their radar."

Damien's backlit face turned toward mine, and I felt the temperature drop ten degrees. "Or you *three*, if ya wanna stay here."

I shook my head, clenching my teeth to keep them from chattering. Trying to outrun a drone sounded like a suicide mission, but as much as it shocked me, I trusted Damien. Without him, I would have died a thousand deaths already.

Without him, I would have welcomed them all.

Pressing his lips to mine, Damien stole what little breath I'd gotten back before moving past me down the stairs. "Jack, tell me when the coast is clear. I'm gonna move these bodies next door."

"Wait!" I whisper-shouted, grabbing him by the shirt and turning him to face me. With trembling fingers, I reached up and unfastened his top button. "Ya can't get blood on this shirt too. It's the only one you've got."

CHAPTER 27

CLOVER

"Here ya are, love. All packed up."

I stood at the bottom of the stairs, clutching Damien's shirt as I stared at the hallway that led to the back door, waiting for him to return.

Turning to face Kate, who was coming down the stairs behind me, I forced a smile as she handed me a military-looking backpack stuffed to the brim. Damien had told me to pack up our things, which I had assumed meant our new toothbrushes and travel-sized toiletries, but Kate must have taken it upon herself to throw in half the pantry as well.

The sight of that backpack reminded me of the one I'd left in Howth. Of my mother's books. Of my mother, period.

She would have done the same thing.

"Kate, this is too much," I said, accepting the heavy bag with a grateful smile.

"I run a bakery. I've got plenty of food. And we've got runnin' water, so you two need the bottled stuff more than we do."

"I don't know what to say."

Kate cleared her throat. It was dark in the stairwell, but I could hear the emotion in her voice as she struggled to find her next words. "I wish ya could stay."

"Me too." I nodded as I slung the bag over my shoulder. "Maybe we can come back, once things calm down."

"Ya mean once we're all speakin' Russian?" Jack added from her place behind the bakery counter. She was using a handheld mirror to look out the large front windows. "Shite. It's almost at the end of the harbor."

I heard the back door open, but before Jack could even draw her gun, Damien emerged from the hallway. My heart stopped, just like it did every time I looked at him. His bare chest was smeared with blood, but the bandages I'd applied to his bullet wounds after our … *activities* the night before were still nice and clean.

Just one more thing I had to thank Kate for.

I felt her bristle at my side. As Damien approached, she dropped her head and stared at her wringing hands.

"It's comin' back," Jack said, watching the drone in the mirror. "Ya better go. Now."

With a nod, Damien turned his full attention to me, and I held up his open shirt with trembling hands.

Once he slid his arms into it, I let go and gave Kate a grateful, grief-stricken hug. "I can't thank you enough. For everything. We'll see ya again, yeah?"

Kate didn't even pretend like that was true. She simply squeezed me tighter and whispered in my ear, "Take care of him," her voice as broken as the dishes she'd cleaned up.

As soon as I released her, Damien stepped into the stairwell and wrapped his good arm around her tiny shoulders. He couldn't pretend like this wasn't goodbye either. The two of them simply hugged in silence until Kate burst into tears and ran back up the stairs.

"It's the shirt," Jack said, her eyes still glued to the mirror. "Go on now. It's movin' fast. Just take this road behind us north, and you'll run right into the train station. I hear the rail union's gonna keeping trains runnin' to help evacuate folks from occupied cities, so … ya might be in luck."

Darting over to Jack, I gave her a full-body squeeze, which she reciprocated by patting me awkwardly on the arm. Damien followed with some military fist bump/back slap combo that she seemed much more comfortable with, and before I could thank her for letting us stay, I was whisked into the hallway and out the back door.

Out of the frying pan and into the fire.

Damien had left the back door of the pub unlocked, and inside, it already looked like a crime scene. Broken glass and furniture littered the floor. Tables and chairs were scattered and knocked over. The place reeked of spilled alcohol from the night before. And when we walked past the stairwell, I glanced over at it and screamed.

"Shite," Damien hissed, escorting me past the man lying face up on the stairs with a bleeding hole between his eyes. "Shoulda warned ya about that."

I could hear the propellers now. The high-pitched whir of a motor at top speed. It sounded like it was almost on top of us, like it was flying as fast as it could.

It heard me.

Oh God, it heard me.

Placing me in the center of the pub, Damien gripped my biceps and bent down to my height so that he could look me in the eyes. "It's okay," he whispered. "It's gonna be okay. Just … stand here and don't fuckin' run."

"I thought we were supposed to run," I whispered back, my voice shaking as he released me.

"Change of plans."

I looked around the pub, but he was already gone. It was just me, standing like an eejit as that mechanical buzzing bore down on me with a speed that made my knees and my bladder threaten to go weak.

I looked around again, Damien's name caught in my throat, but when I turned back to the window, I found a sleek black machine hovering directly in front of it. Like the head of a predator after hearing a twig snap, it rotated toward me and shone its cold, condemning light directly in my face.

Day turned to night. The broken chairs on the floor multiplied, growing into a pile of rubble. And the still, foggy air began to swirl around me, lashing me like the sea breeze over the cliffs of Howth.

"This is a message from President Abramov."

Everything was gone.

"Your city has been captured by the Armed Forces of the Russian Federation."

There was blood. So much blood.

"This is your only chance to surrender. You have ten seconds to raise your hands above your head and follow this device to the nearest encampment."

Hands. I'd found Sheila's hand just a few meters away.

"Refusal to do so will be considered an act of—"

The blinding white light and the drone itself suddenly disappeared, and in its place—just like that night on the cliff—I saw *him.* Only he wasn't emerging from a lake, beckoning me to jump. He was standing right in front of me, in real life, jaw clenched and nostrils flared like a demon.

He squeezed his eyes shut as the countdown began, and his entire body began to shake.

Looking down, I realized that he was holding the drone so that it pointed toward the floor. All four propellers spun like saw blades between us.

I took a step back.

With a strained growl, Damien's face contorted into one of pure agony before the sound of cracking plastic shot through the room like a bullet. Two propellers stopped spinning and fell away, dangling from useless wires as the countdown continued.

In another burst of force, Damien broke the remaining two propellers off, and the sparks that showered over me felt like a celebration. Like a spray of champagne on New Year's Eve.

I wasn't alone anymore. I wasn't going to die. And as long as Damien was with me, I knew that fact would remain true.

Twisting his body, Damien tossed the dismembered drone out the broken window and across the street, where, just before it hit the water, a robotic voice said, "Two."

When he glanced back at me, Damien's shoulders were heaving, his gray eyes were hard as stone, but his lips were parted in relief.

Grabbing me by the back of the neck, he pulled my body against his and squeezed. His heart pounded against my cheek as his powerful arms held me captive. He held me longer than he should have, but not long enough.

It was never long enough.

"They're comin'," he said solemnly, taking the heavy bag off my shoulder and slinging it over his. "Ya ready?"

My chest tightened in panic as he extended his hand, but the moment my palm sealed over his, the moment I felt that surge of warmth and riot of tingles shoot up my arm, my lungs expanded. I sucked in a breath, and together, we ran.

CHAPTER 28

CLOVER

Out the back door, down the alley, and through the vacant streets of Wexford, Damien led me with the stealth and grace of a predator. Because the streets were empty, we could hear the footsteps of every sailor marching from the encampment to the pub, the buzzing propellers of every drone they'd sent out to search for us. But most importantly, we could hear the click-clack of train tracks off in the distance.

Damien knew exactly where to go. We ran parallel to the harbor, catching glimpses of the looming gray warship between and above the buildings we were using for cover. Russian voices bounced down the streets and alleyways between them. But I wasn't afraid. I was exhilarated. Every time Damien pulled me into an alcove to hide or tucked me behind his back while glancing around a corner, my pulse skyrocketed. The scent of him, the heat of his hard body, the defensiveness of his posture, and the soothing security of his touch—it was a high I'd never known. I'd lived in a state of constant fear for as long as I could remember, but with Damien by my side, I felt safe. I felt free.

No one would ever hurt me again.

The realization brought a smile to my face as we darted across a side street and into the doorway of a flower shop, but the scent of decaying roses inside quickly reminded me just how closely the threat of death still lurked.

Damien pointed across a wide intersection to a squat gray building, standing alone along a stretch of train tracks.

Wexford Station.

I'd assumed it would be guarded by rows of machine gun–toting soldiers, checking IDs and taking women as prisoners, but the simple one-platform station sat just as vacant as the rest of the town. The ground rumbled beneath our feet as the next train approached, and once he was confident that the coast was clear, Damien sprinted across the quiet intersection with my hand in his.

"Ey!" a deep voice shouted from the direction of the harbor just before we disappeared around the side of the station.

Hopping the guardrail, Damien helped me over, and together, we ducked into the shadows of the small, covered platform.

A rabble of Russian voices grew louder in the distance, but their cries and heavy footfalls were immediately drowned out by the squealing brakes of the green-and-white train barreling toward us.

I squeezed Damien's hand as I waited for the doors to open, glancing back and forth over both shoulders while Damien simply slipped the gun from his holster and waited in deathly stillness.

When the doors finally opened, we darted into the empty car, and Damien immediately pulled me underneath the first table on the right. We sat with our backs against the wall— Damien clutching his gun and me clutching his uninjured arm— as the sound of collective Russian rage came screaming toward us. I squeezed my eyes shut as the doors began to close, bracing myself for the faces of every man Damien had killed to burst through the gap and exact their revenge. But instead of feeling rough hands around my ankles, yanking me to my doom, I felt the floor rumble beneath my arse as the train lurched forward and the wall vibrate against my back as angry fists pounded on the other side of it. I couldn't understand what the men were shouting, but it didn't matter. A few seconds later, the only thing I could hear was my own relieved, nervous laughter as we pulled away from the station.

I felt like a madwoman, curled up under a table, cackling like a lunatic, but Damien didn't judge me. Didn't call me Crazy Clover. He simply tucked his gun away, turned toward me, and silenced my anxiety with a feral, ravenous kiss.

The collision of our lips felt as strong as a force of nature, like the meeting of two magnets—hard and fast and inevitable. With heaving chests and pounding hearts, Damien and I clung to one another as we devoured each other with panting mouths and grasping hands. I felt safe with him, but Damien felt terrified with me. *For* me. I could feel the fear radiating off of him in waves as he crushed me to his chest and kissed me like I might disappear.

"It's okay," I whispered against his lips, coming up for air. "It's over."

Tilting my head, I moaned as he sucked the side of my neck with the same desperate urgency that he'd shown my lips and tongue.

"I'm right here." Taking his hand, I pressed it to my chest, letting him feel my racing heart.

"I ..." The words left my mind as Damien kissed his way down my chest before removing his hand and replacing it with his forehead.

"Shh ..." I held his head to my breast as his body began to shake in a silent sob.

He'd been so concerned about helping me process what had happened yesterday that it hadn't occurred to me that he'd been traumatized too. That he'd experienced almost all of the same horrors, some worse than mine, and he'd had the added fear of trying to keep me safe while protecting himself.

"Hey," I whispered, running my fingers through his hair. "It's okay. We're okay."

As he shuddered in my arms, I felt both his terror and his relief pouring off of him in torrents. If his protection was my freedom, then my presence was his. He could express himself with me. Be himself around me. Bury his pain inside me.

And I would take it, greedily.

Lifting his face until he was looking at me again, I slid my thumbs under his wet lower lashes before pressing a kiss to his beautiful, miserable mouth.

The sensation was overwhelming. My feelings, my need, my fear of trusting someone this much, my fear of losing someone again—it spilled down my cheeks and salted my lips, the perfect contrast to the sweetness I'd found in this man.

The night before, he'd told me to take what I wanted from him, and what I wanted was this. Every raw, unspoken, terrible thing that lurked inside of him. I wanted to free him of that darkness, catch it on my tongue, and swallow it whole.

When Damien dropped his forehead back down to my heart and I ran my fingers through his hair, I finally remembered what I was going to say before.

"I love you," I whispered, pressing a kiss to the top of his head.

"Angel …" Damien rasped, coiling his arms around my waist. "The way I feel about you"—he shook his head—"there isn't a word for it."

I smiled, knowing that nothing would ever fill me with more joy than hearing Damien Hughes tell me he loved me.

But what I heard next was a close second.

"This train is approaching Castlebridge Station," a digital voice announced over the speakers. "Transfer here for northbound service to Dublin or continue for westbound service to Waterford, Cork, and Glenshire."

CHAPTER 29

DAMIEN

"**D**amien, wake up. We're here."

I hadn't realized I'd fallen asleep until I heard Clo's soft voice. I'd been dreaming about us riding the train like a normal couple, holding hands across the table and smiling about nothing as the southern hills rolled by outside. But we were still very much *under* the table—running for our lives and hiding from Russian militants—and I'd slept through the entire trip.

I knew I was exhausted. I'd been in survival mode for two straight days and been up all night, exerting myself—first in the bedroom with Clo and then in the bowels of her da's ship as I sawed through layers of wood and waterproofing—but I still couldn't believe that I'd let my guard down enough to sleep in a public place. It was dangerous, the effect Clover had on me. The few times she'd let me hold her, touch her, everything else had just faded away. It made no sense. We were in constant danger, but the weight of her body on my chest and the warmth of her breath on my neck tricked me into thinking that nothing bad could possibly happen.

Crawling backward out of our hiding spot, Clover seemed entirely too happy for a girl who'd just spent another day fearing for her life and watching men get slaughtered right before her eyes. She beamed as she helped me unfold my massive body into a standing position. Then, she reached for the heavy bag Kate had sent us with, as if I was going to let her carry it. Plucking it out of her hands, I slung it over my shoulder and pulled her against my good side. There were a few other people on the train now, all of whom gave us sideways glances as they gathered in the aisle, waiting to exit. It could have been because we'd crawled out from under a table, or because there was a gun holstered on my hip, or because Clo was wearing a bloodstained Russian Naval blazer over her sundress.

Or maybe it was because she was the first smiling person they'd seen since the invasion.

"Arriving at … Glenshire Station. This is the final stop for westbound service. Transfer here for northbound service to Killarney, Limerick, and Galway."

Clo let out a little squeal as she clutched my hand and bounced in place. "I've always wanted to come here. That book I read to you in the cave … that entire series is about the folklore of Glenshire. My ma named me after a line from a poem in one of those books."

Clearing her throat, she recited, "*Out where the bluebells grow high as your knee, and the clover and moss blanket every tree, lies a ring made of stone where no fairies dare tread. That's where you'll find him, the ghost of the glen.*"

"The ghost of the glen?" I asked, scanning the platform for soldiers as I forced myself to loosen my grip on Clo's arm.

"The ghost of Glenshire," she replied matter-of-factly. "When he was a boy, the villagers thought he was the son of Satan and shunned him. He hid out in the forest, which, legend has it, is inhabited by fairies and witches and a lake spirit named Saoirse."

"Mmhmm." I was only half-listening.

There were no soldiers. No guards. Just a few dozen traumatized-looking passengers heading up the stairs to the northbound platform, loaded down with suitcases, packs, pets, and children. Where were they going? What did they know that we didn't?

Following the signs for Glenshire instead, Clover tugged me through the turnstiles and into a stone tunnel. A few handwritten posters taped to the walls announced that food and shelter were available to refugees at Glenshire Catholic Church.

"… so when the priest died in a house fire and the boy disappeared, everyone assumed that he'd died in the fire too. That was when the ghost of Glenshire legend was born. They thought his spirit was haunting the woods, waiting for the American girl he loved to return. Isn't that sad?"

I remembered the story. I fucking hated it.

"But the legend was disproved years later when Darby came back to Glenshire as an adult for her grandfather's funeral. She found Kellen alive and well, married him, and they lived quite happily in her grandfather's farmhouse … until they were murdered, of course."

As Clover reached out her hand to open the door at the end of the tunnel, I was overcome with the urge to pull her away from it. It was as if I was watching her reach for a hot stove. Everything in my body screamed that we should go, turn around and take the northbound train, like all the other evacuees. But Clover was happy—after everything she'd been through, this place made her happy—so I bit my tongue and followed her through what felt like the gates of fucking hell.

"Oh my God," she gasped as we stepped out of the station and into a village square. Wind ruffled her hair as gray clouds swirled overhead. "It's sooo cute."

The tightly packed stucco buildings were painted every color of the rainbow—red and green and yellow and hot pink— or they had been, once upon a time. Now, their exteriors were faded and peeling. Dried, dead flowers drooped over the sides of the window boxes. And a few of the businesses were boarded up completely. But Clover didn't see any of that. Or maybe she just saw past it.

Like she did with me.

But I didn't have that ability, and I didn't give a shite about her little folklore field trip. All I cared about was keeping her safe until we sorted out how to get to Boston. If the church was accepting refugees, then they probably knew where to send us to get on one of those American planes or ships. I glanced around until I found a stone steeple topped with a metal cross off in the distance. Guiding Clo across the quiet intersection, I steered her down a winding street that looked like it might lead to the church.

"I wish I had my phone so I could take pictures," she said, walking backward as the square disappeared behind us. A touch of sadness had crept into her voice, but she shook it off and squeezed my hand tighter. "It's crazy," she continued. "Just yesterday, I was in a Russian encampment, thinking I was about to die, and now …" She dropped my hand and skipped ahead, spreading her arms wide as she spun in a circle. The bottom of her yellow dress twirled and lifted, exposing a pair of bruised, scratched thighs that I wanted to lavish with kisses all over again. "I'm in Glenshire!"

Her grinning eyes softened as they locked with mine. "Because of you."

The corner of my mouth lifted as I stalked toward her, and Clo planted her feet, allowing me to catch up. She tilted her head back as I pulled her into my arms, and when I kissed her still-smiling mouth, I decided that maybe Glenshire wasn't so bad after all.

We walked the rest of the way to the church, hand in hand, as Clo pointed at every landmark and explained every shred of lore that she knew about the seemingly uninhabited village. The only proof of life I could see were the hundreds of sheep dotting the valley that stretched out below us on the left side of the road. The landscape looked like a tattered green quilt, and on each patch sat a small house, painted some crazy bright color, just like the buildings in the square.

On the other side of the street, the hills rose up toward a distant purple mountain and were covered in trees. It was strange. I hadn't seen the mountain from the train station, but I felt like I had known it would be there before I turned my head to look. Just like I knew the church would be lurking behind the next curve in the road, and there it was—a simple stone chapel with two massive red doors and a steeple just tall enough to be seen over the trees. The cemetery behind it stretched up the hill at least a hundred meters, stopping where the woods began.

"Wow," Clo whispered, awestruck. "It looks exactly the way I pictured it."

The books. That must be why everything felt so familiar. Clover had read to me about this place.

At the church, several people were gathered around a folding table at the entrance of the cemetery, so Clover and I walked that way. My goal was to find out if anyone knew how to get on one of the American planes or ships and then go there as quickly as fucking possible, but as soon as we approached the table, something at the back of the graveyard caught my eye.

It was a small white house with a door as red as the ones on the church, and the sight of it made my stomach lurch.

I suddenly knew why this place felt so familiar, so evil.

I'd seen it before, in my dreams.

CHAPTER 30

CLOVER

Glenshire.

God, it was so surreal. I was literally walking through the pages of my favorite fairy tales. The colorful buildings, the sheep spray-painted to match their owner's house, the spooky old church ... the woods—it was exactly the way Darby Donovan had described it.

Glancing across the tombstones, I wondered if she and her husband were buried out there somewhere. If so, I wanted to pay my respects before we left.

Before we left.

The thought punched me in the gut.

We weren't just visiting for the day, with a cozy bed and clean clothes and a fully stocked fridge waiting for us at home. We had no home.

We had nowhere else to go.

I noticed that Damien had wandered away from the table and was staring at the priest's house at the back of the cemetery. He was only about ten meters away from me, but that felt too far. I wasn't safe without him, and he wasn't safe without me.

"Name?"

"Hmm?" I turned my head and found a gray-haired priest with puffy bags under his bloodshot eyes standing across the table from me.

"Yer name and date of birth, miss." He handed me a pen and gestured to a clipboard in front of me. "We're tryin' to keep track of all the evacuees."

"Oh." Accepting the pen, I looked around and noticed a few families gathered in groups, huddled over steaming bowls of soup or stew. There had to be at least thirty names on the paper, but some had probably come and gone already.

"I'm Father Sullivan," he said, pulling a metal folding chair out from behind the table and collapsing into it with a groan. He must have been in his sixties, maybe seventy. "Been on me feet all week. Got bunions the size of onions." He smiled weakly. "Once ya check in, head inside and grab yourself some dinner from the kitchen. We got enough lamb stew and soda bread to feed an army, so don't be shy."

"Thank you, Father." I bowed my head, not knowing what exactly was expected when speaking to a priest. I hadn't stepped foot in a church since Ma's funeral. "Before I go, may I ask you a question about someone who used to live here?"

His smile faded. "That someone wouldn't happen to be Darby Donovan, would it?"

"How did you know?"

"She's the only person from Glenshire anybody's ever heard of outside of Glenshire."

"Did you know her?"

"Aye." Father Sullivan narrowed his cloudy eyes at me. "Yer the spittin' image of her, ya know. I didn't think she had any children, but ... everybody's got their secrets, don't they?"

"Oh. No. I'm not her daughter. Just a fan. Her *biggest* fan. I was hoping to see the places she wrote about while I'm here. With the war and all, I don't know if ... if I'll ever make it back."

"That makes two of us, dear." Father Sullivan's face twisted into a heartbreaking frown. "The whole congregation's headin' up to Shannon tomorrow to see if we can get on one of those boats or planes to Boston. This might be the last night any of us spends in Glenshire."

Father Sullivan's eyes lifted to something over my shoulder, and his entire demeanor changed. I didn't need to turn around to know it was Damien. I could feel the warmth of his massive body, sense the magnetic pull that had drawn me to him that night in the sea.

"Father Sullivan"—I gestured toward the man behind me— "this is—"

"The Devil himself," he hissed, clutching the cross around his neck as he shot to his feet, knocking his metal folding chair over in the process.

"Sorry?" I sputtered, watching in bewilderment as Father Sullivan's wide-eyed stare darted from Damien to me, along with the cross that he wielded like a weapon.

"I'd know those demon eyes anywhere." He took a step back, nearly tripping on his overturned chair. "And you." His accusing stare landed on me. "No wonder ya look just like her."

I shook my head as Damien's arm slid around my waist protectively. "I'm sorry, I don't understand."

Father Sullivan took another step back. The hand holding the cross was visibly shaking now. "He should be burnin' in hell for the things he done. If he's here and you're here with him, that means you've forsaken the kingdom of heaven to spend eternity in purgatory with this sinner."

He had dementia, poor fella. Or perhaps he was having a nervous breakdown from the stress of the war and the responsibility of evacuating an entire village. Whatever was going on with him, it still scared me. I didn't like it when men got angry.

I glanced around, hoping to find someone who might be able to help. People were beginning to stare, but no one came forward to check on the old man.

"Father Sullivan, maybe you should sit." I was going to walk around the table to right his chair, but he thrust that cross in my face before I could take a step.

"He's a demon. A murderer. Killed a man of the cloth in that very house." He pointed a knobby, shaking finger at a small white house at the back of the cemetery. "Don't ya see, child? He corrupted ya in life, and now, he's done so in death." Spittle flew from his mouth as he banged his fist on the metal table. "They say he haunts these woods, waitin' for ya to return, but you never left, did ya? Ya turned your back on God to stay here with this Devil."

The ghost of Glenshire. Of course. He thinks Damien is Kellen Donovan's ghost, which means he must think that I'm—

A spatter of water splashed across my face without warning.

"*Vade retro Satana!*" Father Sullivan shouted, slashing a small vial of holy water through the air.

Turning his body to shield me from the spray, Damien snatched the vial out of the old man's hand and slammed it on the table, leaning toward him with a growl.

"Back, Devil!" he shouted, stumbling backward and nearly falling. "Back to the forest with ya! Keep yer evil away from my congregation. Yer not welcome here!"

With my heart pounding and a sudden lump in my throat, I pulled Damien away from the table and practically sprinted through the cemetery. I couldn't get away from there fast enough.

"That's right! Back to the forest with ya!" The raving old coot shouted after us. "May God have mercy on yer soul!"

Gripping my hand, Damien matched my pace, but his stride was longer and much less frantic than mine. I wished the nonsensical ravings of a madman didn't upset me as much as they did, but I couldn't help it. In my experience, when a man raised his voice at me, his hand usually followed.

But Damien wouldn't let that happen.

My pace slowed. My breathing slowed. Damien was there.

He was there, and I was safe.

"You okay?" he asked, wrapping his arm around my shoulders and pressing a kiss to the top of my head.

I nodded, taking a deep breath, as I let my eyes sweep over each tombstone that we passed. One was bigger and newer than all the others. It was shaped like a heart and had two names on it instead of just one. I didn't have to look to know which two names were chiseled there.

But I looked anyway.

CHAPTER 31

CLOVER

Damien stared at the priest's house as we passed, letting me steer him into the woods. I didn't have a bleeding clue where we were going. I only knew that if we went anywhere *other* than the woods that madman was going to come after us with a pitchfork.

"I know that house," Damien muttered, pulling his eyes away just in time to lift a branch and duck under it. "I had a nightmare about it, back in the cave."

"Sorry." I frowned, stepping over a tree root. "You probably had nightmares from me reading those books to you. They're very … vivid."

"Vivid." Damien let out a dark chuckle. "I'm the heir to the largest, most powerful Mafia organization on the planet, and I'm having nightmares over a fuckin' fairy tale."

I pulled Damien's blazer closed over my chest as a shiver ran through my body. I didn't know if it was from the drop in temperature when we entered the forest or the reminder of who exactly I was traveling with.

The only son of a Bratva kingpin.

A deserter from the Russian Navy.

A traitor who'd killed so many of his own men that I'd lost count.

This wasn't going to be as easy as running away to America. The Bratva had endless power, connections, resources. They would never stop looking for him.

Never.

"Hey," Damien said, pulling me to a stop. His silvery eyes, rimmed in black lashes and dark, worried brows, bored into mine as he gripped my shoulders. "You know that's not who I really am, right?"

I nodded, trying to smooth my tense features as I forced a small, reassuring smile. "I know. I do."

"Then, what were ya thinkin' about? You got quiet."

I looked around, finally taking in our new surroundings. The forest was dark and green and soft around the edges. Every boulder and tree trunk—every hard, jagged thing—was wrapped in a blanket of velvety moss. The lake at the bottom of the hill was green, too, mirroring the trees, even through a layer of mist. The light was so filtered by the canopy and clouds that it seemed as though it had no source at all. It simply swirled in the air, like the breeze that rustled the leaves and played with my hair.

It was as if we'd found a portal to a secret world.

To the *otherworld.*

And it was exactly the way I'd pictured it.

"Clo?"

Reaching for his face, already prickly with late afternoon stubble, I pulled Damien toward me and kissed his frowning mouth. Our lips met for only a moment, but in that one held breath, I felt an eternity of stillness, of peace, that I knew I'd never feel with anyone else.

"Let's just stay here," I whispered, my hands sliding from his cheeks down to the hard expanse of his chest. "We can build a cabin, live off of squirrels."

The corner of Damien's mouth curled up, exposing that dimple I loved so much. "I hope you're better at catchin' squirrels than ya are fish."

I smacked his chest with a scoff. "I kept you alive in the cave with my food-catching skills, didn't I?"

Damien's eyes darkened, and his smile disappeared. A sizzle that had nothing to do with the gathering clouds charged the air as his hands wove into my hair, pulling the wind-whipped strands away from my face.

"You did," he said, his voice rough with emotion as he tilted my head back, capturing me in the steel trap of his stare. "You saved me in every possible way, Clo. I owe you my life." Placing his hands over mine, he pressed them harder against his solid, thumping chest. "This blackened heart"—he glanced down the length of his torso—"this bullet-shredded body, every drop of hate pumping through these veins—it all belongs to you."

He'd meant it as a warning, a self-loathing commentary about the extent of his damage, inside and out, but I didn't hear it that way. All I heard were the words *heart*, *body*, and *you*.

"Promise?" I asked.

Damien's stormy gaze collided with mine, and before my smirk could widen into a full-blown grin, he dived for my mouth and kissed it right off.

"Took ya long enough."

Before I finished gasping at the sudden, unknown voice, Damien had already broken our kiss, spun around to face the stranger, and tucked me behind his back.

I peeked around his shoulder and discovered that we weren't where I'd thought we were. I could have sworn that Damien and I had only been halfway down the hill when I'd kissed him, but now, we were all the way at the bottom, standing on the bank of a murky, stagnant lake. In front of us stood an old stone cottage with a thatched roof—the kind people lived in during medieval times—and a woman who appeared to be even older than that. Her body curled like a question mark over a twisted cane and was dripping with the pelts of a hundred woodland creatures, stitched together, claws and all.

I recognized her immediately from Darby Donovan's book, *The Witch in the Woods*—scraggly gray hair, milky-white eyes, that grotesque fur cloak, and a voice that was both high and rough, like a child who'd been screaming for days.

Glancing up at the swirling sky, the gnarled old thing smirked. "She's none too happy with you, young fella. Made a *fine* mess of things, didn't ya?" She clicked her tongue in disapproval.

"To which fine mess would ya be referrin'?" Damien asked, keeping his voice neutral. "I've made quite a few of 'em here lately."

He stood even straighter, causing the sack of food on his shoulder to shift.

The woman's cloudy, pupil-less eyes narrowed at the sound. "I hope ya got somethin' reeeal shiny in there. Ya know how she gets when she's mad."

Damien and I shared a glance, and the old woman let out a cackle that sent a flock of birds tearing into the sky.

"You *don't* know, do ya?"

Her laugh devolved into a hacking cough.

"I … I'm sorry, but …" I took a small step out from behind Damien's body. "I'm afraid you have us mistaken for someone else."

If there was any truth to the book, the old woman was an illusionist and a trickster—a meddling gossip with a flair for the dramatic—but she wasn't malicious. At least, Darby hadn't thought so.

"Mistaken?" she mocked before erupting into another fit of cackles. "I might be half-blind, but I don't need eyes to know that you two bear her mark." Lifting a gnarled finger to the sky, a clap of thunder boomed in response. "*She* knows it too. She's been pitchin' a fit since ya got here."

"Well then, *she* must be mistaken," I stated as politely as possible, assuming that *she* must be this woman's imaginary friend. I knew all too well how real one of those could seem. "We've honestly never been here before in our lives." I glanced around the woods as a deep, heavy dread settled into my stomach. "In fact, I don't even know if we can find our way out."

"*Never in our lives,* she says!" The old woman snorted, doubling over her cane in hysterics and tapping it on the ground, like the slapping of a knee.

"Can you … perhaps tell us how to get back to town?" Damien asked, guiding me back behind him with a strong hand. "Please."

"I'll do ya one better." The old woman closed her eyes as her spine began to uncurl, vertebra by vertebra.

Damien clutched my hip as we watched her body straighten and stretch to a height nearly as tall as the thatch-roofed cottage behind her. And when she reopened her eyes, they were a bright, burning blue.

"Run!" Damien grabbed my hand and bolted up the hill, but we didn't get more than a few meters away before some invisible force—like a wrecking ball made of air—sent us flying backward.

And into the lake.

I braced myself for the lung-seizing cold—I'd only ever swum in the sea, which was freezing, even in June—but the water was cool and still.

Relieved, I began pumping my arms and kicking my legs, eager to get to the surface, find Damien, and get the hell out of Glenshire, but the harder I swam, the faster I sank.

And sank.

And sank.

My muscles screamed as I thrashed against the pull.

My heart pounded.

My ears popped.

But it was no use.

When my feet finally touched the bottom, my eyes flew open to find a trove of glittering treasures spread out before me, illuminated by a pulsing, shapeless, ambient blue light.

Saoirse.

That was the *she* the witch had been talking about. I'd read about her in *The Lady in the Lough.*

Legend had it that Saoirse lived in the village nearly a thousand years ago and was married off to the richest, meanest man in the village. He knew she didn't love him, and one night, in a jealous, drunken rage over some imagined indiscretion, he dragged her to the lake and drowned her. After Saoirse's death and her husband's complete lack of consequences, the other women in the village realized that the same thing could happen to them. They regarded Saoirse as their patron saint almost and began tossing gifts into the lake to earn her favor and protection. They would even bring their suitors for a stroll around the lake in the hopes that Saoirse would judge their hearts and let them know if the man was good or evil.

Generations later, couples began getting married there. They would wade into the water and prick their fingers on a blackberry thorn, shedding a few drops of blood in an attempt to earn Saoirse's ultimate blessing—an eternal, unbreakable bond. But Saoirse only granted that bond once every few centuries, when she found a love that was truly pure. The rest of the time, she was a moody, bitter thing, but she did love a good gift.

The blue glow condensed into a shapeless orb and slithered toward me, plunging the rest of the lake into murky darkness as it gathered around my feet. My heart slammed against my ribs as my panic turned to terror. I had nothing to offer her. Nothing.

Reaching out in all directions, my fingertips finally grazed Damien's, and the moment they did, he held on tight. I could feel him pulling and fighting against the gravity that had bound us to the bottom, but as the light rose up my body, I no longer felt the same sense of urgency. A sense of peace enveloped me, along with that light, like a welcoming hug after a long, hard trip.

I felt Saoirse's presence all around me—the radiant warmth of her embrace, the gentle caress against my cheek, the graceful serenity that washed over me, telling me without words that I was safe. I was loved.

And that I had *definitely* been there before.

My terror melted away, along with my need to breathe, as the most beautiful images flooded my consciousness. They could have been straight from the pages of Darby Donovan's books. A boy with gray eyes, a cottage, a church. A blue-and-white tea set perched on a stump. A rope swing, a blackberry bush, two bloody palms and four innocent lips pressed together in the lake.

Then, the images darkened.

Day turned to night. The boy, now a man. Curls, gone. Smile, gone. But his eyes still warmed when he looked at me. In fact, they glowed like the moon that lit our way as he watched me from the driver's seat of a car that I knew wasn't his. Three freckles slashed across his ring finger, where it draped over the steering wheel. Three freckles slashed across mine, where it draped over his. The taste of vanilla coated my tongue as I watched our naked bodies clutch and claw and cling to one another. As I felt our hearts do the same. Then darker still as gunshots rang out. Screaming. Bleeding. Running. Killing. So much killing.

Then, nothing.

Pressure weighed on my pounding heart as if Saoirse was pressing a hand against it. The blue aura around me brightened, like the tightening of a hug, and what I saw next made my unbreathing chest ache with a loss I hadn't felt since I was seven years old.

I saw that same man again, only he was different. Lighter. Happier. I saw him laughing as I helped him shear a rowdy black sheep. I saw him in a workshop, carving things out of wood, his glossy, grown-out curls held back by a pair of safety goggles. And when he looked up and smiled at me, I saw Damien's eyes in his face. Felt his strength and love and devotion radiate from their silvery depths. Bubbles danced around my body as I struggled to make sense of what Saoirse was showing me, but when they concentrated in front of my stomach, one last image nearly brought me to my knees.

I was standing in a bathroom, staring at down at a pregnancy test—the kind that produced two pink lines if it was positive. I watched that shy second line emerge, silently announcing that my life was about to change, but when I lifted my head, the smiling woman reflected in the mirror wasn't me.

It was the face printed on the inside cover of all my favorite books.

Then, the energy around me shifted violently. The images disappeared, ripped away from me, along with Saoirse's light and warmth as those bubbles darted from my abdomen to Damien's face like a swarm of murderous bees.

I clung to his fisted hand with both of mine as the bubbles engulfed him. Saoirse was hurting him. I could feel it in his jerking arm and see it in the way his body contorted and his head arched back. A helpless scream echoed in my worthless, burning lungs as I watched her exact revenge for something I couldn't remember.

But deep inside, I knew that wasn't true.

I already had remembered. Those images were more than just pictures from Darby's books. They were memories. *My* memories. I'd been there before. I'd met Saoirse before. I'd met Damien, and loved him, and married him ... *before*.

And I'd watched him kill before too.

Saoirse was said to judge men's hearts. To protect the women of the village from monsters like her husband.

But she'd made a mistake. The sweet boy she'd bonded me to had grown up to become a killer.

Twice.

And she was absolutely furious about it.

CHAPTER 32

DAMIEN

My lungs screamed, my muscles seized, and my eyes squeezed shut as a cyclone of glowing blue bubbles poked and stabbed at me with the force of a thousand accusing fingertips. But the physical pain, the powerlessness, the overwhelming need to breathe—it all faded away as a new attack began.

From within.

The sensation was just like the vision I'd had on the ship. That feeling of coming up for air, of breaking through the surface of a dark, murky lake to find myself somewhere I'd never been with a girl I'd never met. Only this time, the redhead wasn't perched in a tree or running through a graveyard or being raped in a kitchen. This time, she was curled up in my lap.

This time, she was mine.

And she was dying.

I knew it before the room finished coming into focus. I could feel it in my chest, in the heart that was breaking just beneath her cheek. It was a crushing, piercing, panicked kind of pain, like the slow closing of an iron maiden's door. I wanted to run, to claw my way out of that vision and back into the lake. I would gladly drown rather than feel that eviscerating pain for another second, but my movements were beyond my control.

I'd been reduced to a helpless bystander within my own body—forced to watch, but powerless to act.

My eyes traveled down the length of the girl's long copper hair and found the bottom of her thick, wavy strands stained red. An unfastened belt snaked between her legs and draped over her upper thigh, but I could hardly see it through all the blood. I'd killed more men than I could count, but I'd never seen that much blood in my life. It gushed from her open wound in spurts, timed with the rhythm of her fading heartbeat.

Darby.

I saw her as a child, bright eyes gleaming as she gazed at me with wonder—the feral boy who didn't speak was never a monster to her, never *Satan's son.* I saw her as an adolescent, felt her lips on mine, and heard a voice in my head tell me that our love was true. Then, I saw her as a woman, funeral dress hiked up to her hips as she sprinted barefoot into the woods to find me.

And she did. She always knew where to find me.

But now, my freckle-faced girl, my sunshine in the dark, my only fucking reason for living … was leaving me.

And it was all my fault.

I couldn't outrun what I was. What I'd done. I'd dragged an angel into hell because I couldn't live without her, and now, God had come to take her back.

Searing hot tears blurred my vision as I watched the movement behind her eyelids go still, felt her final breaths warm my lips. I clutched her sagging body to my chest as the soul inside of it slipped away. And as it did, my pain went with it.

Because I had made up my mind.

If God wanted to take my girl, he was going to have to go through me.

"I'm comin' with ya, angel. Ya understand? I'm not lettin' you go. I'll never fuckin' let go."

I wasn't in control of my words—I was merely listening to them being spoken—but I agreed with every fucking one of them. The pain was unbearable. I couldn't live without her. I wouldn't even try.

Kissing the freckles on her cold left hand—the ones that matched my own—I whispered the blessing I'd heard the day they appeared. According to legend, it meant that she and I had been bonded for eternity. I hoped that was true, but it didn't fucking matter.

Darby had been my eternity since the moment we'd met.

As I slid the knife from my boot, my awareness shifted to something behind me. We weren't alone.

Darby's killer was in the room.

Turning toward him as I lifted the blade into the air, my final breath came rushing in on a startled gasp. Because when I plunged that knife into my own bleeding heart, I was staring into the eyes of a man who'd been born without one.

My own fucking father.

Alexi Abramov.

The woodshop began to flicker and wave as that life slipped away, and the watery hell I'd been submerged in came seeping back into my consciousness.

Falling to the sawdust-covered floor, I watched in horror as Darby's body rolled out of my limp arms. As she landed on her side and stared back at me with vacant green eyes.

As the room dissolved around us, Darby's features began to change as well—the angle of her jaw, the slope of her nose, the shape of her lips, and the placement of her freckles. Her copper hair darkened to auburn, and when my own eyes lost focus and went still—like hers, like my ma's—the last image they saw was a collection of Russian patches blanketing her cold, dead heart.

Clo.

A feral growl clawed its way out of my throat as a blinding burst of rage surged through my bloodstream. Lunging for her, I grabbed the lapels of my blazer and ripped the jacket off over her shoulders. It was like he'd marked her with those patches, marked every woman I'd ever loved, doomed me to watch them all die at his command.

But as I shoved the jacket down Clover's arms, my lungs burning and soul on fire, I realized that she wasn't lying down anymore, and she wasn't dead. Not yet. Her smiling face was bathed in blue light, hair swirling around her anchored body as I stripped the blazer off of it and shoved it into the darkness of the lake.

I expected it to disappear into the abyss, but as I reached for my girl's hand and fought again to push off from the gold- and silver-littered ground, the blue glow darted away from us, diving into the jacket and radiating out through every opening and bullet hole. It was like watching a balloon being inflated. The blazer expanded and smoothed. The arms straightened and bent at the elbows. Beams of light streaked from the cuffs like fingers, fastening each shiny brass button until the fitting was complete. And the moment it was, the moment that shapeless creature stood at attention, proud in its bloodied, bullet-riddled finery, the light went out, the weight was lifted, and I bolted for the surface with my girl in my arms.

I couldn't get out of that water fast enough. As soon as I found my footing, I stood, chest deep in the lake, and clung to Clover's gasping body as I carried her the rest of the way out. The sound of her breathing was almost as beautiful as the sight of her face when I finally dropped to my knees on the bank and drank her in. Where I'd seen death and emptiness only seconds before, Clo's smiling eyes were now brimming with life, overflowing with it. Tears of joy sparkled in the corners as she reached up and cupped my tortured face.

Closing my eyes and leaning into her touch, I tried to convince myself that this was real. That the twisted nightmare I'd just crawled out of was nothing more than a near-death experience—some sick subconscious hallucination triggered by oxygen deprivation. But when Clo pressed her still-grinning mouth against mine, I knew there was more truth to it than I wanted to believe. Because the way she made me feel, the way she looked at me like I was invincible, but loved me like I was already broken, the way she accepted my darkness and trusted me with her light—it killed me. My heart belonged to her now, and the moment hers stopped beating, mine would have no choice but to do the same.

"Clo." Her name was a broken prayer as I dived for her lips—a confession of fear, a plea for reassurance. And she responded with a plea of her own—for more. Clover's soft, needful moans vibrated through my shattered soul as she shifted in my lap and thrust her fingers into my hair.

"It's you," she whispered, grinning against my plundering mouth. "It's always been you."

She was so fucking happy, so alive in my arms, but how was that possible when her blood was still warm on my hands?

Tightening my arm around Clo's body and splaying a hand below her jaw, I focused on the swell of her lungs, relished the rapid pounding I felt against my palm.

But it wasn't enough.

I needed to feel that pulse from the inside. Needed to bury myself in her living, breathing, writhing body until I could no longer remember what it had felt like to hold her corpse.

Until I could no longer smell the scent of blood, mixed with sawdust.

Until I could no longer feel the blade jutting out of my own heart.

Tearing my mouth away from hers, I peeled Clo's dress off over her head and dived for her throat. My teeth grazed her pulsing flesh as she reached for my shirt, unfastening a button for every savage, sucking kiss I trailed down the side of her neck.

Without lifting my head, I shrugged off the wet fabric and wet bandages as Clover quickly unclasped her bra. Arching her back to meet my hungry mouth, she whimpered as I dragged my hands over her soft, round tits, biting the swells like a man possessed before soothing the sting with the flick of my tongue. I didn't want to hurt her; I wanted to devour her—feed from her, drink from her, fill the gaping hole in my chest with her until the bleeding finally fucking stopped.

Clo's whimpers turned to moans that went straight to my cock as I sucked each straining pink nipple from base to tip. My fingertips dug into her hips as I pulled them against me, *ground* them against me, and the subtle scent of her arousal drove me even closer to the brink of madness.

Blinding need exploded through every nerve ending as Clo braced her weight on one hand and grabbed the back of my neck with the other.

"Kiss me," she pleaded, guiding my face toward her waiting lips.

Sealing my mouth over hers, I gripped her full, round arse and stood. Clo's yelp of surprise echoed through the darkening woods as I carried her to a nearby bench and set her down, impatient and desperate and dying inside.

Kneeling before her, I yanked her soaked underwear down her legs and pressed a kiss to her inner thigh. The image of spurting blood and an open tourniquet instantly turned my stomach and twisted the phantom knife in my heart. Hot, angry tears filled my eyes as I sank my teeth into that very spot, needing to taste it, touch it, feel the artery inside, whole and healthy, pulsing against my sucking lips.

Threading her fingers through my hair, Clo spread her legs wider and watched me with trusting, hooded eyes. The sight of her naked body—beautiful and bared to me before the bruises inflicted by other men had even healed—hit me like a match tossed into a can of petrol.

The feral need to consume her flared beneath my skin, and in an instant, I was on her.

Her scent, her taste, her breathy moans, her soft, slick flesh, swelling and quivering beneath my ravenous mouth—all of my senses were suddenly immersed in Clo's pleasure, and for a moment, I was free. Grief rolled off my shoulders in tingling waves as I lost myself between her thighs. With every swirl and flick of my hungry tongue, every thrust of her hips and scrape of her nails over my scalp, the horrors I'd just experienced drifted farther and farther away.

But as Clo's breathing quickened and her body tensed, I found myself right back in the woodshop, listening to her breaths go shallow as she slipped away from me, panicked and desperate to follow her into the dark. Jerking my belt and trousers open, I fisted my cock as I drank from her desire, needing to chase her over the edge, needing to follow, wherever she went.

You jump, I jump.

Tearing my mouth away, I lunged for hers, clasping her jaw as I funneled all of my fucked-up emotions into that singular kiss.

"Wait for me," I begged, tasting her need on both of our lips.

And even through her panting state of arousal, Clo smiled when she kissed me, shattering what was left of my heart. "Always."

Pulling her into a standing position, I took her place on the bench and ran my hands over the swell of her arse.

"C'mere, angel," I growled, guiding her hips down onto me as she held my gaze over her shoulder.

Clo's big green eyes slammed closed the moment I pressed against her slick, warm seam, her body tensing in anticipation.

"Shh ... I've got you," I rasped, my voice breaking at the sensation of her sweet body sucking the head of my cock. "Relax onto me, darlin'. That's it. Take what you want. Take everything I have."

With her eyes still closed and her lip between her teeth, Clo sank onto me slowly, enveloping me in a bliss I didn't deserve but couldn't live without. Once she reached her limit, my gorgeous girl spread her legs wider, leaned back against my chest, and gazed at the gathering mist on Glenshire Lough with a deep, contented sigh. It was the sound of coming home. I knew because I felt it in my chest every time she fucking looked at me.

Sweeping the wet hair off her shoulder, I sank my teeth into Clo's exposed neck and finally felt myself relax.

I could feel her heartbeat *everywhere*—fluttering beneath my sucking lips, pounding against my ribs, pulsing against my fingertips where they cupped her pussy and clutched her throat, throbbing around my swollen cock. Every surge of blood beneath her warm, flushed skin was proof of life. Proof that I hadn't lost her.

Proof that I would do anything not to.

Every move I made was guided by that heartbeat—my slow, deep thrusts; my exploring hands, skimming her breasts, massaging her clit; my tongue circling hers when she turned her head and captured my mouth with her panting lips. There wasn't a single part of me that wasn't attuned to the life pumping through her veins.

And there never would be again.

"Damien," Clo rasped, biting my bottom lip as her muscles began to quiver and her legs began to shake. "Oh God. Ah …"

I thrust into her harder, worked her faster. "That's it, angel. That's my girl. Come. Come for me."

Shaking her head, Clover squeezed her legs shut, trapping my hand between her thighs.

"You can take it, baby," I promised, rubbing her throbbing clit as my cock swelled inside her.

"Oh God …" Clo pulled her knees up to her chest as my arms circled her body, holding her tight. "Damien …"

Turning her sideways so that she was cradled in my arms, I thrust into her from underneath, the slapping of our bodies echoing through the misty woods. I claimed her mouth as her swollen, throbbing pussy began to contract around me violently.

"Oh fuck. That's it, darlin'. That's my girl. Let go. I've got ya. Let go."

Capturing my bottom lip between her teeth, Clo clutched my face and came on a cry that I felt in the depths of my fucking soul. It was the exact same frequency of pleasure and pain that I felt for her—a terrifying, overwhelming, all-consuming force of nature that had the potential to lay waste to us both.

A flood of emotion tore through me like a hurricane, exploding in hot rivers of agony and ecstasy that Clover's body drank with abandon.

I filled her with my darkness until it spilled down her thighs, until I was so blinded by her light that the images I'd just seen could no longer haunt me.

It hadn't been real. I was sure of it.

And I was going to do everything in my power to fucking keep it that way.

CHAPTER 33

CLOVER

Cradled in Damien's arms with the beauty of Glenshire Lough lying before me, I felt reborn. Awakened. Whole.

It was as if I'd gone through life with a blindfold on and Saoirse had just untied it for me. I saw everything so clearly now. Why those books had meant so much to me. Why the fairy prince had seemed so real. Why Damien's soul had called to me from across the sea, and why I'd had a vision of this exact place before I'd jumped.

I wasn't just visiting the setting of my favorite fairy tales.

I was returning to it.

To *him*.

I could have stayed there forever, basking in that revelation, relishing the fact that Damien and I were soulmates, rejoined after two decades of pain and longing, but there was a sense of urgency pressing down on me that I didn't yet understand.

Saoirse hadn't just shown me my past life; she'd given me access to it. Darby's knowledge, her experiences, her hopes and fears—I felt them as if they were my own. This person I'd admired my entire life was inside of me now, living and breathing again. She was me.

And I got the sense that she needed my help.

Our help.

"What are you thinking about?" Damien asked, unease creeping into his otherwise soothing voice.

"Us," I said, lacing my fingers through his. "Do you remember the day we met? We made magic wands out of sticks and hid behind that tree because we were so afraid of the witch." I smiled and pointed at the massive oak next to us. "I thought you were the handsomest boy I'd ever seen. You didn't speak back then, not a word, but I didn't care. I thought it was because you were a fairy, but ..." I shook my head as a new set of memories rose to the surface. My throat became tight with emotion. "Oh, Damien, the things he did to you ..."

Damien didn't reply. He simply pressed his lips to the top of my head and listened. Pushing his tragic past to the side, I tried to focus instead on the woods. On our happy place.

"When you got older, you hung a rope swing from that tree and did back flips into the lake. I never told you, but I was so impressed."

My gaze traveled to the lake, where a shroud of mist had already settled over the surface. "And we had our first kiss right there. The sun was setting, and the water turned pink and orange. Remember? That's when Saoirse gave us these." I lifted my left hand and wiggled my ring finger.

"God, I missed you." Turning in his arms, I curled toward his bare chest and pressed my lips to the side of his neck. "I think I was born missing you, Kellen."

The moment I said his former name, Damien bristled, his arms tensing around my body.

"Come on, angel," he said, kissing the top of my head again. "Let's get you dressed and see if we can find our way back to the train station. We can sleep there tonight and catch the first train to Shannon in the morning."

What?

Lifting my head, I met Damien's concerned gaze with one of bewilderment. "What are you talking about? We just got here. There's so much more I want to see. Like the cottage where we used to play. Remember the cottage? Kellen, it was your favorite place in the whole world."

Damien frowned before smoothing out his features and running a hand over my damp hair. "Darlin'," he said, using a voice that made me feel like a child, "you've never been here before. Neither of us has. All these things that feel so familiar to you … they're from stories. Fairy-tale books."

His words landed in my gut harder than the boots that had kicked me the day before in Mr. McCormick's field.

"I know," I hissed, trying to keep the hurt and anger out of my voice. "I wrote them."

Damien's face fell. He was the picture of heartbreak as his sad eyes bored into mine. "Angel," he said softly, lifting me into his arms as he stood, "I need you to listen to me."

I couldn't see his face as he carried me over to the tree where our clothes lay scattered on the bank of the lake, but I could feel his heart. It was fucking pounding.

"You didn't write those books. They were published before you were born. And your name isn't Darby. It's Clover. I think this place is fucking with our minds, and we need to go. Now."

"Go?" I wriggled out of his embrace, forcing him to set me down so that I could turn to face him. "How can you say that after everything Saoirse just showed us?"

I jerked a hand in the direction of the lake as Damien zipped his trousers and fastened his belt. Then, he took my face in his hands and kissed my frowning mouth.

I jerked away, fighting the urge to slap him.

Without another word, Damien picked my sopping wet dress up off the ground and began wringing the excess water out of it.

"You didn't see it." I shook my head, eyes wide and horrified. "No. No, that's impossible. How did you not see it?"

Damien held the dress out to me, but I refused to take it, standing naked and confused and crestfallen in front of him.

"How?" I demanded, but Damien just ignored me and began dressing me himself.

Kneeling before me, he lifted each of my legs, forcing me to step into my underwear before sliding a soggy runner onto each foot.

"I think it was oxygen deprivation, Clo," he finally said, rising to his feet to help me with my bra.

I glared at him as he slid the straps up my arms, avoiding my gaze by stepping behind me to fasten the clasp.

"So, you did see something," I snapped, cutting him with my tone since I couldn't reach him with my stare.

"I don't know what I saw."

"Yes, you do. Kellen, that was Saoirse. She shows you things. You know this. It wasn't a hallucination. It was real. Tell me what you saw. *Please.*"

"Damien," he corrected softly before tapping my shoulders with both hands. "Arms up, angel."

Spinning around, I glared up at him, feeling crazy, feeling gaslit. But the sadness and genuine concern that stared back told me that he believed what he was saying. He hadn't seen what I had.

I felt like Crazy Clover all over again.

"It was real," I declared to him, to myself, to the forest itself. "Whatever you saw, it was real. I promise."

"Clo." Damien ground the word out through gritted teeth, holding Kate's dress up for me to slide my arms into. "Please. Can we talk about this at the train station? It's almost dark, and we still have to find our way back to town."

Rage and despair pumped through my veins as I reached up and snatched the garment out of his hands.

"You don't believe me."

Turning away from me, Damien grabbed the dripping wet backpack off the ground and slung it over his shoulder, scanning the woods for a way out. He didn't argue with me, and that was what hurt the most.

"Damien"—I tried again, tempering my tone, pleading with him—"please. Please tell me you believe me. Tell me what you saw."

Glancing at me over his shoulder, Damien kept his features neutral as he extended his hand. "Come on, love. It's getting dark."

Angry tears formed in the corners of my eyes, and my chest ached under the weight of his implication. "I'm not crazy."

"I know."

He took a step toward me, and I immediately took one back, shaking my head.

"I'm not."

"Clo, please."

"I'll prove it." My anger turned to desperation as I swung my head from left to right, searching my surroundings for anything that might support my claim.

Glancing up at the branch that I'd been perched on in my vision, I noticed that the rope was missing. It must have rotted over time and …

My eyes darted to the overgrown blackberry bushes beneath that branch, and I practically dived for them, plunging my bare arms into their thorny depths until I found what I was looking for.

"Clover, stop. What are you doing? You're gonna hurt yourself."

Spinning around, I held up the proof of my sanity—a filthy, frayed length of rope.

And Damien didn't react.

"It's your rope swing," I panted. "I told you one used to be here, and look."

Again, Damien said nothing. And that was when it hit me.

"You think I read about all of this in Darby's books, don't you?"

"Clover," Damien sighed. "It doesn't matter what I think. All that matters is—"

"Yes, it does," I interrupted. "Look. Look at this. Come here."

I stomped over to the bench we'd just made love on, remembering something I'd noticed when I first sat down.

"Kellen carved this bench for me—for Darby, whatever. Do you see that date in the middle? June 14? That's the date that Saoirse bonded us, but it's also the date that Russia attacked Howth. We met on June 14, Damien. And those three dots below it? Those represent our freckles." I held up my finger again. "I'm not crazy. You have them too."

I stared at his face, waiting for recognition to dawn, but it was as if he wasn't listening to me at all. His eyes were fixated on the bench. I watched his pupils swoop back and forth, tracing the intricate lines of Kellen's Celtic knot. Turning and glancing at it again, I realized what had him so spooked.

It was the exact same design he'd etched into that sheet of metal back in the cave.

Hope bloomed in my chest as I turned to face him again, but Damien was more closed off than ever.

"That's enough," he snapped, grabbing my hand and pulling me away from the bench as if it might burst into flames. "We're leaving. Now."

As we marched up the hill, it was as if Damien had disappeared into his own mind. He didn't feel me thrashing in his grip. Didn't hear me telling him to let go. He was on some kind of autopilot, and I couldn't snap him out of it.

"Damien, slow down."

Nothing.

"What is going on? Talk to me."

Ignored.

"Damien, look. The cottage."

That did it. Damien's feet rooted themselves to the ground as I barreled into his back. The sun had nearly set, but there was enough ambient light left in the woods to make out the crumbling, vine-encrusted silhouette of a stone structure in a small clearing.

Damien's body tensed as he stared at the ruin. The place that had once been Kellen's sanctuary. His only safe space in a village that had been told to hate him.

Heat radiated off of his body as some unexpressed emotion boiled to the surface. Dread. Hatred. Sorrow. I couldn't tell, but whatever it was, it slithered up my arm like a venomous snake, making me want to break free and run.

Without releasing my hand, Damien walked around to the entrance, and I don't think I breathed once. A flood of memories filled my mind as I waited for him to react.

A tea set.

The taste of vanilla.

A black flight jacket left on the ground.

Black boots, pacing.

And pacing.

And pacing.

The roof was long gone, but the arched doorway remained, and in the shadows of the darkening wood, it felt more like the entrance of a tomb than a playhouse.

Walking backward, Damien pulled me away from the building as if it might sprout teeth and eat us alive.

"It's too dark," he said before turning and marching the rest of the way up the hill.

I didn't know what that meant. Was it too dark inside the cottage? Too dark to find our way out of the woods? Or was it too dark inside his head, where his thoughts seemed to be spiraling and his temples pulsed with every surge of blood from his pounding heart?

Struggling to keep up, I glanced at the sky and noted the heavy gray clouds swirling overhead.

Even that felt familiar.

As soon as we crested the top of the hill, an arch of lightning streaked the sky, illuminating a wide expanse of farmland through the trees below.

An elated sigh burst from my lungs before we started our descent down the hill, both of us moving quickly now for two very different reasons. Sprinting straight through the tree line, I dragged Damien behind me as I raced toward a wooden fence that was broken in more places than it was intact.

The field beyond the fence looked like it hadn't been mowed in decades, and there wasn't a single light on in the house or barn on the far side of the meadow, but I could see every detail in my mind.

Standing beside me, Damien finally loosened his grip on my hand.

I hoped that he saw what I saw. That being here would help him remember, help solidify whatever epiphany he'd been having in the woods.

But instead, Damien breathed a sigh of relief and said, "If we cut through this field, the road on the other side of the house should take us back to town."

My heart sank as a bitter laugh tore through my chest.

"Back to town?" I said, shaking my head. "Damien … we're home."

CHAPTER 34

DAMIEN

Clo was determined to get inside that house, and I knew if I didn't help her do it, I was going to have to carry her kicking and screaming all the way back to the train station.

The place was abandoned and looked like it had been for years. Backlit against the flashing thunderclouds, the shape of it was fucked. The walls buckled. The roof sagged and had saplings growing out of it. But Clover couldn't wait to get inside that death trap, which meant I was going in with her.

The wooden trim was so rotten that I didn't even have to kick the door in. One firm shove was all it took.

I'd planned on making her wait outside while I checked the place out, but before I could enter, something about the barn next to the house caught my eye. It seemed strangely familiar, but while I stood there, staring, Clo ducked under my arm and disappeared into the pitch-black gaff.

Shite.

"Dammit, Clo." I bolted in after her, but hadn't made it more than two steps when the strike of a match stopped me cold.

Illuminated behind it was the awestruck, wide-eyed face of my girl. "I … I remembered where the matches were."

Silence stretched between us as I struggled to rationalize away this new piece of information. The rope, the bench, the cottage … those could all be details in one of Darby Donovan's books—at least, that's what I was telling myself—but the drawer she'd kept her matches in?

There was just enough ambient light from the windows and open door for me to make out the basic lines of a kitchen— cabinets and counters, a sink, a refrigerator.

Of course. Every kitchen has a pack of matches in one of the drawers. Clo just got lucky.

Waving the match out before it burned her fingers, she lit another one, then turned and opened one of the cabinets. I couldn't see what she was doing, but I could hear the match pop and hiss as the light grew brighter around her.

Turning to face me, Clo held two lit candlesticks and handed one to me. "I knew where these were too," she said quietly.

My blood ran cold.

I accepted the candle without a word and followed Clover through the house. Normally, I would have been in front, shielding her from whatever might be lurking in the shadows, but I couldn't see more than a meter in any direction. Clo, on the other hand, moved through the space like she'd lived there her entire life. The only thing that surprised her was when she stepped in the occasional puddle or felt a drip from the leaky roof.

The place smelled like mildew and groaned with every step we took, as if our presence was causing it physical pain.

I felt the same fucking way.

Clover headed straight down a hallway and into a bedroom, where she immediately located and lit at least six more candles as if she could see them in the dark.

I just stood in the doorway and watched as she sprinted around the room, touching every object, smelling them, clutching them to her chest. Every glint of familiarity, every gasp of recognition felt like another hole being torn through my paper-thin veil of denial.

But I clung to it anyway. With both fucking hands.

"Damien, I can't believe this. It's all still here. Nobody has touched a thing since we"—she glanced up at me—"*they* died."

Clover tore through every drawer, every shelf, every shoebox under the bed. There was an urgency behind her actions. An intention. This wasn't just some walk down memory lane. Clo was on a mission, and I didn't fucking like the direction it was headed in.

"I wonder who owns this place now.

"Why has it been vacant this whole time?

"Maybe everyone thinks it's haunted.

"Why on earth would anyone want to kill them?

"I wonder what room it happened in.

"Were they shot? Saoirse didn't show me that part. Why wouldn't she show me? Did she think I'd be upset?

"Oh my God, Darby's journals."

Clo began pulling notebook after notebook off the top shelf of the wardrobe, tossing them on the floor until she found one that struck her as important. Flipping to the back, she thumbed through a section of blank pages until she found the last entry.

"God, her handwriting even looks like mine." She smiled.

Then, her face fell as her eyes swept back and forth across the page.

"She was worried about you. You'd been acting paranoid but wouldn't tell her why." Her eyes found mine. "I know the feeling."

She was speaking about me like I was him again. It was definitely time to go.

Closing the notebook, Clo leveled me with a suspicious stare.

"What did you see? In the lake."

I shook my head, feeling my blood heat and my heart pound at the very mention of that experience.

"Why won't you tell me?"

I shoved a hand through my hair and pushed away from the door, needing to move, needing to bolt.

"Damien, whatever you saw, Saoirse showed it to you for a reason," Clo said. "We are *here* for a reason. And I think that reason is for us to right a wrong. To finally get justice for what happened to them. To *us*."

"The only us that matters is *us*," I said, jabbing a finger back and forth from my heart to hers. "And if we don't get the fuck off this island, we're going to end up just like *them*."

Clo winced and jerked away from me.

Regret roiled in my empty stomach as I took a deep breath and tried to calm the fuck down.

"Maybe not," she said quietly. "Maybe we can stay here, in Glenshire. Use fake names, lie low. It's a small village. The Russians will probably leave it alone. We can get jobs in town—"

"Stay here? Are you fuckin' serious, Clo? This place is pure evil. I can feel it on my skin. I can feel it slithering into my brain. Everything that has happened since we got here has been fucked, and the sooner we leave, the—"

My stupid diatribe died on my tongue as Clo's face suddenly fell. Not because of my shitty tone or my refusal to support her little murder mystery mission, but because something in the wardrobe had caught her eye.

And mine.

Sliding a shiny black flight jacket off a hanger, Clover held it up in front of her with both hands, then hugged it to her chest and burst into tears.

And I almost did the same.

I'd seen that jacket in my nightmare. I knew the weight of it, the way it always felt cool to the touch. I knew that it had orange lining and a tear on the right sleeve. But mostly, I knew the pang of bitterness I felt in my chest every time I was wearing it instead of her.

Sitting on the floor, surrounded by Darby's journals, Clover pressed the jacket to her face—*my* jacket—and wept.

Setting the backpack down, I knelt before her and watched her mourn, unable to speak, unable to bridge the gap between the revelation taking place in my soul and the rationalization that had taken root in my mind.

"I feel so far away from him."

Clover's words were a dagger through my chest, pinning my heart to my rib cage like a fucking ransom note. For the second time in as many hours, I felt that organ bleed out, only this time, death wasn't coming to take away my pain. This time, I had to fucking live with it.

I wanted to grab her face and force her to look at me. I wanted to tell her that he … *I* was sitting right in front of her. That she wasn't crazy. That I was beginning to remember too.

But accepting that reality meant admitting that I was the reason she'd died. It meant admitting that I was putting her in the exact same position again. And I couldn't. Not while her blood was still warm on my hands.

Pulling her into my lap, I held her sobbing body and felt every gasp and shudder like a fist to the chest.

"You have his eyes, but you don't feel like him. Nothing feels like him. He's just … gone. He's gone."

The next words that I spoke came through me, not from me, and it wasn't until Clo's eyes lifted and found mine that I realized what they were.

"*Is fíor bhur ngrá.*"

Saoirse's blessing.

And Kellen's final words to his wife.

Clover's tear-streaked lips fell open, and my mouth crashed into them like the bursting of a dam, flooding her with all of the confusion, certainty, desperation, and terror that my body could no longer contain. A purging of poison that she accepted with pleasure.

Clinging to my damp shirt with both fists, Clo kissed me back with an urgency that rivaled my own, and something inside of me stirred.

Awakened.

And fucking roared.

Breaking our kiss only to peel her wet dress off over her head, I laid Clover down on the pile of scattered notebooks and continued my assault on her mouth as her fingers made short work of the buttons on my shirt and trousers. We seemed to move in synchrony—every swirl of our tongues, every suck, every sigh was a perfectly choreographed dance that I didn't remember learning.

Although I'd spent hours with my hands on her body and my mouth on her mouth over the last two days, it hadn't been enough for me to learn the things I suddenly knew. She'd felt unfamiliar to me—everything had. Every touch, every position had been a first of epic proportions. But this time, when I cupped her tits and traced her perfect pebbled nipples through the fabric of her bra, I knew exactly what sound she was going to make before she made it. I knew the way her moan would vibrate against my lips when I sucked the tender flesh just below her jaw. And I knew the way her back would arch when I kissed my way down her neck, unfastening her bra as I went, and lavished both straining pink peaks with my tongue.

But when Clo unzipped my trousers and took my length in both hands, I realized that she knew me even better. Echoes of some unknown fear engulfed my body in an instant, boiling my blood and seizing my throat, but it passed with every gentle, comforting stroke. Clo touched me like she'd known that I would have that reaction before I did, and the significance of that knowledge hit me like a battering ram.

"Oh, Damien, the things he did to you …"

The shame and rage and nauseating helplessness of a past I couldn't remember ignited my skin, seared my eyes, but Clo was there to soothe it away, to free me from a burden I hadn't known I'd been carrying.

And I wanted to free her as well.

I wanted to use this fire that burned beneath my flesh to make her melt, to reduce her to a writhing puddle of ecstasy so that when she finally cooled, she'd be new again. Cracks sealed. Whole and happy.

Kissing my way down her stomach, I hooked my fingers into the sides of her underwear and peeled them off as Clover's gentle fingers slid through my wet hair.

Her touch felt like home, her thighs, her soft gasps. When I'd tasted her down by the lake, the experience had been a first for me. I hadn't known what I was doing, and I certainly hadn't known how she would respond. But now … it was as if I was operating on muscle memory. I knew exactly what to do, how she would moan when I flicked my tongue against her swollen clit. The way she would arch her back when I swirled it around her dripping entrance, greedily chasing the salty-sweet memories that were just beyond my reach. And I knew when those moans turned to whimpers and her legs tensed on either side of my head, that two fingers, thrust in to the last knuckle, would make her come so hard that her legs would shake, and her hips would buck, and her nails would dig into my scalp.

At least, they would have, *before*.

Now, I kept my hands where Clover could see them. Splayed across her stomach, wrapped around her thighs, pinching and rolling her tight nipples between my fingers. And as her back arched and her breathing quickened, I flattened my tongue and applied more pressure until she did exactly what I'd imagined. Clover clutched my head, sank her nails into my scalp, and rolled her hips against my feasting mouth as the last shreds of my denial burst into flames. My body had just proven what my brain hadn't been willing to accept. That this woman was mine and had been long before I spotted her across the Irish Sea. That I'd loved her before. I'd lost her before. And I'd cut out my own heart for the chance to be here, doing it all over again.

As if I could feel her watching me, I glanced up to find two awestruck green eyes flickering in the candlelight.

Sliding her hand from my hair down to my jaw, Clover lifted my chin as she slowly sat up, never blinking, never once taking her eyes off mine.

I pushed up onto my knees as her massive black pupils darted back and forth between mine. Then, a sweet smile unfurled across her tear-streaked face.

"Kellen," she whispered, her chin buckling as her eyes dropped to my lips.

This time, when our mouths collided, it was Clo's darkness that fed *me*, her despair that I so hungrily consumed. I wanted to take it all from her. All the pain I had caused, in this lifetime and the last. All the pain she'd suffered while we were apart. I wanted to suck it from her parted pink lips, and when she straddled my kneeling thighs and slid her slick flesh along my cock, I knew she wanted to do the same for me.

"Take it, angel," I rasped against her lips. "Take it from me. Please."

And with that whispered plea, Clover held her breath, stared into my eyes, and did exactly as I'd asked.

She took my pain away.

No drug, no anesthetic could possibly compare to the mind-numbing bliss that enveloped me the moment Clover's tight, warm body welcomed me in. Clutching the back of my neck with both hands, she whimpered against my lips as she began to rise and fall, taking me just a bit deeper each time. I kept my hands above her waist—rubbing her tits, cupping her jaw, gathering her hair in my fist—anything that would keep me from grabbing her arse and filling her with one feral thrust like I wanted to. After everything she'd been through, Clo needed to be handled gently. She was too fucking sweet for this world, an angel in the flesh, and I …

I was even less worthy of her than I'd feared.

I wasn't just the man who'd destroyed her life.

I was the man who'd destroyed her life *twice*.

Clover's soft moans of pleasure pulled me back into the present, but it was too late. My pain had returned, along with two lifetimes' worth of guilt and self-hatred.

But the deeper I spiraled, the higher Clo climbed.

Cradling my face with both hands, Clover whimpered against my lips as she finally sank all the way onto me. Stretched to her limit, she stilled and pressed her smiling lips to mine, as close to me as she could physically be, while emotionally, I was as far away as I could possibly get. Clo had found what she'd been missing her entire life, and witnessing that joy, being a part of it, was the only thing keeping me out of the darkest corners of my mind.

She might not have deserved a selfish, murderous piece of shite like me, but my sweet girl deserved to feel good. And I could do that for her.

Using all the self-control I could muster, I grabbed Clo's arse with both hands and slowly rolled her hips back and forth so that her clit ground against my pelvis. Her soft, throaty moans vibrated against my lips as she sealed her mouth over mine, and the sound alone was enough to have my cock leaking pre-cum inside of her.

I wanted so badly to lose myself in her, to pound out all of my fears and regrets and failures until I was nothing more than a sweaty, mindless animal, and my resolve was slipping. With every passing second, my movements grew faster; my pressure increased. Clo's moans grew louder. Her pussy clenched. Nails pierced skin. Fists pulled hair.

But it wasn't until my girl captured my bottom lip between her teeth and cried, "Kellen," that my willpower snapped completely.

Diving to the floor, I sank into her and unleashed everything I'd thought she was too delicate to handle in an uncontrollable torrent of thrusts and grunts and growls and moans. I clung to her body with white knuckles as I tried to exorcise the ghost of my past, and Clo clung to me just as tightly for the opposite reason.

She couldn't get close enough to it.

Digging her nails into my back, Clover sank her teeth into the curve of my neck and whimpered through an orgasm that made her entire body contract around me like a fist. She held me as tightly as she could with everything that she had—her limbs, her mouth, her throbbing cunt—and in that moment, I realized that Clover wasn't the delicate one.

I was.

Because her strength, her unconditional love and acceptance—it fucking broke me.

When I thrust into her fully, a flood of pleasure and unspeakable pain surged through my body, exploding in a river of hot cum and silent, blinding tears. And my angel took it, just like I'd begged her to. She drank my darkness, welcomed it in, but relief never came. The past still festered like a cancer in my soul. I could feel it growing, gnawing at my consciousness. It demanded to be acknowledged. It demanded to be seen.

I held Clo's soft, warm body until her breaths slowed and her eyelids began to flutter. Then, I picked her up and laid her on the bed.

Our bed.

I didn't remember sleeping there. I didn't remember a single thing about that house.

But I remembered the barn.

And it was fucking calling to me.

CHAPTER 35

DAMIEN

Kellen's clothes fit perfectly, down to his boots. But I didn't put on his jacket. That I returned to its rightful owner, draping it over Clo's beautiful, naked body before I tiptoed out the door.

I took a candle to light my way through the house. None of it felt familiar—antique furniture, old paintings, old lamps—but I'd found it in the dark. I'd led us straight there from the lake, and that fact left a sinking feeling in my gut.

Closing the back door as quietly as I could, considering the rotten, creaking doorframe holding it up, I stood on the patio and stared at the looming building to my right.

The entire sky was blanketed with clouds that seemed to glow from within. I couldn't see the moon illuminating them, but I knew it was there, just like I couldn't see what was inside the barn, but I knew it wasn't fucking stables and hay.

I knew.

With every step I took through the overgrown weeds, the scent of blood and sawdust grew stronger in my mind. By the time my fingers wrapped around the door handle, bile was searing the back of my throat. And when I finally pulled the heavy wooden slab open and stepped inside, I did it with my eyes closed and my heart slamming into my ribs.

I didn't need to see to know what I'd stepped into. Every detail of that woodshop was tattooed on my soul. I could picture every tool in the tool chest, the make and model of every gun I had stashed in those cabinets. I could picture the exact size, shape, color, and wood grain of the workbench directly across from me. And I could see the patch of concrete, covered in blood, where I'd held my wife's dying body before I followed her into the dark.

I didn't want to open my eyes. I wanted to turn around and go back into the house and hold my girl, who was very much still alive, until I could convince myself that it had all been a near-death hallucination again.

But it was too late.

You couldn't unknow something.

And I knew, before I even cracked my eyelids and focused on the massive rust-colored stain in the center of the floor, that my worst fucking nightmare had already come true.

I'd failed her.

I'd failed her, and I'd found her, and I hadn't learned a fucking thing.

Because I still couldn't walk away.

Being with me put a target on her back that I was too selfish to remove.

But the thing about targets was, the farther away they were, the harder they were to hit.

So, I would do what Kellen should have done a long time ago. I would get my girl out of the fucking country, put an ocean between us and Alexi, and start a new life as far away from the Bratva as fucking possible.

I would never be able to forget what I'd done.

But I'd spend the rest of my life making sure that Clo never had to remember.

CHAPTER 36

CLOVER

May you be in heaven half an hour
Before the Devil knows you're dead.

"That was my grandfather's favorite saying." I walked up beside Damien and squeezed his arm as he stared at a faded, dust-covered plaque on the kitchen wall.

He was wearing Kellen's clothes—black jeans, black shirt, black boots—and I had traded my damp sundress for Darby's Trinity College jumper and a pair of black leggings. It was so strange to think that we might have been standing in this exact same spot over twenty years ago, wearing the exact same clothes on a different pair of bodies.

Damien's energy was off. He didn't respond when I touched him. Didn't reply when I spoke. After the way he'd made love to me the night before—the emotional catharsis he'd had in my arms—I was so sure that I'd finally gotten through to him. That he was finally beginning to remember.

But when I'd woken up, he'd been gone. And evidently, so was his breakthrough.

"Actually, it was Darby's grandfather, but you know what I meant. This was his house before he left it to her. It's so weird; I don't remember any of that happening. I just … know it."

No response.

"Do you remember this plaque? You've been staring at it for a while."

A single shake of his head.

"Did you sleep at all? When I woke up in the middle of the night, you were gone."

Another shake.

"Damien." I spun to face him. "That's two nights in a row. Other than passing out on the train yesterday, you haven't slept in over forty-eight hours."

Finally returning my gaze with two bloodshot, hooded eyes, Damien simply replied, "And I'll sleep on the train again, on our way to Shannon. You ready?"

"Ready?" My voice was shrill. "I already told you. I'm not leaving. Not until I find out what happened to them. To *us.* That's why we're here, Damien. Don't you see that? The universe brought us here for a reason."

"*You* brought us here," Damien snapped, the force of his words causing him to sway on his unsteady feet. "And we've stayed long enough. I won't lose you again, Clover."

"Again?"

Hope stirred in my chest as those exhausted gray eyes struggled to focus on mine. Gray eyes that Father Sullivan had said looked just like Kellen's. He was remembering. I knew he was.

"When you were captured," Damien clarified, tilting his head back and sucking in a labored breath. "I thought I'd lost you when you were captured … in Howth."

Rage simmered beneath my skin. He was hiding something. I could feel it.

"Please, Clo," Damien begged, closing his eyes. "We have to leave."

"Not until I find out what happened. Saoirse didn't show me. None of Darby's journals give any clues. Something terrible happened here, Damien, and I think it's our destiny to right those wrongs. I'm sorry if you can't see that, but—"

"All I see"—Damien's eyelids lifted, revealing a colorless well of worry as he clasped my hands with weak fingers—"is a girl that I can't live without. I'm sorry if keeping you safe interferes with your little murder mystery, but it's my top priority, now and always."

"Interferes with my what?" I stepped out of his grasp with a jerk, feeling my face heat and my pulse begin to climb.

"You know what I mean." Damien rubbed his temples as his heavy eyelids lost their battle against gravity again.

"No, I don't."

Damien sighed with his whole body. "All of this stuff with Kellen and Darby is just a fantasy, angel. A … distraction from everything that's happened, everything you lost."

His body slumped against the wall while I just stood there, vibrating with anger.

After everything I'd shown him the night before—the bench, the rope swing, the way I knew my way around the house—he was going to ignore all my proof and jump straight to the conclusion that I was some hysterical woman, suffering from some grief-induced mental breakdown.

That I was Crazy Clover, living in her imaginary world again.

"I'm not crazy," I hissed, feeling my hands ball into fists at my sides.

Damien sighed. "I didn't say ya were, love. You're just—"

"And I'm not leaving." I folded my arms across my chest.

"This mystery you're trying to solve, it won't change anything, ya know. It won't bring them back."

"Us!" I shouted. "Stop saying them. It's us, and you know it!"

"No. *Them*. Your family."

Damien's words extinguished my rage like a bucket of ice water as I considered what he was saying. Was I just trying to distract myself from my grief? Was I putting us in danger by staying?

Before I got the chance to answer those questions, Damien's knees buckled, and I had to dive under his arm to keep him from falling. His body was shutting down. The man hadn't slept more than two hours in the last two days, and he was still recovering from two gunshot wounds. He needed to lie down more than he needed me to challenge which one of us was in denial.

"Come on, handsome," I said, steering him out of the kitchen and toward the bedroom. "Time for bed."

Bobbing his head and slurring his speech, Damien protested, but he was too weak and shaky to push me away.

The only words I could make out as I laid him down and unlaced his boots were, "Please, Clo … stop. He's gonna kill you … he's gonna kill you too."

Dear Damien,

I'll probably be back before you wake up, but if not, I went to the church to see if Father Sullivan knows anything. Be home soon.

Love,

Clover

After leaving a note on the kitchen table, I slipped out through the broken back door and into the breezy cloud-covered morning. The sun had risen, but was nowhere to be seen as I gazed across the overgrown meadow at the forest and the purple mountain beyond. The top of it punctured the clouds, mirroring the wound I felt in my chest after my argument with Damien.

I kept telling myself that his refusal to believe what was happening was about him, not me, but when I'd spent most of my life being told that I was crazy, that I should doubt what my heart knew to be true, that my delusions were nothing more than coping mechanisms created by a traumatized child with an overactive imagination … that was easier said than done.

I needed more proof. I needed answers. And I needed them before Damien woke up and carried me, kicking and screaming, back to Glenshire Station.

I couldn't have found my way back to the church before my encounter with Saoirse, but now, I knew exactly how to get there. I just knew.

With one last glance at the mountain, an aching in my heart, and a certainty in my soul, I turned to head toward the driveway …

And found myself face-to-face with a woman staring at me from the other side of the fence.

Clutching my chest with a yelp, I took a deep breath and released it on an embarrassed laugh.

"Sorry," I said, walking toward her through the knee-high weeds with a polite smile plastered on my face. "You scared me. For a second there, I thought you were a ghost."

The woman's laser-focused eyes narrowed with every step I took toward her.

"I could say the same about you, love." A touch of shakiness in her voice betrayed her defensive posture. She appeared to be in her sixties but had the sharpness of someone much younger. A mostly gray braid hung over her shoulder, and her freckled skin was weather-beaten, probably from years spent tending to the sheep grazing in her pasture.

"Ya seem lost." She tilted her head, analyzing me in a way that made me feel like I must have sprouted horns in my sleep. "Do ya need help … findin' yer way?"

Her tone was cryptic, her face guarded, but there was a familiarity about her, a warmth, that I chose to trust.

"No, miss. I know where I am. I'm here to investigate the murders of Darby and Kellen Donovan."

She scoffed. "Bit late for that, don't ya think?"

I smiled weakly and nodded, stopping a few meters away from the fence. "Better late than never.

"I'm Clover," I added, lifting a hand in an awkward, unnecessary wave. "Darby Donovan was ... *is* my favorite author. I just ... want to find out what happened to her."

"What else is she to ya?" she asked, boldly lifting her chin.

My palms began to sweat. "I ... I'm not sure what you mean."

"Ya look just like her, child. So much that I thought you were her ghost. She your kin or somethin'?"

I released a breath and responded with a relieved smile. "Or something."

Nodding slowly, she gratefully didn't press me for more information. "I see. We all have our secrets, don't we?"

"And your name is?"

"Nora. Been living here since the place belonged to Darby's granda. She gave me his flock when he died. Sweet girl, that one. Not a day goes by that I don't miss seein' her."

"Do you know what happened to her? All it says online is that she and her husband were killed during a home invasion."

"That's what they say, isn't it?" Nora sighed.

"Is that not what happened?"

Glancing over my shoulder, Nora flicked her chin in the direction of the barn. "Not unless you consider a woodshop a home."

I turned and looked at the renovated structure. It was definitely in disrepair, but appeared to be far newer than the farmhouse. "That's a woodshop?"

"Aye. Kellen was a gifted woodworker. There was evil in him though. You could see it in his eyes. And rumor had it that he killed the village priest when he was just a lad, but he wouldn't have hurt a hair on Miss Darby's head. He loved that girl somethin' fierce."

"Do you have any idea who did it?"

"None. Nobody does, except for maybe ... Darby's uncle. Eamonn O'Toole. He was some big-shot detective up in Dublin. He came by and spoke to the local guards as soon as it happened, and it was as if the whole thing got swept under the rug. No investigation. No crime scene tape. He just … locked the doors and put a *For Sale* sign in the yard."

"And nobody ever bought the place?"

"Folks out here have a healthy respect for the spirit world."

"So, people think the house is haunted."

"Aye. And the forest."

"This detective, Darby's uncle, do you know where I could reach him?"

"He's a very old man now. Went looney a few years back and has been hospitalized ever since. Probably on death's doorstep by now. Doubt you'll get much out of him at this point."

"I have to try. Do you think I could borrow your phone? Perhaps if I call the hospital—"

"Haven't ya heard, love? Mobile network's down in Dublin. No calls in or out."

"But the trains are still running?"

"For now. Volunteers from the union are keepin' it runnin' so folks can evacuate, but it's just a matter of time until the Russians shut that down too."

"And you wouldn't happen to know the name of this hospital, would ya?"

"Oh, darlin'. If you're thinkin' about going anywhere near Dublin, you'd better think again. The whole city's a war zone now. Look, I don't know what kind of … *attachment* ya had to Miss Darby, but findin' out who killed her isn't worth riskin' yer life."

"Respectfully, Ms. Nora"—I swallowed—"I think that it is."

CHAPTER 37

DAMIEN

Dear Damien,

~~I'll probably be back before you wake up, but if not, I went to the church to see if Father Sullivan knows anything. Be home soon.~~

I went to Dublin to find Darby's uncle. He knows who killed us, but he won't live much longer, so I have to speak to him before we leave for America.

I'm so sorry.

I know you don't believe me, or maybe you just don't want to, but we're here for a reason, Damien. I can feel it. We're supposed to set things right, and I can't do that until I find out what happened.

Please don't worry. I'll be back tonight with answers, and then we can decide what to do next. Together.

I promise.

Love,

Clover

P.S. There's food on the counter from the neighbor.

The decades-old paper practically turned to dust in my fist …

Just before I punched that fist through the closest fucking wall.

The room spun.

My head spun.

And bile seared the back of my throat as I stumbled outside and dry-heaved from the depths of my miserable guts.

The last time I'd woken up and she was gone, I'd had to kill a dozen armed Russians and take another bullet to save her.

Now, she was headed into the eye of the storm, and I didn't have a fucking clue where she was going or how much of a head start she'd gotten.

And this time, it was my fucking fault.

If I had just told her what she wanted to know, admitted to her what I'd seen in the lake, what I knew in my fucking soul to be true, she'd be on a train to Shannon right now with her head on my shoulder instead of Dublin with a fucking target on her back.

Movement in my peripheral vision caused my head to snap to the left and my hands to ball into fists.

An older woman was standing near the fence, watching me as she pretended to pick tomatoes. She'd been so still and quiet that I'd had no idea she was even there, but the moment our eyes met, she became a flurry of sound and movement. Flailing hands muffled a high-pitched yelp as she stumbled backward, away from me and toward the house.

P.S. There's food on the counter from the neighbor.

The neighbor.

Five seconds later, my fist—still covered in plaster dust—was pounding on the front door of a farmhouse that was painted the same shade of purple as the spots on the sheep in its pasture.

The curtains on the window next to the door fluttered before a female voice exclaimed, "Go away!" from inside the house.

"Hello!" I shouted back, dropping my fist. "My name is Damien Hughes. I believe you spoke to my …"

My what? My soulmate? My immortal beloved? My entire reason for fucking living?

"My *wife* earlier."

"I know who ya are," she snarled, her voice loud and clear through the drafty, weather-beaten door. "Be gone, Devil!"

"Did she say where in Dublin she was going? Please … I have to find her." It took all my strength not to put my fist through her fucking door as well.

"She prob'ly went back to the spirit world, where she belongs. Where ya both belong! Get off my porch, demon, before I call Father Sullivan!"

"If you know something, please tell me! You don't understand how much danger she's in."

"I didn't want to believe it when I saw Miss Darby. She seemed so … *alive.* But you … I'd know those eyes anywhere. Death incarnate—that's what you are. Always were, always will be."

"Look out the window again!" I shouted, turning to face the curtains she'd just drawn.

"And why would I do that? You're prob'ly gonna try to steal my soul through the glass."

"Because I can prove to you that I'm not a ghost or a demon or the goddamn Devil himself. Just look out the window. Please!"

Lifting the bottom of Kellen's shirt halfway up my torso, I waited a full minute before the curtains finally fluttered again, which was followed by a gasp so loud I could hear it outside.

"Jesus, Mary, and Joseph, that's a nasty gash."

"Ya can't injure a ghost, ma'am. I'm alive. I swear it."

Nora accepted my explanation with a single nod. "So what the hell happened to ya?"

"The same thing that's gonna happen to Clover if you don't tell me exactly where she went."

Four hours on a train, alone, with zero distractions from my dark fucking thoughts and worst-case scenarios was a punishment worse than death.

And I would fucking know.

Every town and village I passed through looked normal, other than the crushing swells of people crowding the platforms of the trains headed toward Shannon. The buildings and houses were still intact. There were no tanks lining the streets or drones dotting the skies.

Not until I got to the capital.

The smoke was what caught my eye first. It hovered over the city in black and gray tendrils, like a ghost reluctantly leaving a corpse.

And the closer I got to the city center, the more corpselike it became.

Buildings that had once been the backdrop of my childhood were now frail, twisted skeletons, leaking sparks from their severed veins. Their brick exteriors had been reduced to heaping piles of rubble and ash that completely buried the sidewalks and streets. Every car was a gray metal can, dented and hollowed out and smoking from its melted tires. In fact, everything in the entire fucking city was gray, other than the bright orange fires burning among the wreckage.

I couldn't see the fighting from my window, but I could hear it, even over the rumble of the train and the rushing of blood in my ears. Gunshots, machine-gun blasts, and small explosions rattled the windows and vibrated through my chest, each one causing my back to go more rigid and my fingers to squeeze the armrests even tighter. The plastic groaned and cracked in my hands before I finally stood and paced the aisle, looking out every window for an auburn-haired girl or a sign pointing me to St. Patrick's Psychiatric Hospital.

As much as I wanted to mourn for my city, for the home that I'd dreamed of returning to for the last five years, the only thing I gave a shit about as I pulled into Heuston Station was finding Clo and getting the fuck out of there.

I bolted off the train the second the doors began to open and sprinted for the nearest exit, slowing to a walk as soon as I noticed a cluster of Russian soldiers gathered around a laptop. A drone flew in through the open exit doors, docking on one of several charging pads strewn all over the floor.

Fuck.

I hadn't even considered the drones.

They were allowing people to evacuate now, so I assumed these drones were being used for combat, but I knew if one of those soldiers saw a gorgeous redhead walking alone on their laptop screen, they'd switch their device back to Prisoner of War mode real fucking quick.

The only thing that kept me from losing my shit was the fact that she wasn't naked in the middle of that group of men right now. If the drones had found her, these guys would have made damn sure they got a taste before sending her to the nearest encampment.

Or maybe they already had. She did have a two-hour head start.

Fuck.

The smoke that filled my lungs and burned my eyes as I slipped outside was a welcome distraction from the spiraling thoughts in my mind. Keeping to the shadows, I quickly assessed the situation on Steeven's Lane.

After seeing the destruction from the train, I expected to walk straight into a wall of rubble as soon as I left the station, but that part of Dublin was surprisingly untouched. The Russians probably didn't want to risk destroying anything that might be of importance to them later, like transportation hubs or water and sanitation stations or …

Hospitals.

Turning to the right, I ran as quickly and as quietly as my starving, injured body possibly could, listening for drones, suppressing the agonizing urge to cough. My eyes swept across the terrain, scanning for anyone with dark red hair, but there was no one on the street. The fighting sounded close, maybe a kilometer or two away, but it was far enough that it gave me hope.

St. Patrick's Psychiatric Hospital was just up ahead, bordered on all sides by a four-meter-tall stone wall. I remembered it from when I was a kid. It was the kind of place they didn't want people escaping from, and if Clo made it inside, it was probably the safest place in the entire city.

My wounds screamed, and adrenaline surged as I pushed myself to run faster, less concerned with being heard or seen now that I knew where the enemy was and my destination was in sight.

As soon as I saw that the metal gate in the wall was wide open, I felt myself exhale in relief.

Just before an errant rocket brought my entire world crashing down.

CHAPTER 38

CLOVER

"Mrs., em … Donovan? You're in luck. Your uncle is awake and somewhat lucid today. Please, follow me."

St. Patrick's Psychiatric Hospital was being run by a skeleton crew, thanks to the mass exodus from the city, and the few people who'd stayed to care for the patients seemed shell-shocked and vacant. I wasn't sure if it was their desire to care for others or their basic need for normalcy that kept them coming back, but whatever the reason, it was obvious that by this point in the invasion, checking visitor IDs was pretty low on their list of priorities.

I'd given them Darby's name just in case I needed to be a blood relative to visit. Eamonn O'Toole was the only person alive who might be able to tell me what I needed to know, and I wasn't going to risk my chance to see him by letting them know that I was a perfect stranger.

I followed the hollow-eyed nurse down a clinical gray hallway to a door that had to be opened with a key card.

The first thing I noticed was a large window that looked out over Steeven's Lane. Of course, I couldn't see the road through the massive stone wall encircling the hospital, but I could see the taller buildings behind it. At least, the ones that were still standing.

I didn't think anything could affect me as much as the destruction of Howth, but riding through the wasteland that Dublin had become ripped the newly formed scabs off of all of my still-fresh traumas.

I was so close to home, and yet I was homeless.

Images of blood-splattered plaster and a severed hand flashed behind my eyes before I shut them down, taking a deep breath and shaking my head as I stepped farther into the room.

It was small, but sunlit, and spacious enough for some basic institutional furniture and, of course, a TV, which a very old, very frail man was staring at from his elevated position in a hospital bed.

"Good afternoon, Mr. O'Toole," the nurse boomed, getting his attention.

After a second or two, the man's beady blue eyes shifted slowly to hers, and his wrinkled eyelids appeared to be dropping from more than just old age.

"He just had his afternoon meds," the nurse explained quietly, "so he should be nice and calm for ya."

Clearly.

"Mr. O'Toole, this is your niece, Darby Donovan. She came by to say hello. Isn't that nice?"

Dropping her voice to a normal volume again, she added, "Don't be scared, love. This one's harmless. He just has trouble grasping reality sometimes, which, honestly, might be a blessing these days."

I nodded in understanding and held her haunted stare, but it only lasted a second before she turned and headed for the door.

"There's a red panic button on the wall by the bed," she added from the narrow entryway. "Press it if ya need anything."

The door closed with an ominous, automated click, and I suddenly found myself locked in a room with a drugged psychiatric patient in the middle of an active war zone.

I probably should have been concerned about my safety, but my thoughts were split between needing to find out what was in this man's head and worrying about what was going through Damien's.

My stomach soured as guilt ate away at it, but I pushed that aside as well. There would be plenty of time to feel my grief and my remorse on the train back to Glenshire. Right now, I needed to focus. Everything I'd come here for was on the other side of those cloudy, confused eyes.

"Hello, mister—I mean, Detective O'Toole. My name is—"

"Christ almighty, it took ya long enough." His wiry white eyebrows furrowed as an angry spark of recognition flicked across his face.

"I'm sorry?"

"Ya should be. Leave an old man waiting like this, rottin' in this godforsaken place. I was beginning to think you were never comin'."

"I, em …"

"So where to?"

"Excuse me?"

"Heaven or hell? What's it gonna be?"

My heart sank. The man wasn't coherent enough to exchange basic pleasantries, let alone tell me what I needed to know. I'd come all this way, risked my life, betrayed Damien's trust for absolutely nothing.

"You're not gonna tell me where I'm goin'? Why the hell did they send you? They shoulda sent yer ma. She was less of a cunt."

"My ma?"

"She woulda sold me Da's house when he died, but, nooo, the old kook had to go and leave it to you."

Darby.

Eamonn wasn't incoherent. What he was saying made perfect sense, if I were his dead niece who'd come to escort him into the afterlife.

That was it. That was my ticket into the vault of his mind.

"With all due respect, *Uncle*," I said as loudly but sweetly as possible, "I would advise against calling me a cunt when the fate of your eternal soul has yet to be decided."

"Wh-wh-what's that?" he sputtered, sitting up straighter in his remote-controlled bed. "Yet to be decided?"

"That's correct, dear Uncle. The angels selected me to conduct your judgment personally, due to our … unfinished business. They are not happy about the lack of justice that was served following my murder."

"Lack of justice!" he sputtered, clutching his bedsheet with two knobby fists. "What'd they expect me to do? Take on the whole damn Bratva again?"

The Bratva?

Again?

"Thanks to your contract-killin' boyfriend, I'd already risked me arse once to put Alexi behind bars. Got that piece of shite three consecutive life sentences, and he still bribed and blackmailed his way out. What was I s'posed to do? Huh? If I poked that beehive again, they were gonna come for me next. I *had* to cover it up. I had ta!"

"So, a man in the Bratva named Alexi killed Kellen and me? Because you'd helped us send him to prison?"

"A man named Alexi?" he mocked. "Alexi Abramov is no fuckin' man. He's a goddamn disease. A blight on the whole human race. Just look at what he done to me city!"

Eamonn shoved a shaky finger in the direction of the glowing TV on the wall as aerial footage of a decimated Dublin scrolled by on the screen.

Then, his eyes went wide, and his mouth dropped open in horror as he slowly returned his attention to me.

"That's what this is about, isn't it? If I'd been brave enough to go after him again, to put him back behind bars for good, none of this woulda happened."

Eamonn's milky eyes lost what little focus they'd held as he cupped a hand over his mouth and stared into the depths of his own mortality.

"Uncle Eamonn, I need you to stay with me," I continued, using my most soothing voice.

"I'm damned," he whispered, shaking his head.

"Not necessarily," I added. "I just need to ask you a few more questions ..."

That got his attention. "Please," he said, his eyes snapping back to mine. "Tell 'em it wasn't my fault. Tell 'em I couldn't take on the whole Bratva again. Tell 'em there isn't a prison on earth that could hold a man with that much money and power. He woulda gotten out again, and when he did, he woulda come for me!"

"I understand that, Uncle. I do. And I will take it into consideration. Now, can you please tell me why the president of Russia would want to kill a young couple in Glenshire, Ireland?"

"I didn't know this was gonna happen! I swear!" His tone bordered on panic, and I was afraid that I'd lost him.

"Uncle, please answer the question. We're almost done. You're doing grand."

"Really?"

"Yes. Now, please state for the record why President Abramov wanted us dead."

Eamonn nodded and took a few deep breaths. "Alexi wasn't president back then, ya know, but he was one of the top dogs in the Bratva. And Kellen, from what I could gather, was a hit man for the United Irish Brotherhood, back before they became a political party and that rat bastard Séamus Rooney took over. That's another one that I could never keep behind bars. Slimey fuck."

"Uncle, please. Why did Alexi Abramov—"

"I'm getting' to it! Christ. It was never proven, but me hunch was that Kellen had taken out somebody near and dear to Alexi, and as retribution, he came for Kellen's head. The UIB must have sold him out because the two a yous conspired to get both Séamus and Alexi arrested at the same time. Which made yours truly look like quite the big shot back at the station, thank you very much."

Eamonn smiled slightly as his eyes began to drift out of focus.

"You're telling me that my husband was a contract killer for the UIB?"

"Ya didn't know?" The old man laughed until he had a coughing fit. "Kellen was the best hit man I've ever seen! Untraceable. Completely clean. Never found so much as a fingerprint, but me sources on the inside said he was the UIB's number one enforcer. They called him the Devil of Dublin."

The Devil of Dublin. That name sounded so familiar.

I flashed back to the images Saoirse had shown me of Kellen fighting, bleeding, running, killing, and then us happy together in Glenshire. It all made perfect sense now.

The two men currently battling over the fate of Ireland, men who now had entire armies at their disposal, were once a couple of rival Mafia bosses that Kellen and I had tried to stop.

My head was reeling.

"Thank you, Mr., em, Uncle Eamonn." My voice shook as I tried to process this onslaught of information. "You have no idea how badly I … and the angels … needed to hear that. This concludes your judgment hearing. I hereby declare you—get down!"

The last thing I heard before I ducked beneath Eamonn's hospital bed and covered my head was the high-pitched scream of a rocket barreling straight toward us. I didn't look out the window for confirmation—I didn't need to. That sound was carved into the very fiber of my soul like the grooves of a record, a trauma that I was destined to replay over and over and over again.

Just like my life with Kellen.

CHAPTER 39

DAMIEN

It looked like it was snowing.

Smoke and ash and bits of plaster floated down from the sky in slow motion as I ran toward the rubble that, just seconds ago, had felt like an oasis of hope. The building moaned in agony as structures cracked and broke off, shattering on the jagged debris below. And something inside of me shut off. It was as if all access to my emotions had been severed. Logic. Sensory input. Alertness. Planning. That was all that was left. A machine on a mission.

The side of the building closest to me had been destroyed, but the far side was still intact, as well as the main entrance. The only people streaming out of the hospital were in uniform, which meant that the patients were most likely on lockdown. And because Clo wasn't among them, it meant that she was either trapped in the rubble or she was trapped inside a padded cell with this Eamonn fucker.

Grabbing every shell-shocked arsehole I could get my hands on, I asked each one if they'd seen a pretty redhead looking for Eamonn O'Toole. I was met with blank stares or tears or slack-jawed head shaking, but one employee, a middle-aged woman with deep hollows under her eyes, simply lifted a finger and pointed behind me.

I turned my head, expecting to see Clo's big green eyes shimmering with relief as she came bounding toward me, but instead, I found myself staring at a mountain of rubble being torn apart by a dozen frantic people wearing hospital uniforms.

Adrenaline exploded through my bloodstream as I descended on that fucking hellscape like a man possessed. I didn't feel the strain of my muscles as I yanked chunks of metal and concrete and wood the size of cars off the pile. Didn't feel the burning of my lungs or the slicing of my hands as I tossed granite bricks over my shoulder by the dozens. But when I broke through the exterior debris and found a pocket of air under a hospital bed, I felt every sensation in my body all at once.

Excruciating pain.

Paralyzing panic.

Blinding terror.

Murderous rage.

Because lying in a heap, covered in ash and bricks and crumbled plaster, was the body of a woman with long auburn hair.

Wearing a black flight jacket.

I pulled her from the wreckage as gently as I could and ran straight back to Heuston Station with her limp body cradled in my arms. I didn't check to see if she was alive or dead. I didn't even look at her face. I couldn't.

I was just going to hold her until she woke up.

Because she was going to wake up.

She fucking had to wake up.

I knew every soldier on that island was probably looking for a couple matching our description, but with both of us caked in white plaster dust, I was willing to risk being seen by the soldiers at Heuston Station. I was willing to do anything to get Clover the fuck off that island.

But just in case, I entered through the opposite side of the building. My hunch paid off. There were no soldiers on that side, and I nearly wept as I stepped through the free-spinning turnstile and carried Clo's limp body to the westbound platform.

Where a digital sign showed that the next train was twenty-eight minutes away.

Fuck.

There was an empty bench, but I couldn't sit. I couldn't stand. All I could do was pace and hyperventilate and listen for any signs of life.

Because I couldn't fucking bring myself to look.

Twenty-seven minutes.

If her heart was beating, if she was breathing, if she was cold, I couldn't feel it through Kellen's jacket. I couldn't fucking feel it. And that was what scared me the most.

Twenty-six.

My pacing grew faster, my steps larger, my turns sharper. A few of the St. Patrick's staff members joined me on the platform. But they didn't pace. They simply stood and stared at nothing, their shock as potent as my agony.

Twenty—

"Damien?"

My feet became rooted to the spot as I held my breath and listened.

"Damien, I'm so dizzy."

Falling to my knees, I sat Clover on the platform, holding her up in case she was weak, and forced myself to finally look at her.

My heart thundered in my ears louder than the squeals of the southbound train as I brushed the plaster and ash-covered hair away from her face. And there, staring back at me, was the living, breathing embodiment of perfection. A few more cuts, a few new bruises, but that's part of what made her so magical. Clover was a fucking survivor.

"Hi, angel." I forced a smile, cupping her dust-covered face in my bleeding hands. My heart was pounding so hard I could feel it in my neck. "There are some nurses here. Does anything hurt?"

Clo touched a gash on her forehead with a wince before her eyes suddenly went wide. "Damien, I know who killed us! You're never gonna believe it! It was—"

"Shh … I know," I stated, taking her ice-cold hands in mine.

Her face fell, eyebrows furrowed.

"What?" She shook her head. "You know?"

I nodded.

"Saoirse."

I nodded again. "I'm so fucking sorry, Clo. I should have told you. I just … didn't want it to be true." I kissed her knuckles as I prepared myself to admit what I'd been running from.

"It's all my fault. All of it—our deaths, my mother's death, your family's deaths, this entire fucking war. If I'd been stronger, if I'd slit his fucking throat when I had the chance instead of killing myself out of grief, none of this would have happened."

Clover opened her mouth to argue with me, but I lifted a bloody fingertip to silence her.

"I was planning on running from him again, finding a place to hide *again*, but that was what I had done last time, Clo, and it didn't fucking work. I'd still lost you, and when I found your body in that rubble just now …" I shook my head, trying to forget the way her limp body had felt in my arms. "I have to do things differently this time. Like you said in your letter, I have to set things right."

"But … how?" Clover asked, clasping my raised hand in both of hers.

"By killing Alexi Abramov."

She coughed. "That's … that's impossible. He's all the way in Russia. No one can get anywhere near him."

"I can."

"Damien, just because you're in the military—"

"Not because I'm in the military." I sighed. "Because I'm his son."

CHAPTER 40

CLOVER

"*Because I'm his son.*"

My mind raced through every conversation I'd had with Damien in the few short days that we'd known each other. Not once had he mentioned that his father was the bleeding president of Russia.

"You said your last name was Hughes."

"My mother gave me her last name when I was born. She never told me who my father was, and she never told Alexi that he had a son either. Not until she got so desperate for money that she decided to contact him to ask for child support. That was the last thing she ever did. As soon as he found out that he had an heir, he sent his men to kill her and kidnap me. I've been his prisoner ever since."

I was staring into the steely eyes of a hardened killer, but all I saw was the wild-haired fairy prince who'd kept me company in the shadows after my own ma passed. I almost reached out to brush a phantom black curl behind his ear. I'd had no idea what horrors that boy was going to face when he got older. That maybe his home wasn't the otherworld. Maybe it was a living hell, just like mine.

"Jesus Christ," I whispered, trying to imagine the horror of being that man's son. I'd thought Oliver was bad. Damien's father was the fucking anti-Christ. "I'm so sorry."

"It's okay," he said, and I could tell that he meant it. "It was all for a reason. I see that now. Of all the people I could have been in this lifetime, why do you think I came back as Alexi Abramov's only son? Because only his son would be able to get close enough to do what I should have done the moment he walked through our door."

The weight of what he was saying felt like two meters of dirt being shoveled on top of a coffin. I suddenly felt powerless, claustrophobic, unable to breathe.

"Damien, no," I gasped, feeling the station begin to spin. "This is crazy. It's … it's suicide."

Giving me a sad smile, Damien squeezed my hands. "Back in Glenshire, you talked about us being there for a reason, about purpose and destiny. And you were right, angel. I see that now. But getting justice isn't your responsibility; it's mine. I caused this war, and I'm the only one who can stop it."

"No." I shook my head as tears welled in my eyes, clinging to him, clinging to hope. "No, I was wrong. The past doesn't matter, Damien. What's done is done. Let's just go to Boston, okay? We can go right now. The next train will be here in"—I glanced up at the digital sign hanging above the platform—"two minutes. We'll take it to Shannon. Get on a boat or a plane tonight."

Damien simply dropped his eyes to our interlocked fingers, turning them over in his lap.

"Do you hear me?" I asked, my voice growing louder, more panicked. "I just got you back. I can't lose you again."

Lifting his eyes, Damien's face was a terrifying mixture of resignation and indignation. It was probably the same expression I'd worn in Glenshire when he'd tried to talk me out of pursuing my own purpose. And that terrified me even more because, like me, I knew there'd be no talking him out of it.

"You can't lose me at all," he said, lifting our clasped hands and pressing a kiss to the freckles on my left ring finger. "We're forever, remember?"

Tears streamed down my cheeks as I refused to accept what he was suggesting. "No. No. Absolutely not."

"Go to Boston," Damien replied. "Write more books. Maybe one about a Russian prince who kills his own father to stop a war with the kingdom of the girl that he loves." He smiled sadly. "You could call it *The Monster of Moscow*."

The headlight of an oncoming train temporarily blinded me as wind whipped through the station, sending my hair flying all around us.

"You're not a monster," I shouted over the roaring engine and squealing brakes that were slowing to a stop at our platform.

"No, but there's one inside of me," he said. "I feel it crawlin' under my skin. And I'm finally gonna unleash it on the man who put it there."

Beside us, a pair of doors slid open with a hydraulic hiss.

"Damien, don't do this. Please. I don't care about the past anymore. I don't care about settin' things right. If we have to live in the cave for the rest of our lives, I'll be perfectly happy. I just want to be with you."

"Ya will be," Damien said, pulling me to my feet. "Once I finally deserve ya."

Going from sitting to standing made my dizziness return tenfold. I squeezed my eyes shut as a wave of nausea and full-body shivers crashed over me—a product of shock from a very different nightmare that I hadn't even begun to process yet.

And Damien used my temporary disorientation to his advantage.

Steering me by the shoulders, he gave me one last lingering kiss before shoving me backward onto the train.

A second before the sliding doors were fully shut.

Launching myself at them, I tried to pry the doors back open, clawed at the seam, pounded on the glass, but it was too late.

The lieutenant was back, and this time, the only person he was going to hurt was himself.

Turning and raising his arms above his head, Damien shouted something in Russian as the train lurched forward. *Lieutenant Abramov*, *Howth*, and *Wexford* were the only words I recognized, but that was enough to know what was happening.

Damien was confessing his crimes.

Half a dozen Russian soldiers descended upon him with guns drawn just before he disappeared and I careened backward through the hellscape that Dublin had become.

The train was quiet.

Damien was gone.

And the only thing I could do about it was slump to the floor, pull my knees inside Kellen's jacket, tuck my face into the neck hole, and scream until I tasted blood.

CHAPTER 41

CLOVER

*In the hills at the foot of a plum mountain peak
Lies a sleepy old town where the dead never sleep.
The villagers know to stay out of the wood.
That's where the spirits are up to no good.
Especially one, they confess with a shiver.
Born with the Devil inside him, they whisper.
Eyes gray as smoke, hair like black flames.
He killed the town priest and died with him that day.
Damned for eternity, refusing to burn,
He waits in the woods for his love to return.
Out where the bluebells grow high as your knee
And the clover and moss blanket every tree
Lies a ring made of stone where no fairies dare tread.
That's where you'll find him, the ghost of the glen.*

I recited the epigraph from *The Ghost of Glenshire* over and over in my mind as I raced up the hill behind Darby and

Kellen's house. *My* house. It was the only thing keeping me going.

My mother had named me Clover because of that poem. Little did she know that I'd written it myself just a few years before. Or that I was destined to meet and fall in love with the man it was written about. Or that one day, she'd be gone, and I'd be trudging through those very woods alone, in search of that exact same enigma of a man, and that the memory of her voice, reading that poem, would be my only source of comfort in the entire world.

There was just enough daylight left to find my way, but I could hardly see a thing through my incessant stream of tears. The forest was nothing more than a blur of greens and browns, and when I finally crested the top of the hill … purple. Wiping my eyes, I found a sea of bluebells carpeting the woods. Their trumpeted blossoms hung like church bells at noon, swaying back and forth in the summer breeze, but they didn't make a sound. And why should they? Damien was gone. There was nothing left to celebrate.

There was also no trail left to follow, not anymore, but I knew where to go. It wasn't a memory; it was a knowing. A download from the very spirit I was going to consult.

Out where the bluebells grow high as your knee,
And the clover and moss blanket every tree …

Following a row of trees with moss-covered trunks, I came across the cottage ruins we'd discovered the night before. I was definitely headed in the right direction.

Lies a ring made of stone where no fairies dare tread.
That's where you'll find him, the ghost of the glen.

"No, I won't," I whispered to Darby, staring at the crumbling structure where Kellen had always been waiting for her.

But Damien wasn't Kellen. He didn't wait for me. Not in this lifetime. Damien came for me.

He came for me when I leaped off a cliff. He came for me when I was captured. He came for me when I was trapped. And now, it was my turn to come for him.

As soon as I figured out where the hell he was.

The mist on the surface of the water ebbed and flowed, as if the lake itself were breathing.

"Saoirse?" I asked, not knowing what I expected to hear in return.

When nothing happened, I glanced at the cottage on the far side of the lake, wondering if perhaps I should risk another interaction with the old woman, but where I'd seen a quaint little dwelling the day before now sat a crumbling pile of stones that hadn't been home to anything other than squirrels and spiders in centuries.

My mouth fell open as my gaze darted around the perimeter of the lake, but I knew there wasn't another cottage. Just like I knew better than to ask Saoirse for a favor without bringing a gift.

I didn't have a thing to give her, other than the clothes on my back, and as much as she might like them, I needed them more.

Then, I remembered the part in *The Lady in the Lough*, where Darby wrote about the accidental marriage ritual that she and Kellen had performed. Couples would wade into the lake and prick their fingers on blackberry thorns, hoping that by shedding blood together, they could prove to Saoirse that their love was true.

The first time my soul had encountered Saoirse, she'd blessed me, and it wasn't because I'd brought her a gift. It was because Kellen and I had shed blood together and proven our love to her.

Snapping off a particularly thorny twig from one of the overgrown bushes, I rushed over to Kellen's bench and began stripping off my—*Darby's*—clothes. When I draped Kellen's jacket over the intricately carved back, the pang of grief that sliced through my heart nearly brought me to my knees.

After twenty years of waiting, searching, mourning for someone I hadn't even thought existed, I'd finally found him. And I'd already lost him all over again.

The pain was excruciating. It hurt to breathe, knowing that, soon, I would be breathing on my own. It hurt to stand, knowing that, soon, I would have to face a world without him in it. It hurt to be naked without his soft gaze caressing my skin and his lips healing every wound that someone else had caused.

"Saoirse," I whispered, unable to push my voice through the knotted lump in my throat as I waded into her cold embrace. "Saoirse, please. I need your help."

When I didn't get a response, I lifted the twig in my hand and stabbed a particularly sharp thorn into the tip of my ring finger—the one with the freckles.

The blood came slowly, probably due to my dehydration, but when it did, I waded in deeper and swirled my hand on the top of the water.

My heart thundered in my chest, and tears stung my eyes as I waited to be grabbed by my ankles and dragged under water.

What if she was angry this time, like she had been with Damien? What if she decided not to let me go?

What if ...

"Saoirse, please!" I cried, scooping my hands through the water now, searching for a trace of blue, a patch of bubbles. "Please, I need you! Damien's gone! I have to find him. Help me find him!"

But the only response I got was my own voice echoing through the woods.

"Saoirse!" I slapped my hands on the surface of the lake before diving headfirst into the ripples.

The water was colder this time, making my muscles seize and shiver, but I pushed through the pain, peering into the murkiness and finding nothing staring back but a void as deep and wide as the one in my chest.

Coming up for air, I sucked in as much as my lungs could hold before diving in again. Maybe she would be at the bottom. I just had to make it to the bottom. Again and again, I tried to swim down there, but it was as if the lake suddenly had no end.

Once I was physically incapable of swimming another stroke, I hauled my exhausted body onto the bank, collapsed next to the bench, and stared up at the twilight sky through stinging, tear-filled eyes.

They were gone too. Saoirse, the old woman … what if they'd never existed? What if I really was having some kind of mental breakdown? I'd disappeared into Darby's world—her village, her house, her bleeding clothes. All to distract myself from this exact feeling.

The realization that everyone I'd ever loved was gone.

I didn't remember getting dressed or walking back to the house. I didn't know if I'd tiptoed around the bluebells or stomped right through them. I didn't remember passing the cottage or if there was even a whisper of daylight left as I emerged from the woods and waded across Darby's overgrown pasture. My entire awareness had shrunk to the size of a human heart and was now occupying the space where mine would have been if I hadn't left it behind on the bank of the lake.

Now, I felt nothing.

I didn't bother lighting a candle when I got back inside. I didn't want to see another space without Damien in it.

Or Odie.

Or my ma.

God, how I wanted my ma.

As I walked toward the bedroom, I caught myself wondering if Kellen had left any guns in the house.

If the Bratva is going to kill Damien, I can join him, I thought. Like Kellen had done for Darby. I could put an end to all of this suffering and just …

A sudden burst of blue light exploded from the bedroom, illuminating the hallway and causing me to scream and shield my eyes. It was gone in a flash, followed by the sound of glass breaking.

I ran into the room, hoping to see that Damien had found his way home while I was in the woods, but the room was just as dark and quiet as the rest of the house.

"Damien?"

No response.

"Hello?"

Tiptoeing into the space, I crossed the room to light a candle on the bookshelf and heard glass crunch under my feet when I got there. I froze on the spot, waiting, listening, and when I heard nothing but the sound of blood rushing in my own ears, I struck a match.

I was too impatient to light a candle before I glanced down at the mess on the wooden floor. Using the light from the match, I bent down to find a framed photograph shattered at my feet. I managed to set it back on the shelf before the flame began to burn my fingers.

Lighting another, I investigated the photo more closely, and what I saw would have stopped my heart ... if I'd still had one.

A man who looked a lot like Damien, but with longer, wavier hair, stared through me with haunting gray eyes and his arm around the shoulders of a smaller, middle-aged woman. She looked a bit like him—pale skin, light eyes, dark, wavy hair—but unlike him, the woman was smiling. She didn't want to be though. I could see it in the tightness of her features. There was a sadness that betrayed her attempt to be pleasant that struck me as horribly familiar.

"Ow!"

Shaking the match violently, I quickly lit another.

Sweeping the flame over the rest of the photo, I noticed that the two were standing outside of a bakery, and Kellen was wearing a white button-down shirt and a pair of black trousers ...

That looked exactly like the ones Kate had given Damien to wear.

"Shite!"

Lighting one of the last matches in the pack, I studied the woman's face more closely until I was absolutely sure. She had fewer wrinkles than the woman I'd met in Wexford, and her hair was dark instead of white, but the way she carried herself, the way she smiled through her sadness, was unmistakable. She held Kellen like she was already grieving him—and I'd seen that grief firsthand, every time Kate looked at Damien.

Cracking the frame in half on the edge of the shelf, I pulled the photo out and tucked it into the inside pocket of Kellen's black jacket.

Then, for the first time all day, I smiled.

"Thank you," I whispered through the lump in my throat.

And that time, I knew Saoirse heard me.

CHAPTER 42

DAMIEN

I hadn't thought anything could hurt worse than the betrayal and heartbreak I'd seen in Clo's eyes the moment she'd realized what I'd done.

But the physical pain I awoke to was a close second.

I kept my eyes closed in case my captors were in the room with me and reached out with my other senses to try to figure out where the hell I was, or how much time had passed since I'd been beaten unconscious at the train station.

I could tell that I was on my back … in a bed … with my wrists and ankles bound by some kind of padded cuffs.

The temperature was neutral. The room was deathly quiet, as if the walls were soundproofed. And the light illuminating my swollen eyelids felt too white, like a doctor's office or a …

My hunch was confirmed the second I cracked one eyelid open.

Hospital.

Slamming that eye closed again, I directed my senses inward next. Was anything broken? Missing? I felt along the insides of my teeth with my tongue. All there. Toes? Wiggled. Fingers? Accounted for. It hurt to breathe, which I knew from years of getting the shite kicked out of me in the Kletka probably meant that I had a few cracked ribs, and my head and nose were fucking pounding. I racked my brain for any memories from the train station after I'd surrendered, but all I remembered was being shoved to my knees before the butt of a machine gun came down between my eyes.

I didn't know if I'd been out for a few hours or a few days, but if I was already chained to a hospital bed, that could only mean one thing: step one of my mission had been accomplished.

I was back in Moscow, healing up so that Alexi could break me himself.

Cracking both eyes open this time, I scanned the room to make sure I was alone. Then, I did a sweep for anything that could be used as a weapon. I wouldn't get many chances to be alone with my father. During the five years that I'd spent in the Kletka, I'd only seen him once or twice a year. It was too risky for him to leave his iron fortress. It involved armored cars and teams of Kletka-trained bodyguards. When the entire population of your country and most other world leaders hated you, going out in public wasn't exactly a good idea.

When he came for me, I had to be ready.

The room was stark and empty, other than a TV on the wall, a wardrobe, and a chair, which—judging by the institutional gray wall color and lack of art—were probably all bolted down. This was no regular hospital.

This place was a prison.

Hearing the digital beeps and mechanical slide of a door being unlocked, I closed my eyes and focused on slowing my breathing.

"*Prosnut'sya!*" a male voice boomed as two heavy feet stomped across the tiled floor toward the bed.

I'd spent enough years in the Kletka to know that if you didn't wake up right away, you'd get hit, so I immediately opened my eyes and turned to face my unwanted guest.

It was a soldier I'd never met before, high-ranking based on his regalia, but I wasn't familiar enough with Army stripes to know exactly what his position was. I only knew Navy rankings, and even then, not all of them. Alexi had called me a lieutenant and shoved me onto that ship with only a few weeks' notice and training. All he'd cared about was making sure I looked the part, knew how to use the artillery, and would have a front-row seat to the destruction of my country.

Well, mission accomplished, motherfucker.

"Phone call," the man shouted in Russian, handing me a massive satellite phone.

I went to accept it, but my wrist only lifted a few centimeters before the padded leather handcuff did its job.

Instead of uncuffing me, the arsehole with the scowl simply shoved the device against my ear and glared at me as the voice of my nightmares slithered into my head.

"My son."

No.

No, no, no, no, no.

Why was he on the phone? He was supposed to greet me in person, not over the goddamn phone.

Fuck.

"It is such a relief to know that you're alive and well. I hear you took a nasty fall off your ship."

I'd been speaking English again for just over a week, and it was already becoming more difficult for me to understand him. But there was no mistaking the condescension and sarcasm that oozed between every syllable.

"You must have hit your head very hard on the way down because I hear that you also went on a *motherfucking killing spree!*"

I could practically feel the spit flying through the phone.

"Seventeen crewmen. Seventeen fucking crewmen! And for what? Some fucking Irish pussy?"

My blood went cold.

"That's right. I know about your little girlfriend. I know her name. I know what she looks like. And more importantly, so does every soldier in Shannon. If she tries to leave, her ass is mine." He chuckled. "And it's a very, *very* nice ass. You won't mind sharing it with your papa, will you? Ah … I cannot wait to make her scream. I wonder who would be louder, her … or your whore of a mother."

I jerked at my restraints and growled into the phone—a momentary loss of control before I quickly regained my composure. But it was too late.

Alexi chuckled.

"Here's what is going to happen, lover boy. If you were anyone else, I would take seventeen body parts—ten fingers, two eyes, two ears, both balls, and your motherfucking cock— as payment for the men you stole from me, but because it is *my* fucking blood that runs through your veins …"

I swallowed.

"You will not be that lucky."

CHAPTER 43

CLOVER

I arrived in Wexford around three a.m. I'd gotten a few hours of sleep on the train, curled up inside Kellen's jacket under a table where no one would see me. Without Damien around, I realized just how vulnerable I was. How defenseless. My only weapon was the backpack Kate had given me, refilled with some food and bottled water from Nora.

When the train had pulled into Wexford Station, I'd been too terrified to come out from my hiding spot. I knew the Navy crewmen docked in that harbor had drone footage of Damien and me. They knew we'd killed two of their men, and now, I was back with absolutely zero protection. But something Damien had said the last time we were there gave me courage. It was when the battleship in the harbor had started blasting bugle music …

"They play that before lights out. A few patrolmen will have the night shift, but the rest will be tucked away inside the ship until sunup."

I was safe until sunup.

Avoiding all streetlights and keeping to the shadows, I crept along the roads Damien and I had taken together, retracing every step until I was standing at the bakery's back door, which, thankfully, still had a broken lock. There was no way I would have been able to knock loud enough to wake them up without attracting the attention of a drone in the process.

When I tiptoed into the seating area, my throat tightened, and my eyes burned as I remembered Damien chasing me behind the counter where he'd kissed me and fed me pastries. It had felt like a glimpse into the real him—the boy I would have met if we'd been given normal lives. Playful. Sexy. Giving. But the sweetness of that memory faded when I got to the part where I'd freaked out and recoiled from his touch.

I didn't know if Damien had ever seen a *normal* version of me. Everything I did or said was tainted by trauma. Maybe in our next lives, we could just be … us.

Whatever that was.

The second I placed my foot on the bottom stair, a creak echoed through the entire building. I'd forgotten about the squeaky floor, but maybe that would work in my favor. Give them some warning that I was here before I just appeared in their bedroom like a ghost.

"Kate? Jack?" I called out in my quietest voice. "It's me … Clover."

Even over the noises coming from the floorboards beneath me, I swore I heard additional creaking coming from somewhere else in the house.

"Jack?" I whisper-shouted. "Kate?"

Emerging into the sitting room, I glanced around the first floor, which was illuminated from the streetlamps lining the harbor. No sign of anyone, but I heard what sounded like footsteps coming from a room with a closed door on the opposite side of the room.

"It's me, Clover," I said again, a little louder this time, as I crept toward what I assumed was their bedroom door.

Every third or fourth step squeaked. As I reached out my hand to knock, the door flew open, and my startled yelp was silenced by a gun to my forehead.

"Clo?" Jack whisper-shouted, lowering her weapon and clutching her heart with her free hand. "Jesus Christ, woman. You ever heard of knockin'?"

"I was about to," I gasped, my own hand over my own racing heart. "I'm sorry."

"Clover?" Kate emerged from the darkness behind Jack and only made eye contact with me for a fleeting moment before glancing behind me into the sitting room and kitchen.

I knew exactly who she was looking for.

"Damien's not here," I admitted, feeling my chin buckle as I fought back tears. "He … he surrendered to the Russians, and I need your help to get him back."

"He what?" Kate gasped.

"That's a fuckin' suicide mission," Jack scoffed. "Why the hell would a coupla old ladies help you with that?"

I glanced from Jack to Kate and gently removed the photograph from Kellen's jacket pocket.

Handing it to Kate, I watched her expression morph from concerned to completely gutted.

"Because," I replied, "I think he's your son."

Sitting on Kate's blue velvet couch in the dark, I explained everything as Jack made tea and baked muffins and paced the floor and asked skeptical questions … and Kate just stared at the coffee table with her fingertips pressed to her lips and silent tears streaming down her face.

"So, you're tellin' us that the man who was here two days ago is walkin' around with her son's reincarnated soul inside of him … and you expect us to believe that shite?"

"I believe it," Kate answered, her blank stare still firmly in place. "I saw it in his eyes, the way he carried himself"—she turned her head toward me—"the way he looked at you …"

The smile she gave me was heartbreaking.

"I would know that look anywhere." She sniffled, studying my face in the early morning light. "It's you, isn't it? It's really you."

I nodded with a lump in my throat as she pressed a wrinkled hand to my cheek.

"Oh, my sweet girl. Come here to me." Her voice broke as she leaned forward and wrapped her arms around my shoulders. "I missed ya so damn much," she cried. "Thank you. Thank you for giving me my boy back … twice."

I didn't know if it was the validation of having someone finally believe me after a lifetime of being called crazy or if it was the years I'd spent craving the comfort of a mother's touch, but Kate's love broke me wide open.

I wept on her shoulder as all the fear and anxiety and gut-wrenching loss that had been leaking out of me since Damien's disappearance finally came rushing to the surface.

Jack sat on the couch next to her wife, stiff-backed and uncomfortable with our outpouring of emotion. "You actually believe this load of bollocks?" Her words were harsh, but the smirk on her face and the tender hand she placed on Kate's thigh betrayed her arsehole exterior.

Releasing me with one hand, Kate reached out and swatted her partner with a laugh and a sniffle. "Oh, shut up, ya old geezer."

Jack smiled for the first time since I'd arrived before glancing over at me. "Real nice mother-in-law ya got there," she scoffed. Then, giving my knee a firm squeeze, she added, "Come on. Let's get ya some food. Ya can't rescue yer reincarnated husband on an empty stomach."

I hadn't truly allowed myself to feel Damien's absence until I found myself back at their kitchen table. Just forty-eight hours ago, Damien had been right there beside me, comforting me, reassuring me, then risking his life for me—for all of us—when we'd needed him. Now, his chair sat empty.

Now, he was the one who needed us.

And we didn't have the first bleeding clue what to do.

Jack was streaming the news on her tablet again. That seemed to be their morning routine—tea and muffins and the news. I didn't have an appetite, but I needed all the caffeine I could get. And the distraction of a glowing screen was welcome too. At least until I figured out how to find and rescue a man who was probably already being tortured in a secret prison cell in Siberia by then.

My hands began to shake so hard that I had to set down my mug.

"While the Irish military has not yet officially surrendered," a female newscaster for the BBC announced as footage of the hell I'd seen the day before scrolled behind her on a green screen, "our sources report that as much as seventy-five percent of Dublin has been destroyed, and Taoiseach Séamus Rooney was seen boarding a private plane bound for Venezuela late last night."

"Of course he was, the fuckin' cunt," Jack sneered.

"Because Irish President Sean MacSharry, a close UIB ally of Rooney, will neither confirm nor deny that the taoiseach has deserted his position, Russian President Alexi Abramov is declaring a preliminary victory in the war with Ireland. Let's go live to Moscow where—"

"Turn that shite off," Jack barked from the kitchen. She was gripping the edge of the counter with her head between her shoulders. "I can't fuckin' listen to this—"

"Wait. This just in." The female newscaster pressed a finger to her ear and listened. "The press conference is not with President Abramov, but his newly appointed vice president—a position never before seen in the history of the Russian Federation—who I'm being told is President Abramov's son, Lenin Abramov."

If there had been tea in my mouth, I would have spit it out.

The man they cut to—standing behind a podium in a sunlit garden, freshly shaved and wearing a crisp black suit—was the same one I'd seen on his knees, surrounded by six Russian soldiers, just twelve hours before. They'd tried to clean him up, hide the beating I knew they'd given him, but his well-manicured surroundings and appearance did nothing to mask the muscle flexing in his clenched jaw or the deep V between his puffy eyes. Damien was in agony.

"Mother of fucking God," Jack spat, marching over from the sink to get a better look. "That's yer boy. That's fuckin' him!"

"Oh my God." Kate pressed her fingertips to her gaping mouth. "Clover ... is this true?"

All I could do was nod as I stared into the same steely eyes that had turned away from me the day before. They didn't turn away now. They bored into my soul, as if his stare was meant for me and me alone.

"Ya didn't fuckin' mention that he's the son of the goddamn enemy!"

"Jack ..." Kate warned.

"He *is* the goddamn enemy! Look at 'im! Fuckin' VP of Russia!"

"Jack, stop!"

"He has a black eye," I muttered, my fingers hovering over the screen just above his beautiful face. "Under that makeup. Ya see it?"

"The next time I see him, I'll give him a lot more than that," Jack quipped before clamping her mouth shut and shooting Kate an apologetic look.

Bitterness and rage emanated from Damien's entire being as he stared, unblinking, into the camera.

"Citizens of the world," he began in Russian-accented English, his jaw unclenching just enough for him to play the part, "I stand before you today as the newly appointed vice president of the Russian Federation. I, along with my father, am pleased to report that Russia has emerged victorious in our conflict with Ireland, and the evacuation phase of this war is now over."

"Fuck me." Jack finally sat, taking the chair next to her wife.

"From this moment on, anyone remaining on the island formerly known as Ireland must pledge allegiance to President Abramov and the Russian Federation. Failure to do so will be considered an act of treason. Wearing or displaying Irish iconography of any kind, including flags, emblems, or symbols, will be considered an act of treason. And the use of the Irish language, spoken or written, will also be considered an act of treason."

"What about wipin' me arse with the Russian flag? How's yer da feel about that?" Jack spat.

"To help expedite the transition of power, bonfires will be held in every occupied city on the island tonight. Attendance is mandatory. If you do not live in an occupied city, you must travel to one. All Irish regalia must be burned at this time, and all citizens will be required to surrender their passports and driver's licenses to the authorities on-site."

"Oh God," Kate whispered through her fingertips. "Is this really happening?"

"In the coming weeks, new passports and identification cards will be issued to reflect your new Russian citizenship and Russian surname."

"New names! Are you fuckin' kiddin' me?" Jack shoved the table with both hands, causing the tablet to fall flat on its back.

"Failure to attend a burning event or submit your identification will also be considered an act of treason, resulting in immediate detainment and sentencing.

"While this transition might be difficult for some to accept, President Abramov would like to remind you all that it was Ireland's taoiseach, Séamus Rooney, who depleted your miliary in his ill-advised war with Britain, alienated you from your allies, and left the door open for this invasion to occur. Now that it's over, my father would like for all of you to take pride in your new Russian citizenship ... or suffer the consequences."

Jack tapped the screen, pausing the broadcast.

"He's a fuckin' traitor!" she cried, thrusting her hand in the direction of Damien's frozen, vengeful glare.

"He is no such thing!" Kate snapped back in an uncharacteristic show of emotion. "Ya heard what Clover said ... he surrendered to try to get close to Alexi. He's doin' this for us. Including you, ya stubborn cunt!"

"For *us*? Your boy crawled back to dear old da and got a big fat fuckin' promotion—*that's* what he did. Look at him!" She gestured toward the screen again. "That suit costs more than our mortgage!"

Kate didn't look at him. She was too focused on the words spewing out of Jack's fear-mongering mouth, but I looked. And what I saw had me snatching the tablet off the table.

"Damien saved yer life, right here in this bleedin' room," Kate shouted. "He saved all our lives. We have to help him."

Zooming in with two fingers, I studied the garden wall behind Damien.

"What are we s'posed to do, love?" Jack's tone softened. "Book a flight to Moscow and abduct the VP of Russia? We don't even know where they keep the VP. Nobody does. They've never fuckin' had one before!"

Setting the tablet down with shaking hands, I glanced up at Jack and Kate and said the two sweetest words in the English language.

"I do."

CHAPTER 44

DAMIEN

Lift ... flip ... slide ... aaaaand ...
Click.

The repetitive sounds of a leather cuff being unbuckled and re-buckled was the only thing keeping me sane. With nothing to do and no other source of entertainment, I'd spent my hours in isolation plotting my escape. I'd come up with at least four different options, but all of them began with me being able to free myself from my restraints, which I could now do with my eyes closed, thanks to a lot of free time and a metal rod I'd discreetly removed from the paper towel dispenser in the bathroom.

Not that I had any plans to escape. I just needed to know that I could. It made me feel less like a prisoner and more like an undercover assassin biding my time.

Which was exactly what I needed to be.

Press ... latch ... slide ... and ...
Done.

That paper towel dispenser had actually been my first clue as to where I was. When the guards finally let me use the toilet in my new gray cell the day before, I noticed that everything in the bathroom had been bolted down as well. The hand soap, shampoo, and paper towels were all in unmarked metal dispensers attached to the white tiled walls. There were no decorations. No shower curtain or bath mat. But when I dried my hands, I noticed that the paper towel dispenser had a sticker on the side with instructions on how to open it.

And those instructions were written in English.

Alarm bells had immediately gone off in my head, but it wasn't until I'd walked back to the bed—at gunpoint—and caught a glimpse of the world outside my window that the reality of the situation really grabbed me by the fucking throat. A horrifying, nauseating sense of failure washed over me as I stared down at Steeven's Lane—gutted, bombed-out buildings on one side, a massive stone wall on the other, and inside that wall, scattered across the grass below my window, debris from a recent rocket strike.

I hadn't made it to Russia.

I hadn't even made it out of Dublin.

I was right back at St. Patrick's Psychiatric Hospital.

And this time, I was the one trapped inside.

Lift … flip … slide … click.

My surrender had been for fucking nothing. The soldiers at Heuston Station had beaten me unconscious, carried me half a kilometer down the street, and locked me in an empty room in the psych ward until they could get my father on the phone to decide what to do with me.

And his decision had only verified the fact that I didn't fucking know him at all.

I'd expected him to whisk me back to Moscow so that he could see to my imprisonment and torture personally. I'd expected his wrath, his rage, but what I hadn't expected was his thinly veiled pride. My murderous rampage had proven to him that I was every bit as fearless, violent, determined as my old man, and now, he was more eager than ever to continue doing what he enjoyed most.

Trying to break me.

Alexi had thought that a year in the Kletka would do it, but not even five had been enough to make me bend the knee and kiss the ring on his iron fist.

He'd thought that making me lead the charge against my homeland would do it—force me to submit to his power and accept my fate as his heir and successor to the Bratva throne.

But it had quite the opposite effect.

Because I wasn't motivated by fear or power, and my treasonous killing spree had revealed that to him.

He knew now that my sole motivation was protecting Clover Doyle, that I would do anything for that woman.

Which meant that if he had her …

I would do anything for *him*.

I would accept the role of vice president, be his puppet in Ireland so that he never had to leave the safety of the Kremlin. I would strip my fellow countrymen of their identities, their names, their heritage, and their lives if they didn't fall in line. And in exchange, he'd let Clover live when they captured her in Shannon.

But they weren't going to capture her in Shannon.

I might not have known my father, but I knew Clo. There was only one place that girl wanted to be, and it wasn't fucking America. I would bet my life that Clover had gone back to Glenshire. I prayed that she had because right now, that was the safest place for her to be. The Russians would never bother invading a village that small, and Nora would take care of her until she could get a job and save enough money to buy our old house back.

But I was going to play my part anyway, pretend like I believed them when they told me they'd found her, let Alexi think he'd finally broken my will.

Because the sooner he believed that he had me by the bollocks …

The sooner he'd let me get close enough to kill him.

Press … latch … slide … done.

So, I sat in my bed like a good boy, fastening and unfastening my restraints, as I stared at the designer suit hanging from the corner of the TV. I had no idea how Alexi had gotten it to me so fast, but he must have given the soldiers guarding me strict orders not to let it get wrinkled. As soon as the press conference was over, they'd made me change into the institutional-blue T-shirt and trousers that all the other residents of St. Patrick's hospital wore, but I knew that in a few hours, they'd make me put it back on. And that was when my real punishment would begin. When I'd have to enforce the new treason laws that Alexi had just decreed. When I'd have to stand there in my designer clothes and do nothing while my fellow citizens were dragged from their homes and shot in the streets for not cooperating. When I'd have to absorb the hatred in their heartbroken eyes as they used their final breath to spit on my Italian leather loafers.

That would be my real punishment. This was just a security precaution—restraints, solitary confinement, and three Russian soldiers stationed at the hospital to guard me at all times. One was positioned outside my door, one at the front entrance, and one patrolled the perimeter of the building, but there were half a dozen more at Heuston Station that could be there in five minutes if they needed to subdue me.

Not that I was going to fight back. I was going to be such a model VP that Alexi would have no choice but to invite me to the Kremlin for a father-son photo op once my job here was done.

And then I would do what I should have over twenty years ago—I would avenge Darby's death and rid the planet of Alexi Abramov once and for all. I knew I'd never make it out of the Kremlin alive, knew I'd never see Clover's angelic face again, but I would see the next one she wore, and the one after that, and the one after that. It was a blessing I didn't deserve, but I was prepared to walk through hell to change that.

The sound of a digital keypad, followed by a mechanical whirring, gave me just enough warning to re-buckle my cuff and shove the rod down next to the mattress.

"Vice President Abramov," a soldier barked in Russian as he entered my room and stood at attention. "The girl has been located and taken into custody. I have been instructed to tell you that she will not be harmed as long as you—"

The whistle of a bullet being fired through a silencer was the only warning I had before the soldier's forehead exploded and brains splattered across my bed and hospital uniform.

Curling my fingers around the metal rod, I watched as his body fell to the floor, revealing another man, dressed in Irish camouflage and a ski mask, who was now pointing that silencer at me.

"Come on, prince. Let's get ya outta here."

Based on the sound of his voice and the lines around his eyes and mouth, I would have guessed him to be middle-aged or older, but the calmness of his tone and the way he handled his weapon suggested that this was a skilled, experienced soldier. Possibly Special Ops.

"Who are you?" I asked as he holstered his gun and began unbuckling my cuffs.

"A friend of a friend," was all he said before a series of gunshots and Russian shouting echoed through the hallway.

Shite.

If this had been an official Irish military operation, he would have introduced himself with his name and rank, but he hadn't.

This was a rebel attack, and from the sounds coming from the hallway, there were plenty of them.

Just then an alarm began blaring, and a red light started flashing in the corner of the room.

"Stay behind me," he shouted over the siren as he removed the final cuff from my leg.

"Wait! I can't leave!" Panic flooded my veins as my eyes darted around the room, sizing up all of the objects I'd identified as possible weapons during my hours of escape planning.

Alexi was going to think I was behind this. That I'd betrayed him again. Whoever these rebels were, they were fucking everything up. He was never going to trust me after this.

The man's weathered eyes widened. "Why the fuck not?"

Hopping over the railing on the far side of the bed, I ducked underneath and unplugged the power cord.

"Hey! We gotta go!"

Just as the rebel dipped his face below the mattress to see what I was doing, I swept my leg out, taking him out at the knees. He fell backward, landing next to the dead soldier. His head hit the tiles with a sickening crack, but he was still conscious when I scrambled over and wrapped the power cord around his neck. Pinning his right hand down with my knee so that he couldn't grab his weapon, I tightened the cable as he punched me repeatedly with his left hand.

"Damien!" a female voice shouted from the doorway, but I refused to look up until the rebel's body went limp. "What the fuck are you doing?"

As soon as his balled fist fell to his side, I loosened the cord and glanced up as a short, stocky woman in matching camo marched over and swatted me on the head.

"That's my best fuckin' guy!"

"Jack?"

"Yeah, it's fuckin' Jack. Jesus Christ." She knelt beside me and slapped the masked face of the man on the floor. "Paul. Hey, Pauly. Wake up. We gotta go."

"What are you doing here?" I left her to tend to the rebel on the floor as I slid over to the dead soldier and relieved him of his handgun and boot knife.

"Saving your arse," she hissed, helping her friend into a sitting position.

"You shouldn't be here," I said, probably not loud enough to hear over the alarm, as I walked along the wall to the door that Paul had propped open with a cigarette lighter in the doorjamb. Glancing into the hallway, I saw another dead body at one end, but couldn't tell if it was a Russian or a rebel. When the coast was clear, I shouted over my shoulder, "I don't need to be rescued. I know what I'm doing."

"Like fuck ya do," she spat back. "By the time you get close enough to Alexi to kill him, the entire fuckin' country will be speakin' Russian!"

"Wait. What?" I spun around. "How do you know about that?"

"A little birdie told me. How do ya think?"

"Clover?" Darting back into the room, I slid on my knees, through the pool of blood surrounding the dead Russian, over to Jack. Clutching her arms, I locked eyes with her, forcing her to give me her full attention. "You've seen her?" I asked. "She's okay?"

"She's worried fuckin' sick about ya, is what she is. Her and your ma."

"My what?"

"I'll explain in the tunnel. C'mon." Jack stood and helped Paul to his feet. The flashing red light made him wince and dry-heave.

"I can't leave," I shouted.

"Listen to me." Jack draped Paul's big arm over her shoulders and lifted her ski mask to reveal her very annoyed, very tired face. "I wanna kill that son of a bitch just as bad as you. We all do. Right?" She raised Paul's limp hand, and he grimaced. "But I'd like to do it *before* I have to burn all my shite and start goin' by the name Jacqueline Cuntapova the Great."

"Stop!" a male voice shouted in Russian.

Raising my hands over my head, I turned and found a Russian soldier pointing a gun at us, but staring at the face of his fallen comrade on the floor.

His expression turned murderous as he lifted a bulky military phone to his head and barked, "I've got them, sir. They're with the VP—"

A red hole appeared between the man's eyes before I even registered the whisper of the silencer.

"Hold him, will ya?" Jack huffed, lowering her weapon as I scrambled to catch her friend.

Walking across the room, she plucked the phone out of the second dead soldier's hand and held it up to her ear.

"Hello?" she shouted, clamping her free hand over her other ear to block out the sound of the alarm. "Shite. You speak English? *English.*" She cupped her hand over the microphone and glanced at us. "Paul, I need ya to translate."

Paul's head swayed, and his cheeks puffed out as if he was gonna be sick.

"I think he's got a concussion," I said, guiding him over to the bed so he could sit.

Jack's attention fell back to the phone in her hand. "Do … you … speak … English? Ah, grand. Here's the situation. A group of concerned patriots have killed yer men at St. Patrick's Hospital, and—let me finish, fucker! And they've kidnapped your VP."

She pulled the phone away from her ear as angry Russian shouting came pouring out of it.

"Hey! I don't speak Russian, arsehole. Listen. Listen!"

Letting go of Paul with an apologetic glance, I stepped over both dead soldiers and stood at the open door. I tried to listen for footsteps or voices in the hallway, but I couldn't hear a damn thing over the blaring alarm and Jack shouting into the phone.

"If President Alexi wants his son back, he can pick him up tomorrow at noon, in person, in the middle of the Ha'penny Bridge, but only *after* he announces that the new treason laws have been canceled. That's right. We want to keep our flags, *and* our language, and our bleedin' names, ya fuckin' cunts."

Taking a deep breath, I peered out into the hallway and jerked my face back just before a bullet whizzed past it and shattered the doorframe behind my head.

The soldiers from Heuston Station had arrived.

Tapping Jack on the shoulder to get her attention, I held up six fingers and jerked my head in the direction of the hallway.

"Shite," she hissed. "Hey, I gotta go. Remember, Ha'penny Bridge, tomorrow, noon, Alexi can come get his boy in person, or yous all can pick him up in a body bag. Yer choice."

Pocketing the phone, Jack and I helped Paul to his feet. His pupils were blown, but he was lucid enough to stand and hold a gun, so we propped him against the wall out of the line of fire and hidden around the corner from the entryway.

Then, I got an idea.

Holding the metal rod with a white pillowcase tied around the end of it out the door, I shouted over the alarm, "Don't shoot! This is Vice President Lenin Abramov! Do not shoot!"

My father had given me that name the moment I'd stepped foot on Russian soil. Said the name Damien Hughes was "too fucking Irish."

"They're all dead! Don't shoot!"

I walked into the hallway with my arms raised, and half a dozen familiar faces marched toward me, led by the motherfucker who'd knocked me out the day before. I swallowed when I remembered what he'd hit me with and glanced down to see a matte-black machine gun poised in both fists.

Fuck me.

Red lights splashed across their serious faces as I prayed that Jack would know to take the leader out first. I'd already been shot twice. I could probably take a third or a fourth, but not a fucking spray. That machine gun was a game changer.

I could see her in my periphery, preparing to jump out and open fire, and Paul was right behind her, poor cunt. He stood with his shoulder against the entryway wall, still obviously bell rung, but we needed all the help we could get.

Then, with a nod of Jack's head, everything shifted into slow motion.

I dropped to my knees, pulling the Russian's handgun out of my waistband as a hail of gunfire tore through the air just above my head. Aiming for the fucker front and center, I squeezed the trigger, but Jack beat me to it. My bullet sailed over his falling body and clipped the lad standing behind him. I winced as I braced for the wrath of the other four, but their guns had already clattered to the floor, bodies jerking and convulsing as exit wounds burst through camouflage and flesh.

Within seconds, all six Russians were in a bloody heap on the floor, and four grinning, ski mask–wearing vigilantes were hugging and thrusting their guns into the air behind them.

Turning to Jack, who was propped up on her elbows beside me, I let out a laugh and helped her up. "Nice friends ya got there," I shouted over the alarm. "Where'd you find 'em?"

"Special Ops Force." She beamed with pride. "Not bad for a bunch of retirees, huh?"

CHAPTER 45

CLOVER

I paced the length of St. Patrick's Cathedral for the millionth time, crushing a sea of rotten rose petals into the white satin aisle runner under my feet.

The entire gothic chapel smelled like death. There must have been a wedding there on the night of the invasion because every pew and pedestal was draped in white tulle and dead flowers. Every candelabra dripped with melted wax. And every time I reached the altar and turned around, the sun streaming in through the stained-glass windows was a little lower in the sky.

"They're taking too long," I muttered with my thumbnail between my teeth.

"They'll be here soon," Kate replied automatically, never once looking up from the front pew, where she was busily prepping for dinner.

While Jack and I had been coming up with a plan and contacting her military mates, Kate had been working just as hard to make sure that everyone had bedding and food and water for the night. Blankets and sleeping bags and pillows had been set up throughout the cathedral, giving each person plenty of privacy, and meat pies had been made ahead of time and packed in insulated delivery bags from the bakery.

I'd felt useful before the mission began, but once Jack and the lads left through the Poddle—an underground river that ran below the cathedral and would allow them to travel to the hospital unseen—there was nothing left to do but try not to have a panic attack. I probably could have offered to help Kate, but she needed something to do just as badly as I did. I didn't want to take that away from her.

I was just about to turn around again when the sound of squeaky boots on a tile floor echoed through the massive, marble space. Spinning around, I watched as a band of camouflaged men—and one woman—filed in through an arched doorway next to the altar. Their ski masks had been pushed up to reveal their grinning faces, their arms were draped around one another's neck, and their attention seemed to be on a particularly wet member of their crew—a bald man called Finn, I believe.

"Fucker fell in!" Jack chuckled as Kate rushed over and hugged her wife.

"Bah! I was pushed, and ya know it." Finn laughed—or maybe he was Oscar and the bearded one was Finn. I'd only met them briefly before they changed into their tactical gear and disappeared into the Poddle through a manhole outside.

The team had worn black wellies to wade through the underground stream to the hospital, but the man at the back of the group, wearing hospital clothes tucked into Kellen's old combat boots, was wet up to his knees.

"Damien!" I sprinted down the center aisle, satin sliding and rose petals scattering in my wake, and the moment our eyes locked, tears filled mine.

He had his arm around the back of a man called Paul. I remembered him because he seemed to be Jack's favorite, but as soon as Damien saw me, he let go and leaped over the ornate railing separating the pews from the pulpit. He was on me in two bounds, lifting me off my feet and claiming my mouth in a kiss that tasted like tears I hadn't known I was crying.

Eons passed in the span of that kiss, seasons and lifetimes merged and diverged, but not one of them could touch us. Because in that moment, we were timeless. There was no Kellen or Darby or Damien or Clover—those people were tiny fractals of who we truly were—like panes of glass in the ornate windows that were currently bathing our skin in rainbows. We weren't the individual colors. We were the sun shining through all of it.

"You found me," Damien whispered, wrapping my legs around his waist and pressing his forehead to mine.

"I'll always find you." I smiled. "I found your ma too."

Damien's eyebrows pulled together as my grin widened.

"Kate." I nodded toward the pew where dinner was being served. "She was Kellen's ma." Reaching into my jacket pocket, I pulled out the photo and showed it to Damien. "That's why Jack agreed to help. Kate couldn't bear to lose you twice."

I lowered my voice. "Neither could I."

I realized as I watched Damien's eyes roam over the image that he'd never seen a picture of Kellen before.

"The Devil himself," he said, pursing his lips. "He failed you. He failed her." Damien tore his gaze away from the photo of Kate and pinned me with the same haunted, harrowing stare he'd destroyed me with at Heuston Station. "I won't let that happen again," he vowed.

"I know." I smiled, trying to ignore the brutal finality I heard in Damien's voice as I leaned forward and kissed his beautiful, worried mouth. "Because this time, you don't have to do it alone."

Damien's eyebrows pulled together as I pocketed the photo of his former self—a man who had carried the weight of the world on his shoulders—and glanced past him at the group of people who had come to help him bear that burden.

"Come on," I said, tapping his arse with my heel. "Your other mother has been dyin' to see you."

After the longest night of my life, the sunrise still came too soon.

I'd lain awake for hours, listening to a cathedral full of snoring men and Damien's steady heart beating beneath my cheek. Every soft thump had been another grain of sand falling through an hourglass. A ticking clock that was counting down to noon.

And then … nothing. I couldn't see past that. I couldn't feel Damien in the future. Something bad was going to happen. I knew it like I'd known where every candle was in Darby's house. It wasn't a hunch or a case of nerves; it was a fact.

And there was absolutely nothing I could do about it.

I tried to hide my fear from Damien. I only hyperventilated in the bathroom. I kept my trembling hands in my pockets. I spoke as little as possible, not wanting him to hear the tremor in my voice. But the closer it got to half ten—the time when Jack had said she wanted everyone to head out—the closer I came to having a full-blown public panic attack.

At ten, Jack had everyone gather round the altar, where everything they'd taken from the soldiers at the hospital—handguns, a machine gun, extra ammo, a laptop, a satellite phone—had been laid out like Sunday communion. And that was when the chest pain started. I couldn't breathe. I felt like I was having a heart attack. I wanted so badly to wrap myself around Damien and let his quiet strength comfort me, but he would know. He would know I was falling apart, and I couldn't do that to him. He needed to focus. He needed to think positively and be surrounded by calm, confident people. He needed to muster the courage to face the man who'd killed his mother and his wife, and there was no way he could do that if the one person who was supposed to believe in him was acting like he was going to die. My panic could undermine the entire operation. So, I sat in a church pew while they went over the plan, clutching Kate's hand until my trembling knuckles turned white.

I didn't need to hear what they were saying—Jack and I had come up with the plan together before she and the lads from her old unit worked out the details—but I still hung on every word they said, hoping their collective years of experience would calm my nerves.

Damien would meet Alexi in the middle of the Ha'penny Bridge. We'd chosen that spot because it was close to where the River Poddle emptied into the River Liffey, so we could take the underground tunnel there and not be seen. It was also a pedestrian bridge, so there was no way someone could drive up and kidnap Damien while he stood out in the open. And it was at least three meters above street level with railings made of vertical metal poles, so it was more sheltered from a ground attack than any of the other bridges.

Which was why we were going to attack from the air. Brian, Finn, Oscar, and the little guy they'd introduced as Wheezy were all snipers. Or had been, before they retired. Each of them was going to be stationed in the top floor of one of the four buildings closest to the bridge, ready to take out Alexi as soon as he showed his shiny bald head. And just in case something went wrong, Jack and Paul were going to be stationed on the ground on either side of the bridge in case they needed to shoot out some tires … or a driver.

It was a good plan, but something was missing. I could feel it. We had a blind spot. My mind churned over every worst-case scenario, trying to figure out what more we could do, but we were out of time.

With a guttural, "Ooh-rah!" the lads—and Jack—began choosing and loading their weapons.

No.

No, no, no, no, no.

I wasn't ready. They weren't ready.

Everyone was wearing camo and wellies, weighed down with torches and tactical gear, while my sweet, brave Damien was completely unarmed, dressed in a set of hospital pajamas and a damp pair of boots.

I shook my head as he walked toward me and felt Kate squeeze my hand in response.

This couldn't be happening.

Every instinct I had told me to grab him and run. Run back to Glenshire and hide out forever. Keep him safe. Keep him all to myself. But there was an entire country that needed him more than I did.

And we were out of time.

Standing, Kate and I met him in the aisle, where I committed every chiseled angle of this new face to memory. Even the deep purple bruise on the inside corner of his left eye. It was the last time I was going to see it while he was alive.

Damien's pace didn't slow as he stalked toward me. His eyes didn't light up. And when he grabbed me and picked me up this time, there were no smiling kisses, no relief or rejoicing. There was only the rib-crushing embrace of anxiety.

Damien's heart pounded against mine as he buried his face in my neck and took a deep breath.

"Hey," I cooed, smoothing my hand over his soft hair. "It's gonna be okay."

My panic subsided, just enough for me to comfort him, but I could tell it was like the ocean receding before a tidal wave. As soon as he left, the grief was going to come back tenfold and drown me.

Damien shook his head. "I'm not coming back, Clo. I can feel it."

"Shh. Don't say that. You have six Special Ops rangers watching over you. You're gonna be fine." Pulling back, just enough to encourage Damien to look at me, I said, "Hey, two hours from now … Alexi's gonna be dead. And we're gonna have our country back. Right?"

I forced a smile that Damien didn't return.

"I don't know, Clo. I feel like we missed something."

Shite.

My smile slipped as we stared at one another in complete honesty.

"I don't want to wait twenty more years for another half hour in heaven with you." Damien shook his head as his devastated gray gaze fell to my lips.

"Then, don't," I whispered, kissing him first.

"All right, lovebirds," Jack teased, coming up beside us to give Kate a kiss of her own. "Save it for the after-party. We've got a president to assassinate."

Whispering something in Kate's ear, Jack gave her a swat on the arse, adjusted the machine gun strapped across her back, and marched toward the exit they'd come through the night before.

Setting me down, Damien pressed his lips to mine in a way that reminded me of lying on a bed of green grass under a blue sky in a cemetery full of white granite gravestones.

"Remember me," he whispered.

Then, after an obligatory hug for Kate, he was gone.

CHAPTER 46

CLOVER

I stood there for what had to be minutes, staring at the pointed marble arch Damien had just passed through, waiting for my knees to buckle and my wails to start.

But they didn't.

The tidal wave was still gathering strength, and in the meantime, it had left me standing in an emotional desert—an unthinking, unfeeling, unbelieving void where an ocean used to be.

I realized, slowly, that Kate wasn't standing next to me anymore. She was kneeling beside the pulpit, rolling up her sleeping bag as if it were personally responsible for the pain she was in.

"I hate churches," she muttered.

Her dry, wrinkled hands, weathered from years of kneading dough, squeezed the nylon so hard that I thought her knuckles might split open.

"Kellen's da was a priest. Did ya know that?" She spat the information out as if it was made of poison.

I nodded slowly, distantly.

"I was just a girl—" Kate's chin wobbled, but she clenched her jaw and moved over to Jack's makeshift bed.

"They sent me away to have the baby, but I couldn't give him up. I escaped with him, tried to raise him on me own, but ..." Kate shoved the tightly rolled bundles into a camouflage bag, along with both pillows. Tiny muscles and veins strained in her slender arms. "I couldn't do it. I gave him back. I gave him to his sick fuck of a father, thinking he would put him up for adoption."

Falling back on her heels, Kate's face crumpled as she clutched the sack to her chest like a teddy bear.

She needed me to say something. She needed me to function.

Forcing myself to walk up the wrinkled satin aisle runner and the steps to the pulpit, I sat beside her and placed a hand on her knee.

"I'm so sorry," I said, wishing I had access to my feelings. Wishing I could be there for her in the way that she needed me to be. "You raised a good man, I think. I know Darby loved him. The way she wrote about him. He was her entire world."

"I didn't raise him." Kate shook her head, staring at the mosaic tile floor. "No one did. Kellen raised himself ... out there in those woods, hidin' from Father Henry, waitin' for me to come back." She chewed on her bottom lip as something began to stir in my chest. "I was too messed up back then to take care of him ... but then Darby came along, and ..."

Kate's pale eyes lifted to mine. "She saved him."

The ocean floor rumbled beneath my feet.

"I heard what ya said yesterday, about him not being alone this time. But, darlin', Kellen wasn't alone; he had Darby. He had *you*."

The wave of emotion I'd been dreading came crashing down at her words, but it didn't drown me in grief, like I'd feared. Instead, it filled me with hope.

He has me.

That was it. That's what was missing.

Since the moment we met, Damien and I had kept each other alive.

And I'd sent him out there without me.

Giving Kate a kiss on the cheek, I jumped up and scrambled over to the altar, taking stock of everything they'd left behind.

"Clo … what are ya doin'?" Kate asked, a worried tremor in her voice.

"Taking care of our boy," I said with a smile.

CHAPTER 47

DAMIEN

The plan was fucked.

Every aspect, literally blown to shreds. The buildings our lads were supposed to be sniping from were just hollowed-out shells with hardly any cover. Every road leading into the city center was buried under piles of rubble. And it was going to be real fucking hard to meet Alexi in the middle of the Ha'penny Bridge when most of the Ha'penny Bridge was at the bottom of the fucking Liffey.

We'd gotten there early to take our positions without being seen, but there'd been no point. The place was a goddamn ghost town. No cars could get through. No buildings were inhabitable. There was no mobile network or electricity. The occasional drone flew overhead, which we were able to avoid, but other than that, the only sounds in the city were the soft clanking of metal debris floating in the river and the occasional crash as another chunk of bricks fell off a building.

Even the birds had abandoned Dublin.

"Nothin'." Jack shook her head as she reattached a CB radio to her shoulder.

Jack and I had ducked into Merchant's Arch to wait for noon. It was a narrow stone tunnel across from the Ha'penny Bridge with decent coverage and good visibility of the meeting point.

If the meeting point still existed.

Jack had been on the radio all morning, hoping to get in touch with some active-duty Irish soldiers who might be willing to go rogue and help us out or at least provide us with some intel about Alexi's whereabouts in the city, but the channels were all dead.

There was no more fighting. No more bombing. No more Dublin. Jack and her team had considered themselves to be patriots—Ireland's last line of defense—but looking around, there was nothing left to defend. We were too late. And Alexi wasn't fucking coming anyway.

Slapping a hand on my shoulder, Jack squinted into the sun-drenched wasteland outside. "Looks like it's just us, pretty boy."

I nodded slowly. I'd expected the worst, but what I hadn't expected was … nothing.

"He's not comin'," I muttered, and as soon as the words left my mouth, I realized *that* was the real reason why my stomach was knots and my heart was in my throat. Not because I was afraid Alexi would come, but because I was afraid that he wouldn't. I was afraid that I was so insignificant to him that my abduction wasn't worth leaving his precious Kremlin over.

"Ahh, cheer up." Jack gave my shoulder a shake. "He'll be here. Ya matter more than ya think, *Lenin*."

Then, she stared out at the blue sky over the battered city and took a deep breath. "Beautiful day to kill a cunt."

A small light flashed three times from the exposed third story of the building across the river from us. Oscar was giving the signal that it was twelve o'clock. Everyone was in position.

Jack grinned. "Showtime, VP."

Shielding my eyes from the sun, I walked across Aston Quay and up the steps to what was left of the Ha'penny Bridge. It felt like I was walking the plank. The end of the bridge was jagged and scorched, and below it, just beneath the surface of the water, were the pointed white arches that I was supposed to be standing under.

Glancing at the buildings across the river where Oscar, Wheezy, and Paul were stationed, I exhaled heavily. I knew they were in hiding, but part of me had hoped to catch a glimpse of one of them. To see some sign that I wasn't completely alone.

That sign came in the form of a scream.

A scream that had been burned into my brain over the last two weeks.

Clover.

My heart thundered as I spun around, my senses reaching out in all directions. I scanned every building, every burned-out car, looking for movement, a flash of auburn hair, but it wasn't until she screamed again that I zeroed in on her location. Almost a block away, up Aston Quay, a Russian soldier was marching over the piles of rubble in the street, dragging a woman with a bag over her head by the arm.

And sticking out the bottom of that bag was a curtain of dark red hair.

"Clo!" I shouted, bounding down the steps and taking off after them.

"Damien, wait!" Jack hissed from the tunnel, trying not to blow her cover, but I was already gone.

Bricks and plaster flew behind me as I charged up Aston Quay.

Clover's thrashing slowed them down, allowing me to gain on them, and the sounds of her struggle only pushed me to run faster.

Crossing O'Connell Street, she was finally able to get her footing and pulled away from the fucker completely before being tackled to the ground.

"Clo!" I shouted again, a hill of debris crumbling out from under my feet as I fought to get over to her.

"Damien!" Jack called from behind me. "Come back, goddamn it!"

When I finally crested the hill and glanced up, Clover's kicking, screaming body was draped over her captor's shoulder as he disappeared into the building on the corner through a broken glass door.

"Fuck!"

The O'Connell Bridge House was easily two or three times taller than the other buildings in that area, and it was still perfectly intact. It could take hours to find her in there.

If they didn't find me first.

No.

I would find her. As long as I could hear her, I could find her. And I could hear her panicked squeals and grunts of frustration loud and fucking clear as I pulled the knife from my boot and charged in through a hole in the shattered glass.

The moment my feet hit the tiled floor of the lobby, two pairs of arms grabbed both of mine, jerking them behind my back as an unseen foot kicked the back of my knees, sending me to the floor. I managed to hold on to my knife, but it didn't matter. I was completely immobilized and surrounded by at least twenty Russian soldiers as I stared up at the motherfucker who'd dared to put his hands on my girl. The bastard was grinning from ear to ear as he held the back of Clo's thighs with one hand and a small black device with the other.

"Put her down," I snarled in Russian. "That is an order from your vice president!"

The arsehole complied, but he did it with a smirk that made my blood run cold.

Spinning her around, he then yanked the bag off her head.

And her long auburn hair came off with it.

A terrified brunette teenager cowered before me as he pressed a button on the device in his hand, filling the room with the sound of Clo's whimpers and screams. Then, it was filled with the laughter of every man in that room.

Drone footage. That was the only explanation. Clo had had multiple run-ins with the drones in Howth. They must have extracted the audio of her voice and used it to lure me into their hive.

Jack had been right. It was a—

Jack!

Fuck!

I turned and looked over my shoulder just in time to see Jack's sweat-drenched face as she lifted the Russian machine gun to her shoulder and took aim. Throwing myself forward, I managed to duck just before a hail of bullets sprayed into the building, tearing into a quarter of the soldiers in the room before a sickening *click* sounded behind me.

No.

The bullets stopped.

Then started again … in reverse.

By the time I turned to look, Jack was already on the ground, and Paul was running across the O'Connell Bridge toward her. Throwing his gun into the Liffey, he sprinted the rest of the way with his hands in the air, but before he could get to her, three quick pops from a soldier behind me took him out as well. He fell face down in the middle of the intersection, just a few meters away from Jack.

As they hauled me to my feet and dragged me deeper into their hive, I felt every ounce of humanity drain from my body.

I understood now why the villagers had feared Kellen.

Called him the Devil, said he'd killed his own father.

Because he was.

And he had.

And he was about to do it again.

CHAPTER 48

CLOVER

In the hills at the foot of a plum mountain peak
    Lies a sleepy old town where the dead never sleep.

The craggy stone tunnel felt endless—a dark, mildewy, cramped purgatory that closed around me a little more with every labored step I took.

The villagers know to stay out of the wood.
That's where the spirits are up to no good.

It was hard to tell how long I'd been down there, hard to block out the intrusive thoughts telling me I was lost, or worthless, or too bleeding late.

Especially one, they confess with a shiver.
Born with the Devil inside him, they whisper.

The voices seemed to bounce off the walls and echo along the low, arched ceiling, taunting me, making me shiver.

Eyes gray as smoke, hair like black flames.
He killed the town priest and died with him that day.

But I did my best to block them out, putting one soggy runner in front of the other and repeating a poem about finding a boy that I knew I could never truly lose.

Damned for eternity, refusing to burn,

He waits in the woods for his love to return.

All the lads had left behind was a handgun with no bullets, a satellite phone that I didn't know how to operate, and a Russian laptop that couldn't be unlocked without a fingerprint or a password.

But the screen made a decent torch down in the Poddle.

Out where the bluebells grow high as your knee
And the clover and moss blanket every tree

I clutched the open computer to my chest as I waded through the knee-high water, thankful that I hadn't come across any intersections or forks yet. I didn't actually know where I was going.

Lies a ring made of stone where no fairies dare tread.
That's where you'll find him, the ghost of the glen.

I had just restarted Darby's poem for the hundredth time when I noticed a dozen streaks of light piercing the ceiling up ahead. Relief washed over me as I sloshed over to the spot where the light danced on the water, finding a rusty metal ladder bolted to the wall and a manhole up above.

There was no gunfire that I could hear outside, no explosions or buzzing drone blades, so with a deep breath, I climbed up, slid the metal cover off, and found myself face-to-face with a massive stone wall that I'd hoped to never see again.

It felt apocalyptic, emerging from the darkness into the sunlit center of Steeven's Lane. No cars to be seen. No people. No sounds. Just the squish of my sopping wet shoes on the pavement as I crossed the street and passed through the open gates of St. Patrick's Psychiatric Hospital.

Where I stood and stared with my mouth hanging open.

The entire right side of the building was just a pile of rubble. I'd washed the ash and plaster dust out of my hair at Kate and Jack's after catching a glimpse of myself in a mirror. I'd looked exactly like someone who'd been buried in rubble. And now, I knew why.

I'd been trapped in *that*.

My heart began to pound as I approached the landslide that had once been Eamonn's room. Nothing was distinguishable from anything else. It was just destruction—a mountain of it—but as I stared at the pile, picturing Damien digging through the wreckage to find me, day suddenly turned into night.

Bricks turned to stucco.

And I was the one doing the digging.

"Odie!" I coughed harder. "Da! Sheila!"

Wooden beams as long as my arm went sailing across the yard as I attacked the pile, choking on smoke and ash and my own unspoken fears.

"Da, answer me! I know you're in there!"

Lifting half of our once-yellow door with both hands, I hurled it to the side and found my answer lying just beneath it.

A woman's arm, severed at the elbow.

With my da's key ring still dangling from its finger.

Stumbling backward, night turned back to day, and Sheila's arm withered and morphed into a liver-spotted, wrinkled limb hanging from the edge of Eamonn's bed.

I screamed and ran for the hospital doors, glancing over my shoulder in case a nearby drone had heard me.

As soon as the automatic glass doors slid shut behind me, I turned and locked them. Then, spinning toward the front desk, I came face-to-face with a lobby full of shuffling, muttering bodies, all dressed in the same blue shirt and pants that Damien had been wearing.

A man with wild eyes and days' worth of stubble suddenly rushed at me, pinning my back against the doors as he peered through the glass over my shoulder.

"Did they see ya?" he asked, his breath rancid and hands crushing. "Did they?"

I shook my head, pleading with my eyes for the other patients to help but most were completely oblivious. One woman made eye contact with me, then immediately curled into a ball in a waiting room chair and covered her head with both hands.

A large male patient seated at the front desk also noticed what was happening, but the extent of his help was banging a coffee mug on the polished wooden surface as if it were a gavel and shouting, "You're fired!"

"They want our mindssss," the man pressing my back to the door hissed, jamming his forehead into my temple. "They want what's in here."

A scream lodged in my throat as his breathing changed, as his tongue extended from his putrid mouth and slithered its way across my cheek and into my ear.

"Hey!"

I looked up just in time to see a coffee mug hurtling through the air toward my head. Pulling away at the last second, I heard three awful sounds in rapid succession—porcelain hitting bone, porcelain shattering on tile, and a desk being cleared as my attacker launched himself at the man who'd come to my defense. By the time I looked up, the two men were gone, rolling on the floor behind the desk as pained screams and shrieks filled the lobby.

Running past the desk and taking a left, I noticed that red lights were flashing down the length of the hallway, and every single door was wide open. Someone must have tripped an alarm that would free the patients in case of emergency.

I clutched the warm laptop tighter to my chest and broke into a jog as the entire spectrum of human emotion filtered through those open doors, blending together in a laughing, crying, singing, screaming, moaning, snarling riot of sound.

A man leaped from his bed and barked at me until I ran past his door. Another stood naked in his doorway, furiously masturbating. A woman charged at me in the hallway, screaming that I was a man-stealing whore. But I sprinted past all of them, searching, scanning, praying that I found what I was looking for in time.

Turning a corner, I yelped as a hand reached out and grabbed me, pulling me into an unseen room.

"Shh …" The voice was female, and the woman it belonged to released me immediately.

"You're not a doctor," she said, tapping her wrist against the side of her head. "Not a doctor, not a doctor."

"No, I'm sorry."

"Shoes." She gestured at my sopping wet runners. "Doctors wear shoes."

I glanced down at her socked feet and understood.

"Do you need a doctor?"

"The voices." She cringed, tapping harder and harder. "They're too loud. They're too loud!"

My heart broke for her. I was sure no one had been there to administer her meds since the shoot-out.

"What's your name?" I asked, steering her away from the open door and over to the bed, but she was too anxious to sit.

"Hemina," she replied, tapping her wrists against one another now.

"Hemina, this is gonna be over soon. But first, I need to know where the dead soldiers are. There was a shootout here yesterday. Where are the bodies?"

Staring at the floor, Hemina hesitated for several seconds. Then, she took me by the hand and led me out the door. With her as my escort, the other patients left me alone, but they glared and hissed at my feet as we passed.

Doctors wear shoes.

Up a flight of stairs Hemina led me, shushing herself and tapping her head, until we emerged at the end of a long hallway.

That was littered with bodies.

I should have been elated—one of those soldiers might have what I needed—but all I could see, all I could *feel*, were their heavy, bleeding bodies lying on top of mine.

The flashing red lights brightened to white fluorescents, and the hallway narrowed to the size of the space behind the Howth fish market counter. I was no longer dressed and upright; I was naked on the floor, surrounded by a pile of men that Damien had just killed, terrified that, at any second, the unit of living crewmen who'd just walked in would notice me and finish what their comrades had started.

"Shh …"

A gentle tapping on my temple brought me back into my body.

Blinking at the woman standing beside me, I realized that Hemina was soothing me the way she'd soothed herself.

"Too loud," she whispered, her deep brown eyes full of understanding.

It hadn't been a question. She knew.

I'd been trying my whole life to convince myself and everyone else that I wasn't crazy, but what if I was?

What if crazy was just a word that meant something inside of you hurt really, really badly?

What if the only crazy thing about any of us was the lengths we had to go to cope with the pain?

Tears blurred my vision as I held her knowing stare and nodded my head.

Yeah, I thought. *Too fucking loud.*

Looking down, I realized that Hemina and I had continued walking during my flashback, all the way to the pile of bodies. But this time, when I looked at them, the red lights stayed red. The hallway stayed a hallway. And the past stayed in the past. I wasn't lying beneath them, naked and afraid. I was standing over them, living and breathing, all because Damien had come for me when I'd needed him.

And now, it was my turn to return the favor.

CHAPTER 49

DAMIEN

I was the model fucking VP.

Cooperative. Charming. Beyond grateful to have been rescued from my captors and reunited with my Russian brethren.

Yes, I'd burst in, wielding a knife, but only because I'd thought that was the girl who'd killed our comrades back in Howth. I wanted to make sure the soldier who'd captured her had backup. She was extremely dangerous, after all.

They'd accepted my story with suspicious sneers—that wig and voice recording had obviously been used to bait me for a reason—but they kept their mouths shut and fell in line like good little soldiers.

The uniform they gave me helped me play the part as well. It wasn't a perfect fit—it belonged to the hive's captain, who was shorter and heavier than me—and it was for an Army officer instead of a Naval officer, but it would have to do.

Because I had another announcement to make, and my father didn't want me appearing in blood-spattered hospital clothes on TV.

My father.

He was on his way.

I thought of Jack and Paul as I saluted and shook hands with every soldier I passed as Captain Markov escorted me up twelve flights of stairs to the roof. Their deaths would not be in vain.

Because Alexi was arriving by helicopter, and he wanted me up there to greet him.

A tiny flicker of hope sparked in my cold, vengeful heart as I pictured Oscar or Wheezy taking aim at his shiny bald head the moment he stepped out of the chopper, but when Captain Markov led me out onto the roof, I realized just how fucking stupid that thought had been. Twelve stories was way too fucking high for us to be visible to anyone down below, especially when the platform we were on didn't extend to the edges of the building.

I was on my own.

I thought about what Clover had said, about me not being alone anymore, and shook my head in bitter resignation.

Alone was better.

Alone meant no one else would get hurt … because of me.

Captain Markov and I covered our ears as Alexi's helicopter touched down, and it didn't go unnoticed when he took a few steps back, positioning himself between the exit and me.

I might have been Alexi's puppet again, but I would always be his prisoner.

The moment the chopper landed, Alexi tore off his headset, unbuckled his harness, and exited the chopper before the rotor blades even finished spinning.

A rush of adrenaline shot through my veins as I readied myself to attack the second he got close enough, but I quickly realized that there wasn't a single fucking thing I could do. Between him, the captain, the pilot, and a third passenger in the back seat, I was outnumbered and probably outgunned four to one.

"My son," Alexi sneered, placing his meaty hands on my face and kissing me on both cheeks. When he got to the second one, he grabbed the back of my neck and whispered in my ear, "Welcome back." His tone was venomous, his words delivered with a forked tongue. The only thing Alexi was welcoming me back to was his clutches. His almighty fucking control.

"Father," I replied in that perfect Russian his tutors had taught me.

"Today is a great day," he said, holding me at arm's length. Then, he glanced at Captain Markov with a nod of approval. "He looks good. Very good."

Turning me around, Alexi swept an arm out over the decimated city below. "Today, we declare victory and break ground on your new palace. There."

Fuck.

Alexi was pointing at Dublin Castle—one of the oldest, most important buildings in the country and one of the few structures that hadn't been destroyed yet.

"Sergey," Alexi barked over his shoulder at the man who was still sitting in the back seat. His door was wide open, and he was clumsily attaching a video camera to a tripod.

Rushing over, the man stood facing us, next to the pilot, as he set up his gear, sweat beading on his brow as he adjusted all the settings.

"Here." Reaching into his suit pocket, Alexi took out a black device with a red button in the center and extended an antenna from the top corner. "When the red light starts blinking"—he pointed at the camera—"you will stand next to your papa. You will declare victory over the UIB and this entire fucking country. You will announce our plans to build a second Kremlin on the site of Dublin Castle. And then you will blow that motherfucker—"

"Sir!" The door beside us swung open.

And time fucking stopped.

The arsehole who'd roughed up the girl from before—Sergeant Ivanov—stepped out onto the roof, and this time, the redhead in his grasp was no fucking decoy.

She was mine.

Clover's big green eyes softened in remorse as she held my stunned stare.

She was wearing Kellen's jacket, and her leggings were wet from the knees down.

She'd followed us.

Fuck.

"Look who we found lurking outside." The fucker grinned.

"Ha! Perfect!" Alexi clapped his hands together before pulling a cigar out of his breast pocket.

"I'll do it," I said, turning to my father. "Whatever you want. Let her go, and I'll do it."

"I know you will." Alexi beamed, a thick Cuban clamped between his tobacco-stained teeth. "I *was* going to motivate you with the threat of torture, but … you're an Abramov. Tough." He made a fist. "Strong. Torturing your little Irish whore instead will be so much more … effective."

He laughed as he rolled the end of his cigar over the flame of a solid gold Zippo. Then, he puffed on the end until it was lit and exhaled the smoke in my face.

"Ah! This *is* a good day." Alexi wrapped an arm around my shoulders, but I barely felt it.

My entire awareness was fixated on the tearstained face of the woman I loved. The humanity I'd buried in order to do my job came rushing back all at once, stealing the air from my lungs and nearly bringing me to my knees.

My greatest fear had been leading my father to Clover and having to watch her die all over again.

But this was so much fucking worse.

He would never let her go. He would torture and rape her whether I behaved or not, simply because he could. Simply because he hated me.

Well, that made fucking two of us.

"In three … two …" The cameraman pointed at us as a tiny red light began blinking on the front of his gear.

"Good evening," Alexi said in his heavily accented English. "It is vith great pride and triumph zhat I stand before you today, vith my beloved son, to announce historic victory for Russian Federation." He took a deep breath and extended his arms like the dictator he fucking was. "Ireland … is … "

A scream so loud and so primal that I thought it must have clawed its way through the cracks of my own broken heart suddenly shattered the air, giving voice to my grief, my rage, my hopeless fucking agony.

Glancing back at the camera, Alexi laughed awkwardly as the sergeant holding my girl off camera slapped a hand over her mouth and clamped his elbow around her neck.

Clover kept screaming into his palm until her eyelids fluttered closed and her body went limp.

And a red mist of fury clouded my vision.

I lunged to catch her, to pound his fucking face into his skull, but Alexi held me back with a single hand around my bicep. It would be his only warning. If I fucked this up for him, she would suffer.

Greatly.

"We're all very excited." He grinned at the camera, tightening his fist around my arm. "And to celebrate Russian Federation victory over United Irish Brotherhood and ... ah ... *acquisition* of island, vice president and I are pleased to announce ..."

Alexi kept talking, but I was no longer listening. At least not to him. I was listening to what sounded like a swarm of killer bees descending upon us from every fucking direction. The skies were clear, but the sound was unmistakable.

Drones. At least two dozen of them, began spilling over the railings of the building as if it were a hornets nest that had just been kicked.

"Get her out of here!" I shouted, not giving a shit what Alexi did to us anymore. If even one of those things decided to shoot, there wouldn't be a Clover left to torture.

"Is just precaution." Alexi laughed as drones flew in from behind us as well, spotlights on and aimed at the unconscious redhead in the sleeper hold five meters away. "Our technology is state of art."

"Your city has been captured by the Armed Forces of the Russian Federation," two dozen robotic voices recited in unison as they clustered around Clover and the arsehole holding her.

His eyes went wide and cut over to Alexi's.

"This is your only chance to surrender. You have ten seconds to raise your hands above your head—"

"Sir?" The sergeant began walking backward toward the door, Clover's heels dragging in front of him.

"Take her inside!" I shouted.

"Zhey von't shoot." Alexi chuckled, turning back to the camera as sweat beaded on his bald, wrinkled head. "Each drone is piloted by esteemed member of armed forces."

Turning back toward Clover, Alexi gave the command. "Zhis is President Abramov. Stand down. I repeat, stand down."

"Ten."

"Fuck!" Breaking away from Alexi, I lunged for the door and nearly ripped my own arm off when I yanked on the handle and it didn't budge. Jerking it again and again, I kicked and pounded on the metal surface, screaming for someone to open it from the inside.

But all of the soldiers were stationed on the first three floors. No one was up there to hear us.

"Six."

"Is the helicopter armored?" I shouted at the pilot, grabbing Clover's body from the piece of shite whose death I was plotting next.

He was more than happy to hand her over, considering that there were at least twenty-four fully automatic machine guns aimed at her head.

The man glanced from me to Alexi in confusion. I must have spoken to him in English.

Fuck.

Rather than repeating the question in Russian, I simply lifted Clover into my arms and sprinted for the chopper.

"Three."

Our shadows splashed across the interior, backlit by a fleet of spotlights, as I laid Clover's unconscious body on the floorboard.

"Two."

Climbing in after her, I only had time to close one door before I threw myself on top of her, before the final second of our lives was announced by a chorus of machines outside.

Pressing my lips to hers, I waited to feel a barrage of bullets rip my body to shreds, but all I felt as the drones opened fire was the subtle curve of those lips as Clover's hands slid up my back and her legs parted, pulling me closer.

What should have been a deafening eruption of noise as two dozen machine guns unloaded at once sounded more like a distant string of firecrackers thanks to the armor-plated exterior of the helicopter and the blood rushing in my ears. There was no ping of metal on metal. No vibration telling me the chopper was under attack. The drones were definitely shooting at something …

But this time, it wasn't us.

CHAPTER 50

CLOVER

My eyelids were so heavy, but my body felt weightless as a pair of soft lips peppered my forehead, my nose, my cheeks with kisses.

"You don't have to fight anymore. Neither of us does. It's okay."

The voice was as familiar as my own, but it didn't belong to Damien. It was slightly softer but just as sweet. It made my heart just as fluttery, my smile just as wide. I basked in the timbre of it, let it warm my face like the first rays of sun after a long winter.

Those lips touched mine briefly, and the only thing that kept me from missing them when they left was his voice.

"I'm comin' with ya, angel. Ya understand?"

I nodded even though I didn't understand. I didn't need to. All I needed was this.

"I'm not lettin' you go. I'll never fuckin' let go."

His voice broke as he lifted my hand and pressed a kiss to my ring finger, and my eyes shot open in horror.

"No." I was dizzy and weak, disconnected from my body. It felt like I was drifting away from it somehow. Away from him. I wanted to cling to him tighter, and maybe I was, but I couldn't feel my hands.

I heard men laughing and speaking in Russian.

I smelled sawdust.

And I saw blood.

So. Much. Blood.

It gushed out of my leg in bright blue spurts, a fountain of starlight that seeped and spread around us.

And somewhere, far away, a countdown had begun.

Looking up, I drank in a face I'd only seen in my dreams … and in a photograph I kept in my pocket. But I almost didn't recognize him through his agony. His haunting gray eyes were squeezed shut, his loose black curls had been shaved off, and his mouth grimaced as his silent wail echoed in my ears.

"Knife," I whispered, wanting him to fight for us. Wanting him to fix whatever was happening.

But as the countdown continued, his pain only grew. I saw the moment it became unbearable. The subtle smoothing of his features as a decision was made.

And I felt the same sense of peace wash over me when I realized what I needed to do.

Reaching for his ankle, Kellen and I locked eyes as my hand wrapped around the handle of his boot knife and his wrapped around mine.

Then, as the light pooling around us began to swell and pulse, enveloping us in a serene blue embrace, Kellen smiled in understanding.

This time, things would be different.

This time, we'd throw that knife. Together.

"One."

It felt like the dream had started over.

The heavy eyelids. The weightless body. The gentle lips pressed against mine.

But it was real. I could tell by the things that weren't familiar. The scent of my lover's clothes. The muffled staccato of two dozen machine guns firing at once. The sensation of being wet from the knees down.

Wrapping my arms around Damian's body, I smiled against his worried mouth and kissed him back as a euphoric, tingly river of relief rushed into my extremities—further proof that I was not, in fact, dying.

But the way Damien's body responded heated that river, turning it into a lava flow.

My name was an answered prayer on his lips as he unleashed all of his worry, his fear, and his anguish on my welcoming mouth before tearing himself away to look out the window and assess the situation.

Whatever he saw must have satisfied his fear because, soon, his attention was back on me, his hands roaming from my face to my throat to my head to my heart. It was as if he needed confirmation that it was still beating. And it was. My pulse pounded beneath his palm, every swell of blood pressing harder against the surface, trying to get closer to him.

And I felt that same pulsing sensation between my legs, where Damien's body was pressed against mine. Thick and hard and needy. He rocked against me in desperate, involuntary thrusts, and his tongue mirrored that movement, filling me, but not enough. It would never be enough.

My blood was on fire as I tore at Damien's belt, freeing him as he pulled my shoes, leggings, and underwear off in seconds flat.

And then he was everywhere. There wasn't a part of me that Damien wasn't touching, filling, flooding with love. The river of emotion inside of me overflowed, pouring down the sides of my face as my body stretched and my heart swelled, full to bursting with the enormity of the moment, of this man, of my awe and admiration and gratitude for him.

My awareness contracted until all I could feel were the places where we touched. All I could hear was our breathing, our bodies colliding. All I could taste was his love, his relief. And I wanted to live in that liminal space forever—the place between waking and dreaming, where I had him all to myself. Where the outside world couldn't touch us and time didn't exist.

But time did exist, and it was racing. I felt it in every surge of blood, every punishing thrust, every ragged breath and broken moan.

I cried out as he pushed me closer to the brink, mourning the loss of our connection before it was even over. I didn't want to come. I didn't want to ever feel less whole, less overwhelmingly complete, than I did with him inside of me. But our bodies had gone rogue. We'd become desperate, ravenous, frenzied things—clawing and biting, growling and crying.

I tasted Damien's tears on my tongue as he drove into me harder, felt his agony and ecstasy as he stiffened and swelled inside of me. And when his teeth clamped down on my bottom lip and he filled me to my breaking point, I tilted my hips and took even more. His pain was my pleasure, my undoing. I wanted every drop, wanted to suck it from his body until he was free of it. Until it was mine. Claiming his mouth, I whimpered through my orgasm as I clenched and convulsed around his throbbing cock, greedily swallowing every spurt of hot cum and bitter relief that he poured into me.

There were no words exchanged. Only tears and kisses and—when I finally found the courage to open my eyes—long, lingering glances that filled me with joy.

Lifting me up so that I was straddling his lap, Damien wrapped his arms around my waist and buried his face in my neck.

I cradled his head and stroked his hair as I finally allowed myself to look out the window and take in our surroundings.

We were sitting on the floor of a helicopter on the top of a tall building, and outside the window, in a river of blood, lay five male bodies and a still-smoking cigar.

Alexi's corpse was gruesome. He must have been shot at least a hundred times. There was almost nothing left of his head, and his body oozed blood from so many holes that it resembled a weeping sponge. I couldn't look.

Kneeling beside Damien, I kept my eyes on his profile while he stared directly into the pulpy void that had once been his father's face.

"I'm so sorry," I whispered, gently rubbing his back. "I know you hated him, but that doesn't make losing your last parent any easier. Trust me, I know."

Damien returned my gaze with sorrowful eyes, and I immediately regretted my words. He took full responsibility for my family's deaths. I shouldn't have brought it up.

"And I'm sorry that I couldn't explain what was happening," I added, changing the subject. "I didn't expect to be unconscious while it all went down."

Damien's dark eyebrows shot up. "You knew about this?"

I smiled a little too brightly. "It was my idea. I brought the laptop from the cathedral here and gave it to Paul. He speaks Russian, so he was able to operate the drone software."

Damien's mouth fell open. "Paul's alive?"

I nodded, plucking the lit cigar off the ground. "He and Jack were hiding out in Merchant's Arch when I came to find you."

"Wait. Jack's alive too?" His gray eyes glistened as he hung on my every word.

"She's in rough shape," I said, brushing the dirt off the cigar. "Two gunshot wounds and probably some broken ribs, but they were wearing body armor, so they're gonna be okay."

Damien sighed with his entire body. "I saw them get shot. I … I thought …"

"It's okay." I smiled, cupping his face with my free hand. "They're okay."

Nodding as he struggled to process that information, Damien took the cigar out of my hand and inhaled a mouthful of smoke, releasing it along with the grief that had been weighing on his shoulders.

"So, Paul figured out how to unlock the laptop?"

"No … I, em, went and found the key."

Damien side-eyed me as he took another drag.

There was no good way to say it, so I reached into the pocket of Kellen's jacket and pulled out a finger wrapped in a blood-stained paper towel.

"Holy shite." Damien choked out a cloud of smoke. "Where'd ya get that?"

"The hospital," I said, sticking it back in my pocket. "I tried every finger on six dead soldiers before I found the right one."

Damien shook his head at me in speechless awe, and a tingly rush of pride warmed my cheeks. Accepting the cigar in his hand, I took a long puff and allowed myself to enjoy that tiny moment. To savor Damien's admiration and the flavors of vanilla and spice and a sweet, earthy cedar on my tongue.

"Paul used the laptop to call all the drones in the city to Merchant's Arch. Then, when I screamed, it activated all of them at once. He let them target me for the countdown to confuse Alexi, but when it came time to shoot, he switched the target from me to"—I couldn't bring myself to look at the bodies next to us—"them."

Damien's gaze drifted to the bloodbath on the roof, and he held out his hand, silently asking for the cigar.

I passed it over as I watched his thoughts darken.

"I did it again," he said, exhaling a cloud of vanilla-scented smoke. "I fucking failed."

"You what?"

"I had one job, Clover. With everyone distracted by the drones, I coulda grabbed the sergeant's gun when I took you out of his arms. I coulda killed Alexi right then and there, and I fuckin' didn't. My entire life had been leadin' up to that moment, and when I had the opportunity, I fuckin' choked. Again." He glanced at me with bitter tears in his eyes as he shook his head and took another drag.

"Killing Alexi was never your job," I said, plucking the cigar from his frowning mouth and planting mine there instead. The flavor of vanilla custard cream danced at the edges of my consciousness as I pulled away, licking my lips with a smile.

"Never my job? It was my fuckin' life's purpose," he argued.

"No, it wasn't." I stamped the cigar out and held his tortured stare, speaking slowly to make sure that my next three words hit their mark. "It was ours."

Damien's face paled as I kissed his parted lips again.

"You were never meant to do this on your own," I said, cupping his cheek. "If I've learned anything over the past two weeks, it's that we only survive … when we stay together. We only succeed … when we do it together."

I gestured toward the massacre that I was too squeamish to look at. "If you'd shot Alexi, there were four other men on this roof who woulda killed you on the spot. You did the right thing, Damien. You protected me." I beamed, pressing my forehead to his. "And I protected you."

Pulling me into his arms, Damien kissed me with a combination of reverence and relief that was so powerful it bathed the back of my eyelids in a blinding blue light. It filled me from the tips of my toes to the top of my head, and when he pulled away, my body tingled in every place he had ever touched—both in this life and the last.

"You jump, I jump." He smirked, and for the first time in days, I knew everything was going to be okay.

I just didn't know how.

"Damien?" I swallowed. "How are we gonna get down from here without being captured?"

"I've been thinking about that," he said, pursing his lips in contemplation, "and I don't think it'll be a problem."

"Why not?"

He sat me down on the roof next to him and, with one last kiss, walked over to a camera on a tripod a few meters away.

Switching it on, Damien took a few steps back and smoothed his hands down the front of his military uniform before running his fingers through his dark hair. His posture stiffened. His stare went cold. And before me stood a man who was destined for greatness. I'd never seen Damien at his strongest. He'd been injured since the day I'd pulled him out of the sea. Seeing him standing in his full power, healthy and nearly healed, was a religious experience.

"Hello." He spoke in English using his natural Irish accent rather than the fake Russian one he'd used on TV the day before. "This is Lenin Abramov, vice president of the Russian Federation and son of President Alexi Abramov."

Damien repeated his greeting in Russian.

"Less than an hour ago, my father was slain by Irish rebel forces. Based on the order of succession, which was amended yesterday during my appointment to the position of vice president, I stand before you ... as the new president of the Russian Federation."

Holy.

Fucking.

Shit.

CHAPTER 51

DAMIEN

SIX MONTHS LATER

"Good evening. I am coming to you live from the Kremlin with President Lenin Abramov to discuss today's breaking news—that the Republic of Ireland has officially been approved to join the North Atlantic Treaty Organization."

Mia Patel, a veteran news anchor for the BBC, was perched on the edge of her seat across from me in a staged corner of the Kremlin's executive office. I fucking hated being on TV, not because I was afraid of public speaking—after spending five years of my life in a near-constant state of fear, being interviewed didn't exactly scare me—but because of how little I knew about politics. I'd been kidnapped at the age of fifteen and had no education beyond that other than how to speak Russian and kill anything that walked. It really should have been Clover in that seat.

"President Abramov," Mia continued, "you have dual citizenship with Russia and Ireland and are considered to be personally responsible for spearheading Ireland's application to join NATO. Many didn't think it would be possible due to initial opposition from the UK. How did you help broker that deal?"

I glanced across the room at Clover, who was standing out of the way of the TV crew with a proud little smile on her perfect fucking face.

"I can't take credit for the NATO bid," I said without taking my eyes off of Clo. "That was my brilliant wife, Clover's, idea. Clo, say hi."

A camera panned over to her, and I tried not to laugh. I loved making that woman blush. Her freckled cheeks flushed pink as she waved and shot me a murderous glare.

Clover and I weren't technically married—at least not in this lifetime—but she was still my wife. She would always be my wife, and calling her anything other than that felt like a fucking lie.

"After pulling out of Ireland, our goal was to help ensure that they never had to fear another foreign invasion, and joining NATO would give them that protection. Because their acceptance had to be unanimous, convincing the UK to allow them in was crucial, but after speaking with the prime minister, it became clear that UK's issue wasn't with Ireland, nor was Russia's under the rule of my father. It was with their ruling party, the United Irish Brotherhood."

Mia steepled her fingers under her chin. "Yes. Séamus Rooney, the head of the UIB and former taoiseach of Ireland, fled during the invasion and is rumored to be avoiding extradition in Venezuela."

"That's correct. And with him gone, Irish government officials had a much easier time removing the remaining UIB party members and securing their NATO membership."

"Well, congratulations to you—and to your wife—on the role you played in this historic event."

I tried not to laugh as Clover froze in terror, anticipating another on-screen moment, but Mia spared her and kept the questions rolling.

"And what does this decision mean for you personally?"

This was the moment she'd been waiting for. Mia's stoic face perked up as she reveled in the exclusive scoop I was about to give her and the BBC.

Turning to face the camera, I caught myself watching Clover out of the corner of my eye. Nothing had my full attention anymore—not even a worldwide prime-time interview—and it hadn't since the moment I'd first laid eyes on her, across the Irish Sea. Even when she wasn't in the room, part of my mind was never *not* thinking about her. She was the sun that the rest of my life revolved around.

And soon, the rest of my life would require a lot less of my attention.

"It means that I can step down as the president of the Russian Federation."

Clover beamed, and it took all the professionalism I pretended to have not to stare at her gorgeous, happy face instead of the camera.

"I have been holding this position to protect Ireland from being attacked again by my potential successor, but now that the UIB has been removed from office and Ireland has the means to protect itself against future invasions, I can rest assured that they will never be defenseless, or have a reason to be attacked, again. Therefore, the time has come for me to submit my resignation and allow the Russian people to do what they haven't been allowed to do in over a decade—elect a president of their choosing."

As soon as they turned off the cameras and unclipped my mic, I bolted across the room and picked Clover up off her feet. Her auburn hair formed a curtain around our faces, and for a moment, it was just the two of us again.

"We're goin' home, angel." I grinned, tilting my head back so that she could claim the kiss that had been waiting for her since that goddamn interview had begun.

I couldn't have done any of it without her. Clover was more the president of Russia than I was. She was brilliant, organized, eager to learn, and a natural problem-solver. But she didn't want the job any more than I did, so the news that we could finally go home was an absolute dream come true.

The moment I set my girl back down, Mia was there, waiting patiently with a phone in her hand. "Mr. President. Excuse my interruption, but you're gonna want to see this."

Mia tapped the screen and swiped through video after video of people cheering and crying and banging spoons on metal pots throughout the city.

"Our exterior film crew has been sending me footage of the scene in Moscow right now. It would seem that your citizens are very excited about the chance to elect their own president."

Clover and I stared at the footage in awe. When I had become president, we had been terrified that I'd be assassinated, either by the Bratva for my role in rebuilding Ireland, by a challenger who considered me weaker than my father, or by a random disgruntled citizen. It never occurred to us that our ideas would actually be embraced by a country I'd considered to be the enemy for so long.

The Bratva was the hardest to win over. They'd accepted me because they had to—I was Alexi's only male heir, and the Russian Mafia was nothing if not a monarchy—but earning their trust had taken a little more work.

"Mr. President," one of my security guards said in Russian, appearing at my side like a shadow. "The, uh, *package* you ordered has arrived, sir."

Thanking Mia and kissing Clover one more time, I excused myself and followed Igor down to the basement and through an underground tunnel to the Ivan the Great Bell Tower. During Ivan the Terrible's reign, the basement had been converted into a secret prison and torture chamber, which I'd had the pleasure of not needing ... until now.

The tunnel and prison were as dark and damp and cold and barren as the rest of the palace was opulent and bright. But they weren't quiet. Not anymore. Deep Russian voices and booming laughter echoed off the stone walls as I exited the tunnel and emerged into the tower's basement. Cells with metal doors lined the perimeter of the space, and ancient medieval torture devices were gathered in the center, collecting dust like some kind of morbid, forgotten museum exhibit.

But it wasn't forgotten anymore.

Every Bratva elder and high-ranking officer in Moscow had gathered to partake in something I'd been promising to deliver since I'd first stepped foot back in Russia—a peace offering, a parting gift, and proof that no matter how much I'd hated my father, there was a little bit of Abramov in me after all.

Silence fell over the room as I entered, and at least fifty ruthless, sadistic psychopaths—many of whom were my blood relatives—turned to face me.

God, I couldn't wait to go back to Ireland.

"Brothers," I began, thankful that I'd remembered to speak in Russian. I'd had the attention of the entire world half an hour earlier, but that hadn't intimidated me half as much as the cold, calculating stares of the Bratva's most seasoned killers. "As you might have heard, I will be stepping down soon, both as Russia's president ... and also as your leader. It's been an honor, but I think we can all agree that my uncle Yuri, Alexi's brother and one of your most esteemed elders"—I gestured toward the proud, potbellied bastard at the front of the crowd—"is much better suited for the job."

No one argued.

"I've asked you all here because I have a parting gift for you—a token of my appreciation for your loyalty and a symbol of my dedication to your cause."

I wasn't dedicated to shite, except for protecting Clover and Ireland from sick fucks like them.

"Igor, if you don't mind."

The head of my security team, who'd already taken his position next to a prison cell, opened the ancient metal door to reveal a trembling, piss-soaked, red-faced Irishman, bound and gagged and whimpering softly.

"Gentleman, as promised, I present to you the leader of the UIB—the organization that ordered the murder of Alexi's uncle, Dmitry. The organization that had Alexi arrested and imprisoned over twenty years ago. And the organization that was ultimately responsible for his death. Punishing this man was the reason my father went to war with Ireland, and I can think of no better way to express my gratitude than by giving you the satisfaction of finishing what he started."

No one was looking at me anymore. Every head in the room had turned to face Séamus, and if I wasn't mistaken, I thought I saw the piss stain on the front of his trousers darken.

A chorus of laughter and muffled screams echoed through the tunnel as I headed back to the palace, but I barely heard them.

I was too busy loosening my tie and unbuttoning my suit jacket as I pictured all the ways Clover and I were going to celebrate once I made it back to the presidential suite.

Nothing got my full attention anymore.

Nothing except for my wife.

EPILOGUE

CLOVER
SIX MONTHS LATER

Since we'd met, almost every outfit Damien had ever worn was a uniform of one kind or another—the military clothes, the hospital clothes, the endless suits provided to him at the Kremlin. In fact, the first time I'd ever seen him in something that wasn't a uniform was when Kate gave him Kellen's black trousers and white shirt to wear back in Wexford. I still remembered the way I'd sobbed when I came downstairs and found him waiting for me—smiling, clean-shaven, and wearing those clothes. It was the handsomest he'd ever looked.

Until today.

Because today, he was wearing black trousers, a white shirt, *and* my ring on his finger.

Sliding a simple gold band on top of the engagement ring he'd given me the night of his resignation, Damien recited his vows as an audience of seagulls circled overhead and a curious crab wandered dangerously close to our bare feet.

The outfits had been my vision—Damien's simple shirt and trousers and my white lace gown with a handful of bluebells and baby's breath woven into my hair—but being barefoot had been his idea. He told me I'd find out why after the ceremony.

"So, by the power vested in me by … no one"—Paul grinned as he glanced from Damien to me, then back down at his notes—"I now pronounce you … husband and wife. You may kiss the bride."

Jack howled, and Kate sniffled, and all three of them clapped as Damien held my gaze, wrapped a hand around the back of my neck with a smirk that made my insides tingle, and kissed me in a way that would have gotten us excommunicated from any church in Ireland.

Which was why I was so happy we'd decided to have our ceremony on the Eye instead.

And even happier that the rain had held off.

The sky was smothered in clouds as thick as the frosting on one of Kate's cakes, but when I tipped my head back and let the wind catch my hair, the only thing I felt was a single drop of water, right on the tip of my nose.

Followed by Damien's tongue as he licked it off.

"You know your mother is watchin', right?" I laughed, but the sentiment made both of our smiles fade a little.

We were orphans now. Both of us. Kate and Jack were all we had left.

Turning toward them, I finally allowed myself to look at the coastline of Howth, and what I saw took my breath away. The lighthouse was in the process of being rebuilt, using as many of the original granite blocks as they could find at the bottom of the harbor. The fishing boats, turned tour boats for the summer, waved to us as they looped around the island—waiting for the ceremony to be over before they docked with their tourists. And there, on the top of the cliff, in the spot where I used to sit and stare at the spot where I was standing now, was a white stucco house with a lemon-yellow door.

Only now, it had a second story.

And a balcony.

Damien was ready with open arms when I spun and launched myself at him, lifting me off the grassy island and wrapping my legs around his waist.

"Welcome home." He grinned a millisecond before my mouth crashed against his.

"Thank you," I sobbed, peppering his eyes, his nose, his clean-shaven cheeks with kisses. "When did you? How did you …"

"Jack needed somethin' to do while she was on the mend, so I gave her a little project. Two actually."

"Two?" My heart fluttered as I stared into his sparkling silver eyes, alight with mischief of the very best kind.

Damien nodded slowly, holding my gaze with a smirk that would have made my knees weak if I were still standing. "Got the house in Glenshire too."

Glenshire.

My heart simply couldn't hold all of the love and gratitude I felt for this man. This *soul.* It spilled from my eyes as I kissed him again, radiated from my hands as I clutched his face. It coursed through the very marrow of my bones, lighting me up, making me glow.

"Jack's been a little busy."

I turned to find Jack leaning on her cane, trying to look nonchalant but failing miserably, thanks to the massive prideful grin on her face.

"*You* did this?" My gaze darted over to the two-story stunner on the cliff again. "And …" A lump formed in my throat. "And Glenshire?"

"I know some former military lads in the construction business." She shrugged. "Kate decorated, so I apologize in advance for the inside, but the outside's class, right?"

Kate elbowed her wife, who grimaced dramatically and clutched her ribs.

"I can't take credit for any of it, but if ya need a butler, let me know." Paul chuckled, clapping a hand on Damien's shoulder.

Reaching into his pocket, Damien tossed a set of keys to Jack. "Why don't ya give Paul a tour? We'll meet ya there after I show Clo her other wedding gift."

"You got it, boss," Jack said, tossing her wife a quick wink. There was no mistaking the blush on Kate's face as she returned the look with a knowing smirk.

Then, the three of them navigated the rocky shore to the tour boat that was waiting to take them back.

Once Damien set me down on my bare feet and I finally mustered the strength to tear my eyes away from the house on the cliff, I froze mid-step when I glanced over at the beautiful, natural wood–finish speedboat he'd rented.

Because there next to it, staring at me with deep brown eyes, was a single gray seal.

Grabbing Damien's arm, I forced him to stop, and the two of us stood in silence for what felt like minutes.

The seal didn't wink at me. It didn't raise its flipper and wave. But something in it acknowledged something in me, and that felt like enough.

It was enough.

Closing my eyes, I smiled up at the sky.

And felt a drop of rain kiss my cheek.

"Don't look."

"I know where you're taking me."

"Well, ya still can't look."

Hiking my wedding dress up to my knees, I kept my eyes closed as Damien guided me along a narrow ridge through freezing cold ankle-deep water.

Once the ceiling opened up and the familiar crunch of pebbles under our bare feet echoed off the stone walls, Damien wrapped his arm around me and said, "Okay, look."

When I opened my eyes, my body hummed with a sensation I hadn't felt in over a year, one of the most basic human pleasures that I'd nearly forgotten, but that Damien had returned to me tenfold. The feeling of coming home.

Stone walls that my hands knew by touch alone, massive boulders that had been my make-believe furniture, a pebbled beach that, for a few moments every morning, reflected the rising sun like a disco ball … and at the far end, facing the sea and surrounded by candles and rose petals, a gorgeous wooden writing desk … and a matching four-poster bed.

"Damien …" My eyes filled with fresh tears as I glanced up at his sweet smile. "What is all this?"

He shrugged innocently, but there was a wicked gleam in his gray eyes. "My plan was to make you a writing cave, but … when I thought about bringing you here"—he turned to face me, placing his hands on my waist—"and I remembered waking up over there"—he pointed at a spot on the beach behind him—"with you on my chest"—Damien pulled my body toward his until the white lace of my wedding dress was pressed against the black tie of his suit—"and I thought about that kiss, up against the wall, over there"—Damien dipped his head and paused, his lips a breath away from mine—"I decided your writing cave needed to double as a sex dungeon."

A laugh burst out of me but was quickly silenced by Damien's talented mouth. His lips molded to mine, and as his tongue slipped inside, swirling and caressing and dizzying me with need, I was instantly transported back to that night. When I'd finally given in to the undeniable connection I felt. When I'd first tasted forever and recognized its sweetness. When I'd been so crippled with fear that I ruined the moment and spent the night curled up in a ball in his arms.

But I wasn't afraid anymore. For the first time since our souls had collided all those years ago, we were finally safe. Truly free. And ready for a fucking do-over.

Pearls and buttons scattered across the pebbled beach as Damien and I tore the wedding clothes from one another's body, giving in to the insatiable desire we'd tried so hard to deny the last time we were there.

My teeth scraped over Damien's chiseled jaw as I jerked open his belt buckle and unzipped his trousers.

His rough hands palmed my breasts and rubbed my nipples as I stepped out of my wedding gown and kicked it to the side of the cave.

Damien's wolfish smile made my knickers dampen as he gazed down the length of my body. Then, his eyes darkened as his finger hooked into the garter around my left thigh. A phantom memory of a faded dream flashed in my mind—an open tourniquet, gushing blood—but then it was gone, replaced with the ecstasy of Damien's fingertips sliding along the damp satin between my legs.

Clutching his jaw, I pulled his face to mine and kissed him impatiently while he slid his boxers down one-handed. Then, I smiled around his tongue as his warm, rigid length pressed against my belly.

Gliding my hand down his chest, I let my fingertips swirl over the star-shaped scar where his bullet wound had been. Then, I dipped my head and traced it with my tongue. If Damien hadn't been shot, I wouldn't have needed to take care of him, and we might never have reconnected. Some of the most painful experiences of our lives had led to the happiest, and I hoped, as I took him in my hands and traced the length of him with my tongue, that all of the pain was finally behind us now.

That we could stop trying to keep each other alive.

And start trying to make each other come.

The thought made me giggle, and Damien slid a finger under my chin, encouraging me to look up at him.

"Fuck, angel. The sight of you smilin' with my cock in your mouth is the best wedding gift you could ever give me."

Heat flooded my cheeks as I dropped my eyes.

"Don't do that. Look at me, darlin'. I wanna see you."

Emboldened by his words, I held Damien's stormy stare as I gripped the thick base of his cock and took him as deep in my throat as I possibly could. He cursed and gripped my hair as I sucked my way back up, licking a bead of pre-cum from his swollen crown, but he never once took his eyes off mine.

I had Damien's full attention. Always. And the warmth I felt from even his steeliest stares made me bloom like the rays of the sun. Grow. Evolve. I could do anything when he looked at me like that. But mostly, I just wanted to make him smile.

"Fuck." Pulling me up by my hair, Damien slammed his mouth against mine a second before slamming my back against the closest cave wall. He lifted my garter-adorned thigh over his hip and ground his wet cock against my slippery flesh.

"I need you," he panted, breaking our kiss to watch our scarred bodies slide against one another.

Clutching his jaw, I lifted his face to mine. "Then, take me." I smirked.

And he did.

Dragging his length over my throbbing clit, Damien slipped his tongue into my mouth at the same moment that he thrust the head of his cock into my equally needy body.

And I instantly tensed around him.

"Shh …" he whispered, retreating and thrusting again, a few centimeters at a time. "Relax, darlin'. Let me in."

Reaching between us, Damien rubbed my clit with his thumb as he filled me, surging deeper and deeper with every attempt.

"That's my girl," he rasped, dropping his forehead to mine as he watched me stretch and struggle to take him all. "That's my fuckin' angel. Look at you."

Damien lifted his eyes to mine as my hips began to roll in concert with his expert thumb.

"That feel good, baby?"

He licked his lips, and I leaned forward, needing to taste them as well.

Damien granted my wish, kissing me deeply and working my clit until I finally relaxed enough to let him all the way in. Removing his hand, Damien thrust into me fully, and the moment his pelvis pressed against my clit, my pussy contracted around him in pleasure.

"Fuck," Damien hissed, capturing my lip between his teeth.

"What do you want to do, Mrs. Hughes?" he asked, withdrawing and filling me again in one slow, hard thrust. "Because if I have my way, I'm gonna keep fucking you right here against this wall."

"Promise?" I whispered, digging my heel into his firm arse until he ground against me again. It was everything I'd been craving since the last time we were there, another dream that Damien had made come true without me even having to ask.

"God, you're perfect." He smiled before diving for my lips again, and that one fleeting grin was nearly enough to make me come all by itself.

Harder and faster, Damien pounded into me, stone digging into my back as my nails dug into his. Teeth sank into throats. Fingers sank into hair. We weren't afraid to add a few new scars to our battle-worn bodies because we knew that once we used them up, we would just get new ones and do it all over again.

I reveled in the sound of his body pounding against mine as it echoed throughout the cave, as his moans turned to growls and reverberated through my chest.

Lifting my other leg, Damien held me up by the back of my thighs, and with my hips tilted slightly, he was able to fill me even deeper than before.

A desperate whimper punctuated my every panting breath as I reached between us and rubbed my clit.

"That's my girl," Damien rasped, swelling inside of me. "You ready, baby?" He kissed me, thrusting faster. "You ready to come for me?"

"Mmhmm," I moaned, nodding against his forehead as he drove into me harder. Pushed my body to the brink of something magical.

"That's it," he hissed as I whimpered, squeezing him tighter. "Fuck, I can feel you. Let go, angel. Let go. I got ya."

Damien's words were my undoing. Gripping his shoulders, I buried my face in his corded neck as the outside world shattered and fell to his feet. There was only darkness, and the weightlessness of being held in Damien's arms, and a pulsing, euphoric, all-consuming rush of heat as he stilled inside of me and came on a strangled cry.

Without putting me down, Damien walked over to the bed and sat on the edge, filling me fully as I settled onto his lap.

A soft moan left my lips as I gazed into eyes the same color as my favorite place in the entire world.

Glancing over Damien's shoulder at the desk, I noticed a familiar black bag sitting in the chair, and a smile spread across my face.

"My backpack!" I cried. "Damien! Oh my God, are my books still in there?"

He nodded. "Your books, your photos, a few cheap cigars."

"My books." I laughed and shook my head, that sentence taking on a whole new meaning. "I still can't believe I wrote those."

"I can." Damien said, his voice suddenly serious. "You can do anything, Clover. Literally anything."

Gazing back at his sweet face, I ran my hands through his hair and considered our future. "What are *you* going to do?" I asked. "I could turn the shed into a woodshop for you."

Damien shook his head. "I think … I might try for a position on the County Council."

"What?" I couldn't hide the surprise in my voice. "You don't even like politics."

"I don't, but … I want to fix this place … for you. I want to make things right."

I beamed. "Then, you will."

"You know"—Damien smirked, obviously ready to change the subject as his cock swelled inside of me—"I was thinking about your books."

"Oh, really?" I purred, rolling my hips as he ground them down onto him with his rough hands.

"Mmhmm. Should I be offended that you thought I was a fairy when you first met me?"

I laughed. "*That's* what you want to know?"

He nodded, sliding that talented tongue across his smirking bottom lip as he worked my hips a little faster.

"You obviously don't read a lot of romance." I moaned, closing my eyes as he thrust into me from underneath.

"Fairies are the sexiest of all the mythological creatures," I panted. "They're strong and beautiful and fierce and magical."

"Like you," he said, kissing his way from my collarbone up to my jaw.

"Like you," I echoed, threading my fingers into his shiny black hair.

And that was when I realized, as Damien and I chased our bliss without a care in the world, that I'd finally done it.

I'd found my way to the otherworld.

Thank you so, so much for reading The Devil Himself*!*

If you enjoyed this us-against-the-world romance, then read on for a sneak peek of my dystopian romance series, The Rain Trilogy. *It has all the heart-racing suspense, steam, and emotional intensity of the* Devil of Dublin *series, but instead of trying to survive a Mafia war, Rain and Wes are trying to survive a mysterious apocalyptic event. Enjoy!*

ACKNOWLEDGMENTS

This book is a love letter to all the readers who reached out to me after finishing *Devil of Dublin* and said, "We want more Kellen and Darby!" and, "Is there going to be a sequel?" and, "When's the next book?!" and, "Where did you find that Irish voice actor, and can he please, please, please narrate everything you write from now on?!?!"

I had no intention of writing a sequel to *Devil of Dublin*, but as soon as I published it, I began to feel the same way as you guys. I missed these characters. I missed this world. And I began to think, "What if?"

What if Kellen and Darby had another adventure? What would that look like? Should it be a second-generation story, featuring their child? Or should they be reincarnated? OH MY GOD. THEY SHOULD BE REINCARNATED, AND THEY HAVE TO FIND EACH OTHER ALL OVER AGAIN, AND THE BAD GUYS ARE EVEN MORE POWERFUL NOW, AND THEY HAVE ARMIES, AND KELLEN AND DARBY COULD BE ON DIFFERENT SIDES OF THE MAFIA WAR, JUST LIKE ROMEO AND JULIET, AND HE COULD BE HURT, AND SHE HAS TO TAKE CARE OF HIM, BUT SHE HATES HIM BECAUSE HE KILLED HER FAMILY! YESSSSSSSS!

And so, *The Devil Himself* was born. But plotting this epic Mafia/military/star-crossed lovers/reincarnation romance proved to be a lot more difficult than I ever expected. It took me fifteen months to write the first draft of this book. I walked away from it at least a dozen times. It tested me and challenged me in ways that were borderline non-consensual. But it was thanks to a handful of amazing people that I persevered and brought Damien and Clover to life.

Firstly, I have to thank my aforementioned voice actor, Eric Nolan, for being so damn good at his job that people were clamoring for more. I honestly would not have written this book if he hadn't promised to narrate it, so if you enjoyed it, you have him to thank. In fact, the *Devil of Dublin* world has become just as much his as it is mine, to the point that we've expanded the brand to include an entire catalog of fully immersive audio erotica stories over on the Quinn app. Be sure to check them out if you want to hear what else we've been working on.

And of course, I have to thank my real-life book boyfriend, Ken, for holding down the fort while I was holed up in the writing cave for months and months on end. The suffering I did for this book was legendary. I didn't eat. I didn't sleep. I didn't leave my office, except to wander off in the woods, where I would mutter to myself and walk in circles and pray to the writing gods for the next chapter idea, the next plot twist, the next jigsaw piece that would help me complete this seemingly never-ending puzzle. But Ken supported me through it and managed to keep our kids alive until it was over, and for that, he has my undying gratitude.

I'd also like to thank my Irish beta readers/developmental editors—Nicole McCurdy, Adele Halpin, and Alison Clery—for helping to make this story as authentic, accurate, and culturally sensitive as possible. Your insights were absolutely invaluable, and I appreciate you all so much. *Go raibh míle maith agat!*

A huge thank you to my copy editor, Jovana Shirley; my content editor, Traci Finlay; my beta reader, Sammie Nania; and my proofreaders (in alphabetical order), Hanna Calloway, Shanna Leclair, Katie Hague, Rhonda Lind, and Jill Silva. Your timeliness, attention to detail, keen eyes, and gentle honesty are rare and precious things. Don't ever quit me!

And finally, to my readers … thank you for loving Kellen and Darby as much as I did. Thank you for telling your friends and followers and family members and book clubs to read *Devil of Dublin*. And thank you for being so incredibly patient with me while I brought *The Devil Himself* to life. It was definitely a labor of love. I cherish your support; your willingness to go on any wild, weird, genre-bending ride I offer to take you on; and your loving, open-minded spirit. You are the reason I get to do my dream job, and I will never ever take that for granted. Seriously. Thank you.

PLAYLIST

Strap in for a moody, vibey, angsty ride through mystical forests, seaside towns, soul-deep desire, and love that spans lifetimes in this collection of songs that fanned the flames of my burning heart while I wrote *The Devil Himself.*

You can stream the playlist for free on Spotify. Just search "The Devil Himself."

"You're One of Us Now" by Movements
"The Lighthouse" by Halsey
"You'll Be Fine" by Anthony Green
"Daddy Issues" by The Neighbourhood
"Darling" by Halsey
"This Modern Love" by Bloc Party
"Ya'aburnee" by Halsey
"Fail You" by Movements
"Bells in Santa Fe" by Halsey
"Killing Time" by Movements
"Dream" by Bishop Briggs
"When Your Heart Stops Beating" by +44
"Happier" by YUNGBLUD, featuring Oli Sykes of Bring Me the Horizon

"White Flag" by Bishop Briggs
"Dead Man" by David Kushner
"Beach House" by Del Water Gap
"This Love (Taylor's Version)" by Taylor Swift

PRAYING FOR RAIN
CHAPTER 1

RAIN

I'm sitting in a booth at Burger Palace. I don't remember how I got here, or when, but the empty seat across from me tells me that I came alone.

The place smells like classic greasy burgers and fries. My stomach snarls in response.

God, I'm starving.

I glance across the bustling fast-food restaurant at the giant digital menu on the wall and notice four banners hanging on either side of the checkout counter. They're huge, hanging from the ceiling all the way down to the floor. Only, instead of showing pretty models eating airbrushed cheeseburgers, these things look like propaganda for the Antichrist. Each one is bright red with the silhouette of a hooded figure on horseback in the middle. One is holding a massive sword over his head. Another one has a scythe, like the Grim Reaper. One is swinging a mace, and the fourth one is charging forward with a flaming torch. Even though I can't see their faces, I almost feel like their demonic eyes are staring right at me.

This is a fucked-up marketing campaign, *I think, searching the terrifying banners for more information.*

The only text I see on them anywhere is a simple date in bold white font at the top of each one.

April 23.

What the hell?

I look around the restaurant for more clues, but all I find are happy little families sucking soda out of red cups with hooded horsemen on them. A little boy carries a Big Kid Box to his seat with an image of the Grim Reaper guy on it. A little girl licks blood-red ice cream out of a cracked black cone. And, on every wrapper, every poster, every napkin, straw, and ketchup packet, there's the same date.

April 23? *I rack my brain.* April 23. What the hell is going to happen on April twen—

Before I can finish my thought, the lights flicker off and the doors burst open. Wind whips through the small restaurant like a tornado, sending drinks crashing and people scrambling, as four hooded figures on giant smoke-breathing horses charge in.

Suddenly, the banners, the ad campaign—it all makes sense.

Today is April 23.

And we're all gonna die.

Smoke and screams and chaos fill the air as I scurry to the floor beneath my table, backing all the way up to the wall and hugging my knees to my chest.

I can't breathe. I can't blink. I can't think. All I can do it cover my ears and try to block out the screams of mothers and children as I peer into the darkness.

Flames climb up the black-and-red banners, illuminating a wasteland before me. Furniture overturned. Bodies strewed about the wreckage. Severed heads, missing limbs, torsos impaled on table legs. My hands move from my ears to my mouth as I muffle a scream.

Don't let them hear you.

Thick black smoke begins to curl and creep into my hiding spot, making my eyes water and my throat burn. I can hardly see past the table now, and suppressing the cough and the panic building in my throat is getting harder and harder to do.

I know I need to run—I have to—but my legs won't cooperate. I'm stuck in the fetal position, rocking like a child, as I pull my T-shirt over my mouth and nose.

I scream at myself inside my head, but it's my mother's voice that finally gets my ass in gear. "Are you going to stay home all day and wallow, like your father, or are you gonna get out there and try to help somebody?" *Her scolding from this morning rings in my ears louder than the cries of the burning, impaled women and children all around me.*

I want to help. Even if, right now, the only person I can help is myself.

Placing my palms on the filthy floor, I slowly bring my knees down so that I'm on all fours.

I can do this.

Taking one last breath, I straighten my back and prepare to crawl to safety. I can't see the exits through all the smoke, but I can see the two blood-spattered hooves that come to a stop directly in front of me when I take my first step.

I wake up at the tail end of a scream, just like I do every morning. Just like we all do, ever since the nightmares began.

Grabbing my cell phone off the charger, I hold my breath and read the date.

April 20.

I sigh and toss it back onto the nightstand.

I used to feel so relieved when I woke up from the nightmare. Back when I still had hope that some scientist somewhere was gonna figure it out. But everybody on the planet has been dreaming about the four horsemen of the apocalypse coming on April 23 for almost a year now, and we still don't have answers.

After a few months, most of the world's top researchers either resigned in defeat, died from heart attacks, or went crazy from the stress of trying to figure it out. Every day, the news got worse, the crime rate skyrocketed, and eventually, the newscasters just stopped reporting. Without answers or hope or, hell, even fake news to calm us down, most people have just accepted that the world is going to end on April 23.

Myself included.

I still feel relieved when I wake up from the nightmare, but now, it's only because I can't wait for it to be over.

Three more days. I only have to do this shit for three more days.

I drag myself out of bed and groan at my reflection in the bathroom mirror. Choppy, chin-length black hair frames my pale face, the same way that yesterday's smudged eyeliner frames my sunken blue eyes.

Where the fuck did my hair go?

My eyes scan the filthy countertop for a brush and land on my long black braid, still bound with an elastic band, lying in a heap next to an empty bottle of codeine cough syrup.

Way to go, Rain. Get high and cut all your hair off. Real original.

I try to remember what happened last night, but it's not even a blur. It's just gone. Like the hair that I pick up and toss onto my overflowing trash can on my way to turn on the shower.

We've been advised to use our bathtubs for water storage in case our town's supply gets cut off, but the way I see it, if we're all going to die anyway, why not enjoy a hot shower first?

And by *enjoy*, I mean cry under the stream until the water turns cold.

I towel-dry my hack job of a hairdo, throw on a tank top and a pair of plaid flannel pajama pants, and shove my feet into an old pair of cowboy boots. I used to want to look cute when I left the house. Now, I just want to look homeless. Bronzer, beachy waves, cleavage, cutoff jeans—all those things attract attention. The bad kind. The kind that gets you robbed or raped. At least, around here.

As much as I'd like to spend the next three days in bed with my head under the covers, I'm fucking starving, and all we have here is dried spaghetti noodles, a can of lima beans, and a bottle of expired pancake syrup. Our supplies have been running low ever since the gangs took over the neighborhood grocery stores. They'll let you *shop*, but you have to be willing to pay in their *preferred currency*, which, when you're a nineteen-year-old girl …

Let's just say I haven't gotten that desperate yet.

Luckily, Burger Palace is still serving. And *they* take cash. I just have to get in and out without drawing too much attention to myself.

I pick the Twenty One Pilots hoodie up off my floor and resist the urge to bury my nose in the soft cotton like I used to.

I know Carter's scent is long gone, just like him—and thank God for that. The last thing I need is another reminder that my stupid boyfriend chose to spend his last few weeks on earth in Tennessee with his family instead of here with me.

Asshole.

I yank the sweatshirt on over my head, completing my frumpiest look yet, and stomp down the stairs. The scene in the living room is pretty much the same as it is every morning. My father is passed out in his recliner, facing the front door, with a fifth of whiskey tucked in the crook of his elbow and a shotgun across his lap. I'd probably take more pity on him if he hadn't always been a mean-ass drunk.

But he has.

He's just a *paranoid* mean-ass drunk now.

I can't even bear to look at him. I cover my mouth with the sleeve of my sweatshirt to keep from gagging on the smell of piss as I snatch his prescription bottle of hydrocodone off the table.

I think you've had enough, old man.

Popping one of the little white pills into my mouth, I pocket the rest and cross the living room.

I grab my dad's keys off the hook by the front door and lock the doorknob on my way out. Even though I know how to drive, I don't bother taking my dad's truck. The roads are so clogged with wrecked and abandoned vehicles that they're basically impassable now.

Traffic laws were one of the first things to go after the nightmares began. Everybody started driving a little faster, having a few extra drinks, ignoring those pesky red lights and stop signs, and forgetting that turn signals had ever existed. There were so many accidents that the tow trucks and traffic cops and ambulance drivers couldn't keep up, so eventually, they just quit trying. The wrecks piled up and caused more wrecks, and then, when the gas stations closed, people started leaving their vehicles wherever they ran out of gas.

Franklin Springs, Georgia, has never exactly been a classy place, but now, it looks like one big demolition derby arena. I would know. I live right off the main two-lane highway that cuts through town. In fact, the *Welcome to Franklin Springs* sign hangs right across the street from my house. Of course, somebody recently spray-painted a giant UC over the RAN in Franklin, so the sign reads *Welcome to Fucklin Springs* now.

Can't imagine who would do such a thing.

The quickest way into town would be to walk along the highway about a mile or so, but it also feels like the quickest way to get raped or robbed, frumpy outfit or not, so I stick to the woods.

As soon as my feet hit the pine needle–covered trail behind my house, I feel like I can finally relax. I inhale the humid spring air. I listen to the birds chattering away up in the trees. I try on a smile; it doesn't feel right. And I pretend, for just a moment, that everything's okay again, like it used to be.

But, when I step out of the woods and feel the heat of a nearby car fire on my face, I remember.

Life sucks, and we're all gonna die.

I flip my hood over my head and tiptoe around the corner of the library, watching out for the three *R*s: rioters, rapists, and rabid dogs. The dogs don't really have rabies, but so many people have died in the weeks leading up to April 23 that their pets are starting to band together and hunt as a team.

So. Many. People.

Images of those I've lost flicker behind my eyes, dim and grainy, fighting to get a feeling past the hydrocodone. But the painkiller does its job, and within moments, I'm fuzzy and numb again.

When the coast is clear, I shove my hands in the front pocket of my hoodie to keep all my shit from falling out and scurry across the street. Cars and trucks are lurched on the curbs, overturned in the ditches, and abandoned with doors wide open in the middle of the lanes. I try not to think about how many of those cars might still have people in them as I reach out and pull open the Burger Palace door.

When I walk in, I half-expect to see flaming banners and demons slaying people on horseback, but it's just the entire miserable town of Franklin, crammed inside and yelling at each other.

God, it's loud. People who've lived here their whole lives are shoving fingers in each other's faces, arguing about who was next in line. Babies are crying. Mothers are crying. Toddlers are screaming and running around like wild animals. And everybody smells like liquor.

I sigh and begin to make my way to the back of the line when I notice that my third-grade teacher, Mrs. Frazier, is standing at a cash register. It's her turn to order, but she's too busy cursing out Pastor Blankenship, who's behind her in line, to get on with it. I'm sure Mrs. Frazier wouldn't mind if I—

I slip in front of her at the cash register, hoping she keeps screaming long enough for me to order.

"Hi, and welcome to Burger Palace!" A girl wearing a Burger Palace cap and polo shirt beams at me from across the counter. "May I take your order?"

I glance down the line and notice three more employees, all sporting the same exaggerated grin.

What the hell are they giving these people? Molly? Crystal meth?

"Uh … yeah." I keep my voice low. "I'll have a soda and a large fry."

"Would you like to Apocasize that?"

I blink. Twice. "I'm sorry, what?"

"Apocasize it!" She gestures up at one of the digital screens behind her, where an animated thirty-two-ounce drink and bucket of fries are holding hands and skipping around a fire. "It's not like we have to worry about carbs anymore, am I right?"

My eyebrows pull together. "Uh … no, I guess not." I hear Mrs. Frazier call Pastor Blankenship a cunt behind me and know I'd better wrap it up. "Sure, whatever. How much does that cost?"

Perky Polly on Molly taps her monitor a few times. "That'll be forty-seven fifty."

"For a soda and fries?" I blurt.

She shrugs, never letting her smile slip.

"Jesus," I mutter under my breath as I dig in my hoodie pocket for some cash.

Price-gouging pieces of—

I set the contents of my pocket on the counter to sort through them, and with that one simple, absentminded gesture, all holy hell breaks loose. Perky Polly leaps across the counter, clawing at my little orange prescription bottle, at the exact same moment that Pastor Blankenship swipes one long arm out to grab it. Their fists collide, knocking the plastic bottle to the floor, which I manage to get a foot on before it can roll away. But, as I kneel down to pick it up, Mrs. Frazier launches herself at my back and sends us both crashing into the counter.

The entire crowd surges forward, pinning us to the stainless-steel surface as they push and pull and claw at the salvation in my fist with greedy, desperate hands. I scream as one of them rips out a chunk of my hair. I hiss as another rakes her nails across my cheek. I bite and elbow as many others as I can. Howls and grunts and frustrated curses pour out of me as I struggle against the mob. The weight of them is crushing, pushing me down. I curl into a ball on the floor, clutching the bottle to my chest with both fists as I wince and take their beating.

Then, just as suddenly as it began, it stops. The ringing in my ears registers a moment later. Someone fired a gun. Or a freaking cannon from the sound of it.

The room goes quiet, and the crowd freezes, but I don't look up.

It could be a trick. It could be somebody just trying to distract me so that somebody else can snatch my pills. It could be—

I wince as the hot metal muzzle of a gun sears my temple.

"I'll be taking this." I hear the stranger's voice just before a firm hand wraps around my upper arm and yanks me to my feet.

I stand in a daze and face my attackers. They don't even have the decency to look ashamed. In fact, they don't look at me at all. Their eyes, a few pistols, and at least one rifle are all trained on the person holding a gun to my head. They're not mad that he's about to kidnap me. They're mad that he's kidnapping my pills.

"Who the hell are you?" Mr. Lathan, our former postman, growls from the back of the crowd. One of his eyes is squeezed shut as he stares down the length of his rifle, ready to fire.

My abductor shrugs as he walks me backward toward the door. "Doesn't really matter, does it?"

I watch the glow of anger in everyone's eyes cloud over with despair as they take in the meaning of his words.

Today is April twentieth. Nothing matters anymore.

I don't struggle. I don't even turn around and look at him. I let him drag me behind the building and pray that, whatever he does, he does it quick.

So much for not drawing attention.

I realize along the way that I'm limping, but I can't seem to pin down the location of my injury. And my mouth tastes like blood, but it doesn't hurt. And my body feels all floaty and light even though I just got jumped by half the town.

Damn, this hydrocodone is some powerful shit.

I giggle at the absurdity of my situation as the gunman behind me guides me toward a parked dirt bike with the heel of his palm on my shoulder.

"What's so funny?" His voice is soft, just like his touch as we come to a stop.

I turn to answer him and almost choke on my own spit. The words dry up in my mouth as I stare into the mossy-green eyes of a guy not much older than me. A tall, gorgeous guy who should be on a poster in my bedroom, not kidnapping me from Burger Palace.

I expected my captor to be some middle-aged, beer-gutted, gray-bearded, bald guy, not … *this. This* guy is perfect. It's like his parents were so rich that they went to the doctor and selected his DNA from a menu before he was conceived—high cheekbones, straight nose, soft eyes, strong eyebrows, and full lips that he's chewing on absentmindedly.

But the rest of him doesn't look rich at all. He's wearing a white ribbed tank top under a blue floral Hawaiian shirt, his jeans have holes in them, and the disheveled brown hair tucked behind his ear looks like it hasn't seen a pair of scissors in years.

Mine, on the other hand …

I run my fingers through my hacked-off locks, suddenly feeling super self-conscious about my frumpalicious appearance.

My captor raises his dark eyebrows a little higher, indicating that he's still waiting for me to tell him what's so funny.

I think about the painkillers that made me giggle, which causes me to remember all the other stuff I pulled out of my pocket along with that little orange bottle. "Shit!" I gasp, frantically patting my lower belly, feeling for the contents of my hoodie pocket. "I left all my money on the counter in there! And my keys!" I grimace and pinch the bridge of my nose. "God, I'm such an idiot."

"You still got those pills?" The boy pulls back one side of his unbuttoned Hawaiian shirt and shoves his handgun into a brown leather holster.

"Uh … yeah …" I wrap my fist a little tighter around the plastic bottle.

"Good." He flicks his chin toward the dirt bike behind me. "Get on."

"Where are we going?"

He lets his shirt fall back into place and pins me with a look that I can't quite read. It's been so long since I've seen somebody display anything other than the swollen red eyes of despair, the gnashing teeth of mob rage, the panicked twitchiness of fear, or the distant stare of sweet, drug-induced numbness that his calm, focused demeanor confuses the hell out of me.

"Shopping."

I pull my eyebrows together as he strides past me.

"Shopping?"

The stranger stops next to the dirt bike and shoves a black helmet onto his head, ignoring my question.

"A helmet. Really?" I snort. "We only have three days to live, and you're worried about safety regulations. You're not one of those *lifers*, are you?"

Lifer is a term the media coined months ago to describe those disgustingly optimistic members of our society who simply refused to believe that the end was near. You used to be able to tell them apart by their stupid, smiling faces and cheerful greetings. But, now, they look just like the rest of us—mad, sad, scared, or numb.

"I'm not a lifer. I just have shit to do, and it's not gonna get done if my head is splattered all over the asphalt." The boy straddles the black-and-orange machine and turns his masked face toward me. "Get on."

I consider my options. I can't exactly run back into the restaurant and ask for help. I'm in no condition to fight. I might be able to toss the painkillers in one direction and run as fast as my beat-up legs will go in the other, which could work if all he wants is the pills. But then what? Limp home and survive on pancake-syrup soup until the four horsemen of the apocalypse come to get me?

Yeah, I think I'd rather be kidnapped.

JOIN RAIN AND WES AS THEY TAKE THE RIDE OF THEIR LIVES IN THIS EMOTIONAL, GRIPPING, END-OF-THE-WORLD ROMANCE, AVAILABLE HERE:

MYBOOK.TO/PRAYINGFORRAIN

BOOKS BY BB EASTON

STANDALONE ROMANTIC COMEDIES

44 CHAPTERS ABOUT 4 MEN
The steamy memoir that inspired SEX/LIFE on Netflix.

GROUP THERAPY
Hilarious, heartwarming psychologist-client rom-com.

THE 44 CHAPTERS SPIN-OFF SERIES

A shockingly sexy, deeply emotional, darkly funny trip through BB's romantic past.
SKIN
SPEED
STAR
SUIT

THE RAIN TRILOGY

Intense, immersive, end-of-the-world romance.
PRAYING FOR RAIN
FIGHTING FOR RAIN
DYING FOR RAIN

DEVIL OF DUBLIN

A dark mafia romance steeped in Irish folklore.
DEVIL OF DUBLIN
THE DEVIL HIMSELF

FOR UPDATES ON NEW RELEASES, SALES, AND
GIVEAWAYS, SIGN UP HERE:

WWW.ARTBYEASTON.COM/SUBSCRIBE.

AUDIO EROTICA BY BB EASTON

When I'm not writing novels that make your heart race, flutter, and ultimately, soar, the Irish voice actor behind the Devil of Dublin series and I are busy writing and recording short erotic audio stories that have the same effect on a very *different* part of your body.

Each week, Eric Nolan and I publish a new erotic audio under the name The Devil of Dublin, exclusively on Quinn.

Quinn is a platform where content creators from all over the world publish erotic audio stories that are designed to make you, the listener, feel as though you're the main character, fully immersed in all the sexy sound effects, growls, moans, and sweet nothings that come along with whatever spicy scenario we've dreamed up.

To hear some steamy samples from our most popular audios, visit artbyeaston.com/audioerotica or scan the QR code below.

Or, to access our full catalog for free, just head over to the Quinn app or tryquinn.com to begin your free trial.

Happy listening!

ABOUT THE AUTHOR

B B Easton is the *Wall Street Journal* bestselling author of *44 CHAPTERS ABOUT 4 MEN*, the hilarious, steamy, tell-all memoir that inspired the Netflix Original Series, *SEX/LIFE*. Within the first month, *SEX/LIFE* was viewed by 67 million households worldwide, making it the 3rd Most Watched Netflix Original Series of all time.

BB was a stressed-out school psychologist and mother of two when the inspiration to write *44 CHAPTERS ABOUT 4 MEN* struck. Through that process, she rediscovered her passion for writing, became dangerously sleep-deprived, and finally mustered enough courage to quit her job and become a full-time author.

BB went on to publish four more wickedly funny, shockingly steamy, and heartwarmingly autobiographical books in the 44 CHAPTERS series: *SKIN*, *SPEED*, *STAR*, and *SUIT*. Since then, she's been hard at work, writing fictional stories that appeal to her love for us-against-the-world romance, including a dystopian trilogy (*PRAYING FOR RAIN*) , a psychologist-client romantic comedy (*GROUP THERAPY*) , and a dark Mafia romance series (*DEVIL OF DUBLIN*) .

You can find BB procrastinating in all of the following places:

Website: artbyeaston.com

Instagram: instagram.com/author.bb.easton

TikTok: vm.tiktok.com/ZMeEKRLyS/

Facebook: facebook.com/bbeaston

#TeamBB Facebook Group:
facebook.com/groups/BBEaston

X: twitter.com/bb_easton

Pinterest: pinterest.com/artbyeaston

Goodreads: goo.gl/4hiwiR

BookBub: bookbub.com/authors/bb-easton

Spotify: open.spotify.com/user/bbeaston

Selling signed books, mugs, and apparel on
Etsy: etsy.com/shop/artbyeaston

Publishing audio erotica stories under the
name "The Devil of Dublin" on Quinn:
tryquinn.com

And giving away free e-books from her
bestselling author friends every month in her
newsletter: artbyeaston.com/subscribe